Imp Forsaken

Date: 4/27/17

FIC DUNBAR
Dunbar, Debra,
Imp forsaken /

D1715324

Anessa Books, Bethesda, Maryland

ISBN:1493622625
ISBN-13:9781493622627

Dedication

To Dr. Hadley Tremaine (1939-2001), Chairman of the Department of English, Hood College, Frederick, Maryland, who taught me that there is great treasure to be found in what others consign to Hell.

~1~

"What is that?"

The elf's incredulous voice was punctuated by a stab with an especially long branch. He jumped back after poking me, as if he thought I'd leap up through the stick and attack him. It's not that I didn't want to, but, rather, the form I'd managed to create seemed to lack the ability to move about of its own volition. It was a significant design flaw that I'd been unable to correct for the three days I'd lain here in the forest. Luckily, I didn't seem to need food or water. I guess whatever I was at the moment was capable of either absorbing nutrients from the ground or photosynthesis. I couldn't tell.

"I don't know." The other elven scout peered at me, leaning close. He was taller than his friend, his brown hair closer to blond in its tight braid. I had no eyes, but still managed to register a vision of my surroundings and the two scouts cautiously circling my form.

"Is it some kind of pond scum?" I received another jab from the branch. This was beginning to piss me off.

"There's no pond for five miles. I honestly don't know what this thing is; I've never seen anything like it."

I had no idea where the nearest pond was. Since I had no head to raise, and no ability to move, I'd been staring at a canopy of tree leaves, a mossy covered ground, and the red–orange lichen on the trees closest to my ...whatever. Three days I'd been here. The longest three days of my life.

The second, taller elf moved even closer, his face distorted by whatever lens I was viewing him through. I wondered what I could do to him if he touched me. Might be fun to find out. Come here, mister elf.

"Is it a demon?"

The one with the stick poked me again, arm outstretched to its full length, just in case I was, in fact, a demon. I was, but I couldn't seem to do anything demonic right now. Anything beyond oozing all over the ground and soaking up the sunshine.

"Ugh, they are *so* disgusting! I'll bet it is a demon. It would be just like one of them to draw us in close, then leap on top of us."

The one with the stick nodded, not daring to stab me again now that my potential species was in debate. "Remember the rat one last year? I nearly peed my pants."

The taller one snorted. "You *did* pee your pants. Fairy."

I was pretty sure he was slandering his partner's fae race and not his masculinity, although, with elves I think the insult had the same meaning. Clearly affronted, the first elf stabbed me again with his branch. "Let's take it in. We'll net it, just in case."

The other seemed doubtful. "We'll look like idiots if it's some kind of rare fungus and we've netted it."

The pair looked at me for a few moments, considering their course of action and weighing any potential ridicule. I continued to lie there, a gelatinous ooze on the ground.

"I'm not taking any chances," the one with the stick finally said. "Get a bucket and a shovel, and let's take this thing in."

I was scooped unceremoniously into a bucket, netted, and hauled through the woods. My mind raced, going through the potential places in Hel where Gregory might have banished me. I wasn't sure how the whole thing worked. Did I go back to a designated spot? Near one of the gates? My childhood home? I couldn't believe the angel picked the spot himself, since he'd never been to Hel.

More worrisome was that I couldn't feel him at all. When we were near, I'd been able to sense his emotions, read some of his thoughts. Now that our bond was broken, I realized I'd had so much more. There had always been a sense of connection, no matter how far apart we were. It was gone now. I still had the red–purple of his spirit self networked throughout me, but it was no longer tied to him. None of me was tied to him. If I'd had an arm, I would have checked to see if the tattoo was still there. I'm sure it would not have been. Once again, a sense of loss crashed through me. I missed him. I missed my angel. And I missed Wyatt and the girls. I missed Candy and Michelle. I felt so terribly alone.

Once the elven scouts had shown up, my heart sank even further. Not that I currently had a heart. I'd been undecided whether it would have been better to be found by demons or elves. Demons didn't tolerate weakness and would have probably killed me outright. Elves would normally be a better choice, but I'd pissed off almost every High Lord in Hel. My only hope was that they somehow couldn't recognize me, that they'd think I was a strange slimy being, and just dump me back in the woods.

But then, I wasn't sure that was a better scenario. Maybe in time I'd be able to form something more mobile, but if not...well, this pretty much sucked. I really didn't want to spend the rest of my life as immobile ooze, unable to communicate. The only good thing about my return to Hel was that the excruciating pain I'd felt in Aaru had dulled to an achy throb. Something in my spirit–self was scabbing over and recovering. I just hoped it was the parts I needed to survive.

"What should we do with it once we get to Chime?" one of the scouts said. I couldn't tell which one had spoken, since I was deep inside a bucket.

"Let's put it in a cell for a few days and see what happens."

Great. I wasn't sure if I'd be able to live in a dark stone cell. And Chime? That name sounded familiar. I dug through my memories and realized with dread that Chime was in the elven kingdom of Wythyn. Of all the elven kingdoms, that was the absolutely worst place I could have found myself. This past winter I'd cursed at the high lord, Feille, refused to do his bidding then had Gregory yank me out of his grasp. If that wasn't enough, I'd returned to threaten him, blown the top off his fancy–dancy throne then stole my horse back. I could only hope Feille never realized it was me in one of his dungeons, and that I somehow managed to regain the ability to escape before any of these elves discovered who I was.

Eventually we must have reached the city of Chime. Even from the depth of my bucket I could hear the city gates open, the greeting of the guards, the ring of footsteps on stone. Murmured voices grew louder, and I could make out the conversations of those bartering for goods. The noise drifted away, and eventually all I heard was footsteps and the opening and closing of doors.

"So, we just stick it down here? What do we tell the guards?"

My bucket shifted, and I assumed the elf carrying me had shrugged. "That we need a secure place to hold it until we figure out what it is?"

"Riiiight. I'm not about to become a laughing stock. I've got an idea."

I heard a crash, and the elf not carrying me berated someone.

"I'm sorry, sir! I'm so sorry!" The voice was high — either a child or perhaps a young woman.

"Stupid human. A few days in the dungeon should make you less clumsy."

The human gasped and the sound of soft crying accompanied us down another long set of stairs. The temperature dropped noticeably, and I sensed a dusty dampness.

"We're punishing this clumsy human," the other scout told someone.

A new voice replied. "Fine. Glad to see you brought a bucket to clean up any of her — holy Goddess! What is that nasty stuff in there? Ugh!"

I felt my container shift. "Part of the punishment."

We were quickly ushered down the stairs, and I felt the thunk of my bucket hitting the floor. There was the sound of shuffling feet, a soft thud and a whimper.

I was unceremoniously dumped out of my bucket onto a filthy stone floor. The two scouts jumped back and clanged the cell door shut, locking it quickly. Huddled in a corner was a young woman, her scant wrap clothing smudged with the thick dust that lay everywhere. Her terrified eyes looked from the elven scouts to me.

"What ...what is that?" I could hear the fear in her voice and see the emotions flash across her expressive face. No doubt she thought she'd need to eat me, or clean me up, or smear me all over her body for the amusement of the elves.

"It's a demon," the taller elf told her smugly. "We're feeding you to it. First it will encircle you with its poisonous form then slowly creep up your body, searing your flesh bit by bit. Eventually it will cover every inch of you, drowning you as it pours down your nose and throat. But you won't die, because it will Own you. For all eternity you'll repeat this torture over and over until it's all you know."

Fuck, this elf should write novels. I'd buy that one.

The girl made a choking noise and huddled further into the corner, obviously trying to make herself as invisible as possible. The elves laughed and chatted to each other about some wine purchase as they left the dungeon. Assholes — scaring the poor thing like that. Her fear flowed off her in waves, sparking something primitive in me. Her terror was like

---

an aphrodisiac. The demon I used to be wouldn't have been able to resist slowly tearing her apart, trying to draw out as much of that lovely emotion as possible. But all I felt now was sympathy and frustration that I couldn't communicate with her, couldn't reassure her that I had no intention of causing her harm.

In time the girl's sobs tapered off and she looked at me with curiosity. Carefully, she rose to her feet and circled the perimeter of the cell. One of her legs twisted at an odd angle, causing her to shuffle slightly. The elves would never have taken a disabled changeling baby, so her injury had most likely been acquired during her stay among them. She approached, looking cautiously at me, and I noticed two toes missing from her left foot.

She was practically naked, wearing just a thin, plain linen wrap, and I saw a network of ridged flesh, scars in a pattern of lines and crosses, all over her body. Some were old. Others fresh — red and angry. One was clearly in the shape of an elven word. I couldn't quite make it out from my angle, but it looked similar to the symbol for excrement. Although humans on earth sometimes indulged in decorative scarring, I doubted these were voluntary, especially given her other injuries. I couldn't imagine that anyone would willingly put the elven word for "shit" on their upper thigh either.

"Is this some cruel joke?" she whispered, reaching out a tentative foot toward me.

I wondered what it would feel like to have her touch me with her toes, then suddenly worried whatever I was might harm her. Her foot hovered, shaking slightly before she drew it back.

"I'm too scared." Her laugh wobbled. "Although, after everything they've done to me I might welcome death. As long as it didn't hurt too much."

She might not have been brave enough to touch me, but she managed to turn her back on me and carefully examine the cell. It wasn't very impressive from what I could see from my prone position. Stone walls with chipped and flaking plaster were home to scurrying insects. A deep trench circled just inside the walls and door, broken only by a metal–covered grate. I was willing to bet that both the iron–barred door and the metal on the grate were spelled to keep magical and demonic prisoners safely inside. The filthy walls and floor were probably strengthened by runes just under the surface. It looked like a regular human dungeon, but elves took special precautions. Confirming my suspicions, the bars sizzled slightly as the girl accidentally brushed against them. She yelped and retreated to her corner.

Time passed, and I heard the girl's stomach rumble. No food came. Nobody came to let her out. I wondered what they told her owner? Not that he or she would probably protest the human's mistreatment if the scars on her body were any indication. Finally she sighed and shifted, wincing as her hip rolled on the hard floor.

"Looks like we'll be here for the night. Not that I mind. The bright spot of my evening was going to be cold broth strained from the cooking pan, or possibly a half–eaten fruit someone dropped on the floor. The rest of it would be full of beatings and other 'fun'. I think I'd rather starve here."

She smiled, and I saw faint humor in her tired eyes. "Not that you aren't lovely company, Mister Algae. Some of the finest conversation I've had in the last decade."

She got awkwardly to her feet and stretched, shivering in the damp chill of the dungeon. "What have you done, Mister Algae, to anger the elves? Tainted their water, perhaps? Stained their embroidered shoes? Maybe you're just the wrong shade of green."

Nope. I'd threatened to kill their high lord. And if they figured out I was *that* demon, this girl's future would be roses and sunshine compared to mine.

I heard a clang, and the girl evidently did too. She started then dashed over to her corner as fast as she could, huddling in the shadows. Footsteps grew near, and the two scouts came into view.

"I don't see any blood or bones," one commented casually.

The taller elf sighed. "Because she's still in the corner, where we left her. And the demon is *still* on the floor, where we left it. This is stupid, Lyte. Let's just dump it down the drain and be done with it."

Yes, please dump me down the drain and be done with me. Even if I wound up in the sewage system, it had to be better than the dungeon of my enemies.

"No. It's a demon. I'm sure of it."

"Then why is it still like that?" the tall one demanded. "I thought you said it wouldn't be able to resist a human. Why is the wench still alive?"

"Maybe it just needs incentive."

The lock grated, and the door opened, but instead of walking toward me, the elf strode to the human, grabbed her by the arm and hauled her to her feet. She caught her breath, and I tensed as the elf pulled out a knife and slashed her arm from wrist to shoulder.

The girl gasped, biting off a scream. I struggled to do anything — shoot the fuckers with a bolt of lightning, suffocate them with my gelatinous form, anything. I felt helpless — again. Just as I felt when I watched Stab being murdered. What a cruel turn my life had taken that I finally cared and couldn't do anything to help.

"Lyte! Don't kill her. Humans are expensive, and this one has a lot of fun left in her."

The elf slashed her other arm, then did the same to her legs. She stood shaking, dripping lines of red from her limbs. They were shallow cuts, not likely to kill her, but the girl looked like she was on the verge of collapse. She was half starved, probably dehydrated. She couldn't afford to lose any blood, even the small amount decorating her body.

"Idiot." The taller scout curled his lip. "The pond scum doesn't look any more interested in her now than when she wasn't bleeding all over the dungeon floor. I'm done with this nonsense."

He left the cell, his footsteps ringing on the stone. The other scout shoved the human girl to the floor and waved his knife at me. I wasn't particularly alarmed. Poking with a stick hadn't bothered me; I doubted being stabbed would do any damage.

"I know what you are. Let's see if you can resist her now."

He left, locking the cell door carefully and leaving me with a thin girl, dazed and bleeding in a dirty corner. I wished I could do something to help her, to help all of them. I thought of Nyalla, of what she'd been through. Terrible as it had been, it was nothing compared to the life of this poor creature before me. I stared at her, at the defeated look in her eyes and swore that if I could regain any of my powers, if I could somehow manage to even move about, I would help her. I would help them all.

"If only you were an angel, Mister Algae," she sighed, her voice wandering as if she had a fever. "If only you were an angel to heal me, to avenge my hurts and shelter me under your wings. An angel like those in the songs and stories."

If only I were an angel. But I wasn't. I wasn't even sure if I was the Iblis anymore. I was only a powerless imp trapped in a dirty elven prison cell.

~2~

G abriel stood outside the decrepit Cape Cod style house, under the spreading canopy of an ancient maple tree. Cicadas filled the humid summer air with their mating song. Blue light flickered from the windows, illuminating the gray dusk. The angel hesitated, uncertain of the modern protocol of requesting entry into a human's dwelling. Should he vocalize something? Rap on the entrance with his knuckles? One of his angels had told him to push the little beige button beside the door, but he suspected that angel's knowledge might be less than accurate.

Eventually he gave up. *Eldest brother? May I speak with you?*

He felt like a child, or a lesser angel requesting an audience. The uncomfortable feeling grew as his request was met with a long silence.

A moment. I am killing undead at present.

Undead? Necromancy was a lost art, but the humans had made some impressive medical advances lately. Clearly those advances had gone wrong if the head of the Grigori felt the need to temporarily put aside his duties to address the issue. One more thing the humans had messed up in their frenetic evolutionary pace. Gabriel frowned at the window, wondering if intervention would be welcome, or if it would be perceived as a slight upon his brother's ability to massacre animated corpses unassisted.

Just as Gabriel was about to rush the door, it opened. A tall figure stood in the entrance, blocking the light from within the house. With a few words to someone behind him, the angel closed the door and headed toward Gabriel with a relaxed stride. The older angel carried some sort of bag in one hand. It crinkled noisily as he folded the top down.

"This better be good. I've left the fate of the world hanging in the hands of a human with rather poor fine–motor skills."

Gabriel was momentarily distracted by the glossy orange and tan bag at his brother's side. Did it hold some substance that neutralized undead? He'd never seen a weapon like this before, but humans had changed considerably since he frequented their home. Who knew what they were capable of? *Too far, too fast*, he thought with a scowl.

"I've been reading the reports of the two dead angels and have found some unsatisfactory gaps. Since your Grigori discovered the deaths, I'd hoped you could shed some light on what happened."

Any other angel would have shriveled at Gabriel's tone, but his brother just shrugged and opened the colorful bag, shaking it and peering inside thoughtfully. "And this couldn't wait until the next council meeting? These 'unsatisfactory gaps' weigh so heavily on your mind that you risked your purity to venture here and disturb my important work?"

Gabriel tensed, a reflex born billions of years ago, but he refused to let this brother intimidate him anymore. "I'm sure the undead in that house can wait while you turn your attention toward *two dead angels*."

The elder angel sighed, shifting his gaze from the bag to meet Gabriel's eyes. "In the most recent death, the angel was destroyed in an explosion on an island off Washington State. He was not Grigori and did not have permission to be here. Cause of the explosion is unknown."

"Yes, I know that. It's in the report." Gabriel waved an impatient hand. "When will you have concluded the investigation as to the cause of his death, and his reason for being out of Aaru without following proper protocol?"

Gabriel felt the weight of his brother's stare and struggled to continue to meet his gaze. Slowly, the elder angel lowered his eyes to the bag, reaching his hand in and withdrawing a thin, circular object, dusted in orange powder. "We are Grigori. It is not our primary responsibility to investigate fallen angels who have met a just end."

Gabriel took a sharp breath. "And how do you know it was a just end? The report simply says he was here without permission. That alone does not deserve death, unless your standards have become refreshingly strict in the last few days."

"We'll investigate in a fair and impartial manner. In due time."

Gabriel felt his temper rise. "What kind of explosion could have killed an angel? If the humans are starting up that nonsense again, then we need to take action. Really, brother, I didn't expect you to have such a casual attitude toward this."

The elder angel fingered the thin disc in his hand, sprinkling orange powder like fairy dust on the pavement. "As I said, we will investigate in due time. The other dead angel was found in Parral Mexico by one of my enforcers. He left behind his corporeal form."

Gabriel sputtered in frustration. "Yes, yes. *Why*? Is this some new, dangerous human technology? Was it a devouring spirit? If so, I'd expect you would not be standing here playing with round orange things in a bag."

What was *wrong* with him? The brother he'd grown up with would have scoured the earth, sword a–blaze, filled with holy wrath until he'd found the murderers. Especially if there was a devouring spirit at large. The fate of all creation might be at stake, and here he stood as if he just didn't care.

"It was a devouring spirit. He's dead. Case closed."

Gabriel felt words choking in his throat. "*Why* is that not in the report? A devouring spirit strong enough to kill an angel and you just conveniently leave it out of the report? We need to catalog this incident, record the power levels and add the data to our projections. How could you not report this?"

His brother shrugged, turning the orange disk between his fingers. "Guess I forgot. My bad."

Forgot? He forgot? And since when did his esteemed, ancient brother use human slang? Gabriel felt his body shake with rage, but anger was a sin that would move him too far from the precious, balanced center. Clenching his fists, the younger angel took several deep breaths, willing himself to return to a calm and logical state.

"Why was the deceased angel down here? What was he doing, and how did he manage to encounter a devouring spirit? Two angels, down here without permission, both dead — brother, what do you intend to do?"

The elder angel looked pensive as he shoved the orange disk in his mouth and crunched it. "I intend to suggest that angels not journey down here without following proper procedure. It appears to be hazardous to their immortality."

For a few moments Gabriel could do nothing but stare, uncertain whether his brother's action or his words were the most disturbing.

"Did ...did you just *eat* that thing?"

His brother brushed his fingers across his jeans, leaving a trail of orange. "Potato chips with some sort of crab seasoning on them. I prefer the salt and vinegar ones myself, but Wyatt likes these best."

He extended the bag toward Gabriel, who just shook his head in mute astonishment. "Let it be, Gabriel. I will take care of this business, and I promise you will eventually have your full report."

With that, the elder angel dug another chip from the bag, popping it into his mouth before turning to walk back into the house, leaving Gabriel to stare after him.

~3~

Two weeks. At least I think it had been two weeks. There was no daylight in the cell, no way of counting the passing hours, so I was pretty much guessing. Could have been two days, could have been two years. It certainly felt like two years. The shorter elf scout, the one called Lyte, had come back for the girl, furious to find her still alive. She was weak, but managed to stagger out when he'd told her to go. I only hoped someone healed her wounds and kept them from infection. I hoped she'd gotten something to eat, some sort of relief from the nightmare her life had become. I worried that she might have been killed, but perhaps that would have been a relief to her.

Soon after the girl left, Lyte had scooped me back in my bucket and dumped me in another, more filthy cell. I wasn't sure why. This time he'd taken the bucket with him, leaving me alone in the cell with whatever bugs and rodents could penetrate the magical barriers.

Since then, that fucking elven scout had been down ten times to check on me. He'd taunt me, dangle a finger temptingly close then stand back and frown, as if he wasn't sure whether I was animal or vegetable.

I'd made progress. I could feel the bits of my spirit–self knitting together with a hideous network of scarring. That's one of the reasons I felt I'd been down in this cell at least several weeks. Damage like I'd sustained didn't repair quickly. In my semi–liquid state, I could shift myself across the floor.

Mobile pond scum was a step in the right direction but I was more ecstatic that I could now change the composition of my body. I could manage a solid form— some kind of lizard with internal organs and legs. I wasn't the fastest thing in Hel, but I could move, and I had little teeth. I formulated a plan to burst from pond scum into my little lizard being, escape from the dungeon and hopefully manage to get into the forest. I just needed to wait for the right moment.

I still couldn't store raw energy, but here in Hel, that wasn't really necessary. If that skill was lost forever, I'd never be able to return to the realm of the humans, though. There, I'd be defenseless, unable to fix any injury or change my shape or create even the most basic of elements. Without any storage mechanism, I was damned to Hel forever. Baby steps, though. Right now I just wanted to be mobile, and to get the fuck out of Wythyn before they figured out what, and who, I was.

I was trying to convert into something more ferocious, and possibly with a voice box, when I heard the clang of the dungeon door, and footsteps. Quickly I resumed my original state, oozing back to the spot where I'd originally been deposited.

"See? There." It was my elven nemesis, accompanied by three individuals out of my range of vision.

There was a moment of silence while I contemplated the chill of the stone floor, the thick layer of dust stacked high in the corners of my cell. Someone really needed to clean this fucking place.

"It's some kind of pond scum," announced a bored voice. Maybe I wouldn't need to plan a jailbreak after all. Maybe they'd finally let me out, take me in the woods and dump me where I could repair myself in peace. It would really suck if they just power–washed me down the grate at the edge of my cell, although at this point I'd be happy to take that option. I'd no idea where that thing went. I was sure it would not be pleasant, but it had to be better than this boring, filthy dungeon.

"No, look. It's been moving. See how there are marks in the dust on the floor? It's in the same place every time I come in here, but clearly it's been moving about."

Fuck! I hadn't thought about having to cover my tracks. Not that I had any way to do so.

"Rats. Or snakes. Or a breeze." The voice was bored, irritated with the bother.

"No! The footprints are too big for rats, and the pattern isn't like a snake. There's no breeze down here strong enough to move the dust in that pattern. Look at the other cells, they don't have those kind of marks on the floor."

I held my breath. Well, I would have if I had lungs. Out of the corner of my vision, I saw a figure move into view. A human, tall and thin, wearing green robes embroidered with golden runes. He carried a carved yew staff with a blue stone in a claw at the top. He leaned close to look at me through the bars and scratched his gray hair with a bony hand.

"Fine. But if it turns out to be pond scum, I'm going to request that you scoop it up with your bare hands and clean the entire dungeon floor on your hands and knees."

A sorcerer. I'd feared as much, but hearing him address an elf in such a fashion had confirmed it. Sorcerers were top of the food chain among the human slaves and had enough value to rank higher than some low level elves. Probably even higher here in Wythyn, where they were becoming somewhat of an endangered species.

The sorcerer sprinkled a powdered substance on me, and began to chant. I wasn't sure what to do. If I pulled my personal energy deep inside, as Gregory had taught me to do, my physical form would suffer and the change may be noticeable. If I extended myself out as far as I could into my corporeal shell, it would appear realistic, but might register more easily on a divination spell. Unsure, I just kept as I was and hoped luck was in my favor.

It wasn't.

"It *is* a demon," he said, his voice full of wonderment. "How long has it been this way?"

"Two months."

Ugh. Two months I'd been down here, plus the three days I'd lain in the forest before these scouts found me. Did Gregory wonder whether I was alive or dead? Was Wyatt frantic with worry? How were the girls getting on? Did Michelle ever rent that unit on Monroe?

"Are you sure?" The sorcerer turned to the scout, his tone full of skepticism. "It's not very intimidating for a demon to look like a couple gallons of pond scum. I could see one doing this to lure someone in close before changing and frightening them, but I can't believe one would continue with this strange, limited physical form for more than five minutes. They just don't have the patience for this sort of thing."

Tell me about it. This whole thing sucked big time.

"I don't know," the scout replied. "I have no idea why it's still like that, but it's been that way since we found it two months ago."

The sorcerer made a "come hither" motion with a hand, and another person out of my line of vision came forward. Another human — a servant carrying a box. I felt mild curiosity, and a significant amount of dread as I contemplated the possible contents of said box.

"All right." The sorcerer sighed, as if he'd much rather be home in bed, or poring over a huge, leather–bound tome by magical light. "I'll check."

Check what? I was already facing spending the next few months here in this cell, or however long it took until I could successfully formulate a jailbreak. The sorcerer took out a series of colored stones from the box and instructed a hovering guard to open the cell door.

"Are you sure?" he asked nervously, darting a quick glance in my direction. "If it's a demon, maybe you should stay out here."

"It's been pond scum for two months," the sorcerer said dryly. "What's it going to do, stain my robes?"

I doubted I could even do that, but I could change shape and bite his ankle. Unfortunately, with two armed elves and a human, I doubted I'd have much chance of getting out, even in lizard form. I'd hoped to wait until Lyte was down here alone, but I might not have any other alternative than to surprise them and take my chances. Four against one. I didn't like those odds one bit, especially with my current injuries.

The sorcerer motioned the elven guard forward, and I was amused to see the scout happily step aside, making sure the guard would be between himself and the soon–to–be open cell. The guard opened the gate, which slid back with a horrible, rusty screech. These elves really did a shitty job of maintaining their dungeons. Feille should be ashamed of himself.

"Protect me," the sorcerer commanded. The elven guard drew a rather impressive–looking sword, and the scout readied his bow with a cocked arrow. I didn't think either would damage me in my current form — the only advantage to pond scum that I could think of, but they'd skewer me in the lizard form. Could I be fast enough to outrun them? Or should I just hold tight and wait for another opportunity? They'd discovered I was a demon. How much longer until they discovered I was *that* demon?

The sorcerer placed a series of smooth, round stones in a circle approximately ten inches from the edge of my shape, alternating in colors.

Standing back, the sorcerer threw up his hands. "*Blican!*"

Immediately the stones began to glow, sending up a stream of colorful mist toward the ceiling.

"Cennan I beost—hord."

I had no fucking idea what happened, but four pairs of eyes doubled in size as the entire group raced out of the cell, slamming the door shut. In their haste, the door didn't latch, bouncing wide open. I made a split—second decision and transformed into my only other shape and took off. The result would have been hysterical if I hadn't been so deadly serious about getting out alive. All four screamed as if they'd been castrated, the human throwing the box across the room and racing for the door. The guard had more presence of mind and hacked at me with his sword, all the while dancing around on his tiptoes. Two arrows bounced off the ground before Lyte high—tailed it after the human.

That left me with less legs and feet to avoid, although I wasn't sure I would be able to beat the human and the elven scout to the dungeon entrance, and I doubted they'd hold it open for me. Darting back and forth with as much speed and finesse as a lizard could manage, I saw an opening and ran for it. Unfortunately, I only made it three feet before a foot came straight for my head.

I refuse to be kicked in the head without retaliation, so I latched onto the sorcerer's leg, digging my little claws in tight, and bit down. He didn't taste very good, and his frenzied leg shaking was giving me vertigo, but I held on like duct tape to his calf.

"Get it off, get it off," quickly changed to "Don't stab me, you stupid idiot."

I could only imagine the guard, reluctant to get his hands or feet within range, was trying to jab me with his sword. Sure enough, a blade flashed by me, tearing a jagged hole in the sorcerer's robes. Finally, the sorcerer reached down with both hands and grabbed me, pulling with all his might. If I had been a bigger lizard, I might have managed to hold on. Instead, he ripped me from his leg, losing a bit of flesh in the process. I flew through the air and smacked against a filthy wall with a painful thwack, before sliding to the floor. Before I could get my feet under me to rush the door again, it clanged shut — this time catching firmly in the latch.

The elven guard locked me in, hands shaking. The sorcerer muttered a quick spell and a curtain of gold fell before the bars, evidently an added layer of magic to keep me safely inside. Spell complete, he bent over, wheezing as he dabbed his torn robes against a bloodied leg. The human seemed long–gone, but Lyte crept back into view, looking at me nervously through the safety of the magicked door. The very one I'd wanted to bite had run away, and my bid for freedom had failed. I had no idea what the spell had revealed, but I had a feeling the jig was up. At least they'd been frightened enough from my attack to abandon their glowing stones in the room with me. I wondered if I might be able to use them to my advantage. At the very least, they'd make decent projectile weapons. Too bad my two available forms didn't have opposable thumbs.

"I can't believe....I just can't believe it," the elven scout stuttered.

The sorcerer panted, clearly taxed by the unusual physical effort of dancing around with a lizard attached to his leg. "Well, that answers the question as to why she remained a mess of pond scum for two months."

"What do we do?" the scout asked. "I'm not going back in there. I heard what she did last time she was here."

The sorcerer wiped a line of sweat from his brow. "We tell His Lordship, that's what we do. There's a bounty out for her, and he's eager for revenge after what happened last time."

The three backed carefully out of the dungeon, wide eyes on me the whole time. I glared at them as they left, then crawled back into my circle of glowing stones, feeling like lady luck had finally deserted me for greener pastures. They knew who I was, and they were on their way to tell Feille — the very one I'd pissed off beyond any chance of forgiveness. Any day now, he'd arrive for his revenge, and there was nothing I could do. Nothing. I had the choice of either a gelatinous ooze, or a nuisance–sized lizard. I had no demon powers with which to defend myself. Nothing beyond the physical abilities of my two forms. Escape was looking unlikely. I could only wait, frantically try to recover more of my abilities and hope my death would not be particularly long and painful.

~4~

Neutral balance eluded him, even here in his most precious Aaru. A brief moment of peace was all Gabriel could manage before thoughts crashed his composure, filling every space of his being. He tried to clear his mind, to concentrate on the essence that surrounded him. Aaru — so clean and sharp, so soothing in its uniformity. Here, he had no corporeal form subject to physical sensation, tempting him to actions far beneath one of his evolved status. Here in Aaru, there was nothing to disturb him except the tangle of emotions that currently destroyed his concentration.

Two angels dead. Three if he counted the rogue Gregori, his brother, had killed nearly a year ago. It was unheard of. Such casualties had not occurred since the wars. Gabriel still fumed over the death of Althean, a lost soul never given the opportunity for redemption, snuffed out in a fit of rage — justified, but still such temper should have been contained and controlled. Anger was a sin, and angels in their position did not have the luxury of sin — especially not when Aaru simmered with discontent.

Two angels. Gabriel couldn't escape the questions that churned through him. The reports were unacceptably vague, his brother clearly in some bizarre fugue. There were processes, procedures for everything, and the fact that these angels were among the humans without permission disturbed him nearly as much as their deaths. A physical body led to temptation, and humans bore a faint resemblance to those the angels had banished. Two and a half million years was a long time to be alone, and lesser angels could not be expected to resist the seduction of being in the presence of humans.

Were they there seeking the comfort of a warm embrace? Did the urge to create send them to the only outlet available? Or were they, perhaps, formulating rebellion safe from the listening ears of Aaru?

Gabriel

He stiffened in displeasure. The angel addressing him was not a sibling, and even with the addition of the "el" suffix, it was a far too familiar form of address.

Guardian of Truth, Ancient Messenger.

Better. He hardly expected the angel to recite all fifty of his names and titles. Fellow members of the Ruling Council were allowed some latitude, after all.

Sidriel. Gabriel purposely left off all but the basic title, emphasizing the vast chasm of age and level between them.

There was a brief hesitation as the other angel recognized the slight. *Revered one, you wished to see me?*

Now was as good a time as any. It's not like he would be able to find his center until he got the answers he desired.

The two recently deceased angels — what choirs were they from? It hadn't been in the reports, but Gabriel knew if the word was out, Sidriel would have heard. It was best to see if the rumors were true before he wasted time and energy interrogating those with no knowledge of the dead.

The one who left behind a corporeal form, Vaol, belonged to the second choir. The one who died in the explosion, Furlac, was in the third.

Raphael and Uriel's then. Gabriel wondered briefly whether his siblings were aware of their staffs' transgressions. There were sub–levels in each choir, and it was impossible to keep track of the day–to–day activities of every angel. Suspicion gnawed at the angel as he mentally ran through the various levels in each of his sibling's choirs. Were his relations covering up embarrassing indiscretions, or perhaps behind a take–over attempt? It wouldn't be the first time they'd all jockeyed for position, and he doubted it would be the last. No matter how many coup attempts they'd orchestrated over the ages, none had ever succeeded. The eldest was always immovable, the most powerful of them all. But now ...something had changed, and Gabriel got the feeling his brother might have compromised his normally high vibration levels. If he fell, then Aaru would be in a prime state for rebellion.

The second choir has professed ignorance of Vaol's motives for leaving Aaru and flouting the proper procedures, Sidriel continued. *Uriel, the revered interpreter of prophecies, states that Furlac was among the humans delivering a message on her behalf.*

Gabriel felt a wave of irritation roll through him. Raphael was always lax in controlling his angels. He'd been pronounced an Angel of Order upon his creation, but Gabriel had always wondered if there had perhaps been some mistake. Although, as the fourth of five siblings, Raphael had been greatly influenced by his chaotic little brother during his formative years. Either way, he was disgracefully far from center. At least Uriel had owned up to her angel's behavior. Had she circumvented the process to expedite the delivery of her message, or had there been a less innocuous reason she hadn't wanted Furlac's visit documented?

They were both probably there to sin with the humans. Sidriel's tone was gleeful, and Gabriel felt his stomach churn at the eagerness with which the other angel's thoughts turned to improper physical relations.

Do you call Uriel a liar? Gabriel often did, but one of Sidreil's station did not have that right. Ruling Council appointments tended to inflate an angel's head. This one clearly needed to be removed from office, and soon. Gabriel's mind wandered as the other angel sputtered apologies and backpedaled. He wouldn't put it past Uriel to lie. She'd been increasingly sympathetic toward those who sought solace in the arms of the humans. Raphael too.

Nephilim. It wasn't just the sin of physical congress with the humans; it was the creation of offspring with them. Angels lowered their vibration levels with the transgression, but it was humans who truly suffered. A being of spirit, no matter how willing, could never give a human what they truly wanted in a partner, and any children would be different, forced to hide for their long lives, or be killed by the humans that feared them. It was a disaster, a mistake that destroyed human lives.

Reports were vague on the cause of death for these two angels, and choirs were vague on why they were out of Aaru without following proper protocol. What was going on? There was a sickness festering in Aaru that threatened the very structure that sustained them all. With his brother quite possibly fallen, a revolution seemed on the horizon with bloodshed that hadn't been seen since the war. He couldn't allow it, wouldn't allow it. There had been too much chaos in this past year, and it needed to stop.

All it would lead to was pain, and order was the only thing that made the pain go away.

If the rumors are true, then these sinful visits with the humans will come to an end.

Gabriel's attention turned back to the other angel. *What rumors?* Hope flared. Anything that would stem the increasing tide of sin would be welcome. Maybe then they could all get back to normal.

That there is a way to create offspring without violation of the treaty or threat to our spiritual balance.

Gabriel caught his breath. *Impossible. Any such miracle would have been brought before the Ruling Council.*

Sidriel shifted uncomfortably. *I only know the rumors. Perhaps the procedure has not yet been vetted, or there are protocols that must be considered before it is brought to our attention. I don't know.*

Creation. Without unholy contact. Aaru had suffered since the war, evolution had slowed to a crawl, and angels were increasingly rebellious. The terms of the treaty had seemed livable in the bloody aftermath of battle, but with time, the restrictions were like over–tight ropes, chafing sensitive flesh.

We have all suffered with the lack of creation. It would help those who cannot resist the lure of the humans.

And anything that decreased, or even stopped the number of angels who fell, the number of Nephilim born, would be a good thing.

I'm surprised they haven't contacted you to feel out support in the Ruling Council for their cause. I heard that they reached out to Uriel.

It would make sense that they would contact Uriel first. Of all the Ruling Council, she would be the one most eager to support a project that would bring creation once again to Aaru. Memories flooded him. So many had lost lovers and children in the war, but Uriel had lost both. Angels didn't often life–bond. Uriel had. To lose two beings she adored due to war, to wonder if they lived on in Hel or perished — no angel should ever have to suffer so.

It would be a good thing, Gabriel mused, half to himself. *I would support it as long as the method did not violate the treaty or threaten our positive evolution.*

Sidriel paused, as if considering the older angel's words. *I'm not sure how I would weigh in on the issue. If it could be done without compromising my vibration levels, then I might be interested. Of course, I would allow myself to be guided by your august opinion.*

If Gabriel had not been incorporeal, he would have shaken his head. Sidriel's obsequious behavior had reached an annoying level the past few centuries. It was beneficial to have allies, and it certainly was flattering to have an angel hang on his every word, as this one did, but Gabriel had the distinct impression that Sidriel was just waiting for the right opportunity to stick a knife in his back.

I've always regretted not being able to pass along the quality of my being to another, but better remain childless than choose an improper mate in haste.

He felt Sidriel's excitement. *If the rumors are true, you'll be able to pick exactly the qualities you want, and not worry about alliances made in the heat of emotion bringing you shame. Creation without the need to involve lesser beings — it would truly be a miracle.*

Wrong. Something about it just seemed wrong. But curiosity grabbed hold of the elder angel and sparked his interest. Better check it out. He was going to need to investigate these two angel deaths before he could rest, so he might as well look into this intriguing rumor.

Yes. A very welcome miracle.

~5~

I heard the dungeon door clang and felt a familiar sense of dread. Once they'd realized I was a demon, a guard had returned to toss a net over me — a good precaution under normal circumstances, totally unnecessary in this instance. It's not like I could do anything. No melting of prison bars, no ripping my captor's head off and shoving it up their ass. I was pond scum at the time, mostly because in that form my stomach didn't feel painfully empty. There were only so many flies and bugs down here, and I'd managed to eat every one that came within reach.

So I was trapped under the magical restraint as green slime. The worst thing about the net was it kept me from trying to convert. Parts of me were knitting back together, and I worried that without the constant trying, important things would scar over and be lost to me forever — sort of like having knee replacement surgery and being immobilized as it healed. I tried to ooze around the floor, to somehow crawl out from under the net. No such luck. Whatever magic it held attached the thing to me no matter how hard I tried. It also anchored itself to the floor, limiting my oozing range to only a few feet.

It was a waiting game. Eventually Feille would come, and he wouldn't be satisfied beating plant life under a magical restraint for long. Eventually he'd have it removed, and then I'd do whatever it took to get the fuck out of here. I was desperate, and I knew my life was on the line.

Three pairs of booted feet came within my view, following the most ridiculous, jewel–encrusted slippers I'd ever seen. All hail Lord Feille, asshole of Wythyn.

"Arrrgh! That is the most disgusting thing I've ever seen. Are you sure it's her? Why does she smell like that? Why is she in that revolting form?"

I couldn't see above his knees, but I imagined Feille foppishly holding a scented handkerchief to his nose and waving a hand in my general direction. Probably not, although he *was* a bit overdressed for the occasion with his bejeweled slippers.

"My Lord, we believe she chose this form to escape notice. Once again, she was trespassing on our lands. The scouts found her but nearly put her back after two months in the cell, assuming she was some rare form of pond scum. If one of them hadn't insisted on summoning your sorcerer, she would have escaped."

I imagined Feille's eyes narrowing, still holding the handkerchief to guard against my supposedly foul odor. It was probably a gold embroidered handkerchief, scented with an elven perfume — Eau de Midsummer, or some other weird, esoteric scent.

"Where is her horse?" Feille demanded. I could hear the greed in his voice. I knew he wanted my half–demon horse with his teleportation skills. Feille had been pissed beyond belief when I'd demanded Diablo back with the barrel of a shotgun pointed at his elven head.

"She had no horse with her this time, My Lord. I'm not sure the reason for her trespass, or why she chose to do it on foot. Or, rather, not on foot."

"Why is she still like that? You said she knew she was discovered, that she turned into some kind of reptile and attacked you. Why hasn't she changed? The charade is over and there is no sense in trying to pass herself off as a member of the plant kingdom any longer."

There was an awkward moment of silence as I watched three pairs of boots shift nervously on the floor.

"Well, My Lord, she *is* under a net. She is unable to change her form until it is removed." The guard's tone was respectful, but I clearly heard the "duh" underneath his groveling tone. I held my breath as the air crackled with tension. Some elven guard evidently had a death wish. Luckily for him, Feille let the slight go.

"Well, get it off of her. Now! Move it."

There was another awkward silence. "My Lord ...are you sure? She's fast. And you remember last time."

I felt the air thicken, as if we were underwater. Elves had impressive control over their natural environment, and Feille clearly liked to use his skills to remind everyone who wore the crown. "Did I ask for your counsel? No? Then do as I tell you or I'll feed you to her one limb at a time."

I heard a scurry of booted feet and a raspy noise of a key in a lock. I saw the cell door swing to the left, and one pair of boots hesitantly approached. I felt the net lift slightly and saw the boots dash back across the threshold of my cell. This happened three fucking times until the asshole had the balls enough to completely remove the net before racing to safety.

Silence. I would rather Feille think I was thumbing my nose at him than give him the satisfaction of seeing how broken I really was, seeing as how I could only manage one other form — and a rather harmless one at that. Any additional conversion skills that might have returned to me would need to wait until I was alone and could experiment with some privacy. Failure was best experienced without witnesses.

"Why is she still like that?" Feille asked.

Again the shuffling of boots. "I don't know, My Lord."

There was a collective gasp as the fancy slippers approached me.

"Change. Az, you foul–mouthed goat spawn, change!"

I didn't oblige.

A metal tipped stick was raised then brought down upon me, sinking through my gelatinous form to ring on impact with the floor. Again and again it rose and fell, spraying greenish brown bits of me all over the cell walls and ceiling. It didn't hurt, didn't damage me in the slightest. I was rather amused watching Feille's exertions and his growing frustration with his inability to cause me any pain or suffering whatsoever.

The elf lord screamed and threw the staff behind him, narrowly missing the guards who dodged out of its way. "Get a torch. Someone get me a torch."

Another scurry of feet and a mumbled question, then booted feet carefully approached the slippered ones. I saw a flash of light, felt heat as a torch descended to touch my form. Nothing. Curious as to what abilities I'd recovered, I tried to convert energy to water at the edge of the torch and was thrilled to see the flame sputter and die in a rising, thin line of gray smoke.

"I saw that, Az! Don't you think I didn't see that. You change into a human form right now and I'll be merciful. Change and I'll let you live."

Right. The angels might be blind to the perfidy of elves, but I wasn't. Those fuckers lied like there was no tomorrow. Feille wouldn't kill me right away, that wouldn't be fun at all, but I was pretty sure at the end of all the creative torture he wanted me stuffed and mounted on the wall over his fireplace.

"Change. Change, change, change!" he screamed, kicking at me with his fancy slippers. I didn't change, but I did ensure I caked his footwear with enough ooze to cover the pretty jewels. He'd never get the stink out of those things.

He flung his feet around in an amazing impersonation of Riverdance, screaming at his guards the whole time. I felt a bit sorry for them. It wasn't their fault he was trying to beat the crap out of pond scum and failing miserably.

"Get my sorcerers! Where are my sorcerers?"

I heard a cough, which sounded suspiciously like it was covering up a laugh. "My Lord, your one sorcerer is at the capital, working on the project you told him was of the utmost importance."

Oooh, I was fairly certain a guard's head was going to be the next thing flying across the room. Feille casually walked past them all and picked up his staff. Tension filled the room, and the insubordinate guard blanched. His buddies backed away from him as if he had the plague.

"I'm not sure I like your tone."

"I'm sorry, My Lord. I'm sorry," the guard stammered.

It was the last thing he said. Without a word, light streamed from Feille into his staff, and with a blur of speed he rammed it into the guard's throat. It was a quick death. The elf's head exploded into a spray of sand, and his body fell to the floor. Feille carefully wiped the end of his staff on the dead elf's tunic while the others tried not to stare.

"Does anyone else have anything they'd like to say in regards to the number of sorcerers I now have in the kingdom?"

You could have heard crickets chirping in the silence. If I hadn't eaten them all, that is.

"Have my sorcerer come here immediately," Feille said after a significant pause. I had a bad feeling what this project was and why he didn't want to disturb it, but with one remaining sorcerer, he didn't have much choice. "I'll wait for his arrival."

The fancy slippers left. The cell door clanged, and all the footwear disappeared out of my view. Would they remember to put the net back on me? I hoped not. I held my breath until I heard the rusty scrape of the dungeon door closing then let it out. Wait, I had lungs? Carefully, I took another gulp of oxygen and moved myself across the small cell, this time on longer limbs. I felt a weight on my back and the brush of small, membrane–like wings against the ground. Three sets of eyes on long–snouted heads surveyed my surroundings. I nearly wept. This was very close to my first form and physically strong enough to mount a serious attack. I wasn't sure exactly what Feille had in mind, but at least I could make an attempt at defending myself. Converting my physical form had always been a conscious action before, but I was happy to take what I could get.

By the time I heard the dungeon door again, I was able to change rapidly between my three shapes. I quickly reverted to the pond scum, not wanting to show any weakness. Let them think I was just being stubborn. I'd bide my time and take the first chance that came.

A whole host of feet appeared, separated from me by the bars of my cell. Three booted ones, a pair of brown, short boots, and what I assumed were Feille's fancy, slippered ones — this time spring–green with topaz designs. I wondered if he'd had to toss the previous ones. I hoped so.

"She looks just like she did before." The sorcerer sounded confused. "Has she not changed shape at all?"

"She's like this every time I come here," the guard chimed in. "But look, footprints! She must be changing when she's alone."

Dammit! Once again this stupid, fucking dusty floor was giving me away.

"She's stubbornly keeping to that form so I'm unable to punish her properly," Feille snapped. "Make her into something easier to hurt. I can't do anything to pond scum. Make her into a human."

There was a heavy silence, then the sorcerer released a careful breath. "My Lord, transformation spells have never worked on demons. I'd be happy to do your bidding and attempt it, but I must counsel you that the end result will most likely be failure. If she wants to be pond scum, she'll remain that way."

Awesome! They'd have no choice but to leave me here and hope I eventually got bored enough that I complied — or escaped. Normally demons lost any kind of waiting game, but I got the feeling Feille had even less patience than I.

The high lord in question stomped a slippered foot and smacked me through the spelled bars of my cell with a staff. "Do it. Do it now."

There was a flurry of activity, and I saw the door slide open. The sorcerer began to chant, spreading a line of white in a circle around me. Two inches inside was another ring then a triangle inside that. Once finished, he dropped to his knees and began to inscribe a set of runes around the edge of the outer salt circle. This guy wasn't taking any chances. Even if I could convert myself into something deadly, I wasn't getting past two circles and one triangle, all reinforced. Nothing that didn't come from the sorcerer was getting through that.

The rune circle took a while. I saw a wheeled cart and realized Feille had ordered a food delivery. Even though I didn't have a stomach at the moment, the idea of food took over my mind. I'd spent forty years eating human food, and memories of Hunan bean curd, deep–dish pizza, fudge brownies, and fries sprinkled with vinegar were driving me insane. I would have killed for a dozen hot wings at that moment. From what I could see, Feille's food wasn't as appealing as a batch of hot wings.   Still, the colorful fruit, hearty breads, and thin slices of meat made me long for a form that actually consumed food.

The sorcerer's knees made a crackling noise as he slowly rose to his feet.

"Be a lot easier if there was more than one of us," he muttered to himself as he surveyed his work.

Feille had a habit of losing sorcerers. And mages, and apprentices. Regardless of the minuscule odds of success, a large number of his magical staff tended to cut and run. Personally, I believed the cause of the exodus to be his winning personality and collaborative management style. I'd retrieved a number of sorcerers and mages for him in the past, but I wasn't always good at bringing them back in one piece. That fact deterred future runaways, but many still took their chances. That Gareth guy was still at large, as far as I knew, up somewhere in Eresh with his apprentice. I'd killed the sorcerer Feille had sent to work with the angels. From the comments of his elven staff, I was fairly certain this guy was the only one left. He probably had a dozen or so mages, but few of them would be skilled enough to advance to the highest level, and it often took decades.

Taking a scroll from his pouch, the sorcerer set it at one side of the circle on top of two twigs: one of willow and one of maple, both crossed to form an "x".

"Stand back," he commanded.

There was a backward shuffle of feet, and I was amused to see Feille's jeweled slippers edging safely behind a set of large boots. Pussy.

"*Neadian lil–hamma.*"

The scroll and twigs burst into blue flame. I felt a surge of energy rush into me, cold and sharp. Parts of my spirit self expanded, ripping and tearing the scars that were mending my wounds. It was agonizing, and if I'd had a mouth I would have screamed. The energy swelled. I felt as if I might burst apart. The salt triangle around me glowed red and bubbled; the inner circle began to smoke. I writhed on the floor, shifting my semi–liquid form around in search of relief. I felt an explosion and, at first, wasn't sure if it was me that had combusted or something else. Oh shit, not this again.

Then the overfull feeling receded and I tried to hold still, shaking inside the pond slime that housed my spirit self. The triangle of salt was gone, in its place a deep groove of black etched into the floor. The inner salt circle had fused into a ring of gray. I was in pain. As much pain as I'd been when Gregory had snatched me from death and gated me to Aaru.

"That's as powerful as it gets." The sorcerer's voice held a note of resignation mixed with curiosity. "It should have at least forced a brief change."

"Do it again," Feille insisted.

I didn't think I could survive if he did it again. Everything was raw and open, split between thick lines of scarring. Was I back to square one? Had this undone the little progress I'd made so far? Or perhaps, broken me so completely that I'd never function again?

"With all respect, My Lord, I cannot do it again. I'll need an additional scroll, and more salt. Plus the result will be the same. Our magic just doesn't have enough power to force a demon to change form."

"Then use the demon energy we have in storage. That should work."

Crap. I wondered how much they had, and if it was sufficient for their plans. I'd hoped when I blew up the facility that everything went up with it, but they must have been sending a supply over as they collected it.

There was an awkward silence. "My Lord, you have us working on other things with that. Our shipments have temporarily halted. Shouldn't we conserve what we have for ...you know, the coming events?"

"We can spare some, and we'll be getting more soon. I want her transformed into a human, and I want her to stay that way."

Getting more soon? So Feille knew about the destruction of the facility. The fact that it was in the process of being rebuilt made me realize that this went far deeper into Aaru then the two angels working with Baphomet. There had to be another angel, or even more, involved to start up the process again so quickly. How long would it take, and would I be able to somehow reach Gregory and alert him in time? I hated the thought that I'd sacrificed myself for nothing, although at least I had bought everyone some time. I just needed to let Gregory know what some of his angels were up to, and warn the demons of what was coming their way.

"My Lord, I am not sure even that will work. I think something is wrong with her, that she may be broken or injured somehow."

Feille strode into the cell and stabbed at me again with the staff, careful to keep his precious shoes away from me. "She's not injured; she's just a rude, insubordinate, stubborn imp. She's doing this deliberately, to defy me and avoid punishment."

"My Lord, we haven't even tested this out on anything beyond a few Lows. Perhaps we should just leave her as she is and wait for her to change on her own. I hate for us to waste resources, and I have concerns what might happen using the new magic on one with her unusual skills."

Feille snarled, and I saw the staff whirl past me to whack the sorcerer in the leg. "We're about to use it on demons far above her level. It better work on her."

"Yes, My Lord." The sorcerer sighed. He clearly had no choice in the matter. No wonder so many of them ran away.

"Dismissed," Feille told him. "Go prepare and be back here in twenty-four hours."

The sorcerer caught his breath, and I got the feeling that twenty-four hours wasn't nearly enough time for him to do what he needed. I knew it wasn't nearly enough time for me either. Who knows how much progress that stupid spell of his had undone.

"You too. Everyone leave."

The guards hesitated then left, wheeling the food cart along with them. With a screech of the dungeon door, it was just the two of us in the cell. Feille and I. I tensed, waiting for the stick to fall. Even though it didn't hurt, I still didn't like the idea of being beaten.

"Az, Az," he said, his voice soft. "You're only delaying the inevitable. Keeping to this disgusting form may save you from pain today, but it will only mean a future of woe. Change your shape and I'll give you a quick and painless death."

He lied. And I didn't want a quick and painless death; I wanted to jump on him and rip his head off with my bare hands.

The slippers approached, right to the edge of the outer circle. I hoped he breached it — the only thing containing me at this point. Not that I could do much to him, but I really wanted to ruin one more pair of slippers, or perhaps bite his leg.

"No? Maybe you should reconsider. Once you're in human form, I'm going to collar you. Know what that is? It's a device that will keep you from changing form, using any kind of demon attack, or fixing any of your injuries. You'll be as weak and vulnerable as the human flesh around your demon soul."

He didn't just have a stash of demon energy to fuel his magic; he had collars. It wouldn't matter one bit to me in my current condition, but I shivered, thinking of what would happen if those collars wound up on high-level demons. It would shift the entire power structure of our society. It would be so easy too. All he'd have to do was throw a big festival and give a bunch of them out as gifts, all blinged up to the max. We are such suckers for gifts, and even the most ancient among us wouldn't hesitate to put on a gaudy bauble. We're demons. Top of the food chain. A simple necklace would seem nothing compared to our powers. Our hubris would be our downfall.

"Then I will stripe your skin with acids, tear long lines of flesh from your body, insert burrowing beetles into every orifice. I'll heal you myself, just enough so you don't die, but not enough to relieve the pain."

Yeah. I'd had worse. These elves were pansies. If I could just manage to convert to a more fierce form, I'd fuck this guy up big time. But I worried that whatever the sorcerer had done had put me back to square one. I was terrified I might not even be able to manage the lizard form anymore.

"When my troops ride into battle, I'll make sure you watch. Maybe I'll actually drag you out to see the carnage, watch the vultures pick the flesh off the bones of your household. I've already taken control of Li, Allwin, and Tonlielle. Cyelle and Kllee are already lining up to sign an alliance with me. Once that's done, we'll conquer the demons. They'll serve as energy sources for us. Mindless, restrained in collars and chained in cells, only kept alive to supply us with their power. With their power, I'll take the northern elven kingdoms and rule all of Hel."

Not if I could help it. The elves might fall to his might, but the demons wouldn't go down easy. Controlling us was like herding cats — really big cats that shot lightning and threw fireballs and started plagues and decimated crops. He had a finite supply of demon energy right now, and an interruption in his supply chain. I needed to do something to ensure he couldn't collect from any demons within Hel — ever. Here the energy flowed thick and heavy all around us. It was so easy to pull it in. Even a Low could supply him with an infinite source here in Hel. I had to make sure he never got his hands on one of us. Of course, I couldn't do much as pond scum.

"And we'll sell them to the angels. Yes, that's right — angels. When I'm done playing with you, I'll drain you of every drop of energy then pull you apart like meat from an overcooked roast. I'll section you, put you into special storage containers and sell you to the angels."

Fuck him and the horse he rode in on. My new mission in life was to see this elf dead — before breakfast, if at all possible.

"Or maybe I'll keep you alive and use you as my personal pet. I'll keep you collared and chained like a dog by my side. Maybe I'll pull your teeth, cut off your fingers. I'll feed you nothing but human flesh. I know you're fond of some of them. I'll find them, make them watch as I torture you, and you can watch while I eviscerate them before your eyes. You'll be forced to choose between starving and eating their flesh."

And they said we were evil. This guy needed to die. He really fucking needed to die. I lay silent, in my pond scum form, and fumed. I could do nothing right now. Nothing. And after that fucking sorcerer had messed me up, who knows how long it would be before I repaired enough to warn the demons, and Gregory. I'd never been the most powerful demon, even as the Iblis, but this feeling of helplessness enraged me.

"No? Well, Az, we'll see how loud you scream after tomorrow. Rest easy, dear friend."

The slippers retreated and the cell door closed behind them. I heard his footsteps as he exited the dungeon and the screech of the door as it closed. What could I do? I needed to get out of here and kill that motherfucker, but I wasn't in any state to take him on right now. At the very least, I needed to escape to let the other demons know of his plans, to warn them about the collars. I also needed to somehow let Gregory know that the angel I'd killed wasn't the only one involved in this little "project", but I wasn't exactly mobile at the moment. If only there was some way to stall Feille, to delay his attack until I could regain enough of my skills to take him out.

I tried once again to change my form into the reptile shape. I was in so much pain, the dull ache had once again become a sharp blade of agony lancing through me. I tried to concentrate and transform — tried to create legs, a head, eyes, anything. Nothing. The only good thing that had come of this was that the thick scarring that was restricting some of my newfound abilities had loosened. I had become more flexible, but it didn't do me any good if I couldn't convert or store energy.

I wasn't getting out of here anytime soon, and I couldn't think of any way to get a message to Dar or any other member of my household. No one came down here but that asshole

Lyte, the guards, and the crew with Feille. So a warning was temporarily out of the question. I needed to somehow delay Feille. Smash his store of demon energy, destroy the collars, disrupt the magic necessary to use either of them.

The sorcerer. He was Feille's only sorcerer. I'm sure there were still some mages and apprentices, but he had one sorcerer. If I killed him, Feille wouldn't have the magical ability to go against the demons. He'd need to wait until a mage came up to speed, or he could transfer and train a sorcerer from his new kingdoms. It might buy me six months, it might buy me a year. But how to kill him?

Pond scum couldn't do much. Maybe if he ate me, but I doubted that would be a possibility. If he had an open wound, I could probably infect it, but that would take forever, and I didn't think he'd get close enough for me to transfer any bacteria or virus. I'd just need to watch and take any opportunity I could find to kill him.

A twinge of guilt went through me. Wyatt would not approve, and I wasn't sure I did either. I was reluctant to take an innocent life, and this sorcerer was a victim. He was a slave, living under Feille's iron thumb and, no doubt, wondering if every day would be his last. He had some job security in that he was the only sorcerer that the high lord had. Feille wasn't likely to kill him — yet. Once he fully absorbed his conquests, he'd have their sorcerers. And he could demand tribute from the allied kingdoms as well. Once that happened, this guy's life would be hanging by a thread.

I toyed with the idea of trying to win him to my side, but I didn't have any way to communicate with him. Plus, I'm sure his fear of Feille would trump any juicy deal I could make with him — it's not like I was in a great bargaining position. I hated the choice I was about to make, but the man was a tool that would be used to take down all of Hel. If his death would prevent it, or delay it long enough for me to come up with a viable plan, then he needed to go. Someone needed to do the dirty work. Guess that someone was going to be me.

~6~

G abriel looked at the woman walking toward him, then beyond her to the humans playing in the sand at the surf's edge. He could smell the ocean's salt, its mix of life and death, a mini cosmos in its own liquid sky.

"A coffee shop would have been nice," the woman huffed. "My physical form isn't equipped for this sort of activity."

"I always pick the shore. I'd think that over billions of years, you would have realized that."

The woman plopped down beside him, spreading her legs out in front of her. The sun glinted off her red hair, turning it the color of flame around her pale face. It was odd that only two of them could create red hair. The one a dark auburn, then this one a bright crimson. Gabriel had tried, but the only color he could manage was deep black. Flexibility in corporeal forms was not a strong skill for Angels of Order.

"Still female, Uriel? Bit off the median, aren't you?"

Angels tended to alternate genders fairly regularly, always keeping within a tolerable distance of their balanced center. With a new Iblis, they'd found themselves compensating, sliding further right of an acceptable mark, especially when in close proximity to her. It irritated Gabriel, who continued his excessively masculine form outside of her presence, as if he chose this of his own free will. Uriel did the opposite, forcing herself into a painfully feminine form even when in Council meetings.

"I like being female. It's been a while since I was. If it troubles you, I can change."

"Don't bother," he replied. If she changed, he'd need to alter his form to balance. It just wasn't worth the effort. Increasingly, nothing seemed worth the effort, no matter how hard he fought against his ennui. There were pinpoints of light — fighting with that horrid imp, investigating rumors of sin and stamping them out. Thoughts of Sidreal's conversation rose in his mind. Creation might be just what he needed to feel alive again.

Alive. The last time he'd felt that way, it had all come crashing down. Balance and order were safer, less painful, than feeling alive.

"You have the papers?" the woman asked, jolting Gabriel from his thoughts by bringing up the reason he'd given her when he'd requested this meeting.

Gabriel flicked a wrist, and a stack of bound documents appeared in her hand. "Obviously, this information is to be kept between the two of us."

She lifted an eyebrow. "I assume so, given that we're doing this outside of Aaru."

Gabriel glanced out to sea, where the water met the horizon. At one time he'd enjoyed coming here, assisting the evolution of a lesser species. It was a noble purpose. Now, there wasn't a day that went by when he didn't think of wiping the slate clean. Raise the mighty sea and wash them all away. It would be a fitting end to a terrible tragedy.

Humans had become terrible creatures. It was disheartening how such a promising species could veer so far from their right evolution. They'd messed this one up terribly, and it would be a shame to wipe them out. Increasingly he wondered if they could ever be brought back into the fold. They were too far from center, almost as far as the demons. He felt a pang remembering the Angels of Chaos the demons had once been. Never centered, but still with good in their hearts. He couldn't say that about what remained of them, and he wasn't sure he could say that about the humans either.

"It seems we have once again lost our Adversary," he commented. He'd been there when his brother brought her in, broken and barely alive. He'd felt sorrow, and wasn't sure if it was for his brother or for the half–dead demon he'd developed a distasteful affection for.

Uriel placed her energy seal on the last page of the paperwork, and it vanished from her hands. "Don't count the Iblis out yet. She's a lucky little imp."

Gabriel shrugged, trying for a casual tone. "Doesn't matter if she lives or dies, it's not as if she can hold the office from Hel, and she's unlikely to return."

"I think you're sweet on her," the woman teased. "Better get your own though; I doubt our brother will share."

He hid a smile. No, his brother most definitely wouldn't share. Still, as fun as it was to bully the little imp, he couldn't understand the attraction. "He's breaking the rules, dear sister. All of Aaru is whispering about his treason."

Uriel took in a sharp breath. "Be careful what words you choose, brother. He is powerful and he has loyal allies."

Gabriel watched her carefully. Her mannerisms, her words all seemed sincere. If his sister had lied about Furlac's purpose among the humans, she was hiding it well. She was not typically the one who would formulate rebellion. The top position in Aaru had never had appeal for her. The few times she'd gone against any of her brothers, it had been in defense of an ethical ideal — or to protect one she loved.

"Do you defend him? Support him in this madness? Yes, the Adversary is allowed a certain status by the treaty, but he takes it too far. She'll cause him to fall, if she hasn't already, and that will rock Aaru to the core."

Uriel smiled, and he saw a soft light in her eyes he hadn't seen in millions of years. "Let him be. He's carried the weight of Aaru on his shoulders for as long as I can remember. He deserves some happiness."

Happiness. Gabriel felt a stab of pain. Happiness was a fleeting thing, never worth the agony that remained when it fled.

"It will create jealousy, dissent."

Uriel frowned. "Yes, there will be envy. I too experience that sin, but that doesn't mean I can't also feel joy at my brother's happiness."

Gabriel turned to look out at the waves crashing on the shore. It was hard to feel joy when the sin of envy blackened his own heart.

"His blatant connection with this demon will open the door to sinful behavior among all the angels. Not that I blame him," he added. "We've had no procreation since the split. Some are desperate."

"There are a few angels who continue to mate with humans, but it's not as widespread as you think, and we punish the transgressors. Most would not dream of such an act."

"What alternative is there? Seize and bind a demon, use it as vessel? They are no longer angels, and the prospect is just as abhorrent as mating with a human female. We are trapped in a cage of our own making."

Out of the corner of his eye, he saw Uriel clench her hands together. A twinge of guilt speared through him — this was an open wound for her, and he was cruel for bringing it up.

"No one forced us to write that treaty. No one forced us to continue the war to its inevitable conclusion. We made our choices, and now we must live with them."

"Everyone except our illustrious brother. He evidently can violate the treaty and procreate, while others must abide by the choices we made. Nice how he gets to break the rules."

"Are you questioning our brother's motives?" she asked hotly. "He *loves* her. Do you even remember what that sacred emotion felt like, Gabriel? Is this the sin of jealousy talking or do you really think his interest in the imp is strictly as a vessel for offspring?"

He couldn't help a grimace of irritation. Uriel was such an optimist, always a romantic.

"No, I'm sure he's head over wings in love. I'll admit though that this is one of the most difficult effects of the war to reconcile myself to — never being able to create another being."

He felt the weight of her stare on him. "Creation. Not love. You missed your chance to pass on your oh–so–impressive angelic traits before the war, and now you regret that there will be no opportunity to do so. That's the empty spot in your heart?"

Her words cut to the bone. "Don't tell me you wouldn't jump if the opportunity to create presented itself," Gabriel said.

Uriel lowered her head, picking at a tiny grain of sand as she hid her expression from him. "Yes, but it's the joining I miss the most. That sense of closeness, when I become more than an angel. It's the nearest I've ever been to divinity."

"They're not angels anymore; they're demons. Love is off the table, as is joining. You'll need to find divinity through right order and meditation, just like the rest of us." He hadn't meant his words to be so harsh, or his tone so bitter.

Her entire body tensed, and her head snapped up, eyes flashing. "I've seen a lot of miracles in my five billion years. I won't give up on love, and I won't give up on creation."

Here was where he had to tread oh so carefully. "We may never be able to experience love again, but maybe someday we could manage to find a way around the problem of creation."

Uriel shot him a suspicious look. She didn't seem surprised at the premise, but he couldn't gauge which way she stood on the issue.

"I've heard rumors that we could see creation again in Aaru."

The redhead gave a short bark of laughter. "Such a positive outlook. I hadn't expected that from you."

"Would you, Uriel? I know there will never be a spirit to replace Haka, but would you seek to create again?"

They sat for a moment, Uriel's eyes on the humans playing below while Gabriel watched her. Both her lover and her only child had been Angels of Chaos. The war had split families, but Uriel had lost so much more than most.

"Yes," she said softly. "I would very much like to create another life. But to do that, we need an Angel of Chaos — a demon. We severed that tie nearly three million years ago. We knowingly committed ourselves to this path. Unless there is a possibility of immaculate conception, proof that the process does not violate all we hold dear, I won't break my vow."

Her voice held two million years of pain. He knew, deep inside, she longed for a different choice, to return to a happier past before the war.

Gabriel drew a line in the sand with his finger, trying to keep his tone casual. "Then I guess we should pray for immaculate conception."

Again they sat in silence while Gabriel allowed his words to sink in.

"Do you think she is Samael's offspring?" Uriel asked unexpectedly. "The imp? Our unconventional Iblis?"

Sharp pain stabbed through Gabriel's chest. "No."

He offered no explanation. He'd fought fiercely with Samael, as only close brothers can, but even with the war that divided them, he refused to believe his youngest brother had fallen so far as to interbreed with other Angels of Chaos. He never would have contributed to the monsters such inbreeding produced.

"So what are your thoughts on the report?" Gabriel asked, shifting the topic back in a safer, less painful direction.

Uriel breathed a tired sigh. "Two angels dead. That's three this year including the one our beloved brother dispatched."

"Althean was one of his Grigori. Even though he wasn't in the fourth choir, it was still within his scope to deliver justice."

The woman chuckled. "That sounds like approval. Be careful, dear brother, lest I think you actually support our eldest sibling for once."

"Just because it was his right, doesn't mean I agree with the justice he delivered," Gabriel protested. "Death was an extreme verdict, especially given our inability to produce more angels. Althean could have been rehabilitated, given sufficient time and attention."

Uriel shivered. "Death was probably more merciful."

Gabriel waved a hand dismissively. "But it's not Althean that concerns me. He was Grigori and had every right to be walking among the humans, even if his actions weren't sanctioned. These other two angels were away from Aaru without permission, one of them yours."

He felt a wave of power from his sister, gritty as the sand they sat upon. "Furlac was delivering a personal message for me. His death had nothing to do with his errand. It was simply an unfortunate accident."

Gabriel's eyebrows rose as he looked at Uriel in disbelief. "He was murdered, dear sister. Pray enlighten me as to who killed him, and how it had no connection to his clandestine visit on earth."

Uriel glared at him. "I do not know who killed him. I've recused myself from the investigation due to my conflict of interest. I'll read about it in the final report. All I know is that I sent him on a peaceful mission and he never returned."

Gabriel couldn't help the harsh laugh that escaped him. She lied. If she wasn't planning a rebellion, what was she up to? Could it be that his own sister found the idea of human companionship too tempting to resist? Was she perhaps hiding a Nephilim of her own, or one born to an angel in her choir?

She snarled at him, and he felt the abrasive scrape of her power, like a rasp against his flesh. "I mourn. He was a loyal member of my choir. I'll thank you to understand my sorrow and respect the tragedy of our loss."

He personally felt no sadness, no sense of loss over this angel, but he inclined his head in apology for his callousness. "Then what about Vaol? Raphael's angel. He left a body behind without a mark on it. How did he die? Who could have done such a thing? "

Gabriel watched his sister closely to see her reaction.

"The Grigori are investigating this death. I believe they suspected a devouring spirit, which is in keeping with the manner of death."

"And the thought of a devouring spirit loose doesn't bother you? I find it hard to believe you could be so casual about the prospect." He shook his head. First his brother's odd behavior, and now Uriel's indifference. What was going on?

"Of course I'm concerned. I have great faith in our brother and his Grigori to contain the matter. If he is unconcerned, then there is no cause for worry."

Gabriel frowned — was she aware that the monster had been slain or was she just oddly unaffected by the thought of an imminent apocalypse?

"The timing of the two deaths would lead me to believe they were connected, and the fact that the deceased's choir is not cooperating requires added scrutiny in the investigation."

Uriel waved a hand in irritation. "You see conspiracy where this is none. Their deaths were not at all similar. How could there be a connection between an angel delivering a message and one whose life was taken by an abomination?"

Gabriel winced. A devouring spirit was something they all feared. Eventually, one day, one would escape them and all life as they knew it would cease. The end would be upon them.

"But why was he with the humans? Raphael claims in the report that he has no knowledge of the angel's purpose, and his choir refuses to cooperate."

Uriel closed her eyes and shook her head. "Maybe he was tempted to sin. Maybe even tempted to find a loving connection with a human woman and produce Nephilim. Maybe he just wanted to catch the last episode of Mad Men. Our rules are inflexible and many of the lesser angels chafe under the restrictions."

Gabriel stiffened. He understood temptation better than most angels. That Uriel was so casual about the shortcomings of others never failed to irk him.

"But he's dead. Why cover it up unless whatever he was doing is still ongoing and something that is forbidden? There is no shame in having a fallen angel in your choir, unless the entire choir knew of and supported his actions."

He watched her closely, but she just appeared ...tired.

"I don't care. I just don't care anymore. Is that wrong? I see how happy our eldest brother is with his little imp and I find myself wanting to throw away all I've held dear for the past two and a half million years and find one of my own." She rubbed a hand over her brow. "Maybe I'm just weary. I'm old, and things are not like they used to be. There's too much chaos in the universe to hold fast to a philosophy of strict order."

"Now who is it that voices treasonous thoughts?" Gabriel said softly.

"If over half of Aaru thinks the same, than how is that treason?" she replied. "Perhaps it is a natural turn of events. A return to equilibrium."

"We have equilibrium," Gabriel snapped. "And I, for one, will not sully myself with humans or demons. Until someone can present me with a viable alternative, a way to combine myself with the necessary portion of spirit to produce offspring without actually having to join with one, then I will hold fast to my principals."

Uriel shook her head, once again gazing down at the human children at play. "Then pray mightily, my brother. Pray mightily."

~7~

I spent the next twenty–four hours trying to ignore my pain and force myself to convert energy into matter. Even though I couldn't manage to change my form, if I could turn raw energy to fire or lightning, or produce an explosion, at least I'd have an offensive ability. I may be pond scum, but I'd be bad–ass pond scum. The biggest problem I seemed to be having was holding onto enough energy to produce a decent–sized result. I could spark and shock, rumble the floor below me, but nothing bigger. Raim had been able to directly convert large chunks of matter into energy and produce a lethal burst, although he couldn't hold or store the energy. I couldn't manage even that.

I heard the dungeon doors open with a sense of dread. Whatever was coming my way was going to be painful, and there was nothing I could do about it. The large group of feet approached my cell and stopped. I envisioned them staring at me, as if I were an animal at the zoo and they a bunch of second graders on a field trip.

"She needs to be moved to a different cell," I heard the sorcerer say. "The floor here has been compromised — it won't properly hold the magical enchantments to perform the rite."

There was a series of mumbling, and a voice finally spoke. "How are we supposed to move her? I mean ...look at her. She's not exactly solid."

"Well, how did you get her here? I'm sure she didn't appear from nowhere into your dungeon." Feille's voice was impatient and sarcastic.

"A bucket. And a shovel." I recognized the scout who'd brought me in.

"Then why are you standing here, staring at her? Get to it."

There was a flurry of activity, and a few minutes later, my cell door opened. I heard the scrape of the shovel, and felt myself dumped into a bucket. It was all very undignified. From the confines of my container, I felt the vertigo of being lifted, then a rocking motion as whoever carried me swung the bucket to and fro. Another cell door clanged open, and I was deposited onto a cold, hard floor, just as dirty as the one I'd been in for the last few months.

It took a few seconds for whatever sense I was using to visualize my surroundings to stabilize. When the world righted, I saw all the shoes a healthy distance away on the other side of the cell bars. They'd left the door open, but retreated in case I decided to attack.

"She seems determined to ride this out," one of the guards commented. I'd landed at a slightly different angle and could actually see more than their feet this time. At the distance they all stood, I could make out their faces, although I calculated that within three or four feet, I'd be unable to see anything above their hips.

"Yeah, I thought for sure you were going to get electrocuted, the way you tossed her in that bucket," one laughed. I really wanted to. If only I could.

Feille gave them a fierce glance and the laughter abruptly stopped. "Is there enough room surrounding her for your circles and runes? I have a feeling she's waiting to pounce, and I want to make sure you're safe."

I knew his concern was strictly because this man was his only sorcerer, and he couldn't afford to lose him. I'd need to watch carefully for any opportunity to make my move. Not that I might be able to take advantage of it. My only hope was that this insane spell actually worked, and didn't kill me in the process. If he managed to turn me into a human, I'd be more vulnerable physically, but better able to grab whatever I could reach and beat the shit out of everyone. I loved a good melee, and I was hoping one was in my near future.

The sorcerer stepped forward, once again surrounding me with a serious amount of salt — two circles and an inner triangle, as before. With a grunt of pain and an awkward movement, he knelt down and began his circle of chalk runes. I felt a twinge of guilt. This guy wasn't young, and he was crawling around a cold stone floor on his knees twice in two days. He was a slave, a man who had no option but to follow Feille's orders. I felt terrible for what I needed to do.

Done with his runes, the sorcerer stood stiffly and motioned to one of the guards, who brought a box over. The sorcerer pulled a variety of stones from the box and placed them at the four directional corners outside the rune circle, chanting as he went. Granite for north, turquoise for east, red jasper for south, and jade at the west. With both hands massaging his back, he retreated to survey his work. I tensed, waiting for the ritual to begin, and was surprised when he dropped to the ground and began another round of runes outside the stones. This guy wasn't fucking around. Whatever he planned to do, it was going to be big — big enough to require six layers of defense.

That done, he stood and mumbled an incantation, too soft for me to hear. The air crackled and I felt walls of power encase me in a sphere that went through the dungeon floor to whatever was below and up past the roof. Worry pushed at the edge of my mind. I began to doubt I'd live to see daylight.

The sorcerer motioned, and a guard came forward, carefully placing a glass vial into his hand. The contents swirled and churned, a pearl–white with streaks of gray. The sorcerer muttered a few words under his breath, and I wasn't sure if they were part of the spell, or an entreaty to his deity to protect him from the contents.

"*Lethafa wurthan.*" As he spoke, sorcerer threw the vial onto the ground, smashing it just outside the last rune circle. The pearly–white and gray vanished in a puff of sparks that melted the shards of glass onto the stone floor.

Assent to it. I had a fraction of a second to ponder the words. Was it a command for me to bow down to the spell? If Gregory hadn't been able to compel me, I doubted elven magic could. Then I realized as a stream of cold seeped into me, like an icy drug through veins, that it was the spell itself commanded to ride on the back of the demon energy, to act as a harmonious pair. The cold was unpleasant, but not painful, and I felt a sensation I hadn't in so long. The energy stayed within me, held inside my spirit being by the sorcerer's magic instead of passing through my frantically grasping fingers as it had since my near death experience. It was a tiny amount compared to what I was used to holding over the last forty years, and it felt odd. Normally, I stored raw energy as a compressed mass near my core, but this was spread out all through me. It reminded me of when I'd battled Raim and had exceeded my storage capacity, raw energy flooding along every part of my spirit being. Was that what had triggered the incredible need to devour everything? If the sorcerer's spell made me repeat that experience, I wasn't sure I could return from it like I'd done before. Especially without Gregory here to center me and pull me from the brink.

The sorcerer motioned again and another vial was pressed into his hand. "*Lethafa wurthan.*" Once again I felt the icy magic and the energy pour through me.

This continued for four more vials before Feille spoke.

"How much are you going to use? I thought just one vial would do the job." His voice sounded uneasy, probably calculating what his remaining stock was and if it would be enough to complete his goals of world domination. I knew what he was thinking — if it took this much to force one little imp to change forms, how much would he need to bring the entire demon race under his thumb? I hoped it was more than he had.

The sorcerer hesitated. "My Lord, the collected energy was from Low demons, and although she is an imp, she has a huge capacity. If we don't use an adequate amount, we risk wasting it all for no results."

Feille scowled. "How much? How much do you need?"

The human wiped a bead of sweat from his forehead. "Umm, two, possibly four more."

The elven lord narrowed his eyes, shifting his gaze from the nervous sorcerer to me. "Do it."

The sorcerer broke four more vials before he finally backed away. Backed far away. They all did. A few of them edged sideways out of my view. Feille usually was a coward, hiding behind magical protection to do his bullying, but this time he stood just a few feet behind the sorcerer, arms crossed as he watched intently.

"Neadian lil–hamma."

Same words, different result. This time I felt something ignite inside me, moving along the icy cold magic and pearl–colored energy. There was a burst of color, a flash of creation as atoms formed and molecules came together. I was vaguely aware of the energy I held pulling together in a knot, then rolling like molten lava in an underground fissure. I felt pressure build, passing the limits of comfort and crossing into agony. Something was going to give, and I had a feeling it would be me. Cell reproduction went into overdrive. I felt like a sausage on the grill about to explode its casing. Just as I thought I could take no more, the energy exploded as a fireball into the dungeon.

Oddly, my spirit–self, and whatever physical form currently held me, were unaffected. I watched in interest as the triangle, two circles, runes, stones, and outer circle of runes were swept away. Iron bars melted, the floor and walls blackened, huge cracks appeared every ten inches, like a pattern. Chunks of stone fell from the ceiling, smoking as they hit the floor. Figures vanished in the flame. I saw Feille, protected from the heat somehow, thrown against the back wall, bouncing hard and landing on the floor in a heap. The sorcerer, equally protected, slid along the floor to crash beside him. Damn. If I was going to explode and die in a fiery blast, I'd hoped to at least take the pair of them with me. But they appeared only stunned, and I felt ...fine.

I looked down and saw hands. Two hands attached to arms, breasts, belly, legs, and feet, all familiar. It had worked, and as happy as I was to be mobile, I was just as unhappy to realize whatever Feille had planned for the demons would probably work too. I grabbed at the energy in the air around me, thrilled that I could grasp and hold a modest amount. I still had no demon offensive skills, but was confident they would be possible in my near future. Right now I was a human, fragile and without the ability to fix any wounds, but mobile. And I didn't need demon abilities to fight and kill. Forty years among the humans had taught me I could be just as lethal with my own bare hands.

It might not be much, but I'd take it. Jumping to my feet, I sprinted across the hot dungeon floor, feeling blisters form on the bottom of my feet. Seeing the sorcerer defenseless, an old man in a crumpled heap of embroidered robes, I had a second of doubt. I didn't want to kill this man, but I desperately needed the time his death would buy me. Jumping on him, I pressed a shin across his neck, my full weight on his windpipe. He came to with a start, and struggled. I pressed down harder, hearing the thud of hurried footsteps on the stairs beyond the blasted dungeon doors, seeing Feille stir just a few feet away. Killing him this way wouldn't work. Elves have healing abilities second only to angels, and Feille, or even one of the approaching guards, could resurrect the sorcerer with a flick of a wrist. I planned to do something drastic. Something to make sure there wasn't enough of a body to resurrect. I just didn't want the sorcerer to be conscious for it.

Finally, I saw the light go out from behind his eyes, felt the relaxing of his body under mine. Feille lifted a hand to his head. The guards threw themselves against the melted dungeon door, trying with magic and might to create an opening. I grabbed the largest rock I could find from the partially collapsed ceiling and brought it down over and over on the sorcerer's head, hearing the sickening crunch of bone and feeling the soft give of the tissue beneath.

I heard a scream of fury beside me. I didn't stop. I pounded the rock into what no longer resembled a human head until the whack of a staff against my side threw me off the sorcerer and against the wall.

Feille stood before me, wielding the staff like a golf club. My side throbbed from the impact, and a deep breath sent a sharp pain through me — at least one rib broken. With a snarl that would have done a demon proud, Feille reversed his grip on the staff and beat me with it. Blows rained down on my head and body as I frantically tried to grab the weapon.

"You spawn of Satan, you lowly piece of offal. I'll drag you behind me in chains for centuries, impale you in the square for everyone to beat. I'll kill everyone you know while you watch."

"You're next, Feille," I promised, rolling about as I tried to evade his blows and snatch something I could use as a weapon. The only thing handy was the staff smacking me on my back and head. I managed to roll onto my knees and get to my feet, all the while trying to grab the staff as I deflected it with my arms.

We danced in time to the clanging noise of the guards trying to gain entrance to the dungeon. My hands and arms were numb from the blows, and I was pretty sure I had a few fractures in addition to the broken rib or two. Trying to ignore the pain–induced nausea, I narrowed the distance between the high lord and me, causing him to back up in order to get the best impact out of each swing. If I didn't get that staff from him soon, he was going to tire of beating me and employ whatever magic he'd used to explode the guard's head on me. While he screamed in rage, I left myself open to a particularly hard smack to my left side, rolling along the length of the staff to bring Feille's arm around my body with his momentum.

I might not be able to fix myself, but I still could tolerate pain better than any human. Disregarding the broken bones and bleeding, I finally managed to wrap my arms around the staff and Feille's arm. He yanked the staff backward, punching me in the lower back with his other hand. My grasp slid, hands slick with blood.

Feille spun about with typical elven agility, and my hands slipped along the length of the staff until I stood two feet from him, each of us holding an end of the staff. The elf spun about again, and I flew, like in a game of crack–the–whip, to smack against the dungeon wall. My hands slid further and I would have lost my hold on the staff if my grip hadn't caught the round crystal mounted into the end. I braced myself against the dungeon wall and yanked back, twisting as I pulled. The staff flew from Feille's grasp. Instinctively he covered his head as a protective light burst like a bubble around him. I swung the staff past him, tossing it to the side, and dived at the elf lord. Fuck the staff, I wanted to feel my hands wrapping around his neck.

The dungeon door fell to the floor with an almighty clang. Six inches from Feille, the bubble around him sparked with an arc of electricity and I flew back, convulsing from the shock and hitting the stone hard enough to knock the wind from me.

I heard the guards, and saw Feille put out his hand to halt them. "Hold back. I'll take care of her myself."

Like hell he would. I staggered to my feet, taking tiny breaths in an attempt to get my diaphragm back in action. The bubble around Feille faded, and he taunted me, waving a finger to motion me forward.

I rushed him. Well, staggered toward him, actually. He let me get within five feet, then raised his hands with a shimmer of green. I dove, trying to reach him before whatever spell he'd cast activated. Just as I touched his robes, I felt vines wrap around my legs, yanking me backward and to the ground. They grew from the stone floor; gray and hard at the base, gradually becoming a tough, woody green that bound around my body like iron. I struggled, gasping in pain as the rope–like strands tightened against my broken ribs and cracked bones.

"My Lord, where shall we put her? Half the dungeon has been destroyed, the spells securing it compromised."

Feille's voice was calm, as if he'd been taking tea in the garden and not fighting for his life. "One of the end cells. Pick whichever one is least damaged. I'll personally repair any breached areas."

He walked toward me as I struggled in the viney embrace, sparking little bits of demon energy in an attempt to burn through the restraints. Reaching inside a hidden pocket of his robe, he pulled forth a silver circle —one that I recognized with dread. With a smile, he closed it around my neck, the vines parting for him as he secured it.

"I'd like you to stay this way, Az, in this soft vulnerable human form. I'd also like you to enjoy your injuries a bit longer. You'll assume the shape I want you to. You'll only heal when I allow it. From this moment on, you will have less power than the lowliest of my human slaves. How does that feel, Az?"

"Won't stop me from killing you." I spat at him, my only remaining way to show defiance. "It may be a week, it may be two, but eventually you'll slip up, and I'll be waiting. You're a world–class fuck–up, Feille. You won't live to see the year's end; this I promise."

A flicker of uncertainty flashed in his eyes, quickly hidden as he motioned the guards forward. They exploded into action, kicking and hitting me as I lay bound and defenseless. I hovered in a delirium of pain, trying to keep from passing out as they dragged me and heaved me into another cell. Feille examined the protection around the bars and walls with a glowing hand, while I tried to look menacing with my swollen eyes and puffed lips. Finally, he smiled at me and closed the door with a clang.

"Sleep well, Az. You've forced me into a difficult choice with your actions tonight. Unfortunate for me, deadly for you. Too bad."

He and the guards left the dungeon, and the vines binding me crumbled into dust. I breathed deep and tried to settle into a comfortable position. Whatever Feille had planned for me wasn't worrying me at the moment. I'd bought myself the time I needed by killing his sorcerer; now I needed to figure out how to get out of here — which wasn't going to be easy broken, injured, and with this damned collar around my neck keeping me from using even the small amount of demon skills I'd managed to recover. But as that ballsy southern woman had once said; tomorrow was another day.

~8~

Gabriel nudged an old banana peel with his toe. This kind of back alley thing was far beyond what any angel should have to experience. He hated being this close to the humans, so near their areas of commerce. He'd thought about rejecting the odd invitation, debated whether accepting showed an unseemly desperation, or revealed his willingness to move beyond his comfort zone to entertain the interesting proposal. Was this something he wanted to consider personally? Not that it mattered. He still had a duty to make sure nothing about this secretive enterprise violated angelic law or jeopardized their vibration levels.

He'd been running in circles, trying to get to the bottom of the two deaths, all for nothing. Ruling Council meetings had been suspended indefinitely; the reports from his eldest brother were far overdue. For an immortal, two months should be a wisp of time, but patience never came easy to Gabriel. Especially this past year, when it seemed every second dragged on like eternity. He was at a frustratingly dead end with the matter of the deceased angels, but this was something he could turn his attention to.

"Exalted one."

The voice came from behind him, down the alley, to the left. Gabriel didn't turn around. An angel of his status didn't greet others this far down the hierarchy.

"I regret that a lowly being such as I has been sent to speak with you, but you must understand that in matters as sensitive as this, discretion and secrecy are necessary."

Gabriel gave a sharp nod, refusing to face or speak to the angel.

"We have heard that you may share longings in common with some of us. Longings that we are hoping to alleviate."

Gabriel hesitated, finally turning around. In order to find out if these angels were behaving lawfully, it might be best to pose as a potential client. But a conversation about his having a burning desire to create wouldn't be suitable with such a lowly angel as this. Why had they sent him? Was this an insult, or were they just being cautious, as he claimed?

"Speak plainly," Gabriel barked out, deciding to go for 'insulted'. "I have no time for double talk."

A figure emerged from the shadows. Gabriel didn't recognize him, and there was nothing to indicate which choir he belonged to — just a low-level angel, nervously shuffling his feet as he approached.

"There are some who have taken on a project that will result in angels being able to procreate."

"If you're trying to sway my vote on the issues of Nephilim, you're wasting your time," Gabriel warned.

"No, no," the angel waved his hands. "My superiors would never condone breeding with human females. They seek to find a way to increase the angelic ranks."

"That's impossible. We've had a complete separation of our kind. Breeding would violate our treaty. Such contact with demons is not allowed."

"We would never promote such a thing." The angel waved his hand as if clearing the air of such thoughts. "This would not involve any relations that would compromise your vow following the war. There need be no contact with them at all."

Gabriel pondered his words, glancing out of the filthy alley into the sunlit street beyond. "An immaculate conception," he mused.

"Yes, yes! There is a way to separate demon essence outside of their physical shape and to combine it with the requisite amount of angel to create a new life."

The elder angel shook his head. "We don't form. It's not just a matter of providing essence, it's the problem of what happens next that is insurmountable."

"Nothing is insurmountable. That hurdle has been overcome. All of Aaru will be invigorated by new life."

"And there's some swampland in Mesopotamia you'd like to sell me." Gabriel drawled. "First there's the issue of *getting* the demon essence. Then being able to store it properly so it doesn't degrade. Then the insurmountable obstacle of forming. That doesn't even get into the issues of the end result. What happens if the child is an Angel of Chaos?"

His heart skipped a beat at the thought. What a moral dilemma. Would they drop the newly formed angel off in Hel, like an unwanted pup? Would they find a way around the treaty and be able to keep it in Aaru? His mind wandered to memories of his youth, of his youngest brother shocking him with a bolt of lightning and flying gleefully away. *Catch me, catch me.* And catch him he always did. No matter how agile Samael had been, Gabriel was always faster. But none of this mattered. His brother was lost to him forever, and there would be no more Angels of Chaos.

"We have done it," the angel insisted. "A few tweaks to perfect the process, then we'll need assistance and support to get the approval of the Ruling Council before we begin to offer the service to a select population."

"I need to know the details of the project, the exact process. I can hardly support something without ensuring it truly is in keeping with our laws and ethical standards."

Gabriel heard the other angel shifting nervously from side to side. "I'm afraid I am not privy to the details, Exalted One. You must understand that there are also concerns regarding confidentiality and patent. Those involved have invested significantly and would not want others to set up their own operations."

Gabriel understood the concerns and need for confidentiality, and he too would not want the process to be easily duplicated, even if it were a lawful one. There would need to be a suitable application process, to ensure only the most holy of angels were allowed permission to proceed. Of course, it wasn't just the general angelic population these individuals should be worried about. There was a good chance the Ruling Council would seize their invention and regulate all phases of creation as a matter of public good. They must have thought long and hard about whether to legitimize their enterprise and risk the heavy hand of the Ruling Council in their business, or run it illegally without approval and risk terrible punishment. Still, he couldn't support anything so blindly.

"I'm not lending assistance and support to an unsubstantiated pipe–dream." Gabriel stepped forward to meet the angel's eyes for the first time — pale, pale gray eyes in a golden face surrounded by a halo of white hair. "Bring me some proof that any of this is possible, that it won't either violate the treaty or negatively impact our positive evolution, and I'll consider it. Until then, this is all wasteful gossip in a back alley."

The angel nodded, bowing as he stepped backward to vanish from the dark passage. Gabriel gazed around at the line of trashcans overflowing with fragrant plastic bags. He hated it down here. He should just go back to Aaru where he could shed this painfully sensitive corporeal form and relax in seclusion. It had been centuries since he'd wandered the streets and observed humans. He'd become increasingly disillusioned with reports of their impulsive, selfish, un–orderly behavior. When the post for head Grigori came up ten thousand years ago, Gabriel gladly passed, knowing even then he'd not be able to stand close contact with the humans for any extended period of time. It wasn't just the terrible temptation of a physical form, it was how he had begun to see Samael in the eyes of each one he met. Odd how his youngest brother and the other Angels of Chaos had vehemently opposed giving the gifts of Aaru to the humans, and yet the species was becoming just like their detractors. Here, on earth, it seemed chaos was winning out over order. No wonder the demons loved to come here.

On a rare whim, he stepped out of the alleyway, blinking as the blinding light of the midday sun hit his eyes. Tall brick and concrete buildings stood in an endless row to either side and across the busy street. Cars whizzed by, barely missing the ones lining the curb, the six feet separating them from the buildings a floor of cement. The only nod to nature was a sickly tree, allotted two square feet of cigarette butt laden soil at the edge of the sidewalk. A woman in uniform walked past him, checking parking meters as she went.

Normally he attracted a lot of attention. In the past, he'd have a crowd of humans following him around within moments of his arrival from Aaru. Demons blended in with their ability to copy human forms to a molecule. Angels stuck out, always looking somewhat non–human. Some covered for it with a charisma that allowed humans to believe what their eyes told them was wrong. Gabriel always preferred the opposite approach — to exude an aura that made humans just not notice him. It was as if he wasn't there at all.

He watched the uniformed woman write on a slip of paper and slip it securely on the windshield of a parked car before he turned to walk down the street. They'd lost so many angels in the wars. Not as many as the rebels had, but still enough that his heart ached. After the war their numbers had stabilized. Immortals had no need to bear offspring. No deaths, no births— it seemed at the time a proposal they could live with. But now...Part of him hoped this mad scheme was legitimate, that once again he'd see creation in Aaru.

It wasn't just the continuance of the angelic race, it was the loss of new life that was eating Aaru from the inside out. There had been that terrible fiasco with the tenth choir. Angels still fell into sin by breeding with human females. Their evolutionary progress had slowed to a crawl. Of course, that was to be expected. As one approached divinity, advances would be more difficult to achieve.

To create once again. To select traits and qualities from oneself and imbue a new being with them. It was a heady thought — one he hadn't allowed himself to have in millions of years. If this angel was right, if there was a way to produce offspring without sullying principals, then everything would change. Perhaps this would be the very thing to breathe life back into Aaru.

Three angels dead in one year. He was still irked at the loss of Althean. The rogue had exceeded his reach, but Gabriel could certainly sympathize with his frustration. One dead at the hands of a devouring spirit. But the other— what had happened to him? Dead not a week later in a mysterious explosion. Angels were a hearty bunch. It would have taken one heck of an explosion to kill one.

A sting on his arm jolted him from his thoughts. Before he could turn, another barrage of thin, small objects bounced off his head and body.

"Get out of here. Go home. We refuse to submit to your oppressive presence."

Gabriel swatted away the objects and stared in surprise at a young bearded man, standing in front of a large cardboard box beside a dumpster. He held a bag in his hand suspiciously like the one Gabriel's elder brother had carried, but instead of eating the chips, he was using them as projectile weapons. Their triangular form was more effective than the round ones would have been, but they still were a less than ideal missile.

"You can see me?"

The man threw a few more chips at the angel before stopping. "Of course I can see you. Angels and demons everywhere, coming and going, disrupting our lives. Go back to where you belong, and leave us alone!"

It made sense that there would be a congregation of angels and demons in this particular area, what with one of the major gates just a few miles away. Still, the fact that this human recognized him for what he was and seemed unaffected by any aura or glamor amazed Gabriel.

Another handful of chips hit Gabriel's face. "Stop throwing those things at me," he commanded, pushing four billion years of power into the compulsion.

For the first time in his long life, it didn't work. The human screamed at him and rushed Gabriel, throwing chips and eventually hitting him repeatedly with the empty bag until the angel fled back out into the street. What was wrong with this man? Humans had clearly changed since he'd frequented here. How could angels fall to sin with ...this? Were his brother's enforcers regularly subjected to this sort of attack? Had those two dead angels, possibly down here on an unholy visit, been assaulted with food items and chased down the street?

Gabriel came to an abrupt halt as the idea came to him. If he really wanted to get to the bottom of the murders, he needed to do it here, not in Aaru. This is where they had come; this is where they had died; this was where he would find the answers he sought. Unpleasant as it would be to walk the earth, he'd discover more here than in the labyrinth of political cover–up among the angels. Perhaps there were humans like the violent one in the alley who had witnessed the murders. Perhaps there were clues left behind. If his brother's Grigori refused to make this a priority and investigate in a timely fashion, he should do it himself.

A bell rang and Gabriel started. A stream of children ran from a brick building set further back from the road then the others. They all wore identical clothing — long navy shorts that came to their knees, and white button–down shirts with a crimson–and–black–striped tie. They tore down the entranceway, slowing as they rounded the corner on the sidewalk and parting around Gabriel as if he were a stone in a fast moving stream. They were all male children, he realized. Human genders were difficult to discern in their young, but he somehow knew this. Opening his mind, he let their thoughts flood him, crashing into him with a calliope of emotion —tests, parents, dinner, an itchy rash, the cute neighbor girl, fear, anger, joy, sorrow. He was used to hearing the communications of a thousand angels at once, but the raw passion in these children's minds left him shaken. Two of them ran up behind a third and knocked him with their shoulders, tripping him and laughing as he fell.

Smelly worm. Know—it—all. Hope he never comes back. Hope he moves.

Gabriel caught his breath at the volume of hate and closed his mind with a snap. Even their young were corrupted. Nothing had changed. Being here among the humans as he investigated the murders would be one of the most painful things he'd ever done. There was no way he'd be able to endure any extended time among these creatures. He should leave this phase of the inquiries to the Grigori after all. It wasn't his job to do this. He'd leave it to those better suited to dealing with the humans and go back to Aaru where he belonged, away from the temptation and constant reminder of how evil could permeate even the most promising of species.

Again he thought about a great cleansing, about starting over with another, but then a wave of guilt went through him. It was the angels' fault this had happened — the tenth choir, the original Grigori fallen and lost to sin, giving humans gifts they were not ready to accept. The angels had been punished, some of them still in the process of rehabilitation, but the damage had been done. How could he fully blame them, though? They'd been without Angels of Chaos for over two million years, making it oh—so—easy to slide into depravity. And the humans were so very tempting.

No joining. No creation. No chasing little brothers through the air in retaliation for a strike of lightning. How could a decision of virtue and morality have gone so wrong? There was no way to undo the past, but perhaps, if that angel were correct, there was some hope for the future. And then, maybe, they could finally leave the humans to whatever future the Creator had in mind.

~9~

I awoke to a world of pain. I felt like I should be dead. Each breath stabbed through me, my face was swollen, my arms completely purple and green. It was just as well I wasn't dead. Being inside a decaying body wasn't much better than being pond scum. Although, if I could animate a dead body, I might be able to terrify the elves enough to escape. I can't imagine what they'd think having a zombie in their midst. Demons always died when their physical forms did, and seeing what would appear to be a dead human shambling about would probably cause mass hysteria. I chuckled, envisioning the panicked elves, and immediately wished I hadn't as blinding pain shot through my chest and back.

I had two fractured vertebrae, a bruised spleen, two cracked ribs and three battered ones, a concussion, and more bruises than a heavyweight boxer. Oddly, the hairline fracture of my right femur, and shattered ankle I'd noted last night had somehow repaired themselves. How had I managed to fix injuries in my damaged state with the collar on me? Was the thing perhaps defective? Maybe my damaged spirit–self was repairing faster than I'd thought possible.

And what the fuck was I going to do now? I'd killed the sorcerer, and I was positive that all the elves in Hel couldn't put that guy back together again. Not even Gregory could bring him back to life. But the advantage his death bought me wouldn't be worth shit if all I could do was lie here, a mess of broken bones and purple flesh. By the time it took me to heal naturally, Feille would have another sorcerer transferred from one of his conquered kingdoms and up to speed.

Wallowing in pain and frustration, I was surprised to hear the slam of a door. The elves must have fixed the dungeon. I couldn't really tell, since every sense was clouded in discomfort. I heard voices and caught my breath. Feille and a voice I thought I'd never hear along with his — Taullian. The two elves approached the glowing bars of my cell, accompanied by half a dozen elven guards and as many human magic users. I glanced over at the humans, dismayed to see that from their robes, two appeared to be high–level sorcerers. It seems the time I'd bought myself had been less than I'd hoped. I hadn't expected Feille to act so fast, or for his archenemy to do such an about face.

Wythyn and Cyelle had fought since the elves had joined us in Hel. They shared no common borders, separated by another elven kingdom along the northern two–thirds of the kingdoms, and by demon lands at the southern portion. Still, they'd managed to inflict damage on each other with spies, surprise guerrilla attacks, and theft of riches. The last two millennia had seen an uneasy truce between the kingdoms, even more uneasy once the younger Taullian took the throne after his predecessor died following a mysterious wasting illness.

"In bed with the enemy, Taullian," I said, my voice slurred with pain. "I always knew you were weak, but I didn't expect you to be so eager to have Feille fuck you in the ass."

Both elves stiffened in anger. They should have been used to our vulgarities by now, but elves never learned.

"I know what's in the best interests of my people, Az. And a peaceful treaty is far from what you're implying."

Nice words, but he was full of shit and he knew it. Taullian's ruling style alternated between democratic and bossy. He'd always been seen as weak compared to his more fierce neighbors and had been unable to completely quell unrest in his kingdom. Half his kingdom would probably welcome Feille. A peaceful treaty was his only choice, but it would be a short–lived peace if I knew Feille.

"This treaty just delays the inevitable, Tally–boy. Once this asshole gets his feet on the ground, your head will be the first to roll."

"One more word and I'll cut out your tongue," Feille snapped. "And you won't be able to recreate another with that collar on."

Little did he know I probably couldn't recreate one without the collar on. Still, I uncharacteristically obeyed, wanting to find out exactly what these two had up their little green sleeves, and what it had to do with me. Did Taullian know about Feille's project? Did he know how fucked they'd truly be if Feille was able to get his hands on a vast store of high–level demon energy?

Taullian curled up a lip as he scrutinized me through the bars. "Looks like you did your best to kill her. She looks like a black and blue pretzel."

Trust Taullian to have all the good similes at his disposal.

"She's alive. I have no idea why. Trust me, I tried with all my might to kill her. Even after my guards beat her, I made sure I got in a few more hits just to be sure. But here she is, alive and breathing."

"Why isn't she in a net? Don't you worry she will overcome your magical protections? Does the collar you mentioned perform the same function?"

Feille grinned at me, his smile sadistic. "The collar restricts all her demon abilities and renders her no more powerful than a human. Unlike a net, which restrains her physically, this collar allows us to have all sorts of fun with her."

Taullian looked doubtful. "I've seen her in action. I'm not so sure I want her to be able to have control of her limbs."

Feille made a derisive sound, but an uneasy look flickered across his face. "You're an elf and a high lord. If you can't control a rebellious demon, you're not worthy of the throne."

Brave words from someone who I had intimidated into returning my horse, someone who I'd nearly bested with only "human" strength.

What were these two doing together? They hated each other. Feille had said that Taullian was on the verge of signing an oath of loyalty to him, basically handing over his kingdom in return for peace. I hadn't believed it. Surely Taullian would have strung Feille along only to launch a last moment attack. I couldn't see him ever bowing his head to Feille's reign. Was he as weak as everyone had thought, or did he have something sneaky up his sleeve?

Taullian ignored the other elf's barb and shook his head at me. "How am I supposed to enact my own vengeance when she's hanging onto life by a thread?"

Well, he could heal me then beat the shit out of me himself. Although I wasn't sure elven healing powers would work on demons. I hadn't heard of it ever being done before. We always fixed ourselves, except for the Low, and no one cared whether they lived or died. An angel had healed me, several times. Perhaps elves could too.

Feille sighed. "She stubbornly refuses to fix herself just to spite me. Give her enough pain, drive her to the edge of death, and suddenly she'll do it. Trust me."

"Hmmm." Taullian sounded skeptical.

"She spent over two months in the form of pond scum, hoping to escape detection. Even after we discovered who she was, she refused to change. We had to employ drastic and costly measures to force her into this human form, and even then she didn't learn her lesson."

Taullian moved as close as possible to the glowing bars of my cell, frowning at me. "Are you sure? Maybe she's broken."

"Do you want her or not?" Feille snapped.

"Yes. We have a deal."

Taullian's subdued tone with its note of resignation revealed his difficult position. His dispassionate gaze roamed over me, cataloguing my injures I assumed. "Two?"

"Two," Feille confirmed. "Level twelve or above.

Taullian nodded. "As you wish." His voice was subservient and defeated.

Well, this was out of the frying pan and into the fire. I'd just dispatched Feille's only sorcerer, but the elven lord quickly recovered. From the conversation, I gathered he was trading me to Taullian for not just one, but two high–level sorcerers. Instead of months, I'd only have weeks at the most to get the warning out, and I'd be as unlikely to do it from Taullian's dungeon as from Feille's.

Feille and about half the guards left the dungeon, leaving Taullian and what I assumed were his staff. I heard a heavy sigh.

"Unlock the gate."

My heart leapt with futile hope. I may be collared and facing a high lord, six magic users, and three elven guards, but those odds weren't as daunting as one might think. Demons lived for risk. Unfortunately, as I was currently a black and blue pretzel, the odds were too unfavorable, even for a reckless imp.

"Net her," Taullian said.

Fuck. Collared and netted. Pond scum or living dead girl was looking better and better. The guard came toward me, and I shot out a hand to grab his ankle. He gasped and jerked, pulling easily from my grasp and kicking my face. It was a glancing blow, but combined with my current injuries it was too much. I retched, but there was nothing in my stomach to vomit. I was too physically weak to take any advantage. I felt the net fall over me, itchy against my bare skin, the magic like a thousand pricks of a nettle.

"Can you heal her?" Taullian's voice sounded disinterested, as if he were asking a purely academic question.

There was silence for a few moments as the figures moved around me, assessing. "I don't know, my lord. We have some healing spells for humans but have never had to use them on a demon before. They always fix themselves."

There was a moment of silence. "We will remove the net and the collar to give you an opportunity to fix your physical wounds. If you even look like you're about to attack us, we'll kill you. Do you understand?"

"Yes." I doubted I could fix myself. I might be able to transform myself into healthy pond scum or a lizard, but I was terrified that if I left this human form, I'd never be able to assume it again. I'd killed the sorcerer who'd transformed me into a human and had a bad feeling I couldn't do it myself. I'd try my hardest to fix any injuries, but if I couldn't, I'd remain like this until they healed naturally.

"My Lord, I advise you not do this. Wait until we have her safely back in Cyelle. I don't trust her."

"We can't move her like this. I don't want her to die before I have a chance to make her regret what she's done to me and the elves of Cyelle."

I felt their disapproval and fear, but they obeyed, lifting the net and examining the collar around my neck.

"How ...how do we remove this thing?" one of the guards asked, running a finger around the circlet in search of a catch. "I've never seen anything like it."

"Let me."

I recognized that voice and blinked in surprise to see a mage I knew come forward. Kirby. He avoided my gaze and instead knelt down to examine the circlet.

"It's a form of angel energy," I told him, my voice raw. "Attached to a magical device similar to your nets. There are tiny gaps in the energy — the biggest is where the catch is."

Kirby's eyes met mine, and I was warmed by the sympathy in them. "Is there an incantation? How do I get it off?"

I shook my head, wincing at the pain rattling through my skull. "Not sure. Mages can remove and attach them, and I've seen elves do it too, so I think it's a physical sort of latch. Whatever it is, I've never been able to activate it."

"Got it," Kirby said, his fingers halting along the back of the collar. With a snap, he'd removed it and held it before him in wonderment. "Tricky bit of magic. Anyone can latch it, but it takes a human or elf to allow the physical latch to release."

The guard got up and backed away. Kirby gave him a quick glance and did the same. "You should be able to repair yourself now."

Yeah. In theory. I closed my eyes and reached within myself, gathering the energy from the air around me. I'd done this a million times in my life. Created new molecules, replace all the damaged structures with new ones. It was as easy as breathing.

But it seems breathing was the only skill remaining to me. I felt a spark, gloried in the creation, then felt it all slip away like water through my fingers. I tried again, and again, hearing the uneasy movements of the elves and magic users as they watched me.

"Perhaps Lord Feille was speaking the truth? Why would she remain injured like that?"

Idiots. But I'd rather they think me obstinate, or playing some convoluted game, than know how damaged I truly was. I tried again. Little improvements, but nothing major. Ribs were partially repaired, spleen good as new, concussion on the mend. If I had a few days, I might be able to fix everything on my own. This was definitely progress, but taking a few days to repair injuries could spell the difference between life and death.

"Leave. Everyone except Sylvia. Wait for me outside the dungeon."

I heard a collective gasp at Taullian's command and knew he must have silenced any protests.

"I am perfectly capable of defending myself against one little imp. Go."

I opened my eyes and saw the guards leave, Kirby casting me a quick look as he went with them. Taullian approached, a female magic user by his side. She looked uneasy, clutching a wand tightly in one hand, bunching her robes in a fist.

"Cover me," Taullian said, and Sylvia pointed a nervous wand at my head.

The elf lord bent down, a golden glow covering his hand as he ran it a few inches over my body. "She's managed to partially repair her wounds," he mused. "But I wonder....."

I felt a sizzling warmth beneath my skin, heating me down into my spirit self. His hand reached down to probe my shoulder, then down along my side. "I can't really tell, but I suspect some injuries are beyond the flesh," Taullian commented to the mage.

"I definitely cannot heal her spirit being, my Lord," she pronounced, her tone respectful but assured. "I could try the human healing spell and see if it restores her corporeal form to health."

The elf lord glanced up at her, his expression admiring, as if she were a valued piece of art. "You are my best healer, Sylvia. I have no doubt you could restore her physical self."

She beamed. "I would be happy to try, my Lord."

Taullian hesitated a moment. "No." His voice sounded oddly distracted. "Save your magic. You'll need everything you've got soon enough. I'll do it myself."

I caught my breath. Elves were very private about their magic and their abilities. When needed, they always relied on their human mages and sorcerers. Beyond my recent fight with Feille, I'd never actually seen one use any of their gifts and had no idea the extent of their powers.

"Leave us." Taullian commanded. His deep voice lacked its usual firmness.

"Are you sure, My Lord? Should I net her first? Put the collar back on?"

"Leave us." This time he sounded tired.

Sylvia jumped to her feet, robes swaying around her legs in a blur of embroidered blue. She bowed deeply before Taullian and left. The dungeon door clanged, and I felt a hand on my shoulder.

"I am a fool to trust you once again, Az," the elf told me. "Twice you have bitten me — once literally, and once in deceit and treachery. Yet the enemy of my enemy is my friend, and I would dearly love to hurl your chaos into the battlefield."

Under normal circumstances, he would be a fool to trust me. Right now, I was far more interested in him healing me than attempting to take him out. That could wait until five seconds after he healed me.

As his hands moved down my body, I felt warmth seep through my skin and deep into my bones. It was pleasant, and my mind floated, feeling relief from pain. Everything tingled. It was like being mildly drunk, buzzed from a few shots of vodka. There were no words in his spell like there were in human magic. My flesh rolled against bone, bone slid against flesh, knitting and healing in a dance of golden warmth. My mind cleared and I saw Taullian as he continued to work his hands along my body, hovering them a fraction of an inch above my naked skin. A golden glow shone as a buffer between us, glittering like dust motes in the morning sunlight.

My eyes traveled up him as he worked, taking in the draped clothing all elves wore, fresh and unwrinkled. They were always that way. Weeks of travel, and they never stank of sweat and dirt, never looked greasy or in need of a bath. Their clothing always looked freshly laundered, their hair shining and clean. But his face — the elf lord looked as if he'd aged three centuries since I'd seen him last. His mouth was a tight, narrow line, skin creased at either edge, his eyelids heavy — dark underneath and slightly swollen. Lines ran across his forehead and dove down into a deep V between his brows. He was an asshole, just not as much of an asshole as Feille. Maybe he was right and the enemy of my enemy could be an ally.

"There," he pronounced, rising. He didn't look at my face, didn't even bother to meet my gaze so intent on him. "At least I can be confident you'll survive the journey now."

"We're not going to gate?" I'd decided to hold back on my impulse to attack him and attempt an escape. His staff were right outside the dungeon, ready to race in if needed, and I had a feeling Taullian would be of more use to me alive.

He shook his head. "I can't waste the magic or my people's energy."

He fingered the net and the collar, and I held my breath, trying to decide if it would be in my best interests to let him confine me with them, or fight for short–lived freedom. Luckily I didn't have to choose. He dropped both back onto the stone floor.

Without another word, he left, shutting the cell door firmly behind him. I had no idea when we were supposed to travel. I was starving, but otherwise physically fine. If only my spirit self were as fit. Everything inside my flesh ached with a dull throb. Scar tissue was once again forming over the sections that had cracked and re–opened with the sorcerer's spells, and I felt an uncomfortable tightness once again. My stomach growled loudly as I lay naked on the cold stone floor. Would I ever be right, or would I spend the rest of my life with little more than the skills and abilities of the human form I now wore? If so, it would probably be a very short life.

~10~

Taullian and his traveling party came in the next morning, bringing an array of food. My stomach clenched at the smell, and I hated them for torturing me so.

"Feed her," the high lord commanded. "Then we will discuss transportation options."

Kirby came toward me in a swish of robes, a platter of food in his hands. He looked good — tired and stressed, as they all did, but pretty much the same Kirby I'd seen before. I had made good on the favor I'd promised when I'd last seen him, delivering to his parents both his note and the marble he'd been carrying when he'd fallen through the elf gates. It had been one of the hardest things I'd ever done. I hated seeing the pain on their faces, imagining how I'd feel if it were someone I loved, long gone and presumed dead. Kirby met my eyes and gave a nearly unperceivable shake of his head. Here, at last, was someone on my side, someone I could trust. He could let Dar and my household know where I was, have them contact Wyatt, have Wyatt warn Gregory. I slumped in a relief I hadn't felt in months.

"Just drag her behind the horses," one of the elves mentioned. I started, realizing they were debating my transportation.

Taullian pursed his lips. "She'd take injury and be unable to fix herself in the confines of the net. I don't want to risk removing it for her to repair her injuries."

Why was he covering for me? He knew I was struggling to repair myself, and here he was, blaming it all on the net and his safety concerns so his elven staff didn't know how dire my situation really was. Why?

"Here." Kirby pushed the plate toward me. I didn't even bother to thank him, so intent was I on shoveling the contents into my mouth. I was starving and beyond my physical needs; I hadn't had the joy of consuming food in months. The sensation of it in my mouth, the fullness in my belly all felt incredible.

"My Lord, a net can be modified so she can walk," another elf said.

"An excellent idea, but it will delay our journey considerably and our time is running out."

An excellent idea? I choked on the slab of cheese. What the fuck? Elf lords ruled with an iron fist, or they didn't rule for long. Where was this collaborative Taullian coming from?

Kirby went to pull the plate back, and I snatched the remaining food from it, cramming it in my mouth. He chuckled.

"There will be more, I promise. Just hold tight and keep silent. He needs you. Desperately needs you."

Needs me? What. The. Fuck?

Kirby cast a quick sideways glance at his lord. "I've told him things. He doesn't trust you, but he's out of options. You're all he has left."

Before I could swallow my food enough to speak, Kirby had taken the plate and walked back to the others. Four scouts, skilled in forest travel, two mages, and four guards. Not the biggest entourage I'd ever seen with an elven high lord. I assessed Taullian, surveying his posture and expression. He still looked drawn and tired, tense as a strung bow, but there was something calculating in his air. Could this small group be his way of appearing harmless to Feille?

"My Lord, I could give up my horse and she could ride across his back. Llualia has a strong mount that can carry two of us as I lead the demon on mine. We can use the collar on her, now that we know how to put it on and remove it."

I felt Taullian's approval. Actually felt it. The glow of his elven magic radiated from him and the others leaned toward him in a strange sort of bonding I'd never seen before. It made me realize how little I really knew about the elves, how secretive they had been about their powers and society while seeming to reveal all.

"By the Goddess, I think that will work. Thank you, Spriggh for your offer, and thank you Llualia for allowing your mount to carry double during this long journey. I truly appreciate your dedication and loyalty."

It seemed to be an over–the–top speech, as if he were laying it on too thick, but I didn't get that feeling at all from Taullian or his elves. They accepted his praise like a corporate team, ready to get out the flip charts, ven diagrams, and call in for a lunch delivery.

The six–day trip from jail cell to jail cell was uneventful and uncomfortable. Riding from sunup to sundown draped over the back of a horse with my head and arms dangling down one side and my legs the other wasn't dignified. And it fucking hurt. Bound and wearing the collar, I had a limited a range of motion and was unable to fix any bruises or pulled muscles. I couldn't stretch my limbs or relieve the pressure against my abdomen for hours at a time. By day two I was thinking this qualified as one of the most horrendous forms of torture ever. I made a mental note to remember it.

My new captors had the courtesy to let me off the horse when they made camp, dumping me in a centralized area to better keep an eye on me. I had food and water, and at least the collar allowed me to see what was going on, unlike the elven nets. The view from the back of the horse had not been very enlightening, but once the elves, and few humans with them, settled in for the evening, I observed. The first night, everyone carefully watched their words, glancing frequently over to me, but by day three, they'd begun to ignore me. I held as still as I could, quiet and unthreatening in my chains and tried to glean as much information as possible.

It wasn't much. The elves were scared. Worried what Feille would do to their kingdom even with the treaty. They grumbled that Taullian hadn't made a stand against Wythyn's aggression like a proper high lord should, but they still followed him, still kept some hope in their hearts that he'd pull through for them. The humans were mostly silent, casting defeated looks at each other. I knew what their fate would probably be. Feille would claim them all as spoils of war, as some sort of tribute, taking them from their current owners and gifting them to his key supporters. Nyalla had detailed Wythyn's uncaring attitude toward humans, and I'd seen it firsthand. Even those with magical ability were treated as animals. Tolerated ...until they stepped out of line, then "justice" was swift and brutal.

Kirby and another mage were the highest ranking of the humans, and I watched them move among the elves, sharing casual conversation before moving off to sit by themselves. They weren't the same level as the other humans and not welcomed fully by the elves. It had to have been a lonely existence.

All talk was on the fate of the kingdom, of their families, of what their futures might hold. There was no mention of Feille's scheme to move against the demons, or his larger plans to eventually take the Northern elven kingdoms. For a megalomaniac like Feille to keep such grand schemes secret, there had to have been a weakness. Something wasn't ready, or wasn't working quite right. Otherwise he would have shouted it from the rooftops. It gave me hope that perhaps I had a bit of time beyond that which killing his sorcerer had bought me.

I couldn't see the city in the distance as we approached, couldn't see anything beyond the forest under my horse turn to grassy field, then to a well–worn dirt path. There were shouts of greeting. We halted as the gates were opened. Then I had a lovely view of the cobblestones under my horse as we made our way through the city streets toward Taullian's palace. They untied me and hauled me, still shackled and collared, off my horse. Netting me, which was a completely unnecessary precaution, they proceeded to drag me along a rough, hard floor to yet another dungeon. The gate clanged behind me, and I wondered if they intended to keep me in the collar and the net.

I felt hands on my neck and instinctively lashed out, hitting the restraining edges of the net.

"Hold still," an elven voice told me, sounding unusually sympathetic. "We're removing the collar so we can study the magic behind it."

Of course they'd want to figure out something so intriguing. I felt relief as the collar clicked from my neck, assuming they'd leave me netted in the dungeon until Taullian came back to do whatever he wanted to do with me.

"*Cleofan.*"

I guess not. The net dissolved from me. I slowly stood, stretching cramped, stiff muscles. The dungeon seemed much the same as the one in Wythyn. Stone walls. No windows. Big metal bars that glowed with magic.

I turned and saw Kirby outside the closed gate, two guards by his side.

"Would you please leave me to have a private word with the Iblis?" he asked the guards. I barely controlled my surprise. Asking to be alone with me? That was really going to raise suspicions. But instead, the two guards exchanged looks then glanced at me.

"We appreciate your kindness to our kin, Tlia–Myea," one told me. "May the Goddess continue to grand you her favor."

I didn't know much about "continue". I think whatever deity had once smiled upon me was long gone at this point. Still, I watched them leave, no doubt positioning themselves just outside the dungeon door, ready to race in at the slightest sound of trouble.

"I delivered your note and marble to your family," I told Kirby, fingering the skin where the silver collar had been around my neck. "They were relieved that you were still alive, although they were very upset about what had happened."

"I know." The mage grinned. "The marble — it was a gate relay. We've been working on them for the last decade, trying to find a way to establish permanent, movable, interdimensional access points that are unnoticeable until activated. I've been able to go home to visit and be back before anyone realizes I'm gone."

Holy shit! That was huge. Gates were always either open, like the elf traps, or doorways that were visible and usable to anyone with the skill to activate them. A stealthy gate, activated briefly only to melt into its surroundings, was an amazing feat of magic. The implications hit me. Forget the demon powered magics of Feille, this was the real ultimate weapon. To be able to appear right before your enemy, kill him and vanish before anyone ever knew — that was far more valuable than the brute force that Wythyn held. Did Taullian realize he had such a thing at his disposal? Perhaps there was more to this elf lord and his quick acquiescence than I thought. I could tell Kirby wanted to talk about his family reunion but all I could think about was the storm on the horizon.

"Does Taullian know about this? How many of the elven kingdoms have something similar?"

Kirby tilted his head, his expression quizzical. "Yes, of course he knows, although he has no idea I've been using it. No other kingdom has it that I'm aware of, and the entire project is of the highest secrecy. If I weren't a level twelve mage, I wouldn't know of it."

I walked toward the cell bars, feeling a sizzle like a static shock as I drew near. "Really bad shit is about to hit the fan, Kirby," I told him, keeping a respectable distance from the bars. "This thing with Feille is bigger than anyone knows."

He nodded. "No one believes he'll keep his end of the treaty. He'll stabilize Li, Tonlielle, and Allwin, then tear through Cyelle like a hurricane. Everyone knows what life will be like if he takes control of the kingdom, and it will be ten times worse with him as ruler of all six of the southern kingdoms."

"Bigger," I told him, ignoring the sizzle of the bars to lean closer. "He has something that will give him control over demons. Once he gets his elven power base, he's going for all of Hel. Including the northern elven kingdoms."

Kirby stepped back in shock. "No. He can't. There's no way he can possibly overcome the ancient demons. Maybe Lows and imps. Possibly mid–level plague–bringers, but not the ancients. Once they see what he's up to, they'll band together and crush him."

I didn't have time to get into the absolute lack of cooperation among the demons in Hel with him. "Trust me. You guys need to make a stand. You need to use this stealthy gate thing to get an army on his doorstep and take Wythyn down as they sleep. The northern kingdoms won't do anything to support you until it's too late; they won't bother. It's all up to Cyelle."

"We don't...." Kirby hesitated. "I don't know what his lordship intends. He's not an aggressive ruler. He spends most of his energy on infrastructure, research, and cultural preservation. I respect that, I really do, but he's not the kind of lord for subterfuge or overt attack."

I rubbed my hands over my face. Fuck. The sole hope of the southern elves, the northern elves, and the demons lay in the hands of a social feel–good politician. No doubt he thought the treaty was a reasonable compromise, preserving the peace of his kingdom at the cost of only his pride. He'd still be thinking that when Feille lopped off his head and executed half his people.

"We traded two of our sorcerers," Kirby continued. "We only have one left, and three high level mages. Not enough to wage war, even with a gate relay. I believe you, I really do, but I don't know what I can do to help."

He was a mage, and a human. There probably wasn't much he could do. Except....

"Can you get a message to my household? A message to Dar?" I pleaded. "Let him know what I told you. I want them to prepare for Feille's attack."

The elves were a lost cause, but I wasn't going to give up on the rest of Hel. There might be nothing Dar could do either, but at least the demons wouldn't be surprised. If they believed him. If not, then at least Dar and my household wouldn't be surprised. Dar was stronger than he let on, and he had the kind of subtle influence centuries of wheeling and dealing had brought.

"I'll try," Kirby said doubtfully. "It's not easy to get a message out right now. Wythyn is watching us carefully. And I'm a human; I don't have much leeway in travel outside the city, let alone outside the kingdom and into demon lands."

"Try. Please try. Tell them what I told you about Feille's plans, and ask them to tell Wyatt to let Gregory know that there's more to what happened to me than we thought. That there are others in Aaru involved."

Kirby looked confused. "Tell Dar that the Wythyn elves are going to attack the demons, and Wilson needs to tell somebody there are others involved with the angels?"

Close enough. "Wyatt. And Gregory."

He nodded, and I had no doubt that the message was going to be garbled beyond recognition by the time it reached Dar. Fuck. I needed to get out of here.

"Why did you come back?" I asked the mage, curious. "You could just disappear one night, go home and never return." He'd had a way out, a way back to his parents, and he'd returned.

"I belong here. I enjoy my work. I have friends and colleagues. I have a life here, valuable skills and interesting opportunities for advancement. What would I do as a mage back home? I'd wind up delivering pizzas and living in my parents' basement."

"But you'd be free. Doesn't that count for something?"

"Yes, but it's not worth the trade-off. Other humans might choose differently, but I have value here. The elves respect me, even if they are pompous jerks sometimes. I'd miss my magic, the forests, the festivals, my friends. This is my home now. I just want to be able to see my parents every week or so, not give everything up to return there."

It was the same as Nyalla had said. There was no going home for so many of these humans, even Kirby who had family that loved him. If they'd choose to stay in Hel, then I needed to make sure they could carve out a decent life here. It's not like anyone else gave two shits for them. Besides, they were mine. *Mine.*

"You know what will happen to you humans if Feille takes over?" I asked softly, remembering the girl the guards had thrown in my dungeon cell. "I've seen how the elves there treat the servants, and I don't think the mages have it much better."

Kirby whitened, looking like he was on the verge of puking up his lunch. "I know. We won't have it quite as bad as the servants will, but there will be no more socializing amongst ourselves, or free time. We'll be on constant lockdown, every movement accounted for, every spell component logged and signed out. His sorcerers are on every hour, every day. They achieve amazing feats of knowledge and magic, but no one can take that kind of pressure for long. Escape winds up looking like a good option, even with the probability of death by a demon bounty hunter."

"What will you do, Kirby?" I knew what I'd do. I'd fight to the death, just like so many of us did two and a half million years ago in the war with the angels. And if I was given a choice, I'd take eternal exile over a life of subjugation.

The mage's jaw clenched. "I'll fight for Taullian. It's the best option I've got. And if we lose and I'm still alive, I'll leave and spend the rest of my life delivering pizzas."

I felt a surge of something powerful in my core. I loved humans. The gifts of Aaru, every fuck up that had happened since then — it hadn't been a mistake. They were the perfect blend of order and chaos. If the angels couldn't see that, they were a bunch of blind idiots. A crazy idea formed in my mind. If I had my way, the only pizza Kirby would see would be one he was about to eat.

"If you hear anything more about Taullian's plans or the situation in the elven kingdoms, can you find a way to let me know?"

"Yes, although I may not know of anything until events are already in motion. Communication has been locked down tight, and we're all in the dark."

I nodded and watched as he turned to leave.

"Wait," I called after him. He stopped and retraced his steps. "Why did Taullian trade two sorcerers for *me*? His need for vengeance can't be so strong that he would weaken his kingdom to see me suffer."

Kirby thought then shook his head. "He knows how erratic you are — like chaos personified. We all think he plans to throw you at Feille to distract and occupy him while he's launching some sort of attack. It's not good strategy that I can see, but then again, we're not exactly prepared for war. We might be wrong, though. Possibly he thought Feille was going to take the sorcerers anyway and he might as well get something out of the deal?"

And that "something" would be a chance to get back at one of his least favorite demons? I doubted I was worth two sorcerers. I thought on Kirby's words as he left. Maybe Taullian did have some elaborate plot up his sleeve. But why did the high elf heal me in the dungeon? Why had he continued to feed me and ensure a reasonable amount of comfort in transit? Why wasn't he flaying the flesh from my bones right now? Did he really intend to catapult me at Feille like some kind of demon warhead? That would really suck, given my current, broken state. But it may ...it just may play into this crazy idea I had brewing.

I didn't have long to wait before Taullian himself came to visit.

He stared at me though the bars. I stared back, wondering who would be the first to break, the first to speak. Imps are not well known for their patience.

"Feille, huh? I'd heard you were a weak ruler, but I never imagined you'd bow down to Wythyn without so much as an arrow fired. You have truly made a deal with the devil."

He smiled. It was genuine, but it never reached his eyes. "I haven't yet, but I'm about to."

"And what good am I? A diversion to make you happy in your remaining days? Torturing me is your idea of a last meal for a condemned high lord?"

He sighed and shook his head as he watched me. "My father would roll over in his grave if he knew what I'm about to do. 'Never trust the demons', he always told me, and yet here I am, about to negotiate with the demon I trust the least." He shrugged, the smile twisting at one corner of his mouth. "As the humans say, 'the devil you know'."

Negotiate? Well, that sounded a whole lot more promising than torture and execution. "I'm all ears."

He glanced briefly at my ears, then scowled. "Not funny, Ni. Not in the least bit amusing."

Ni. Short for Niyaz, my childhood name. No one called me that anymore, besides Leethu. The name triggered a wave of memory from my childhood — of rolling in the mud at the edge of the swamps, of hiding in Oma's house from my cruel foster siblings, of frolicking with brave elf children in the woods. Shit. That little elf boy I'd played with all one summer, letting him chase me and shoot me with arrows.

"I didn't mean to bite part of your ear off," I said slowly, trying to gauge his reaction. If I was right, no wonder he didn't trust me. "I was just a child, an overexcited child. There was no malice in what I did."

He waved a hand. "I know. Demons will be demons. My father warned me to stay away from you, but I was curious. I liked you, and I wanted the other elves to see how brave I was, chasing demon young through the woods."

"I kept looking for you," I told him honestly. "I'd hoped you would come back to play again."

Taullian shook his head, his eyes hard as they met mine. "No. You may have not intended to kill me, but you would have. There is too much risk dealing with demons. Their emotions rule their actions, any loophole in a deal will be exploited, and treachery is inevitable. I learned my lesson that summer long ago. Well, I thought I did, but even after your betrayal with the demon spawn this winter, I've returned to deal with you again."

I sighed. This was going to be very one–sided. He'd never trust me, and the whole situation over the elf/demon hybrid job wasn't exactly putting me in a good light.

"So what do you want me to do in return for my life and freedom?"

"Help me kill Feille."

I laughed. Laughed until tears spilled down my cheeks. It's what I'd planned on doing anyway, but a good demon never gave away any bargaining chips. "You're fucking kidding me! I'm broken. I could bleed to death from a paper cut. How do you envision I perform this assassination?"

Taullian frowned. "You exploded his dungeon, killing two elves. You crushed his sorcerer's head with your bare hands."

"I used a rock that had fallen from the ceiling," I corrected. "And the explosion wasn't me."

Well, not intentionally me. Whatever that sorcerer had done with the demon raw energy had triggered it. I simply facilitated, and lucked out that it had any kind of destructive effect.

"It took three guards to take you down. You'd overpowered Feille and were throttling him."

"Uhhh, no. The guards were stuck on the other side of a melted dungeon door. Feille smacked the shit out of me with his staff, then roped me with a bunch of vines he grew out of the stone floor and proceeded to beat the shit out of me again."

Taullian leaned close to the bars. I noted they didn't sizzle for him. "I've seen you in action, Az. There may be some doubt as to whether you are the Iblis or not, but you're one fierce fighter. You play dirty, throw yourself into a battle like your life means nothing. Feille fears you. I fear you. Nearly every elf in the six southern kingdoms fears you."

I threw out my hands in frustration. What part of broken did this guy not understand? "Fine. I'll put it on my to–do list. Anything else? Endless riches? Eternal life? The universe at your feet?"

"Help me restore the kingdoms."

I'd been joking about that universe thing. I stared at him a moment. "You want to take Feille's place? Rule over six instead of one?"

Now it was Taullian's turn to laugh. His was short and bitter. "I want to, but I doubt I can. I don't have his force of will. I'm weak. I can barely hold my own kingdom together."

"Your guards seem to respect you. Your humans speak highly of you." I remembered my conversation with Kirby at the party, how he'd gone on and on about how progressive Taullian was, how the kingdom was surprisingly kind when it came to their laws regarding the treatment of humans. And although he'd admitted Taullian was no warrior just now, he still seemed to hold him in high regard. They were treated like shit, as Nyalla had been, but at least they didn't suffer as bad as in the other kingdoms.

"Elves respect force and power. And humans ...well, they don't matter."

"They do," I argued. "'They're clever and resilient, and they accomplish great things in collaboration with each other. You must have a thousand humans here. Give them equality and see how hard they fight for you, see what kind of army you have."

His eyebrows shot up. "Humans? They are cowards. Even my mages and sorcerers, skilled as they are, won't assert themselves in the least."

"Perhaps they are convenient cowards. Give them your respect and friendship, treat them as peers and see how brave they really are."

He stood abruptly, spinning on his heel to leave. "Demons lie. And humans are weak cowards."

"One attacked an angel for me," I shouted after him. He halted halfway to the door, his back still toward me. "To save me. He is my friend, my lover, and he attacked not just any old angel, but one of the Ruling Council."

Taullian turned. I couldn't read his expression from the distance.

"To save me," I repeated. "Because I treat him as an equal. I treat him with love, respect, and friendship. I have other humans who would do the same, humans I call my friends. If a demon can inspire this, you can too."

He stood in the dim light of the dungeon watching me, faint light from the illuminating globes dancing off the silver and gold embroidery on his clothing. His chest rose and fell with a deep breath then he turned and walked out, closing the door behind him with a careful 'snick'.

Kill Feille. Maybe in a few centuries, when I'd regained whatever of my powers I could, but not now. But it had to be now. I had no time to wait, no time to grow strong. The humans, the elves, the demons — it would all be lost if I waited. I looked down at my body, clothed in a borrowed shirt and pants from the elves. I'd extoled the strengths of the humans to Taullian, now it was time to put my money where my mouth was. I might be no better than a human right now, but I was still me on the inside, where it counted. I had to do this. For the humans, for demons who didn't give a shit about me, for elves who hated me. I had to do this, because some things were worth dying for.

I thought about Kirby's marble. If I could just get Feille alone, surprise him at a moment when he'd let his guard down, I might be able to kill him. I was good at killing, and it would be a great feeling to have Feille's neck snap under my hands. I think even Wyatt would approve.

Yes. I'd kill that asshole of an elf lord. As far as restoring Taullian's kingdom, that was his job. Without Feille, there'd be a scramble for power. Every elf for himself. If Taullian couldn't pull his shit together for his own people, then he didn't deserve the crown on his head. But the humans ...they deserved more. And I'd help them if it was the last thing I did.

~11~

Meandering cobblestone streets separated the weathered brownstone row houses and provided a quaint ambiance of yesteryear. They also acted as an effective speed deterrent, Gabriel noted as he watched the cars inch along, vibrating even at slow speed on the uneven terrain. Pedestrians walked by, eyes downward to avoid an ankle sprain. It was especially amusing to watch the female humans in their high heels tip–toeing across the street. This town looked the same as when he'd last visited it a thousand years before — maybe a little bigger, certainly much less odiferous. Not that he could smell much of anything with his purposely inhibited sensory organs. All the better to avoid the temptations of the corporeal world.

Gabriel approached a table and sat down opposite an olive–skinned man whose dark brown hair was combed back, curling at the edge of his shirt collar. This angel was better than most at reproducing a human form, and that alone made Gabriel suspicious. He too could produce a convincing form, but there was a price. Driving his spirit so far into the flesh, committing himself so fully, created a painful sensory overload. Eventually, angels could get used to it; come to enjoy it even, but it threw them off balance. It pushed them away from their righteous center, and it made all those forbidden things so hard to resist.

He recognized this angel as one of Uriel's, and not a minor member either. He'd petitioned to change from Sidreal's choir to his current one a few centuries back. It was typical for angels to make strategic moves as they gained prominence, and the third choir was known for being one of the more welcoming. This particular angel was one to watch. There had been talk of his potential candidacy for a Ruling Council slot in the next hundred years or so.

"Tura. Where's Uriel?"

He was making a joke about his sibling's fondness for coffee shops and was surprised to see Tura stiffen, his hand white on his coffee cup.

"He's not here. Did you expect him?" Tura relaxed back into his chair, the movement oddly forced.

"*She.* Uriel seems to fancy being female lately."

Tura shrugged. "Really? I haven't seen him ...err, her in a long time."

Was that a lie? Gabriel watched the angel toy with his coffee cup and decided to let it pass. Angels didn't often see the heads of their choirs on a regular basis. Even though Tura seemed strangely nervous at the mention of Uriel's name, Gabriel wasn't here to interrogate him. Not at the moment, anyway. This visit was all about information, and he wouldn't get any if he took a hardline approach with this angel.

"I've heard you have some interest in our project." Tura continued. "We could use a supporter at your level. An angel on the Ruling Council giving it his backing would make things happen faster."

"It's a far–fetched notion. A fantasy that will only end in madness and broken dreams." Gabriel waved his hand, turning his face from the other angel dismissively. It wouldn't do to appear too eager.

"But here you are." The words hung in the air.

Gabriel observed the cars rumble slowly by. One small and blue vehicle had four grown men stuffed into it, their heads practically hitting the roof with each bump. Where were they going? Sharing a ride to work? Heading off to some sporting event? The angel shook his head, irritated at his own curiosity about human lives. Slowly he turned to face Tura.

"Yes. Here I am." It was a fine line, dancing between interest and aloofness — draw him forward, push him back.

They sat in silence, Tura rubbing a finger along the edge of his coffee cup, Gabriel looking about with casual interest at the other café patrons. With a sigh, the younger angel put his cup down and reached for something under the table. Gabriel couldn't help a quick smirk of amusement. If this were a human across the table from him a thousand years ago, he would have expected him to pull a knife. But Tura was an angel, and above the need for human weaponry, and he was too smart to try anything against one of the Ancient. No, to go up against even one of the brothers, an angel needed an army at his back.

Instead of a knife, Tura pulled out a glass tube and slide it across the table toward Gabriel who picked it up and admired the iridescent green swirl that churned about inside.

"Genie in a bottle," he mused, feeling the instant pull of attraction.

Except the demon wasn't in a bottle but some strange glass tube. There had been times when human magic users had been able to bind demons, pull their spirit selves out of a corporeal form and house them captive in a vessel. He'd always found it quite amusing. Usually they snared the imps and tricksters, the ones whose curiosity left them open to capture. Sometimes the demon would remain there for decades, centuries even, until whichever human owned them at the time accepted their bargain for release. Favors. Everything came down to favors with the demons, usually in the form of three wishes. Sadly, the humans were too much like their captives and often wound up dead and Owned following the genie's release.

"Not quite. This one is not worthy of such as you, but we can easily find one that is. And it's only a portion, not the entirety of the spirit being."

Gabriel peered closely at the contents of the tube, carefully extending his spirit–self to examine it beyond the restrictions of his form's physical senses. An imp would be below him, far below him, he thought, feeling a twinge of irritation at his eldest brother's folly, but this demon in the tube wasn't even an imp. It was a Low.

"Why do you show me this portion of a Low?" he asked, his voice harsh with distaste.

"It would violate our treaty to join and breed with a living demon," Tura said, extending a tanned hand for the vial. "This is simply the portion you would use to create new life. It's more than enough, actually, but we would supply the extra to ensure a successful birth."

How in all of creation had they gotten it? Gabriel swallowed down the bitter taste that rose in his throat. Dead. They'd killed a Low demon and parted him out for breeding. It wasn't a genie in a bottle; it was a severed body part in a bottle.

"You killed him, chopped him up into bits and stored the parts?" His voice was gruffer then he would have liked. Why should he care? They killed demons all the time — the ones that violated the treaty and crossed into the human world. Might as well put them to good use.

Tura drew back, and Gabriel felt the atmosphere chill between them. "Of course not! That would be barbaric. Demon essence is needed to breed. It would violate the treaty and our vow to have an actual breeding exchange with a live demon, so this is the solution." Tura peered at him, obviously trying to gauge his reaction. "I cannot divulge the identities of our contacts, but we have a system of donation in place."

Donation? "Without naming names, how is this donation brokered? You do understand I need to ensure compliance with angelic law. Breeding aside, we should have no contact with demons unless they break the treaty, and then only the Grigori are allowed to dispatch them. How would that scenario lend itself to a donation?"

Tura grinned. "It's quite complicated. Humans act as our go–between on this side of the gates and elves on the other. The elves compensate the demons, humans compensate the elves, and we, in turn, compensate the humans for their efforts."

Humans. Once again, they were meddling in human lives, involving them in matters beyond their abilities. Humans were the sole link to the elves, and the elves were the only beings in Hel that could truly be trusted. But the involvement of the very species they were supposed to be shepherding toward a higher existence wasn't the only troubling point in this project.

"This is all very interesting, but the main hurdle is in the formation. Angels can't form. And donated bits of demons can't form."

Tura shifted in his seat, again picking up his coffee cup. He hadn't taken a drink from it, and Gabriel was beginning to think it was a prop, something to occupy his hands during nervous moments.

"We've overcome that obstacle. The method is proprietary information, but I assure you it is lawful."

"So you've created new life using a Low sample and...?" Gabriel asked. What angel would seriously consider combining their essence with a Low? The very thought made him shiver in disgust.

"A volunteer. I know what you're thinking. The results were destroyed, and now that we've been successful with a Low, we'll try with more reputable demons. Those offspring we'll keep."

It made sense. Lows would be plentiful and cheaper to use in experimentation. No sense in wasting good demons on testing. Still, the idea made something inside him knot in protest.

"What happens if the result is ...you know, an angel that would not be allowed in Aaru per the treaty?" Gabriel tried to keep his tone casual, wishing he too had a coffee cup to toy with.

"'We're working to perfect the technique so only Angels of Order are produced. Right now, offspring are already predisposed to order, and every test has resulted in the desired offspring. In the remote chance that an Angel of Chaos is born, we'll send it to Hel."

Gabriel had a vision of a helpless angel, dropped through a gate and quickly set upon and ripped to shreds. Everything blurred, and he nearly rose from his seat. Clenching his teeth, he smoothed the tablecloth before him and tried likewise to smooth his emotions. Samael. Was this a fate he would have wanted for his brother? Newly formed and discarded in hostile territory?

"I can guarantee there are some on the Ruling Council that would not approve of the project unless creations of order were a guaranteed result."

Tura nodded. "We are close. By the time we present, we'll have that guarantee."

"So why all the secrecy? It seems to be a noble purpose. It doesn't violate the treaty or threaten our positive evolution. You should have plenty of support and backers in this endeavor."

Again Tura shifted in his seat, running a finger around the lip of the white, porcelain cup. "You certainly know, Ancient One, that there are some in Aaru who would not approve of this, who would feel it skirts too close to the limits of our vow. There are also others who have begun to regret their actions in the war and the subsequent treaty. Time has dulled their memories, and they would disapprove our project."

Gabriel nodded. Aaru was a realm divided, and the last two millennia had seen an increase in unrest. There were those who secretly held sympathies towards the demons, and on the other side there were the isolationists. A storm was brewing, and these factions threatened to tear Aaru apart once again, just as the war had so long ago.

"Even more," Tura continued, "can you imagine what would happen if we announced we had a method of creation? We'd be overwhelmed with requests — demands for the opportunity. Once we have the technique perfected, we need to ensure an appropriate method of evaluation and a waiting list. We wouldn't want every angel to have this opportunity, only those deemed most evolved, those with the highest vibration level."

"Of course." It wouldn't do to have Aaru overrun with inferior offspring. Before the war, breeding had been a long, drawn–out affair involving petitions, negotiations, and detailed deliberations. Sometimes after a century, a pair would walk away from a contract, unable to agree on terms or specifics of formation. Even with Angels of Chaos in Aaru, creation had been a rare and celebrated event. This would change all that. There would need to be rules and standards put in place.

"So, what would you require of me?" And that unspoken other half of the sentence — what will I get in return?

Tura smiled, his shoulders dropping as he let out a relieved breath. "Merely to assist us as needed, Ancient One. We've had a small setback. We've lost a few of those who were to supply us with donations. We will continue to fine–tune the technique with the stock we have. We hope to be receiving a higher quality of demon donations within the next six months."

"I cannot commit to something so vague," Gabriel cautioned. "You need to be more explicit in what help you'll need or I won't guarantee you'll have my assistance."

"We may need you to cover for us. The angels working on this project are not Grigori and may be questioned as to their brief and occasional presence among the humans to collect donations. Most importantly, we would request your support in presenting our findings to the Ruling Council when we have confirmation of success."

Gabriel caught the surprise, before it creased his face, and schooled his expression into calm disinterest. Were the two murdered angels, who'd been among the humans without permission, somehow involved in this? It was a farfetched idea, and far more likely they'd journeyed out of Aaru to sin with the humans.

"I can present your findings before the council and ensure your work continues without scrutiny until it is time to organize a rollout," Gabriel vowed.

Tura shook his head. "We want to present the findings ourselves. We have a team of dedicated angels. I know, Ancient One, that angels such as I are not allowed in the presence of the Council, but it would mean a great deal to those who have worked so hard in the service of order. To look upon our highest angels, to tell them of our work, would be the highlight of their immortal lives."

Gabriel hid a frown. Normally he struggled with the sin of pride. Not so much as his eldest brother, but enough. Tura's speech should have filled him with a sense of his place within Aaru, blinded him to all reason with its subservient and adoring tone, but it didn't. It rang false, and that allowed Gabriel to keep his wits about him.

"Of course," he said magnanimously. "I would be happy to sponsor you and your team at a Ruling Council meeting."

Tura smiled, the first genuine smile he'd had during the meeting. There was a hint of triumph in the smile. He took the glass vial from the table and stood, bowing low to Gabriel before vanishing.

The angel sat back in his chair, picking up the coffee cup Tura had been holding and running his hands over it. Smooth, but with a slightly porous feel to its white surface. He felt the clay, the liquid within, the traces of energy from the angel that had held it. The meeting had gone well, but Gabriel still wasn't satisfied. As things stood, he might not hear from Tura until they were ready to present to the council, and that was unacceptable. He needed to know more; he needed to be involved.

Smiling slightly, he dipped a finger into the liquid in the cup. Acidic and dark, burned beans steeped in water then strained. What the humans found to like about this was beyond him. All these trips here were taking a toll on him. All the smells and sights, the emotions were pulling him, calling to him with their siren song. But still, he delayed returning to Aaru. Perhaps, just perhaps he'd stay a while and watch. Just observe as he used to so long ago.

~12~

I languished in my cell another two weeks, occupying myself by carving obscene pictures in the stone walls with my eating utensils. The only regular visitors I had were the elven guards that accompanied the humans who brought my food. They didn't trust me enough to send a human servant into the dungeon solo. Neither elf nor human spoke to me in spite of my repeated attempts at banal conversation. The humans seemed curious like they wanted to linger, but the guards always hustled them along.

I tried making extra limbs, scales, claws, elongated teeth, all the while terribly anxious that if I changed into something else, I may not be able to return to my current, human form. A human with four legs or fangs might be ho–hum in Hel, but I could hardly walk around Earth like that. And I clung with all my might to the hope that I'd be able to return to the people I loved. I shouldn't have worried — nothing came of my efforts. The only thing I managed was grow my hair and nails at a quicker rate, which made me hope that the ability to quickly fix injury wouldn't be far behind.

Worse was my realization that I could no longer manifest my wings. I mourned them the most and feared deep in my heart that I'd never have them again. Few demons could create them at all, but I'd always had wings. They were part of my first form. I'd flown before I could properly walk. The permanent loss of my wings would be a terrible blow. I fretted that my stolen flights above the Potomac River and flying with

Gregory through the ice fields in Alaska would be the last times I flew unassisted.

Finally, I heard the door to the dungeon open and a sound I'd been waiting for — many feet on the stone floor. Taullian came into view wearing a more subdued, leather version of his usual attire. Gone were the gilded robes, in their place was form–fitting, body–concealing protective clothing —practical and, at a distance, undifferentiated from the ones his guards wore. Clearly, whatever the elf lord had planned, he intended on being right in the thick of things with his people. Maybe he wasn't such a wiener after all.

"So what's the plan?" I asked, careful not to get to close to the bars. I'd already zapped myself on them dozens of times in the past few weeks. It always hurt like fuck but didn't seem to do any lasting injury.

"We'll move in two weeks. We have a magical device that will allow us to gate in and take them by surprise. There are some final logistics, then we're ready."

He didn't look ready. He looked like a man about to face his death.

"Can we speak privately?" I asked.

He nodded and dismissed the guards with a wave of his hands. A few were reluctant to leave, glaring at me as if they expected me to erupt in violence the moment their backs were turned. I didn't blame them. I was sure their past experience colored their opinions about demons. Little did they know, I could do nothing to hurt Taullian beyond hurtling my fork through the bars at him.

"Once we gate in," he continued. "I'll need you to make your way to the palace to find Feille and kill him."

"Yeah," I drawled. "There's a bit of a hole in that logic. Feille is the worst coward I've ever seen. He's happy to beat the shit out of someone or bully them safely behind wards and protective circles, but when there's a threat to his being, he crumbles like a two–month–old cookie. Within seconds of a surprise attack, he'll hide and have every sorcerer on his staff ensuring his personal well–being. I need to get him somewhere he can't run to safety."

"I could possibly get you into his personal chambers, but I can't guarantee it."

"That, and have me go first. The rest of you can move once I'm in. Give me a few moments, then you can cover me with the commotion of your attack."

Taullian nodded. "We'll need you to fight with us after he's dead. He has supporters, and although not everyone agrees with his policies, there will be resistance to rule by Cyelle."

Ah, so he was thinking big. Yes, I might actually end up liking this guy after all.

"Unless you're willing to wait for me to fully recover from my injuries, I doubt I'll be of much use to you."

He contemplated that a moment. "Agreed, but you'll need to get out of the palace and the kingdom somehow. It would be in your best interests to ensure we win so you'll have safe passage."

Right. Normally, I'd sneak out as something small and eight–legged, but it would be harder to accomplish my usual stealthy exit as a human female. There was a good chance I'd be killed, and although I'd become rather adept at surviving inside a corpse, I hadn't yet managed to animate it. Plus, I couldn't change my physical form. The prospect of spending centuries inside a rotting cadaver, waiting to recover lost skills, wasn't appealing. Staying alive was a top priority, just behind killing Feille.

"I'll do the best I can, but beyond Feille, I'm not promising anything."

"Good. We have a deal then. I hope I'm not making a terrible mistake in trusting you."

"Nope. You can completely count on me," I told him cheerfully. From his grim expression, he knew I was lying. I'd help him, but I had my own agenda, and that came first.

"If the Goddess shines her favor upon us, we'll be a free kingdom by the end of the month."

Taullian didn't look very confident about having his goddess' favor. In actuality, he looked rather ill, like a man marching to his death. Not good, since his troops would need to feed off his confidence to fight with any valor.

"I think you need a whole lot more than the favor of your deity. What's your battle plan?"

Taullian lifted his nose in disdain. "I'm hardly going to tell you my battle plan. Trust doesn't go that far when it comes to demons."

Fair enough. "Then let me tell you what I'd do. Not that I'm particularly skilled in warfare, but I have spent the last nine months listening to really long, boring tales of battle strategy from an angel. I zoned out for most of them, but I think a few things soaked into my memory."

"An angel?" Taullian interrupted. "Of all the ridiculous lies, that one is the most unbelievable I've ever heard."

Taullian knew I'd been bound. It was the one thing that had saved me from winding up dead or in jail over the whole hybrid baby fiasco. He obviously didn't think that servitude extended to the kind of instructional conversations Gregory and I had together. I'm sure ours was the first to cross the line from angel and bound demon into friendship and more. With tightness in my chest, I glanced down at the underside of my arm. Gone. No tattoo of a sword with angel wings at the hilt. No link to my angel beyond the disconnected red purple of his spirit sitting like an alien presence throughout my damaged self. I shook off the crashing sense of loss and refocused. I'd mourn later, but now I had things to do.

"First, I hope this technology of yours that gates us all in is undetectable. I'm sure it is when it's not in use, but once someone makes the hop, will it set off any alarms? Because that is going to affect your timing."

Taullian shook his head. "It registers a small energy blip, but nothing significant enough to set off alarms. Of course, I'm not positive the sensitivity of the Wythyn alarms, but I've got a good degree of certainty we'll arrive unannounced."

Phew, that was a relief. I didn't want sirens going off all over the palace with me trapped in Feille's bedchamber.

"Then I'd use intel to figure out the best time to transport my assassin and give her a set time to do the deed before all hell broke loose. If she kills him too early, the palace will be in a state of alert looking for the killer, and the army would lose some of the element of surprise. If she arrives too late Feille will be safely behind twenty layers of runes and circles."

Taullian's expression was blank, but I could tell he'd already thought of this.

"The actual attack needs to be swift and bloody. They'll be shocked and not have time to adequately evaluate the threat, so there's a good chance with an immediate high body count, the rest will just lay down their arms."

He still wore a blank look. Good.

"I'd have a plan for post battle, to ensure any little uprisings over the next month are quickly squashed. The best bet would be to get everyone back to work immediately — business as usual kind of thing. Make them feel like not that much is going to change day-to-day. That you won't be taking their lands or their wealth, or lowering their status in any way."

A flicker of interest appeared in his eyes.

"And one more thing, to really seal the deal. Use your humans. It will expand your fighting force. If you offer them freedom, a livelihood in Cyelle, or perhaps even a small sub-kingdom of their own if they want, they'll jump to serve your cause."

"I'm not using the service humans," Taullian sputtered. "Aside from the mages and sorcerers, they're unskilled. They can't fight and won't make a good army. They don't have the speed or martial talent the elves do."

"But they have one advantage — they're invisible. Elves speak freely around them, relax around them. Beyond the mages and sorcerers, humans aren't a threat. They're overlooked, discounted, and underestimated. I bet you think they all look so similar that a new human wouldn't even register on your radar as out of place."

"What good does that do me? I can see the intelligence gathering opportunity, but I wouldn't trust them to get it right. Receiving the wrong information is worse than no information at all. And what would they do in a fight? Beat the elves over the head with a loaf of bread?"

I shrugged, unable to help a wicked smile. "They poison the bread."

Taullian gasped, his eyes horrified. "Only demons do such things!"

"Yeah, right. That's why you have a taster at every diplomatic event. Demons poison, but I'm sure elves do too."

The high elf sputtered in outrage. "I refuse to lower myself to the level of a demon."

"Feille will. He'll do anything to achieve his goals, and if you're not willing to go that far, that's your weakness. He'll use it against you."

"A leader without scruples is no leader."

This was beginning to sound like an argument Wyatt and I had over and over again.

"Scruples are fine, but when your people are in danger, when there are innocents to protect, someone has to do the heavy lifting. You're no leader if you're not willing to dirty your soul to save your people from having to do so."

I winced as it came out of my mouth, thinking of the two sorcerers I'd killed. Pawns. There'd been a lot of collateral damage lately. Was I justifying my actions so I could sleep at night, or was this really what I believed?

"I'm not sanctioning the poisoning of others, and I'm not using humans. They'd be arrow fodder, dying left and right."

"Then teach them. The elves won't recognize the threat until they've got a knife through their hearts. They'd never expect a human to attack them. Just give them some instruction and proper weapons and they could do great things."

"No." Taullian rose to his feet. I thought convincing him to use them in his war would bring about the end I wanted, but it was time to cut straight to the point.

"I want their freedom. I want you to provide them with part of a kingdom and resources to have their own society. I want you to close down the traps and stop enslaving them."

He froze, his mouth open in astonishment. "What are you talking about? You're a demon. You've done far worse things to humans than any *elf* ever has."

"I like humans. They're mine, and I won't let you enslave them any longer."

He started to laugh, and spun on his heel to leave. "What do you plan to do about it? You're in no position to bargain."

"Neither are you. You need me to assassinate Feille. This is my price. You want me to fight? This is my price."

He turned briefly, a condescending smile on his face. "Your *reward* is your freedom and your life. I hold all the cards here. Yes, I need you, but not at that price. I'd rather let you rot in my dungeon for the rest of your life."

I watched him leave, leaning dangerously close to the magic–enhanced cell bars. If I ever regained some of my ability, I could blow up the elven gates. They'd rebuild, so I'd need to do it over and over, discovering the locations then sneaking into each kingdom to disable them. I could spend the rest of my life in Hel trying to free humans, one at a time or in small groups. Where to put them, though, that they'd be safe from both elf and demon raids? Plus, I'd have a huge price on my head. Eventually someone would get lucky, or I'd get unlucky. No, the only way to human freedom was to gain buy–in from the elves. Taullian was my best bet. Nyalla said he was the most sympathetic to their plight compared to the neighboring kingdoms. He was the only elven lord who punished serious mistreatment of humans, the only one who legislated a minimal standard of care. But my only hope was not proving to be willing. What could I do to change his mind?

~13~

"This has got to be the worst place on the entire planet," Gabriel muttered to himself as he swerved to avoid a large group of human teens, walking sideways and backwards as they chatted excitedly. Usually his projected "avoid me/ignore me" compulsion created a safe, ten–foot human–free zone around his form, but the teens seemed immune. Actually, everyone seemed to be immune — a fact he attributed more to the anomalies of the location than anything to do with the humans who were shopping here.

The gate hadn't originally been in the middle of a shopping mall. When they'd built it, most of the world was a frozen block of ice. The mountains had been bigger, and the ocean wasn't as close. And of course, the humans hadn't filled the area with their buildings, roads, cars, and chaotic lives. Gabriel paused, eyes unfocused as he remembered. If he imagined where he stood without the humans and their busy work, the landscape really wouldn't be that much different. Another image danced across his memory, from when these beaten–down mountains had been jagged peaks and when volcanoes stretched north to south. He'd flown among the summits, observing life below, playing in the thermals. Samael had always dared them to dive into the lava and out again. Fire had never been Gabriel's strong suit. Samael's either, he thought. It was the brother he was here to see today that was the one skilled in all things flame and heat.

Gabriel found him next to the gate, which at the moment was in front of a busy sandwich shop. The other angel stood still and calm, as if meditating in the midst of all this chaos. His dark, reddish–brown hair was an unkempt mess of big curls, his arms crossed in front of his chest. The humans glanced at him as they walked by, their eyes full of adoration. They'd never remember seeing him, just that sense of joy and peace dancing across their souls in the middle of a day's shopping. It irritated Gabriel that his eldest brother encouraged the humans so, that he seemed to enjoy their brief attention. Angels were supposed to remain aloof and distant, only monitoring the humans, not giving them brief moments of grace. They'd had enough grace — too much too soon, and look where it had gotten them.

"Are you watching the gate?" Gabriel asked, incredulous that a member of the Ruling Council, an archangel, could be doing such a thing.

"Yes. The guardian needed a break. I believe she is off getting some lunch."

Gabriel choked, his eyes wide. "What? A break?"

"Mmm," the elder angel nodded. "I've been rather hard on her lately. It's the least I could do."

Gabriel shook his head in disbelief. "She shouldn't be eating. It's a violation of angelic purity standards. It's a sin."

Broad shoulders lifted in a shrug. "It's a minor infraction. Besides, she's a guardian. Her vibration level is not where I could require rigid adherence to standards."

"Her level shouldn't matter. Standards are standards. How do you expect her to attain positive evolution if you bend the rules for her?" Of course, he'd seen his own brother eat something recently. They were all slipping from their right order, falling and encouraging others to do the same.

"She's not slaughtering humans, or having sexual intercourse with them. She doesn't even socialize with them. She's isolated down here with no companions." A brief look of pain crossed the elder angel's face. "Well, not any longer. Let her have her lunch. Besides, it's not like any of us are experiencing positive evolution. Not for two and a half million years."

Gabriel winced. "I don't agree. You need to hold your staff to higher standards. And you should be setting an example, not eating these crab chips and leading others to sin."

His brother turned to face him, black eyes calm and emotionless. Gabriel felt a shiver down his spine. Not this again. The brother he'd both loved and hated had died inside after the war, leaving this cold, dispassionate angel in his place. The last year he'd thought whatever spark lay dormant inside had come to life, but now those eyes were once again empty, black.

"Do you wish to take over here as head Grigori, brother? I'm sure the Council would vote in your favor if you have such a need to set things right."

Gabriel felt panic tighten his chest, locking his breath for an instant. No. He couldn't. An extended period of time here? Tens of thousands of years watching the humans evolve and regress? Never again. Not after what happened last time.

"No," was the only word he could manage.

A fleeting smile crossed his brother's face as he turned again to watch the gate. "Then tell me, what is so important that it brings you from the safety and comforts of Aaru to brave the horrendous world of the humans?"

Gabriel flushed slightly, hating the condescending tone. It had always been this way as the middle angel of the five . He'd not been young enough to indulge, nor old enough to respect.

"We've lost three angels in less than a year."

Again, that brief smile. "Why yes, my brother. How very astute of you. I commend you on your excellent math skills."

The younger angel ground his teeth. "You killed Althean. The other two died within weeks of each other, and the latest reports are *still* unacceptably vague."

"I thought they were particularly well written. What sections are you objecting to this time?"

"The section that deals with cause of death of the one in Washington State." Gabriel sneered. "Have you found out anything further since we last spoke? Are you even bothering? He's an angel. We don't die from ingesting bad shellfish or stampeding elephants."

"*Was* an angel," his brother corrected. "He lost his corporeal form in a massive explosion and had insufficient time to create a new one before coming apart. What's not to understand?"

"Who caused this explosion? Demons? Something internal to the planet? Humans? If the latter, we need to consider eliminating them and devoting our time to another species."

The older angel shook his head. "Gabriel, you didn't used to be so pessimistic, so quick to condemn. Where is your faith?"

Gone. A long, long time ago.

"So, a meteor strike? Spontaneous combustion?"

"Explosion of origin unknown. The humans claim it was a remote campground that fell to an unfortunate meteor strike. Some claim it might have been some sort of secret human military facility. An angel was there as were approximately two–dozen humans, some of them with magical ability. Of course, further investigation is hindered by the fact that the entire island is no more."

Gabriel frowned. "Have you discovered why he was there? What was he doing that involved such contact with humans and magic?"

A cup of soda slipped from the hand of one of the humans walking by. With a flash of speed, the elder angel snatched it and handed it to the girl. She smiled in thanks and walked on.

"I've no idea why he was there. Enjoying nature, perhaps, and struck down unexpectedly? Or if the other report is true, I'd assume that whatever he and the humans were working on was highly explosive."

"But not inherently destructive?" Gabriel urged his brother to continue. There were things he wasn't sharing, and it bothered the younger angel.

"Nuclear power for energy would be my guess."

Fission. The humans were so careless with it; just as bad as the demons. Gabriel looked intently at his brother. Humans with magic. If one was a sorcerer, there was a good chance a demon was on his or her tail. He wasn't sure why, but demons seemed to be quite eager to hunt down humans with significant magical ability. An angel chasing a demon chasing a sorcerer? But why would an angel visiting illegally risk exposure by attacking a demon? Or risk death by attacking a demon high enough to be storing a lethal amount of raw energy? Unless the demon was doing something so heinous that the angel sacrificed himself to prevent it.

"So what about the other one? How did he come into contact with a devouring spirit?"

"No idea."

"Well then, what *do* you know?" Gabriel snapped. "Did any humans witness the murder? Were they murdered by the devouring spirit, too? Did they just vanish from the face of the planet?"

"The Iblis claims there are wild gates. If so, vanishing is a possibility."

Gabriel gave a short bark of laughter. "The Iblis also claims that her hellhound eats her four–nine–five reports. She's a demon. She lies."

The older angel shrugged, clearly declining to comment further. Gabriel let the silence stretch on past the point of comfort, staring at his brother as if he could force him to provide the answers, but he wouldn't budge.

"Fine," the younger angel sighed. He wasn't done with this one. If he had to walk among the humans and investigate himself, he'd do it. He'd hate it, but he'd do it.

The gate shimmered slightly, and the pair tensed, ready to leap, but nothing came through. A few seconds later it returned to its dormant state.

"Defective?" Gabriel asked. He'd never really bothered much with the gates. It's not like he expected any of the elves to come through. Maybe in a few million more years, as newer generations forgot the past and became interested. They'd always been curious, willing students sitting at the angels' wings. Such a shame things had gone so wrong during the wars that the elves had chosen Hel. They'd be back, though — of this, he was certain.

"No. The elder angel motioned toward the gate. "Young demons test to see if their skills are developed enough to activate a passage, or older demons trigger for a quick look to better strategize a crossing. When they come through, they're swift, and they often employ distraction techniques."

Gabriel looked around him, his brother's voice fading into a monotone drone as it always did when he went on these dull lectures. Gates weren't his problem. He didn't care.

"Have you seen Uriel lately?" he interrupted.

Disapproval flowed in waves from his brother. Yes, Gabriel was rude and insubordinate. Nothing new there. "Not since the last Council meeting. Is he well?"

Gabriel snorted in disgust. "She. She insists on maintaining this ridiculous female appearance. It's unseemly and not centered."

A low chuckle burst from the older angel. "I thought that was just for the meetings, to show how strong he was against the unbalancing influence of the Iblis."

"Evidently not. She says she feels like being female for a while. I'm concerned for her evolutionary path."

His brother rolled his eyes. Rolled his eyes! Where in the universe had he gotten that mannerism?

"I'm serious. She suffered greatly when Samael di ...when we lost Samael."

"We all did." The elder angel's voice was raw with pain, as if it had just happened yesterday and not over two million years ago.

"Yes, but she also lost her only child. A brother, a life partner, and a child. I fear for her. She's not stable, and now she has this bizarre insistence on being female."

"You're often female. So is Rafi. I would be, too, if I could."

True. Gabriel used to switch often, but lately he'd felt the rightness of a male form. And although his eldest brother had always been male, he was more extreme than usual. Far more. His entire center had shifted drastically. It was that imp.

"So what happened to our Iblis? She's surely repaired herself enough that she can return from Hel and resume her duties. Her reports are long overdue."

Gabriel didn't think it was possible for his brother to look that way. Fury and agony. Sorrow and fear. Gabriel had felt the very foundations of Aaru shake with his brother's emotion when he'd appeared with their Iblis half–dead in his arms. It brought back memories that frightened him, of his brother with tattered wings, the blood of Samael coating his sword. "I mean no disrespect, dear brother," he added softly, feeling as if he were suddenly treading over ground laced with landmines.

"Yes you do. You cannot stand to see me happy when your insides rot and fester. She is hurt. Gravely hurt and possibly dead. And if you speak of her with that flippant tone again, *you* will be the one to feel my sword."

Gabriel took a sharp breath. For all their differences, for all the animosity burning like a slow fire inside him, he did love his brother. And he never would have wished this kind of pain on him, not again, not after Samael. They'd all grieved, but the eldest of the five had gone deep into the pit of his sorrow. So deep, none of them thought he'd ever make it out again. To lose his little imp after all he'd been through.... It was cruel for the strongest among them to be tested so.

"I deeply regret my words, and my tone. Is there a way you can find out if she's alive? If she's repairing herself? Can I assist in any way?"

Not that he could. None of them could cross the gates to Hel. The demons were chaos incarnate; they could break the treaty without any moral pain. Angels of Order were not so flexible — especially the ancient ones.

"Her human toy has her communication mirror. He is in touch with her household, but they have heard nothing of her. Nothing."

Gabriel shuddered, feeling his brother's pain, accepting a share of it as a sibling should. "But you are bound. The pair of you. You should know if she did not survive."

The older angel shook his head, turning away from the gate. "I had to banish her. The bond is broken."

Gabriel frowned in confusion. "But the bond was two ways. She carries part of your essence. You should know."

"I don't," he hissed. "I had to break my connection, to sever that part of myself. I can't feel her."

The last words were raw with agony.

"Why?" Gabriel asked. "There was no need to sever her side of the binding to banish her. And you needn't fear she would take advantage of you. She may be a demon, but you are far more powerful and could easily resist."

His brother shook his head, looking toward the lighted panels that made up the ceiling of the mall. "She may need that portion of me. It was my gift to her — a gift of love. I only hope she realizes and uses it if she needs."

Gabriel felt ice run though him as he stared in shock at his brother. "What ...what are you talking about?" A demon could not "use" angel essence for anything but breeding, could not use it to repair themselves or heal injuries. Unless …unless they were the very worst abomination.

"She devours, Gabriel."

He caught his breath. The elder angel's tone was accepting with an odd fondness as though he were discussing a strange quirk. "But you cannot allow her to live! What if she brings about the apocalypse? Your job is to stop that from happening."

"Perhaps my job is to allow that to happen. All things begin and all things end. Hopefully not today, but I'm coming to realize that as powerful as we think we are, there are forces and rhythms we can never overcome."

Gabriel stared. "What is *wrong* with you? What happened to you?"

His brother's mouth twisted into a wry half–smile. "I met an imp, and everything changed."

The universe was truly doomed. The Angel of the Apocalypse, the Angel of Eternity had fallen in love with a devouring spirit. They were all doomed.

~14~

A few hours after Taullian left, lunch arrived. At least I think it was lunch. I was having a hard time telling the time of day. I sighed, eyeing the medium—rare slab of roast, surrounded by colorful vegetables and half a loaf of crusty bread. It looked good, but what I wouldn't give for a dozen jalapeño bites and a cold beer. As I dug in, I turned my thoughts from the humans to what I needed to do to not only gain my freedom, but prevent Feille from taking the demon section of Hel.

Taullian had said he might be able to send me into Feille's personal quarters, but I knew he couldn't guarantee the elf lord would be there at the time. I'd need to stay low and play a waiting game until the opportunity presented itself to make my move. Patience was always a weak spot for me, and remaining undetected would be a serious challenge given my present state of brokenness. Normally, I'd change myself into a small, unobtrusive insect and lay in wait, but I was unable to alter anything about my form. I only hoped there were enough tapestries and wardrobes to hide in or I'd be right back where I started — battered and bleeding in Feille's dungeon. Or more likely, dead. I couldn't fix myself and I couldn't defend myself. An elven child could probably take me down right now.

Then there were my doubts about this new relay technology. Kirby had been using it with no ill effects, and the elf lord assured it was stealthy, but this would be the first time it was ever tested to Taullian's knowledge. Wythyn might have some kind of alarm system that would be set off by the activation of a magical gate, especially one within the royal chambers. Plus, Taullian was trusting that one of his sorcerers would be able to place it in the private areas, but he had no way of knowing exactly where or if it had been accomplished. For all I knew, I'd be transported into a garbage bin, or the middle of a party.

I ate and entertained myself thinking of all the inappropriate places I could find myself. Most amusing would be popping in on Feille when he was getting busy with some lady friend. Or maybe male friend. I'd never watched elves fucking before. Might be worth delaying the assassination to observe a little.

I was pushing the plate aside and getting ready for a nap when I heard an explosion. It sounded fairly close, and even through the thick dungeon walls and doors I could hear the flurry of activity. A rat ran by my cell, only to pause and turn, his red eyes shining with an unholy light. Even before the rat vanished and he stood before me in the form he'd worn all our childhood, I knew him. I'd always know him, no matter what shape he took.

"Dar! What the fuck are *you* doing here?"

"Rescuing your ass. What does it look like I'm doing?"

Oh no, this was all wrong. I'd needed to convince Taullian to accept my deal. I needed to take out Feille before he attacked, and this plan was the best chance I had to gain access to him. This was the most untimely rescue ever.

"No Dar. I need to stay. I appreciate this, really I do, but there's something I have to do here."

"We can discuss this later. Come on, we've got to hurry." He reached forward with clawed hands to open the gate and squealed, leaping backward.

"Dumbass," I told him affectionately. "Do you seriously think they'd keep a demon in a regular old cell? Now get out of here. If I'm not back in a few more weeks, then you can come rescue me."

"They're coming. We've got to go right now." His voice sounded harsh through his furred, fanged snout.

He raised his hands. Before I could stop him, he blasted the cell door open with a surge of energy. Magic doesn't like to be breached in this fashion. Instead of a melted lock, there was a rolling fireball of melted iron that flew along the length of several cells before exploding bits of hot metal everywhere. I shrieked, trying to shield myself with the empty food platter, but agonizing splashes hit my exposed feet and arm.

"Get it off, get it off," I screamed, trying to flick away the burning bits and scrambling to get out of my smoking tunic. I was going to burn, burn badly, and it would take me days to fix myself.

"Oh you baby. Stop with the drama already," Dar announced, striding through the flaming chunks and grabbing my arm. I could hear the dungeon door slam open, feet racing in response to this new explosion. I could feel Dar yank me to him, heard a soft "snick", but all I could concentrate on was trying to save my fragile flesh from damage.

"Glah ham, shoceacan."

A button. Where the fuck did Dar get a button? At least the magical transport had extinguished any remaining sparks clinging to my body and pants. I had a series of painful blisters up one arm and a few on my legs that looked rather serious. From the smell, a good bit of my hair had burned off. I was naked from the waist up, but luckily the tunic I'd thrown off and the dinner platter I'd used had shielded me from the brunt of the blast. It could have been worse — much worse.

"Dar, you ass. Are you trying to get me killed?" I pulled away from him and saw that I was home, inside the crumbling, yellow stone dwelling I'd bought with my trust fund once I'd reached the age of maturity. I'll bet it was bursting at the seams with all the additions to my household.

"Well, that's gratitude for you." Dar grinned and yanked my hair, raking a claw against my bare stomach.

"Ow! Cut it out, Dar! Don't damage me; I can't fix myself right now." I didn't tell him that I was beginning to fear I'd never recover any significant conversion skills, that I'd be trapped in fragile human flesh with no way to quickly repair any injuries.

"Sorry, sorry!" He backed away, paws upraised. "Wyatt told me you'd been seriously damaged, but you know how these humans exaggerate everything. Can't even break one of their bones without them screaming and crying like they're dying or something."

Wyatt. Longing hit me like a fist. "You spoke with Wyatt? Does he know I'm okay?"

Before Dar could answer, the door burst open, and nearly forty demons of all shapes and sizes poured into the room, all talking at once and trying to lay a paw or claw on me. Dar shooed them off, acting as a bodyguard. Aside from the top few, household members were supposed to remain a respectable distance back with eyes lowered, but relief over my obvious survival overcame all social niceties. They had to have been worried— a household without a master was vulnerable, and I'm sure they all thought I was dead after hearing from Wyatt.

"I'm fine, I'm fine," I lied, waving my hands for silence. "I just need a few moments with Dar, and to contact my human household, then I need to have a meeting with all of you."

"Can I stay? I'm so glad to see you alive and in one piece, Ni–ni." Leethu's pheromones slid over my skin in a caress, raising goose bumps and causing other physical reactions south of my waistband. She'd added tiny gold scales over the skin of her human face and body. They shimmered in the light; beautiful accessories on the stunning succubus. Leethu might not be the easiest houseguest, but I trusted her and would be a fool not to utilize her extensive knowledge of the elven kingdoms as well as her shrewd mind.

"Yes. Leethu and Dar. Everyone else go get ready for a big party tonight."

There were cheers and the crowd raced out, empting the room as quickly as they had filled it.

"Ni–ni, can you fix your injuries? Wyatt said you were damaged and may have not recovered all your abilities yet."

I looked about, to make sure we were alone and couldn't be overhead. "Not really. Right now I can fix myself, but it takes a few days at the very least. I can't hold more than a tiny store of energy, and I can't convert matter in any significant amount."

Leethu sucked in a breath. Both she and Dar looked at me in horror. If this got out, I'd be killed by any random demon who felt like it. My status would drop so far that no weregeld would need to be paid for my murder. My household would likewise be on the open market; either snatched up as lesser members of other's groups, or killed themselves.

"What will he do?" Leethu murmured to Dar.

"He can't find out." Dar murmured back

"Who is 'he'?" I demanded. "Who can't find out?"

I knew no one should know of this, that it was dangerous if a head of a household was basically powerless, but they seemed to feel there was a particular threat from someone. They jumped in guilty surprise but ignored my questions.

"Surely you'll recover. It's only been a few months, and you've managed this human form. That requires skill." Leethu ran a finger down my arm to illustrate, and I shivered at her touch, even with all my painful blisters.

I hesitated. "Maybe. I'm not giving up hope. I didn't create this form, though. When I first arrived, all I could manage was some kind of weird pond scum and a lizard. I stayed that way pretty much until a sorcerer performed a spell on me. I've been this way ever since."

"Well, pond scum is something. Can you go back and forth between that form and the one you have now?"

"I'm afraid to try. What if I can't change back?" Suddenly I was eager to be alone, where my failure would be my own and not the cause of fear and worry to my household.

"If a sorcerer can get you to change into a form that comes from one of your Owned beings, it means you still have that ability somewhere," Dar assured me. "They just facilitated it. It's there. Just give it time."

"I don't have time. I need to take out Feille right now. He's got a weapon that can bring all of Hel under his thumb — demons included."

Leethu and Dar exchanged worried glances.

"Mal, you can't go after him right now. You've got a commitment you need to uphold."

I stared at them as I searched my brain, trying to determine what the fuck they were talking about.

"Ahriman," Dar prompted. "He showed up a few weeks back with your contract. You're his now for the next millennium. We're all his."

I felt as if someone had squeezed my head in a vise. I'd forgotten all about the breeding contract, the one I'd signed when Dar had brought Nyalla over from Hel. Crap, I had no time for this now. How could I delay it, or get out of it entirely? Ahriman would hardly want me in my current condition.

"Actually, Ni–ni, we were very grateful," Leethu said. "If he hadn't put us under his protection, many would have died. Dar would have been fine, he's run his own household before, and I always have offers, but the others...."

She was right — over two months with rumors of my death flying about. I thought about Baphomet's household, of Raim's, of all the Lows I'd taken under my wing. I'd signed the contract, and Ahriman had already begun making good on his end of the deal. I had no recourse now, and this wasn't a demon I could possibly defy.

"Why would he press forward on the contract with me missing and presumed dead?" I asked, my heart feeling like a lead weight in my chest. It was one thing being owned by an angel, but something completely different being owned by Ahriman. Dread of my future with the ancient demon wasn't anywhere near the sick feeling I got when I contemplated what Gregory would think. I hoped he never found out. I hoped that I could somehow keep all this from him.

Dar tilted his head, looking at me with curiosity. "He's the one who found you, who got me the elf buttons and sent me in to do the rescue."

I shook my head, trying to clear the grim visions of my future with the demon. He'd offered me a good deal, including a considerable amount of freedom and added status for my household. He'd protected them when they were vulnerable. I needed to just get through the next thousand years and complete my contract. It shouldn't be so terrible. So why was I feeling like I was on a short march to the guillotine?

"I need to take out Feille and help stabilize the southern elven kingdoms," I recited woodenly. Maybe I could ask Ahriman for permission to do this. He should approve of an elf assassination, and if I worded the other request well, perhaps he'd allow it too.

"You're in no shape to be taking out anybody right now," Dar said, his tone unusually gentle. "Lie low, so no one knows how bad you are, and let the elves take out their own garbage."

"Not when the garbage is about ready to spill all over our lands," I argued, rubbing my face with my hands. "This is important. I can't sit back and recuperate while he drains demons and enslaves us all."

Again those glances, as if they thought I was a crazy invalid they needed to humor.

"Ni–ni, I know you want to kill him, but just wait a bit, until you're stronger. Concentrate on regaining your abilities so you can fulfill the contract with Ahriman, and leave all this to someone else."

The pair of them were pissing me off.

"I might not recover," I shouted. "I'd rather go down fighting, trying to do something, than live the rest of my life helpless, trying to cover it up to keep my household safe."

"You have time. Feille is not going accomplish this in a few months," Dar urged. "Mal, I know you. This is not the end. You'll recover and be the same badass little imp you were before. Don't run off on a suicide mission right now. We need you. Your household needs you."

He reached out to grab my arm, and with a movement that was purely muscle memory, I zapped him with a shot of energy. It was a disciplinary burst, as I'd do for a naughty household member, or a friend that had gotten out of line.

Dar jumped back — not because the tiny zap hurt, but because it was completely unexpected in someone as broken as I. I stared at my arm, my heart leaping with hope at the sudden appearance of this ability. Not that this development would help much, unless Feille had a really bad heart and a faulty pacemaker. Wondering, I pulled energy from the air around me and tried to hold on. It was like trying to capture oil in cupped hands. The energy slid around, escaping my grasp and pouring back into the air, but in the end I did have more than I'd been able to hold since my injury. It was better than nothing.

"See?" Dar puffed out his chest as if he'd performed a miracle. "We just need to get you pissed off and you'll be good as new. Talk to Ahriman, recuperate, then go after the elf guy later. Easy."

I doubted it would be easy, but perhaps there was some truth in what Dar said. Taullian said two weeks, which wouldn't give me much time to recover enough to begin my contract terms with Ahriman, let alone be in fighting shape.

When I acted instinctively in anger, I made more progress than when I fussed over my injured areas and obsessively tried to use them. Maybe there were new pathways forming and I just hadn't made the proper connections yet.

"All right," I acquiesced. "Let me call Wyatt first, assure him I'm okay. Then I'll go speak to Ahriman and discuss the timing on the terms and conditions of our contract."

The pair of them breathed a collective sigh of relief.

"I have a message for you from your angel too," Dar added, making a pained face at the word 'angel'. "According to Wyatt, he has commanded 'Eat me'."

I choked back a laugh. How very Alice in Wonderland of him. Would I grow until my head hit the ceiling? Or perhaps the command was an erotic one. Leethu seemed to think so from her knowing smile.

"Oh Ni–ni! You have to get me an angel too. One who is not quite so scary, and perhaps doesn't smack me against the wall like yours does to you. Hopefully, he will want me to eat him too."

I had a vision of Leethu at a Ruling Council meeting and smirked. I'd send her after Gabriel just to watch him squirm. Considering Gregory's command, I touched the red–purple of his spirit that networked through me like tiny roots. It had always been unresponsive, refusing to do anything beyond summon the angel to me. But now it couldn't even do that. Did he mean I should devour it? He'd told me never to devour again, but perhaps this was an exception. Leethu and Dar watched me expectantly, but I was reluctant to attempt anything in front of them. I didn't want them to see me devour and really didn't want them or anyone else to know about the angel I'd stolen and kept inside myself for the last year. I trusted them, but this was something private.

"I promise I'll find you both an angel to eat," I said, running through likely candidates in my head. Gregory would kill me, playing matchmaker between our kind, ambushing some poor angel and subjecting them to the affections of my siblings.

The two left the room, excitedly brainstorming all the painfully delectable things they would do if they had an angel to 'eat', while I looked over at the huge communication mirror propped against the wall. It was three feet wide and six feet tall, with large colored stones to accommodate the bigger extremities of my first form.

My finger hovered over the milky–white stone, and I wondered what time it was. I'd had no idea in the dungeon, and hadn't asked, or even had a moment to peek outside after I'd arrived here. It could be three in the morning for all I knew. But even if Wyatt was asleep, I knew he'd want me to call him right away. I would if our situations were reversed.

"Dar?" His voice was sleepy across the device — was he actually sleeping next to the mirror? Had he been afraid to leave it for the last three months?

"Wyatt. I'm here. I'm okay." It was a bit of an exaggeration, but I had a feeling he'd consider my current state "okay."

"Sam? Sam!" His voice cleared of sleep then choked with emotion. "Gregory told me you almost died, that he banished you to Hel and broke your bond to try and save you, but when we'd heard nothing from you, when even Dar didn't know if you were alive or dead, we feared the worst."

I felt burning in my eyes as my vision blurred. "It was a close thing, Wyatt. I won't lie. I managed to survive, but the elves caught me and threw me in a prison for months. Dar did a jailbreak and I just arrived at my house."

"We've been so worried. Are you all right? Did you fix whatever injuries you had?"

I took a deep breath, wondering how much to tell him. I didn't want to worry him needlessly, it's not like either he or Gregory could do much to help me right now. "I'm in my human form, but I haven't regained the ability to change my shape or do much at all. Right now, I'm less than a Low. It's going to take some time."

Maybe all of eternity. And who knows if I'd ever be able to store energy so that I could fix and create physical forms outside of Hel, let alone recover any kind of defensive or fighting skills.

"Come home, Sam. We'll take care of you until you heal. All of us."

I wanted to. I wanted to feel his arms around me, see the girls, run with Candy in the woods, plot out my rental empire with Michelle. I wanted to see my angel. But there were things I needed to do first, and a commitment I'd made that needed to be fulfilled. Soon — if I survived, and if Ahriman kept his end of the deal, that is.

"Wyatt, did Gregory find out what happened to me? Did he tell you the elves were using their sorcerers in a pact with some angels to harvest us and divide us between them?"

He caught his breath, and I knew the angel had either not discovered what went down on Oak Island or had spared him the horrid details.

"It's Feille, that asshole elven lord who had Diablo. He's got a new magic fueled by demon energy and plans to take over all the elven kingdoms. He's already conquered the southern ones. Then he plans to move against the demons and take all of Hel. He'll chop us up, keeping some of us as batteries to fuel his magic, draining others, and sending shipments of us to a group of angels to use for breeding. I can't leave until I stop him."

I felt his misery across the mirror. "I understand, Sam. You're the Iblis, and this is something you have to do. Please call me at least once a day, though, and let me know that you're okay. I miss you so much. When I thought I'd never see you again..." His voice choked off into silence, and I knew.

"I promise I'll come home as soon as I can, Wyatt. I'll either contact you myself or have Dar or Leethu call you if I'm unavailable."

I heard him take a ragged breath and I closed my eyes, imagining his warm skin against mine, the feel of his breath in my hair.

"I love you," I said.

"I love you, too," he replied softly.

We held there, the line open, neither one of us wanting to break off. I still had Ahriman to talk to, my household to rally, Taullian to convince to fulfill my plan to let the humans go. But it could wait just a few more minutes while I imagined I was beside Wyatt, wrapped in his arms.

"I'll drive down to Columbia Mall and have the gate guardian let Gregory know," he finally said. "Amber can recognize her and can find the gate. That's how I usually contact him, although he comes every few weeks to check if I've heard any news of you."

"Thank you." It was far more than I expected. I knew they disliked each other, but perhaps the threat of losing me forever had brought them together. "Can you tell him what I told you? And that there are more angels involved in this than the one I blew up at Oak Island? For his ears only. I don't even know if I can trust the gate guardian with this kind of info."

"I will, Sam."

I took a deep breath, my heart aching. "I need to go talk to a few people then do some planning. I'll call you tonight, or in the morning. Fuck, I don't even know what time it is."

"Five in the morning here. Although, I don't know if time is the same where you are."

"It's close, usually within a few hours. Our days aren't as consistent in length as yours are."

Again we hesitated, and I reached out a hand to the mirror, wishing that I could reach through it and touch him, feel the sleepy warmth of his tan skin, the morning stubble on his cheeks.

"Talk to you soon, Sam. I hope I'll see you soon. I love you."

"I love you too." I touched the milky-white stone.

My heart felt like someone had clamped it in a vise and my lungs were tight with sorrow. I stood for a moment and stared into the mirror at myself, having a private pity party. Unfortunately, I couldn't indulge myself for long. I needed to see Ahriman. Thankfully he wouldn't mind my half-naked, burned body and signed hair. Demons don't put much stock in formality. Besides, in spite of my sudden rise in status, I was still an imp. He shouldn't expect much in terms of physical presence from me.

With a sigh, I turned away and walked out my front door into the blinding, red heat. I had a long walk ahead without my wings and needed to get going if I hoped to be back home before nightfall.

~15~

G abriel walked the paved street of Parral, invisible to the humans, his white wings extended to catch the warmth of the sun. On one side of the road, a series of cement block and adobe buildings stood in a straight line. This wasn't a wealthy neighborhood, yet it wasn't a ghetto. Working class, he would have said. Parked along the street were older–model cars with splotches of gray primer and mismatched tires. The wrought iron fencing guarding the houses from the public sidewalk and street was rusted and missing much of the decorative scroll work. Children's toys were strewn across lawns like confetti, echoing the bright paint on the houses.

There was a shimmer of light halfway down the street in front of a yellow–block convenience store, and Gabriel saw an angel appear, walking toward him with purpose. He flared his wings in a subtle display of status toward the younger angel and waited to be addressed.

"Ancient One. I am greatly appreciative of the audience you grant me, although, I am perplexed as to why we are meeting at this particular location."

Tura seemed nervous, looking about him as if he feared to be seen, even cloaked as he was from human view. Gabriel remained silent, allowing the other angel's discomfort to grow as he watched. After a quick glance at the houses beside him, Tura's eyes strayed across the street, at the broad, green expanse of park. Finally he wrestled himself under control, assuming a disinterested air as he faced the elder angel.

"I'm researching a matter for the Ruling Council," Gabriel said, his tone casual. Why would Tura be bothered by this location? A café in Italy, a park in northern Mexico — why was he nervous? "A report that I feel warrants additional scrutiny."

Tura's wings twitched as if he didn't know where to place them, belying the polite expression of interest on his face. "A report? Can I assist in any way?"

Gabriel reached down to pick up a stone. "No. It is not a matter that concerns one of your level."

Tura lowered his eyes, flushing slightly at the insult, his hands beginning to mirror the nervous movements of his wings before he clenched them into stillness.

"Speak," Gabriel commanded, tossing the stone across the street and into the grass of the park. "I have no time for idle conversation."

The other angel watched the stone's trajectory before turning his gaze back to Gabriel. "We are almost ready to present before the Ruling Council but need additional demons to complete our research. We'd prefer to show our august leaders high–quality results, but all we have in storage is from Lows."

"What are you requesting of me?" The only demon Gabriel had met in the past few decades was the Iblis, and she was an imp. "I don't have a supply of demons tucked away somewhere for you to use."

"We would like the assistance of a liaison from your choir. Someone to facilitate the supply through the gates and to transfer it to Aaru."

"Why do you need my help for that? Isn't there someone in your enterprise that can do this?"

A wry smile lit Tura's face as he shook his head. "The process for angels to gain permission for repeated trips is prohibitively long, and we're reluctant to journey here illegally, especially given the recent, shocking deaths. You have angels assigned to the Grigori. We're hoping you could request one of them do this as a small, side duty. It would not require a burdensome amount of time."

Gabriel considered the request. It would violate no angelic law. Even assigned to Grigori service, his choir was still under his command. He would just need to choose which of his angels would be most suitable. "I will arrange for one of my angels to meet you here at nightfall."

Tura's face was a mixture of relief and anxiety. "We are most grateful, Ancient One."

"When would you like to schedule the presentation before the Ruling Council?"

Tura chewed on a lip thoughtfully. "Would two rotation cycles be sufficient time to call the meeting?"

Six days. Odd how he was automatically translating into earth–time. Old habits were so easily revived. "Will you be demonstrating or presenting an actual offspring?"

"Noooo. I think it best we discuss the project at a high level."

Gabriel frowned. Why wouldn't they want to solidify their case with some proof of success? Nothing would sway the Ruling Council like seeing a newly created angel. Unless Tura lied, and the whole thing was a farce to stir up volatile emotions in Aaru that were currently barely contained.

"Have you *truly* been able to perform a successful formation? Did the creation survive in or outside of Aaru? Was it stable and worthy of the effort?"

"We have produced successful formation that would survive in Aaru until it can develop enough to manifest a physical form. But since we have the very lowest of demons, the offspring is not worthy at this point. We hope to try next for something even an archangel would be proud to call his own."

Lovely rhetoric. Gabriel sensed he told the truth, but that there was something lurking behind the angel's words.

"I want to see proof of creation, ensure this is a possibility before I schedule a meeting."

Tura schooled his face in an expression of regret. "Right now the offspring has not been suitable. Everything we created was destroyed. We need higher–level demons before we can present anything to one of your stature."

Gabriel frowned. Unsuitable. Because it was of a Low? Or in spite of Tura's assurances earlier, had there been Angels of Chaos produced? Neither sat well with Gabriel. What criteria had Tura and his partners used to decide on life or death for a newly formed offspring? It bothered him that this angel had made that determination. It bothered him that Tura showed no remorse, no hint the decision had cost him any moral pain.

"I thought you had a steady supply of these demons. What happened?"

The younger angel shifted, again darting a quick look around him. "The humans facilitating the exchange proved unreliable. Our supply chain was temporarily disrupted while we replaced them. It was a brief setback, and we are due to receive higher–level demons as soon as the next rotation cycle."

"Then why can you not produce a sample of your success at the meeting? It should only take a moment once you have the demon essence you desire."

Tura shifted his wings. "Please understand, Ancient One, we do not wish to promise this only to present an unacceptably low angel, or worse yet ...one of *them*."

A cold chill rolled through Gabriel. Yes. What would they do if Angels of Chaos were created? The idea both frightened and excited him.

"You assured me that wouldn't be a problem."

"It won't. I vow that the only angels produced will be those of Order. I'm just concerned that with the short time frame we will not be able to create something worthy of the

Ruling Council. If they approve of the project, then of course we will produce proof of successful creation. Members of the Ruling Council will have first access to the technology."

Gabriel frowned. Instinct warned him to delay the presentation until there was proof, but this meeting seemed to be the only way they'd truly find out the details behind Tura's project, and be able to determine whether it fell within angelic law or not. It wouldn't hurt to schedule the meeting to discuss the theory. They could always put it to committee or ask for a follow–up if Tura's reports were ambiguous.

"We will need to see the tools in order to evaluate both the feasibility and the lawfulness of your project," he warned. "Be prepared to show us both the storage mechanism, to ensure there is no degradation of the demon essence, and your method for formation. We'll need to spend considerable time discussing the ethical implications of an unsatisfactory creation, as well as any barriers to eligibility for the program."

Turas nodded as if he were one of those bobbing dolls Gabriel had seen on the dashboard of a car.

"Of course, Ancient One. Of course." The angel vanished with a quick bow.

Glancing toward the park, he thought again of Tura's anxiety when he'd first arrived. The cause may have been anything, but it was an odd coincidence, especially since the park was the very location the body of one of the recently deceased angels had been found. Still invisible, with wings tucked behind him, Gabriel crossed the road and hopped the embankment, dropping lightly to the grassy park a few feet below. It was a pretty spot with colossal trees and wandering dirt paths. Wooden playground equipment stood to his left on a large bed of mulch. To his right was a cluster of picnic tables with a small hibachi grill and metal trashcan, painted bright blue.

Pivoting, Gabriel walked toward the playground, painfully aware of how terrible it would have been had a dead body been discovered by human children racing for the swing sets. In some neighborhoods, that may have been a normal occurrence, but this was not one of those neighborhoods.

"Back so soon? Will we ever be free of you?"

Gabriel pivoted, hearing the words in Spanish from underneath the dappled shade of a towering tree. There sat an ancient man, gray curls tight against the sides of his head, encircling a bald pate. His eyes were white with thick cataracts. Beside him sat a cane, a brown bag with a banana protruding from the top, and a thermos.

"Abuelo, I'm sorry to disturb your restful outing. I will not be here very long." The man must have heard his footsteps on the path, even though Gabriel was cloaked and normally moved with the silence of a shadow.

"You've come about the dead angel," the man continued. "Drained, he was. Devoured until all that remained was a physical shell. The angel that came to collect him could barely tell he was one of theirs, but I knew."

"Can you see me?" Gabriel asked in astonishment. "How do you know all this?" It wasn't just that the man's vision was obviously severely impaired, but that Gabriel was cloaked. No human should be able to see him. And he was fairly certain that any of his brother's Gregori who came to collect the corpse would have likewise been hidden from human eyes.

"Angel of Water and Ice, of course I see you. I am not blind." His voice rasped with a deep, throaty laughter. "I see many things, and others do not see me at all."

Gabriel could imagine that was true — tucked under the tree in the shade, he was practically a part of the bark, his aura blending completely with the surroundings.

"Please tell me what you know of the dead angel, Abuelo. I will be very grateful."

The old man shifted on the bed of moss that was his seat, looking pleased that someone was actually interested in what he had to say.

"An angel brought the body. He flew in, wings outstretched, cradling the man in his arms. It was a beautiful vision. Then he landed and tossed him onto the ground by the swings and flew away."

Gabriel stared in astonishment. "An angel brought the body? Not a demon? Where was the fight with the demon?"

Demons devour, and not very many of them either, thankfully. If this man were to be believed, he had the sensory skill to know the angel died by devouring. But why would the body have been moved? Demons didn't bother with that sort of thing, and the man had clearly said an angel had brought the body here.

"An angel," the man said, his voice indignant. "I can tell the difference between an angel and a demon."

"Then why would an angel bring the body here?" Gabriel wondered out loud. Without the actual crime scene, the angels investigating would have no way of tracking or tracing the offending demon. It was a wonder his brother had been able to find and dispatch the devouring spirit responsible. And it was no wonder the report had been so vague.

The old man shrugged. "Perhaps he did not want other angels sniffing around the scene of the death. Perhaps these angels have their own secrets to keep."

Indeed. "What happened after, Abuelo?"

The man spat at the ground, carefully avoiding the banana and the thermos. "I could not believe he threw the body to the ground with all the care of someone tossing a cigarette end out a car window. Disrespectful. If my family treated the dead in such a fashion, I would be ashamed. After the angel left, I went to investigate the corpse. He was an angel, devoured straight from his physical being."

Gabriel looked again toward the swing set. "Was he discovered by humans? Children?" He prayed that hadn't been the case. Humans may have become detestable creatures, but a young child was still sacred and close to grace.

145

The old man laughed, revealing a set of loosely fitting dentures. "They would not have seen him. Only I saw him."

Ah, so the corpse had been cloaked. Interesting that the angel dropping the body off had taken the time to cloak it from the humans.

"Another angel arrived to retrieve the body the next morning. I saw her arrive and had to hurry as quickly as I could to get a better look at what she was doing."

The next morning? Someone was alerted then, and with angels, anonymous tips were not possible. Someone knew, and Gabriel was determined to find out.

"She stayed with the body until another angel arrived. I liked her. She grieved. Paced back and forth the whole time."

"Can you describe them?" Gabriel asked, doubting the man could with his nonexistent eyesight.

"Of course! The angel that dropped the body off was soft and golden with wings of pale yellow edged in white. The woman angel was strong. Her eyes flashed with anger and sorrow. She had brown hair and wings like a barn swallow. Brown, with long white points at the end."

Asta. He didn't know the other angel, but Asta was one of the Grigori, an enforcer who'd been assigned only a few–hundred years ago. She was part of the first choir — his choir. Was her grief just sorrow over the loss of an angel, or did this one mean something special to her? Did she know the deceased and possibly the one who brought his body to this location? Asta was a promising young angel, one he could trust. She'd also be an ideal liaison for Tura.

"Gracias, Abuelo. May I restore your sight in gratitude for your assistance?" It had been centuries since he'd offered this sort of thing. Centuries since he'd felt inspired to offer.

The old man waved him off. "My eyesight is just fine. It's these other humans you need to be worried about."

He did worry. In spite of all his efforts not to, he worried too much. And that was the problem.

~16~

It took me about four hours to reach Ahriman's city house. He had residences everywhere, but this one was particularly imposing, rising high in a sheen of dark gray stone veined in red. It was visible from miles away. Patchine wasn't the biggest city in Hel, but it was strategically located between the deserts of Dis and the swamplands. My house was closer to the swamplands. If I'd had my way, it would have been right in the marshes, but few demons would have agreed to follow me there.

Huge black metal gates rose twelve feet around the residence, separated from the house by a courtyard full of sculpted stone. Gates would never keep a demon out, but this one had a magical fire that licked along the decorative twisted bars and curlicues along the top. I eyed it, uncertain how I was supposed to get in. A small demon with backward—bent legs and a wart—covered body nodded in greeting as he strode by me, pushing the gate open and walking right through. The fire parted for him, and I assumed he was part of Ahriman's household. I wasn't. Or was I?

I approached the gate, suspending my finger above the fire. It didn't move, and I was reluctant to risk a burn with my abilities on the fritz. Looking in vain for a doorbell, I was relieved when I saw the warty demon come back out and walk toward me.

"Hello," I called. "Is Ahriman here? I'm Az."

This whole thing was terribly awkward. How was I supposed to introduce myself or state my purpose? I didn't feel right calling myself his consort when we hadn't confirmed the deal face–to–face, and it would be weird to tell this little demon I was here to discuss a breeding contract with an ancient one. Suddenly I felt like I'd made a terrible misstep in protocol by not sending a proxy, or at the very least my steward to request an audience. Showing up at his door unplanned, with my hair half burned off, and my skin covered in blisters probably wasn't doing much for my street cred. I'd be lucky if they didn't run me out of town with a fireball launcher.

The demon hesitated, a look of surprise crossing his face as he quickly shoved a chunk of meat into a pocket. Great. He thought I was a beggar at the door. Impressive consort I'd make. Ahriman was liable to rip up the contract. The thought gave me hope.

The demon took a deep breath, as though what he was about to say pained him. "Niyaz, Az, Jahi, Ereshkigal, Malebranch, Mal Cogita, Samantha Martin, I welcome you to our home."

He'd neglected to include one of my names. My very last one. I didn't really want him to say it, though, didn't even want him or Ahriman to know it. Only my angel called me that name. Only he had that privilege. No one else, ever.

"Ahriman is in Eresh at the moment, but I'll alert him to your presence. Please come in and enjoy our hospitality until he arrives."

I wondered how long this was going to take. Eresh was in the very north of Hel. Of course, a demon as old as Ahriman probably could transport himself just as Gregory could.

"Sure. Sounds good." I waited for the demon to open the gate so I wouldn't fry the shit out of my skin going through. He just stood there, cocking his head to the side as if perplexed with my delay.

"Since I'm not yet a member of your household, your alarm system doesn't recognize me," I told him, putting out a finger toward the flame as if to illustrate.

"I apologize," he said, hurrying to open the gate. "By your appearance, I assumed you enjoyed a bit of burn."

He wasn't joking. Many demons did. I would too if I wasn't in this terribly sensitive human flesh and completely unable to repair myself. I walked through the open gate and stood and waited while the demon closed it then followed him up the courtyard path to the house.

The term "house" didn't do the place justice. Instead of doorways, huge broad–arched entrances, big enough for a being with significant wingspan, were strategically placed at all four stories. The upper ones had narrow cantilevered balconies to slow an aerial approach before entering. The entire building appeared to be shrouded in shadows, even with the bright sun above. The red veining pulsed slightly on the gray stone, giving the illusion that the structure was alive.

Interesting bone sculptures lined the path, which likewise seemed to be a mixture of crushed bone and shell. A few sculptures still had flesh clinging to them in shreds, surprisingly free from scavenging insects or decay. It seems Ahriman didn't like to share his kills with anyone, even those assisting a natural process of decomposition.

The demon led me through the huge arch on the first floor and down a hallway to a small side room. It was oddly cozy, with seats in numerous shapes and sizes to accommodate a variety of demon forms.

"I'll bring you some refreshment and entertainment," he said, bowing as he backed out of the room.

The chairs weren't the only interesting things here. Tables of different heights, covered with gouges and claw marks, sat against the walls. The ornate carpet design was complimented by a variety of blood spatter patterns. The walls looked as if they were finger painted with a grisly variety of bodily fluids. Ahriman's decorating style appeared to be 'early

149

psychopath'. I sat on one of the chairs only to realize that the hide covering the cushions bore a striking resemblance to one of my old school mates. As I wondered whether my contract period would end in my becoming part of the dé cor, the demon returned with another, both of them carrying trays.

Each sat a tray on a different table, then the demon who'd escorted me through the gate, and to the house, gestured to them.

"Refreshments," he announced, as if I might be in doubt as to the purpose of the meat piled onto the metal disks. "And entertainment." He gestured to the other demon.

I stood, shocked as he left the room, closing the door behind him. The other demon waited in front of the table, his arms clasped behind him, eyes to the ground in submission. He was a Low. I shouldn't have been surprised. Elves might offer me a basket of rats for entertainment, but Ahriman's was a classy household. I'd be expected to do whatever I wanted to this Low — break him, fuck him, kill him. Anything.

It had been too long since I'd lived this life, and I'd changed. I couldn't hurt this little guy.

He stood in his servile stance for a few minutes before peeking up at me, a perplexed frown on his furry face. "Do I displease you in some way, Consort? Would you perhaps like to chase me?"

The familiar urge tickled like a faint memory in the back of my mind. I always loved to chase, but I couldn't do any harm to him once I caught him. His expression turned to hurt, his posture drooping further. I was insulting him by refusing to harm him, implying that I felt him too weak and fragile for a demon such as myself to enjoy properly. I remembered the satisfaction of leaving a higher–level demon's house; my limbs barely attached, and burns covering the majority of my body. I would leave my injuries unrepaired for weeks, proudly displaying that another demon had found me worthy and I'd been tough enough to survive it. I knew that's what he wanted.

It would raise his status with his peers, ensure his position within the household, give him a sense of pride.

I couldn't do it.

"I'm sorry. You look like you'd be quite an enjoyable playmate, and there was a time when I'd happily chase you around the room and gnaw your flesh down to the bone, but I'm not that demon anymore. Why don't you join me in eating some of this food, and we'll chat."

His shoulders drooped even lower, and he refused to look in my direction, but he nodded, walked over to the table and placed a handful of meat into his broad, flat, snout–like jaws.

"What is your name?"

He looked up at me with a startled glance before turning again to stare at the meat. "Bwoof."

I wasn't sure if his name really was Bwoof, or if his full mouth had garbled the word. I decided to go with it.

"What do you do here in Ahriman's household, Bwoof?"

Again he looked at me, swallowing hard before answering. "I'm a Low, Consort. I do whatever I'm told."

That was a bit snarky coming from a Low, but I hadn't exactly done anything to inspire his respect, in spite of my honorary title. Bwoof's posture returned to the traditional deferent pose, but he reached out and quickly crammed another handful of meat into his mouth. I wondered if Ahriman fed his Lows, or maybe this meat was of a much higher quality than he would normally be given.

"Nice weather we're having, huh?" I wasn't sure what to say to him. As a Low, his duties were to endure whatever the others in the household did to him, and run minor errands, usually ones that would result in either dismemberment or death. I could hardly ask him if he liked his service here, or if Ahriman was a good master.

Bwoof shot me another perplexed look. He clearly thought I was weird, and his initial dismay at my rebuff was ebbing away. It wasn't him; it was me. There was obviously something odd about me.

"Wfthr hot nnn drwy," he mumbled, stuffing even more meat into his already full mouth.

I contemplated making some comments about sporting events, or yet more observations concerning the weather, when I noticed faint black smoke spiral in a thin, twisted column. As I watched, it grew thicker and darker. I was wondering if something were on fire, when Bwoof noticed it too. He spat the contents of his mouth onto the rug and assumed a posture of servile attention, facing the smoke column.

The room dimmed in dramatic effect as the smoke billowed into a black cloud, swelling to the ceiling before swirling back down to the floor. It was thick and greasy, smelling of burning flesh and hair. My host had arrived, and he was making an entrance with style.

The oily dark coalesced in a bipedal shape with glowing red for eyes. Slowly, the smoke merged into flesh, equally black with the same oily sheen. Dusky wings snapped outward, flexing before they settled into a more restful pose. They were typical demon wings; leathery with claws along the edges, and prominent bones at the ridge and supports. Ahriman's were black, with an unusual stippling that increased along the edge. As he walked toward me, I saw a small piece of black drift to the floor from the edge. A feather — a tiny remnant of the angel he used to be so long ago. I had a feeling that was the only piece of his angel–self that remained.

He halted and frowned, his red eyes leaving me to stare at the Low to the side. "Was the entertainment not to your liking?"

His voice sounded dry and raspy, as though he hadn't spoken out loud in eons. The little demon in question shook and I felt a stab of anxiety, worried that Bwoof would be in trouble for my social breach.

"No. I mean, yes. Very much so. We talked. Had conversation. He's quite personable. I'm just a bit tired and not really in the mood. Perhaps later. He's very appealing, and normally I would be happy to break off his limbs or something like that."

Ahriman ignored my babble and shot out an arm, removing Bwoof's head with a quick snap of his fingers. The body tumbled to the ground where it convulsed and spilled fluids across the ornate carpet. I hastily swallowed a quick gasp of shock and horror. I'd been living among the humans so long that I'd forgotten this sort of thing happened regularly here, that no life was sacred and could be thoughtlessly ended at the whim of a more powerful demon.

I'd failed him. If I had hurt him, done some physical damage to him, then perhaps he would not have been killed. Even when I tried to do the right thing, innocents still wound up dead. I realized there was a possibility that Ahriman would have killed him anyway, that it was his right as master to take the life of any household member for no reason at all. I tried to tell myself it wasn't my fault, but in my heart I felt differently. I should have put aside my own changed values and done a distasteful deed for the good of another. I hadn't, and now Bwoof was dead.

Schooling my face into a mask of indifference, I picked up a chunk of meat and stuffed it into my mouth, struggling to chew the tough fibers with my human teeth. Ahriman glided toward me, his forward movement faster than the sway of his legs indicated. I choked a bit on the meat, hastily swallowing the mass with a dry throat as he halted mere inches from me. Would my headless body be the next on the floor? I was aware I didn't exactly look like consort material at the moment, but after all, he was the one who'd presented a breeding petition to an imp.

You appear to have enjoyed your stay with the elves, he commented, abandoning verbal skills in favor of mind speech. His claw examined my blisters. I winced as he lanced one, digging the talon into my flesh as the sore oozed and bled down my hand.

"The food sucked. Other than that it was a total hoot. Elves are such fun."

Elves are of little importance to me, he announced with a wave of his hand. *You're late. You were due to present yourself to me nearly a month ago.*

"I apologize for my tardiness," I told him, feeling like a naughty schoolgirl. "Time slipped away from me, especially in the dungeon where it is hard to keep track of the daily cycles."

He nodded, tilting his head in an undulating movement. *Yes. I, too, sometimes find it difficult to keep track of time.*

Silence pressed thick and heavy between us as he continued to examine me with his glowing red eyes and sharp–ended hands. I was grateful he was no longer stabbing me with his digits, but the scrutiny was beginning to make me feel rather ill.

I have heard rumors that you are enslaved to an angel, bound to him for service. You'll understand if I ask for proof of your ability to agree to this contract?

I nodded, my mouth dry as dust. My tattoo was gone, my bond broken. Would the contract have been declared null if I'd been bound at the time of signing? Of course, I had no proof of that with my currently free status. It was probably just as well. If he had found me bound, his anger would have been considerable. I shivered slightly thinking of what he might have done to me and my household.

He held out a black, smoky hand, fingers ended in long needles of nails. I placed my hand in his, and he gripped my wrist tightly, twisting it to look up the inside of my arm. I knew only smooth flesh met his gaze.

I am relieved to find you unbound. Not that I expected otherwise. Angels no longer bind us, and even if they did, they'd hardly be likely to bind an imp.

I overlooked the insult. It wasn't terribly hurtful given that he'd presented a breeding contract to one of my status. Clearly, I had attributes that warranted a higher consideration than my demon type.

Dropping my arm, he walked to the sideboard and poured himself a drink from a stoneware jug. I shook my head at his offer and tried not to wince as he kicked Bwoof's head aside, returning to me.

Az, in good faith of our contract that you've agreed to by signing my breeding petition, I have already shielded your household. They have been spared attack and theft by the weight of my name and protection.

"Thank you," I stuttered after a long pause. He seemed to expect a response, and I wasn't sure what to give him. It had been so long since I'd been here in Hel, playing the games demons played, and I'd never had contact with someone of this high level.

In return for exclusive breeding privileges of my choosing, I offer you the position of consort. I will embrace your household within my own, protect them and provide for them as a master. You will be allowed freedom of movement, including trips among the humans if your behavior is such that I grant my approval. You will be allowed to retain all of your current funds and possessions as separate holdings. The term of our contract is one thousand years.

I couldn't breathe. I just couldn't. Everything inside me locked up and I struggled to present a composed façade. I couldn't let him think I was panicking over this whole thing. I needed my wits about me to negotiate and clarify the terms. This was the last chance I had to carve out some independence in what would be a gilded cage.

"You will not have the right to discipline my household staff," I told him, trying not to look at the headless body on the floor. "Any issues you have with them should be directed to me for remedy."

He was silent a moment, considering, before he nodded.

"Breeding privileges will not exceed ten occurrences in the duration of the contract period."

No. His voice was like a whip inside my mind. *Unlimited. I need the flexibility to produce the specific type of offspring I'm wanting.*

My temper flared, overwhelming my judgment and paltry survival instincts. "It shouldn't take you unlimited breeding chances to figure out how to achieve what you want. I'm not turning into a puppy mill bitch just because you can't mix and match genes properly."

And now I probably was going to be a dead demon. I tensed, refusing to lower my eyes for the blow I knew was coming. Instead, he reached a hand forward and ran a needle–like claw down my face, licking the blood from it as I tried to control my breathing and heart rate.

One thousand then. That's one occurrence per year. I doubt I'll actually use that many, but it satisfies my need for flexibility and should keep you from feeling like a puppy mill bitch.

A slight sigh of relief escaped me. "I am concerned that my autonomy of movement and ability to tend to my human household across the gates is subject to behavior standards and your approval. I want full control over that portion of my life."

He laughed. The sound chilled me all the way through. It was like a rusted echo of long forgotten mirth. *Az, you are notorious for vanishing and refusing to come when called. You were even late in appearing for our contract. How can I possibly trust you to be where I need you to be?*

"I'm an imp. I can hardly be held to your behavior standards — it's not within my nature. And I have responsibilities that may require me to make timetable changes. I can vow that I'll inform you if the need to reschedule something comes up."

Ahriman sighed. *You no longer have responsibilities beyond those I give you. I'll take your imp nature into consideration, but it's high time you learned to be a demon. You've had plenty of opportunity to play with the humans. Time to grow up.*

"Six months of each year on Earth." Fuck, I was beginning to sound like I was begging.

No. One week per decade.

"Three months per year concurrent."

Three months per year concurrent, as long as you appear when requested and do not directly violate any command or order I've given. If you do, all visitation privileges are off and you will lose your freedom of movement.

This was as good as it was going to get. "Done. But that doesn't include my duties to appear at Ruling Council meetings or other meetings necessitated by my position as Iblis."

Ahriman jerked his head upward, his red eyes filled with surprise. *An imp, the Iblis? What an amusing idea. Yes, of course I will allow those duties to take priority, but you'll understand that I first need to see proof of your assumption of the office. I'll need to see the sword.*

Fucking sword. I hadn't been able to summon the thing since before I'd been held captive on Oak Island. I'd needed it desperately, and it had abandoned me. Doubting I could make it appear, I tried. Nothing. No sword, no feathered barrette, no shotgun. It refused to appear in any of the forms I usually saw it. I couldn't even feel it near. It was gone, abandoning me as it once had its original master.

"It's been a little shy lately," I told him, well aware he thought I was lying about my possession of the sword. "It will come later."

Probably not. I doubted I'd ever see it again. But if I was no longer the Iblis, why did I still feel the weight of the office, the crush of responsibility? And to be honest, I'd grown to rather like being the Iblis. Huge reports aside, I enjoyed interacting with the angels, shaking up their order with my presence. Sword or no sword, I was still the Iblis, although, if I couldn't convince Ahriman of the fact, I'd not be able to make any meetings for the next thousand years. Hopefully they'd hold my spot for me. I couldn't see anyone else wanting it. It had been vacant for nearly three million years before I came along.

Well, once it comes to you, please let me know. Until then, there will be no special exceptions for Iblis duties.

I felt the noose tightening around my neck. There was only one more thing I needed to address.

"I've made a commitment to do some things for one of the elven kingdoms. An assassination, then fighting for them in a war."

I held my breath and watched him raise a thin hand to run along his jaw, lightly tapping a long finger against his coal black lips.

How very interesting. Normally I would be in favor of any outing that involved bloodshed and assassination, especially of elves, but I'm afraid I must decline your request. You're late in presenting yourself to me, and I find I do not want to delay the start of our contract period.

"There is some significant impact to the demons if this particular elf lives," I hinted, hoping to lead him along, spark his curiosity. His red eyes glowed with interest, and he nodded for me to go on.

"There is an elven high lord that plans to take over all of Hel. He has already seized the five southern elven kingdoms, and his sorcerers worked with rogue angels to develop a method of draining us of energy, of completely restricting our ability to repair injuries, change form, or defend ourselves. After that, he kills us, parting our spirit–selves out to send to the angels. If he continues unchecked, he'll rule all of Hel and the demons will be nothing but slaves."

A deafening silence met my words. I squirmed, suddenly realizing how farfetched it all sounded. The elves had been living side by side with us for nearly three–million years without any more than the occasional squabble. Their kingdoms had changed rulers and boundaries quite frequently over the history of our coexistence, but there hadn't been any actual wars between our kind. Ever.

Internal elven issues are not my concern, Ahriman announced, his thoughts smooth and emotionless. *If this high lord conquers all the elven lands as a tyrant, his actions mean nothing to me.*

"But he has this technology," I protested, desperate to explain the threat. "He'll grab groups of Lows and drain them to fuel his weapons against us. The elven kingdoms will fall first, and then we'll be next. And he's selling us out to the angels!"

Ahriman shrugged. The movement left a faint trace of blackened smoke hanging in the air over his shoulders. *I care not if this elf takes Low demons, or even if he takes entire households. The weak will fall, as always, making room for the strong.*

"But if we ...I mean *I* don't move against him now, he'll grow strong enough to attack the high level demons and defeat them."

I doubt that, he cut me off. *No elf will ever be strong enough to take on a high–level demon and win, even with an army of sorcerers and this mysterious technology. No. Not allowed. You're stalling, Az, as you always do.*

"But I...."

No! You are forbidden. You will not participate in this elven war, and you will not, as appealing as the idea is, assassinate this high lord. Am I understood?

I lowered my head. "Fine. Shall we move on, then?"

This was the next stage of the contract negotiations, where he told me what types of attributes he was looking to produce in his offspring, and what portions of my make–up he favored and admired. I only hoped the things he wanted I still had the ability to give him.

No such luck.

I greatly admire your energy storage capacity and would like progeny to have that attribute as well as your detailed conversion and matter creation ability.

I no longer had those skills. They were lost, gone, shredded away when I nearly died. Who knew when, or if, they'd ever return. There was nothing for me to give him. He was going to kill me.

But most importantly, he continued, unaware of my mini panic attack, *I want my creations to devour.*

I caught my breath. I knew he was aware of the devouring — his messenger had told me so back in Atlantic City and assured me that my disgusting habit wasn't a deal breaker. I'd never expected *that* would be the very thing Ahriman would consider most important. Deliberately creating a devouring spirit? Most demons tried very hard to avoid passing on any inclination to devour.

Of all your admirable traits, that is the one that must be present in full degree with each exchange of spirit.

Weird and kinda creepy, but I still had that ability. At least I thought I did. I hadn't tried devouring since my terrible injury, but I felt the familiar, gnawing hunger, right there beneath the surface as always. Perhaps he wouldn't kill me after all.

Those who formed you did an exemplary job with your devouring drive and ability. Why they saw fit to put such potential into an imp, I have no idea. I intend to rectify that terrible mistake.

So much for 'admirable traits'. It seems I was a 'one good trait in a huge ball of shit' in Ahriman's opinion. Imps aren't very high in the demon hierarchy, but the insult still stung.

But your ability to devour ...such hunger, barely within your control, coupled with your ability to store a vast amount of energy ...you truly are remarkable. I long to examine you, see how your creators put you together in such a way and still gave you a measure of control.

Oh no — there would be no examining. If he got that close, he'd *really* find out the extent of my devouring ability, and I wouldn't be sorry. No one got that close except for my angel.

"This is a breeding contract," I interrupted. "Not a dissection one. You will receive the portion of my spirit per our agreement, but you will not be allowed any intimacy beyond that."

He smiled, a puff of oily black curling from his body. *Of course not. But as we grow to know each other and you begin to understand the value there is in being my consort, you may change your mind.*

My stomach turned at the thought. Demons don't join, but Ahriman was old enough to have remembered when we did such things with angels before the war. He could keep that little fantasy to himself because I wasn't going to be angel fucking with him. Not now, not ever. Ick.

"I need some time to wrap up matters within my household. Can I have two months before the start of our contract?"

That creepy smile turned to a frown, the smoke increasing slightly. *No. You're late already, and you should have taken advantage of the time you had, rather than playing around with elves.*

"I'm not ready." My mind desperately searched for some reason I could give him to stall. I needed time to take out Feille at the very least. "I've ...I've got some enemies I'm torturing and I don't want to rush things."

He paused, once again tapping his chin with a long finger. *Ah. Yes, these things should not be rushed. So few things bring joy anymore that we should all savor the moments that do. Two weeks.*

I swallowed. Two weeks to assassinate an elf lord. Two weeks to try and convince Taullian to free the humans. Two weeks to regain whatever skills and abilities I could so Ahriman wouldn't kill me for deception in contract.

"Thank you. I appreciate the extension."

It seems we have a deal. Ahriman seemed rather pleased. I, on the other hand, wanted to throw up.

He held out his hand and once again I placed mine in his. The long fingers close around my wrist, snaking a curl of black up the inside of my arm in a caress. This was the final act that announced to all of Hel our partnership. The demon moved in close, his physical form a mix of solid and vapor as he raised my arm upward. A memory flashed — me pressed against an abandoned gas station wall, terrified as an angel bit down on my arm. It seemed so long ago, and yet here I was again, this time with a demon, but equally terrified.

The foul smoke of him choked me, heavy and thick in my nose and lungs, leaving a greasy sheen where he touched my skin. He bent forward and opened his mouth, unhinging the lower jaw and extending several rows of serrated teeth. The whole process was painfully slow, and I got the impression he was deliberately delaying for effect, enjoying my discomfort and fear.

His teeth hesitated over the soft skin of my upper arm, right where the other tattoo had so recently been, and he rubbed his spirit–self along mine in a sudden grope. I recoiled within my physical form, trying to remain as far from his as possible. Ahriman chuckled and bit.

Gregory's bite had been a painful pleasure, quickly shifting into all pleasure. Ahriman's was all pain. His teeth shredded like a shark's, but the tearing of flesh was only part of the agony. His smoky aura burned, spiraling down through my physical being to mark my spirit–self. No matter what shape I took, the mark would be there. Even without shape, my spirit–self would bear the mark for one thousand years, or until negation of the contract by death of either party, or by mutual agreement.

Unlike the angel's binding, this one didn't network deep within me. I felt no particular connection to Ahriman, no real bond. This was simply a way to mark me as his. Other household members would bear a sign of ownership, but this was a consort mark. In theory, I should be afforded especial respect. In theory, I'd be considered nearly a partner, able to represent Ahriman in certain matters. In theory.

As he pulled back, he snuck in another quick grope, which I was too slow to avoid. I'd need to watch this guy. Breeding contracts didn't include this sort of thing, but I got the feeling Ahriman was going to set his own rules, and that he wouldn't be above breaking our contract terms if he was particularly motivated. I'd just need to make sure I didn't give him that motivation, which might mean expressing disinterest at intimacy rather than a more intriguing revulsion. I wouldn't want to set off any predatory instincts, of which I'm sure Ahriman had many.

He stepped back, and I forced my eyes up to meet his glowing, red ones.

I will see you in two weeks, Az.

"Two weeks."

His physical form shuddered, dissolving into thick, black smoke that rose in a tall column then dropped to spread wide across the floor. With a flash of light, the smoke was gone, and I stood in an empty room with a platter of raw meat and a decapitated corpse. One thousand years. At least it wasn't an eternity.

~17~

By the time I'd walked the four–hour trek to my home from Ahriman's it was late afternoon. I was exhausted and starving for something beyond raw meat or elf food. My house was lit up like a Christmas tree, and I remembered I'd promised my household a party. If someone had managed to get beer and hot wings, I was going to kiss them.

I walked through the door to face a group of expectant demons. Dar and Leethu stood toward the front, as their status allowed, eyeing me with raised brows and big eyes. I knew what they wanted to know. Turning over my arm, I showed them the raw, chewed underneath with an indistinct black smudge. The entire room erupted into cheers. Demons grabbed each other, crushing ribs and head butting so hard I heard the cracks of skulls. Dar and Leethu enveloped me in more gentle hugs. I was the only one not happy about the next thousand years.

"Oh Ni–ni! I worried ...I mean, I know how you are and was concerned you and Ahriman might not come to an agreement. I'm so happy for you. You truly deserve this."

I winced at the thought that I deserved a thousand years of servitude to a demon as cruel and unfeeling as Ahriman. There would be pain, quite possibly rape, and maybe even death. I hoped that I deserved better than this.

I felt Dar's furred snout against my cheek. He pulled my hair with his usual sign of affection and made a snapping noise in my ear. He, of all my household, should understand. He'd been my friend, my closest sibling for as long as I could remember. Pulling back, his beady, crimson eyes looked into mine.

"It will be okay, Mal," he said gently. "You'll see. You've just been with the humans too long, and it will take you a while to come back to being a demon. A consort! To Ahriman! Just think of what that means. No more worrying about other demons trying to kill you, no more jockeying for position or status. All of Hel will be at your feet."

I had an uncomfortable feeling that instead I was going to be crushed under Ahriman's feet. I didn't obey, was disrespectful and spent nearly every waking moment in some sort of hot water. Gregory was a stick in the mud but he loved me in spite of our differences — or perhaps because of them. I doubted Ahriman would be so willing to change. Instead, I could see him bending me to his will until I shattered into a million pieces.

I took a deep breath and ran a hand over Dar's face, tugging at his whiskers. It was done. I'd go on being an imp, being Samantha Martin, and whatever happened, happened. As always, I placed my future in the hands of fate, hoping that luck still continued to smile on my antics with her favor.

The play fighting slowly wound down as the demons turned toward me, their faces happy and expectant. Party. That's right, we were supposed to party. I stared back at them, wondering what to say. I felt trapped, desperate.

"Food, drink, games and mischief. Let's celebrate."

The room erupted again, and Leethu danced off to gather drinks. Dar hesitated, tilting his head as he eyed me with concern.

"You okay, Mal?"

I forced a smile. "Yeah. I just need a few moments alone to absorb it all. Can you run this shindig for me? I'll be back before dawn."

He hesitated, his eyes searching mine. "If you need me, you ask. Anything. I'll always have your back."

This smile was genuine. "Thanks, Dar."

He headed off into the crowd and the party began in earnest as I snuck off, out the back door, down a nearby lane and out through the grasslands toward the swamps. It was early evening, and if I jogged a bit, I could make it to the edge of the marsh.

The swamps are unforgiving to human flesh. I tried to ignore the relentless bites of the insects, and how the sharp reeds tore at my legs as I waded through the muddy water. Bitey fish that thrived in the murky shallows darted around my feet, tickling with their whiskers. I longed to grab one and eat it but I was afraid it might be poisonous to my human stomach. I'd have no way to negate the poison, no way to fix any damage it did. How did humans endure this life, constantly walking the tightrope of survival? It was nerve wracking continually trying to censor my behavior to keep alive and healthy.

Sitting down, I let my ass sink into the soft mud and felt the water rise up around my breasts. Ahriman. Two weeks. In two weeks Taullian would make his move against Feille, and I would waltz into a gilded cage for a thousand years. And if I defied the ancient demon and tried to kill Feille, that gilded cage would turn into something far more unpleasant.

Why bother? The elves hated me. I didn't owe them shit. Taullian was an ass, Feille even more of an ass. I'd met a few that seemed okay, but what had they ever done for me? If I were in trouble, none of them would lift a finger.

Ditto for the demons. With the exception of Leethu and Dar, most of my household would sell me out without a second thought. I knew in my heart that none of the demons would pay my warnings any heed, none of them would care if others were taken, drained, killed — especially if the ones being targeted were Lows. That was the way of my kind — everyone for himself. Individuals would surely fall; it would only be through combined strength that we could possibly hope to defeat the combined force of six elven kingdoms.

Why bother? I should enjoy my remaining two weeks and just let the chips fall where they may.

I sat up higher in the cool water, feeling the strands of slime cling to my skin. Kirby. All the humans would suffer even more if Feille ruled all the elves. That poor human girl from my cell — was she still alive? How many more would end up like her? It seems like I was the only one in all of Hel that cared about their plight. And the Lows.... I thought of the one who had been trapped in Columbia Mall, now in my household, as well as the Low who couldn't do more than change colors. I thought of Stab. I owed him. I'd promised to save him, and I'd failed. What happened to him should never happen to another Low.

But Ahriman.... I shuddered, the water suddenly feeling uncomfortably cold. He'd forbidden me to interfere in this matter, and if he found out I'd defied him, the punishment would be horrific — not just for me, but for my household. I'd need to protect them and be willing to accept the probable consequences of my actions, even while trying like fuck to ensure I got away scot–free. I wasn't sure I could do that. In fact, I was fairly certain I couldn't. I may be an imp, but I did have a modicum of common sense, a tiny bit of self–preservation instinct.

Closing my eyes, I tried to put it all out of my mind, to relax, forget about the insects and the reeds, the blisters that covered my body, my lower digestive system rebelling against whatever meat I'd eaten at Ahriman's house. The mud sucked at my sinking feet, soft and slippery. Sweat beaded across my forehead and rolled down my face, pooling between my breasts, and under them. I felt my hair, damp and heavy against my back.

I'd spent most of my childhood in the swamps, hiding from Paquit and other siblings that loved to torture me. It was the one place I felt safe. My very own Garden of Eden. My past and childhood seemed right within reach, as if it were happening concurrent with the present, with the endless intertwined threads of my future. I could stay here forever. Hide from the elves, Ahriman, all the stupid responsibilities I'd collected over the last year.

I relaxed in the swamp and watched the moons drop below the horizon, waited until the pink of dawn turned blisteringly hot. A splash as a bitey fish leapt above the water. Insects burst into song. The mating call of a Svelton sounded, and then a reply. Noise filled my ears and joined with the sensations against my skin, the smells of swamp in the hot sun filling my nose. With a sigh I opened my eyes and stood, making my way out of the swamp and back toward my house. The time to spend eternity hiding in the swamps, or under rocks, had long passed. Too many had died; too many still suffered, and I found that I got a major charge out of setting things right, evening the score. But there was one person I needed to consult, the one who had become my moral compass. I might not always take Wyatt's advice; I might not always agree with him, but he grounded me. He made me human, and I valued his opinion.

The party was still in full swing when I returned, a significant amount of furniture smashed and being used as makeshift weapons. I snuck through my own house, kicking everyone out of the room before turning to my mirror.

"Wyatt, did I wake you?" I tried to figure out the time. Was it afternoon there, or four in the morning?

I heard him laugh. "Since when have I gone to bed at noon?"

Many times, in my arms, after a few hours of passion. I closed my eyes for a moment, willing the ache of longing away. It was no time to let my feelings for Wyatt overwhelm me.

"I need your advice."

His voice became serious. "What's wrong, Sam? Is it something to do with the elves?"

I swallowed, wondering how I was going to explain this to Wyatt. "It's a demon. Remember that breeding petition I showed you? The one from Ahriman?"

"Your top contender? Yeah. Gregory didn't approve. Not that it mattered. You said you weren't going to accept any of them."

"Well, as they say in the mafia movies, he made me an offer I couldn't refuse."

Wyatt was silent for a moment. "Did he threaten you? Us? Your household?"

"All of the above. I figured I'd have time to weasel out of it, but then everything happened in Alaska and Washington. Now I'm here in Hel, and there's not much I can do but make the best of a bad situation."

"Can Gregory...?"

"No!" I panicked, just thinking of his reaction. "Don't let him know. There's nothing he can do, and I don't want him to worry."

"I'll never see you again, will I?" His pain came through the mirror like a tangible thing.

"I'll be allowed some physical freedom, and regular visits through the gates. It won't be much, and I'll understand if you don't want—"

"Stop it. Don't even think that. I know we had our rough spots, but there isn't a day I don't regret not making things right between us — especially after I thought you'd died. I love you. I'll always be here for you. That's all you need to know."

I couldn't see from the tears in my eyes. "Wyatt, I have a horrible choice. Ahriman has forbidden me from interfering with the elves. If I do and he finds out, I'll not leave his dungeon for a thousand years — maybe longer. If I don't interfere, innocents will suffer and die. Low demons, the most vulnerable among us, will be dissected, and no one will care.

The humans will be tortured and played with, killed when they are too broken to serve."

"It seems like you've made your choice, Sam."

I thought he'd be sad, but underneath his sorrow, he sounded proud. I didn't want him to sound proud. I wanted him to beg me not to do it, not to risk myself on this fool's mission. I'd already sacrificed enough. Let someone else step up to the plate.

"I don't want to," I whispered. "I'm afraid of what Ahriman will do to me."

"So, you'll just be a good little consort, obey the powerful demon and defer to him on all things? How long do you think that's going to last?"

I winced. I was an imp. "Probably about three days, if I'm lucky."

"Yeah. And even if you do manage to stay on his good side, how long do you think it would be before Gregory found out?"

I looked down at the black smudge on the underside of my arm with a sick feeling. "The moment he saw me, he'd know."

"How will you feel when you're under Ahriman's thumb, watching Lows systematically killed, humans tortured and tossed to the side? What happens to your household when Gregory grabs you on your first visit and refuses to allow you to return?"

I was damned either way. There were no good choices.

"Make the choice that will let you sleep at night, Sam. Make the choice that will console you when it's your darkest night."

I heard his unsaid words — make the choice that would make him proud, that would make Gregory proud. And work my ass off to make sure Ahriman never found out I'd disobeyed him.

"I may never see you again, Wyatt."

There was a few seconds of silence. "You will. I know you will. Before the end of the year, you'll be jogging with Candy, mixing it up with those angels, naked with me on a blanket in front of a roaring fire. Oh, the things I intend to do to you."

Now this was a far more promising conversation. The dark clouds around my heart lifted somewhat. "Please tell me about these things you intend to do to me while we're naked on a blanket," I teased.

"First, I'll take off your clothes, slowly easing them down and kissing every square inch of your skin as I go."

"Mmm, do I get to take your clothes off too?"

"Only when I'm done. I want my hands and mouth on every inch of you."

I smiled, touching the mirror as if I could reach through it to him. "Me too. I'll drink vodka shots from your belly button. Find something delectable to lick off your cock."

"No hot sauce," he interjected.

I laughed. That had been rather disastrous. Poor Wyatt. "Chocolate?"

"Whipped cream, honey, strawberry sauce." I could hear the heat in his voice.

"With a cherry on top?"

"With you on top."

Top was my favorite spot. "I love you, Wyatt. I'll call you every night, and if there comes a time when I don't call, know that I'm thinking about you."

"It will be okay, Sam. And I love you, too."

I turned away from my mirror, hoping that Wyatt was right. I'd made my choice, but I still had to talk to Dar and Leethu, to make sure my household was safe no matter what went down.

"I have two weeks," I told the pair of them after finding them squabbling over who could insert a chair leg furthest into another demon's ass. "Two weeks to do this thing with Feille and report to Ahriman."

Dar caught his breath, and Leethu's lovely eyes widened in alarm.

"Forget about the elves, Mal," Dar urged. "You need to focus all your attention on regaining your strength and lost skills. What if he wants thing's you've lost? You need to make sure he's happy with the bargain he made. Let the elves deal with their own shit."

"I can't forget about it. I nearly died trying to escape these guys. I know what Feille plans to do, and I'm not going to let him go through with it. Too many demons and humans will die if he does."

Leethu tilted her head, looking oddly bird–like in spite of her tiny scales. "Is Ahriman in favor of this? We need to have his approval before going forward."

I didn't blame either of them. Ahriman was powerful, and all of our futures depended on retaining his favor. I hesitated, realizing that it wasn't just me I was risking, it was my whole household. So I carefully skirted the truth. "Are you kidding? An elf assassination and a chance to kill a bunch more elves? It's a dream come true."

Dar raised an eyebrow, clearly not convinced. I saw him waiver, torn between his love of a good fight and fear that we'd wind up worse than dead at Ahriman's hands. I knew he was dying to get in some action. Like me, he'd always enjoyed messing with the elves. "How many of his household is he sending along?" he asked, his voice full of suspicion.

I squirmed. I was a terrible liar, and I didn't want to get my household in trouble. Technically, our contract didn't take effect for two weeks, and I fully intended to be back at Ahriman's door on time. Hopefully he'd never know. If he did, I was counting on my taking the heat since he'd agreed any transgressions from my household would fall on my shoulders. Even with our contract, I planned to make sure all of them were far away for the next thousand years.

"I'll coordinate with Ahriman's household," I lied. "Can one of you approach Taullian and arrange a meeting? I'm sure he's pissed about my rescue, so we'll need to assure him that we still want to fight under re-negotiated terms."

"I'll do it," Dar chimed in. "Leethu is still on his shit list. Not that he likes me any better, but at least I'm not suspected of fucking elves and knocking them up."

"Just the one," the succubus protested. "Although I have gotten to third base with quite a few."

It's a wonder Leethu was still alive. If she was so good at tempting the stoic elves to sin, then she might be able to do the same with angels. I eyed her, thinking I needed to get her alone and see if she could give me some pointers. I'd happily take third base with Gregory. For the time being, anyway.

"I also need one of you to go to Eresh to find a sorcerer. His name is Gareth. He's one of Feille's runaways, and he's somehow managed to carve out a place for himself among us."

Dar blinked in surprise. "Gareth? He's in Dis. That's who Ahriman got the elf buttons from. He's been selling magic items and scrolls to the demons. Got quite a nice little setup."

"I'll go," Leethu announced. "Do you want a meeting with him, or to purchase something in particular?"

"A meeting. I'd go myself, but I'm limited to this human form and it would take me precious days to get to Dis. Can you have him come here in the next day or so?"

Leethu nodded and I turned to the rest of my household. They'd begun smashing various bits of furniture over each other's heads, some jumping on top of others and choking them. It was like a pay-per-view wrestling free-for-all.

"Hey! Everyone! Pay attention!"

"We're going to continue celebrating in just a few minutes but first I want to let you all know of an upcoming opportunity to go to battle."

The demons looked at me blankly, a few of them whispering to each other. Demons hadn't fought together in an organized group since the wars two–and–a–half–million years ago. I had a sinking feeling they'd become incapable of any kind of organized, team activity. That's okay. There were other ways to fight.

"We're gonna go kill some elves," I said, with a fist pump. The room erupted into cheers.

"This is completely optional. There's a good bit of danger involved and a chance that you might not make it out alive. If you don't want to take the risk, it's fine. You can stay home."

I faced thirty–seven perplexed faces. Demons love to fight, gladly risking their lives for a good brawl. We were always aware that every moment could be our last, but self–preservation was at the bottom of our priority list.

"There will be some elves we can't kill." Groans of disappointment from everyone. "But they'll be easily identifiable. I'll let you know — a color or possibly an item they have. Those elves are off limits, but others are fair game."

The demons cheered again, and I tried to think of a way I could structure this to limit civilian casualties and keep it from turning into a sea of carnage — demons don't always know when to stop.

"Rules." More groans. "There will be a certain area where killing is allowed, and a time limit. Stay within the rules of time, killing area, and allowed targets, and the demon with the most kills gets a prize. Break the rules, and face the punishment of my choice."

There was some grumbling, but it was respectful. Everyone knew how creative I could be in my punishments. More than one demon had been sentenced to spend a week in the muddy swamps, living off bitey fish and rushes while being mercilessly stung and bitten by various insects. The swamps were my favorite place, but few demons shared my love of muck.

"What prize? What prize?" one of the demons squeaked in excitement. I looked and saw it was the little Low I'd taken in after killing Haagenti, the one who couldn't do much more than change colors. I hoped he stayed behind. I didn't want to see him dead. I didn't want to see any of them dead, but for demons, this war would be an especial treat.

I ran though my inventory in my head, trying to find something suitable. "Scroll of invisibility."

Again the room erupted into cheers, demons bouncing up and down, smacking each other with any available furniture.

"Wow, I want that," Dar said.

I laughed. "You've probably got four of your own already. You've got more shit than any demon I know. Plus it's a bit unfair. You're the best fighter in a hundred miles."

Dar puffed out his furry chest in pride. It wasn't idle flattery — he was the best fighter I knew. Sneaky and strong, with a great sense of strategy. I had no idea why he stuck with me for all these centuries. He could have probably amounted to so much more on his own.

"So, who's with me?" I asked.

Dar and Leethu shot up their hands, and the room was filled with waving limbs. There was no turning back now. I only hoped I could do what I needed to while keeping them all safe.

~18~

Gabriel stood on the bridge overlooking the Chicago River, car–clogged streets flanked on both sides by walls of skyscrapers. A promenade full of joggers hugged the riverside below him, the only thing of nature besides the sluggish green–brown water. The river seemed subdued as it made its circuitous route past the buildings on its way to Lake Michigan, but Gabriel knew better. Water. It was persistent, flexible but strong. Given enough time, it would break any opponent, breach all attempts at containment. It was the only thing that made this oppressive city of humans bearable.

"My Sovereign."

A figure knelt on one knee before him, golden–brown hair sliding across her bent shoulders to curtain her downturned face.

"Rise, Asta, lest the humans wonder why you are on your knees in the middle of a walkway."

She jumped to her feet, golden skin nearly hiding the blush that flushed her cheeks. In her enthusiasm, the angel had clearly forgotten she was fully visible while Gabriel was not. *At least she'd had the presence of mind to hide her wings*, he thought as he glanced at them, visible to his eyes — an intricate pattern of shades of brown, the long flight feathers startling white in contrast.

"Sorry. So sorry," she stuttered breathlessly. "I haven't seen you in almost a century, Ancient One, and I forgot myself in my excitement."

She *was* excited, the white of her wings twitching against the pavement, her eyes, the same color as her hair, lifted to his in respect. A century was nothing to an angel, but time always seemed to slow when one was among the humans. Gabriel could understand her joy in seeing him, the head of her choir. It must have felt like an eternity since she had been in Aaru.

"Asta, you have been Grigori for nearly two centuries now. I have some questions to ask you, and a task to request of you, but I must first know if your loyalty is primarily with me, or with my brother?"

She caught her breath, her eyes wide. "With you, Ancient One. As always."

Gabriel couldn't help a rare smile. Her voice rang with truth, her aura a clean, shining white. Asta was one of the youngest angels, created barely before the wars began. It wasn't unheard of for angels to petition to change choirs, to shift their allegiance to another. Knowing that she'd remained one of his even after reporting to his brother filled his heart with gladness. Loyalty was a highly prized virtue.

"Then what can you tell me about Vaol's murder? I was informed you found the body."

Asta bit her lip, pausing before she responded. "He was devoured, his corpse left in a park near some children's playground equipment. Thankfully, the Eldest One managed to catch and kill the abomination before he was able to do additional damage."

"How did you know he was there, Asta?" he asked gently. "Who informed you of his death?"

She looked at him in surprise. "No one. I was told there was a demon there. A plague demon. I flew to the town — that's how concerned I was. When I arrived, I found him." Asta clenched her hands, her eyes filled with horror. "He ...the extraction wasn't a clean one. There were bits of him remaining in his corporeal form. That's how I knew who he was."

Gabriel winced. "You knew him? Were you friends?"

She hesitated then seemed to come to some sort of decision. "In Aaru, he was merely a passing acquaintance, but over the last decade he was often here among the humans. Vaol frequented the Seattle area, although he traveled to the east coast of the continent. I'm assigned to the mid–west but had been asked to cover the west coast in addition to my usual territory. That's where I met him. I wouldn't say we were friends, but we did see each other on occasion."

"He was not authorized to be out of Aaru among the humans. Why was he here?"

Asta looked at him, her eyes filled with guilt. "I do not know, Ancient One. I don't want to speculate on his motives, or slander the dead without adequate proof of misdeed."

"Very noble, but his being here without permission is also a sin. A minor one, but still, it should have warranted a report. Did you let your superior know of his infractions?"

Asta shook her head, crimson once again staining her golden cheeks. "I'm sorry. There is so much sin here along with an overload of tempting sensation. The small things begin to seem acceptable. That is no excuse for my lapse in judgment. I beg your forgiveness."

Gabriel placed a hand on her hair, sending a soothing tendril of blue out to calm her distress. "Stronger, older angels than you have done far worse. All will be forgiven."

She breathed a sigh and relaxed slightly. "I only have another year of service before I return to Aaru. I'm afraid I need the cleansing only my home can offer."

Gabriel smiled once again. "We will welcome you back, Asta, and honor the work you've done here. In the meantime, I ask that you serve me as well as my brother by facilitating the transfer of some objects between the gates and Aaru."

Her expression grew wary. "The gates? Whatever comes from Hel has no place in our sacred home."

Should he trust her? If she was going to be a liaison for Tura, she should be aware of what was happening.

"I tell you this in the strictest confidence. A group of angels has found a way to create without unholy contact or violation of the treaty. Demon essence will be delivered through the gate to you, and you will deliver it to a contact in Aaru." He watched her stunned expression turn thoughtful. "I'm sure you understand how sensitive this whole matter is. If it becomes general knowledge that creation is once again possible, all of Aaru will dissolve into riots."

"Yes," she breathed. "I will gladly serve you in this capacity, my Sovereign. And I will maintain the highest level of secrecy."

"You'll be meeting Tura or one of his staff in Parral at sundown — the same place as you found the deceased angel." Sorrow flashed across her eyes, and Gabriel remembered one question that she'd not yet answered. "Who was it that informed you about the presence of a plague demon in Parral?"

Asta took a deep breath, releasing it as she shifted her weight from one foot to the other. "Furlac. An angel of the third choir."

~19~

Dar went with me to meet Taullian. We were each allowed to bring one other to the meeting. I wasn't surprised to see the elf lord with a sorcerer by his side. The gathering was at a clearing in the Western Red Forest, the buffer lands between the elven kingdom of Cyelle and the demon grasslands that surrounded the Maugan Swamp. Taullian had prepped the site with a large table — gently constructed to retain the look of wild growth. Two seats were at either end, and on top was a spread of food. It was a good strategy. Demons enjoyed food almost as much as they loved gifts.

Dar kept glancing over at me. He'd been doing this since he'd seen me this morning. The party had run into the wee hours without either Dar or Leethu, who had headed out to arrange the two meetings for me. Leethu wasn't back yet, but Dar had shown up bleary–eyed in the morning, letting me know that Taullian wanted to meet right away. I hoped that was a good sign.

"You look good," Dar whispered.

I knew it was more than a compliment on my attractive features. Somehow my human form had managed to fix itself overnight. All the blisters had disappeared to be replaced with smooth, tanned skin. The chewed up part of my arm with Ahriman's mark was likewise unblemished, save for the dark smudge, like a smear of charcoal on my flesh. Even my burned hair had been replaced with thick, glossy, brown locks. I felt strong, a small store of energy within me, available as long as I didn't try to hold on too tight. It churned through my spirit being, shining out through my eyes with an unholy light. I might have looked like a demon, but I didn't feel quite like one. I felt ...different.

"Lord Taullian." I bowed as I spoke. "I appreciate the audience, especially on such short notice."

The high lord sat and gestured for me to do the same. "Az. I am surprised you contacted me. Now that you have your freedom, there is no motivation for you to assist me."

"Oh, but there is." I leaned forward in my seat and picked up a spoon, twirling it between my fingers. "I'm still willing to assassinate your enemy for you, and fight on your behalf, but there is a price."

He'd flinched when I reached forward, but quickly relaxed. A spoon was no weapon, and I was well aware I looked non–threatening in my human form.

"And that price is?"

"I want all the elf gates in the kingdoms under your control to be dismantled. Never again will you trap unsuspecting humans and keep them as slaves."

He laughed. "You can't be serious."

"Second, there will be no more changeling swaps in any of the kingdoms under your control. No more human babies will be stolen from their parents and brought to Hel."

"But how are we expected to replace the humans who die? They don't live very long, you know, and we render all of them infertile upon puberty so there are no issues of loyalty."

"And no longer will humans be subject to involuntary sterilization. All humans in the kingdoms under your control will be granted their freedom and be given a subset of a kingdom of no less than the value of eight million hecals. They will be considered citizens and given all rights and privileges as such."

Taullian shook his head, a smile turning up the corner of his lips. "And for this you will make me a god? Grant me eternal life and all the riches of Hel? Really, Az, nothing you offer me could possibly make me consider such a preposterous request."

With a feeling of déjà vu, I showed him the underside of my arm. He frowned, and his sorcerer leaned in close.

"What happened to your other tattoo? The one from the angel?" he asked.

"My Lord," the sorcerer murmured. "That is a consort mark. She is Ahriman's partner."

Taullian's eyebrows shot up, practically into his hairline, as he looked from me to his sorcerer. "Ahriman?"

"Yes, Ahriman," I confirmed. "For one thousand years, we have pledged in contract to each other. I am his consort, and I speak with his authority."

It was a huge exaggeration, but what Taullian didn't know wouldn't hurt him. Dar, thankfully, kept a composed face. The consort clause did give me status, but my brother was fully aware of its limitations.

"If, and only if, I win and hold all six kingdoms, I'll grant the humans the peninsula. Only the ones who wish to go will be free. Ones that want to stay will remain under the same restrictions they have now. This excludes any humans in the mage program — they are ours. The freed humans are on their own. They'll not be considered elven citizens or afforded any rights by us. We keep the gates and all humans who come through them as well as changelings."

"Humans that stay with the elves always have the option to leave without hindrance. Mages and sorcerers and all others in the training program are included. No sterilization. No traps ever again. No changelings."

Taullian's eyes narrowed. Out of the corner of my eye I saw his sorcerer watching the back and forth like a tennis match, his face hopeful.

"We have invested significant time and resources into these magic users. I won't just give that away."

I shrugged. "If the freed humans remained part of your kingdom, and were given citizen rights, you could tax their magical products and recoup your training costs. Dude, you can't have things both ways. Either let them go and eat the training costs, or welcome them as part of your kingdom."

I could hear his teeth grind from across the table. "My elves would never go for it. I'd have a revolution on my hands. It's going to be hard enough getting them to swallow giving up their servants, let alone forcing them to treat them as equals."

"Boohoo," I mocked. "Such a hardship, considering another species to be an equal, worthy of respect. I'm sure your elves would much rather be under Feille's thumb. He's always been so friendly toward Cyelle. He'll give them big welcoming hugs and everyone will live happily ever after."

Every muscle in Taullian's face tensed. He knew there would be mass executions, that once Feille fully shouldered the mantel of his kingdoms, he'd ensure their obedience through fear and death.

"Now, in a time of desperation, elves may agree to this, but once the crisis is over, they'll rebel and demand their humans back."

I took the spoon I'd been twirling, and with a burst of speed and energy, slammed it halfway through the table. The handle quivered, the wood surrounding it smoking slightly.

"Then man—up, grow a set, and be a king, for fuck sake. Set the rules and enforce them, you fairy."

The sorcerer sucked in a breath, but he did nothing to stand between his king and the demon who'd just jammed a spoon through a table and insulted him. Perhaps he was scared, but I was thinking his loyalties might be divided, especially with the fate of his own people in the balance.

Silence stretched between us, and I wondered if I'd gone too far. Dar shifted slightly, coming into view on my right and motioning with his hand as if he were patting the ground. Wait. Let Taullian make the first move. I'd thrown the glove in his face; it was his turn to respond. It would do my position no good to break the silence and either backtrack or push too far forward.

"Any free human practicing magic is subject to a special tax, regardless of where they reside. The humans are on their own with the peninsula as theirs. No sterilization, but any human child born to those serving elves must be bought–out if the parents choose freedom. No on the gates."

"How the fuck are they supposed to buy out their children?" I erupted. "They're slaves. They don't have any wages or possessions. No deal. Fuck you and fuck your little problem. Have fun when Feille has your head on a pike at the edge of the Western Red Forest."

I stood up. The sorcerer's eyes widened. Taullian scowled.

"Who will care for these human children while the parents work? Who is expected to pay for their food and shelter?"

"They're *babies*," I argued, thinking of Tlia–Myea. "I've seen elves make a huge fuss over a new changeling. Don't feed me this bullshit about what a hardship it is to have a cute little baby, or toddler, running around. You guys eat that shit up."

I stood still while the high lord glowered at me and the sorcerer turned rather red from holding his breath.

"All right. But no on the elf gates. Never. We need the humans, and this is our only way of getting them."

"Elves have been in Hel for two and a half million years. The last four thousand you've been bringing over human slaves. You can't tell me how indispensible they are. That's just crap. You survived without them before and you will again."

Taullian thumped a fist on the table. It was the most forceful move I'd seen from him so far. "No. The gates are off the table and so are changelings."

I smiled. It wasn't a nice smile. Taullian shivered, covering it up by taking a sip of wine from his goblet.

"Deal. Of course, I'll find the gates one by one and destroy them myself. Not just the traps either. It's going to be mighty hard to do a changeling swap when you've got no gates."

The elf's eyes nearly popped from his head. "Don't be ridiculous. You can't do such a thing. Only angels can close a gate."

I shrugged. "I didn't say close; I said destroy."

Taullian gave me a skeptical look and turned to his sorcerer.

"Unlikely," the man commented, eyeing me nervously.

"Humans disabled an angel gate with a fifty megaton bomb," I mentioned casually. "Now, that's a fuckload of energy, and I'm probably one of the only demons that could manage it. It's one of my superpowers — storing a fuckload of energy and blowing shit up with it."

Well, it had been one of my superpowers. Now all I could manage was cramming a spoon halfway through a table. But they didn't have to know that.

"I thought you were broken?" Taullian sneered "You couldn't fix yourself a few days ago, and now you expect me to believe you can blow up an elf gate?"

"Do I look broken to you?"

His gaze roamed over me. I could see he was undecided. Had I lied before, claiming permanent injury to convince the elves to lower their defenses so I could escape, or was I lying now?

Taullian again looked to his sorcerer for guidance. "Is it possible for a demon to do this?"

The human wiped a bead of sweat from his forehead. "The ancient ones used to be able to create and dismantle gates, and they might still have that skill. In my knowledge, demons born since the banishment have never been able to, but it may be possible."

Taullian narrowed his eyes at me. "Her. Do you think she could do it?"

"If she could, the magical blowback would destroy a square mile. From what I've heard, an angel could survive it, but all but the most powerful demons would die. Kill their corporeal form, and they die too."

True, but I was the exception to that rule thanks to the instruction of a certain angel. I could live inside a corpse, but I'd learned the limitations of my abilities, especially after my near–death experience on Oak Island. I couldn't just go in with force, blow up a gate, and expect to survive it, but with some strategy and planning, I could ensure I was protected from the magical blast. Of course, this whole thing was a massive bluff since I could barely blow out a candle right now, let alone destroy a gate.

"Magical blowback? Now that sounds like a whole lot of fun." I grinned. "I've blown myself up before and come through just fine. I'm no angel, but clearly I must be a demon of some substance. Which is probably why Ahriman chose me as his *consort*."

That last bit was my attempt to remind them that I was special, that I was powerful and someone they really wanted to have on their side. I was a terrible liar, but for some reason, this particular deceit went through.

Taullian let out a huge breath. "Deal. But Feille dies, I rule all six kingdoms, and you or your agents assist until all six are stable."

I glanced at Dar who gave a brief thumbs–up. He loved this sort of thing. My brother, the general.

"Deal."

Dar stepped forward. "If I may?" he asked with a bow in my direction. Poser. I nodded.

"My Lord, there are reasons I believe you will prevail against Feille in spite of his more numerous forces and disproportionate military funding. He is a dictator. He's spread too thin trying to manage his own kingdom and four conquered ones."

Taullian nodded, a look of respect in his eyes. "Yes. That's why we were allowed to pay tribute and sign a treaty. I made it clear we would fight hard, and he doesn't have the resources right now to take us down."

Dar's nose twitched in agreement. "But once those four conquered kingdoms are under control, their rebellions crushed, their leaders executed...."

"Cyelle is next." Taullian's face darkened. "There will be no warning. We'll be murdered in our sleep, a new regime in place by sun–up. That's why I must move now."

Dar leaned in, red eyes deepening to crimson. "But how should you rule six elven kingdoms?" he said, his voice soft and deep. "Each one so very different in philosophy and custom. Will they be six, or one?"

Taullian's frown had a worried edge to it as he raised a hand to smooth a stray golden hair from his forehead. "Six." He sounded uncertain, almost as if he were asking a question instead of replying to Dar's.

Dar bounced his head in vigorous approval. "Wise choice. Consolidation would be a painful, bloody, and costly process. What will your governance model be?"

I had no idea what the fuck they were talking about, so I composed my face into what I hoped was a wise expression and tried not to doze off.

Taullian hesitated. "A Cyelle representative on their council. There will be certain laws they must follow, and a tribute, but beyond that, they can enjoy self–rule."

"But what do they get in return? What keeps them from tossing your ass to the side and telling Cyelle to go fuck themselves? You don't have the military might to force them to comply; there must be some benefit worth their cooperation."

"A pact of non–aggression, and the promise of military support? Protection against invasion?"

Those were clearly questions. Taullian was floundering, reminding me of Kirby's comments. He wasn't a military leader, that wasn't his strength. He was a civil leader, preserving culture, building stable infrastructure, supporting innovations in magical research and fine arts.

It gave me an idea. I wished Leethu was here, though. She was the expert.

"How about a program for knowledge sharing? Economy of scale in multi–kingdom projects? Cross–cultural arts and festivals? And a dedicated team comprised of representatives from each kingdom to address matters significant to you all, such as fertility, forest preservation, sacred spaces?"

Dar stared at me in shock. I didn't blame him; I sounded like a fucking angel. I guess all those Ruling Council meetings were eating away at my brain. A bright light came into Taullian's blue eyes, and he raised a hand to tap thoughtfully on his cheek.

"Would that be enough?"

I shrugged. "Give them an accounting of exactly what their "tribute" is going towards, so they can see it's in support of projects that benefit them all. Might work. Might not. Either way, it's better than lopping off heads for the next century and worrying about a knife in your back some day."

Dar smoothed the back of his paw across the side of his face and along his whiskers. "That shit would never work with demons, but it might with elves."

He was right. Demons might have their little quirks regarding hobbies or pet projects, but ultimately it came down to power and force. I hoped we hadn't influenced the elves too much in that regard.

"I'll take it under advisement," Taullian said after a thoughtful pause. "How many demons shall we expect to fight alongside us?"

I knew what he was thinking. Ahriman's household was huge, encompassing nearly every geographic area of the demon territories. Of course, Ahriman's household would not be attending this event — just me and my forty crazy followers.

"I'm afraid I can't be specific," I told him. "Surely you understand that Ahriman must continue to appear uninvolved in this matter. It wouldn't benefit his reputation to be seen assisting an elven lord."

Taullian frowned. "How can I plan the attack? How can I determine what positions to put the demons in?"

I tried to summon up every bit of aloof snobby attitude I could muster. I thought of Gregory and how he treated the others on the Ruling Council, how he brushed off their questions with authority and confidence.

"You cannot expect them to fight under *your* direction," I drawled, trying with every ounce of me to project an angelic disdain. "Demons don't do organized warfare. Give me some way to identify your troops, so they don't get killed in friendly fire, and trust us to do it all from the shadows."

"They will all wear a band of golden yellow fabric on their right arm," Taullian said, after a moment of consideration.

I nodded. "When do we strike?"

"Two months.

My heart plummeted. I'd be tightly within Ahriman's grasp by then. "No, it needs to be next week. You need to strike now, before Feille has any time to gain info from spies, or consolidate his power base."

A look of fear shot across Taullian's face, but he set his jaw and took a deep breath. "One week. I will have the relay device delivered to your residence along with the specific time frame you'll have to do your job. I'll also send you the coordinates for the attack. I won't be able to transport your army there, so I'll give you ample time for them to travel independently and infiltrate the kingdom."

I nodded. "We'll be ready."

Taullian stood to leave, his sorcerer pulling a transportation button from his robes. "Oh, and Niyaz? If anything goes wrong, it will be *your* head on a pike at the edge of the Western Red Forest."

He and the sorcerer were gone before I could reply, leaving me with a table laden with food and impaled by a spoon. I turned to Dar who was looking at me, an expression of admiration and amusement on his face.

"You are so fucked, Mal."

"Tell me about it." I grabbed a loaf of bread off the table and stuffed a piece of dried fruit into my mouth. I hated to let decent food go to waste, and although it wasn't hot wings, it was better than a lot of the food back at my own house.

"How are you going to pull this off? I can tell when you're lying. I may have been too inebriated last night to catch it, but it's clear to me now that Ahriman doesn't know anything about this. He won't be sending any troops, and he probably would be pissed as fuck if he knew you were up to this. Am I right?"

I swallowed the fruit, my mouth suddenly dry. "You're right."

"That elf is expecting an army, not forty demons, half of which are Low and can't fight their way out of a paper bag. I'm good, but I can't single-handedly kill hundreds of elves, and what is Leethu going to do? Fuck them to death?"

She could. And they'd all die happy, too.

"If you don't want to do it, if Leethu or any of the others want to back out, it's okay."

Dar let out a breath, rubbing his paws over his face. "Mal, we're not letting you do this on your own. You know better than that. And the other demons are thrilled with the chance to kill something, especially an elf. Just tell me you've got a plan. Please tell me you've got a plan."

"I've got a plan," I mumbled, my mouth full of fruit. "Trust me."

Dar threw out his hands, looking at the sky in exasperation. "I do, Mal. I always trust you. I follow you into the most horrendous, poorly–thought–out, disastrous scenarios, because, in the face of terrible odds, you always come out smelling like roses. But this time ...what the fuck, Mal?"

I swallowed the huge lump of fruit and crammed more into my mouth. It was actually pretty good stuff. "I've got a plan. Trust me.

Dar ignored me and kept going. "And if that elf doesn't have your head on a pike, Ahriman is going to. What the fuck were you thinking, throwing his name around like that? Consort does not mean equal. You can't commit his household to this thing. No one in their right mind would believe he'd send his people in to fight for an *elf*. He's going to be furious you used his name and dragged him into the middle of this mess."

"After the fight, I'll need you to help Taullian stabilize the kingdoms. Take one, the most troublesome one, because you're that good, and help his deputy get some order. Leethu can take another one. She's not much of a fighter, but she can maneuver her way around politics like nobody's business, and she knows elven power structures like the back of her webbed hand. Taullian can handle one personally, and hopefully the other two won't be much trouble. I don't have any other demons in my household I trust to do this sort of thing. The others can help you, or maybe I'll send them up to the mountains to pester the trolls for the next thousand years."

Dar froze, his eyes knowing. "You're sending us safely away, so we don't suffer Ahriman's wrath once he's found out what you've done."

My brother knew me well. "He could easily guess that my foster siblings are my weak spots. I fear he'll kill you both to punish me, and even though any household discipline is supposed to be mine to deliver, I worry he'll kill every last one of you."

We looked at each other, knowing the truth in my statement. I longed to lighten the moment, to hit him over the head with the loaf of bread, or declare he was a worthless shithead that didn't mean anything to me, but I couldn't. We'd gone far past that in our centuries together, and no longer needed to pretend. I'd never forgive myself if anything happened to Dar and Leethu. Especially Dar, who had let me down over and over again, but had always come through at the last minute, when it really counted. As demons go, he was the most loyal of anyone I'd ever known.

"He might kill you, Mal," Dar said softly. "Ahriman is cruel, and you're just an imp."

He might, but I was counting that his greed would keep me alive. "I've got one thing he really wants, and if I'm dead, he doesn't get it. There's a reason he was so insistent about my accepting his breeding petition, and he wants to ensure he gets a lot of chances to produce the offspring he wants."

Dar tilted his head to the side, his bright-red eyes confused. "But you're still terribly injured. There's a good chance whatever he wants is something you won't be able to pass along to any progeny."

I smiled, although the irony of the situation twisted it to a grimace. "He wants devouring. Not just a little either, he wants the whole enchilada. And that's one of the few things I still have. Unfortunately."

A choking noise came from Dar's long snout. "Devouring? No one chooses that deliberately. That's not creating a demon — it's creating a weapon."

Dar's voice trailed off, a look of shock on his rat–like face. "A weapon. He wants a weapon, but one he can control. Mal, you have a massive ability to devour, but you've always been able to control it. If Ahriman had a demon like that under his influence, he could take anything he wanted."

"Yes, he could." I had a good idea what Ahriman wanted this weapon for. I'd suspected the moment he'd insisted on any offspring having that particular skill. Now I just had to make sure that over the next thousand years he didn't get exactly what he wanted.

"Hel?" Dar shook his head. "He's ancient. He fought in the demon wars. If he wanted to rule Hel, he could do it now, without a devouring spirit. Why bother to go through all this if he wants Hel?"

"Not Hel," I told him, my eyes intent on his. "Aaru. I suspect he wants to take back Aaru."

~20~

While I waited for Gareth to show for his meeting, I mulled over my conversation with Dar. Aaru. I couldn't imagine any other reason for Ahriman to want to create a demon with a strong devouring spirit, one he could control.

But why would Ahriman want Aaru? Did he want to destroy it and the angels as revenge for his banishment so long ago? A strong devouring spirit could certainly accomplish that according to Gregory, but there was an enormous risk that Ahriman wouldn't be able to check his weapon once activated. I thought of how I'd felt, up on Devil's Paw, how nothing mattered but sucking in everything around me like a demon vacuum. Was his thirst for revenge suicidal? Did it include the destruction of all creation? I wasn't sure.

Of course, Ahriman might just want to use the threat of his devouring demon as a way to rule Aaru. If he could manage to pull the demon back after a terrifying demonstration, he'd have the leverage needed to enact a coup. I shook my head, wondering why anyone would want to occupy Aaru. The place sucked big time. Corporeal forms continually dissolved; there was nothing to see, nothing to hear, nothing to touch. It was a sensory wasteland. And it was filled with angels — angels who had all sorts of draconian rules and impossible–to–follow procedures for everything. He was better off here, and Hel was his for the taking if he'd just lift an ancient, powerful finger. Of course, few demons wanted to rule an entire planet of beings. Too much work. It would suck all the fun out of life, although, Ahriman was an ancient and might have retained some of his personality from when he was an Angel of Chaos.

With a powerful devouring spirit as his right hand, he could ruin the place, kill angels and scatter the rest. Even those who fled and survived would find themselves consigned to a corporeal existence. No Aaru would mean no place where they could exist as a pure being of spirit. They'd be damned, exiled, just as they'd done to us. Of course, he'd need to be able to control this weapon of his, and I suspected a devouring spirit strong enough to overcome the Ruling Council and smash Aaru would be one Ahriman couldn't rein in at the end of the day. Revenge made for reckless decisions. I remembered Gregory's prophecy of how a devouring spirit would bring about the apocalypse, the end of all creation. Would Ahriman find vengeance as sweet if it cascaded a chain of events that ended in the annihilation of all life — himself included? Maybe his hate had been festering so long that he just didn't care anymore.

Gregory would never allow it, I thought with a surge of admiration and pride. He was unbelievably powerful, but so was Ahriman. Yes, the demon had been on the losing side of the wars, but failing to win once didn't mean he couldn't succeed this time. And Gregory might be taken unawares. He'd always been a tower of strength, but since I'd come into his life he was changing. Would he hesitate a second too long? I felt a twinge of guilt that the love he had for me might have compromised his safety and that of all of Aaru. In spite of my slander, I was developing an odd affection for the place. In some way it was mine.

Which left me caught in the middle. How could I keep to the terms of my breeding contract and not be party to the monster Ahriman wanted to form? If we'd agreed on just a couple of occurrences, I could sneak defective bits, or useless traits over to him. He didn't devour. He was relying on me to provide what he wanted. How long could I deceive him? One thousand years. One thousand occurrences. He'd catch on eventually.

There was a burst of light and a man appeared before me. He wore sensible gray robes that hummed with the magic of the runes embroidered along the edges. His bald head was unusually tanned and dotted with brown age spots. Fierce dark eyes met mine from under a bushy white brow. He was clearly well fed, but there was power under the extra weight. Most sorcerers spent all their time in lightless rooms with their noses glued to books, or practicing their art. This guy got outside and did physical things.

"Gareth? Welcome to my home," I stood and offered my hand. He looked at it, as if he expected me to hand him something. "Sorry." I withdrew the hand and bowed instead. "I've been with the humans a very long time and they clasp hands when they greet each other."

He held out his hand, mirroring mine. "Like this? I would be very interested to learn the customs of my people, as well as more about their culture."

His tone was formal, wary, but contained a wistful quality.

I took his hand in mine. "There is significance in the tightness of the grasp, the proximity of the two individuals, and the distance the hand is raised and lowered. A handshake can be a simple greeting, or it can convey status and intention."

He nodded with a terse smile. "Good to know. How should I address you? Some tell me you're the Iblis, others say you're not."

That was the million–dollar question. Was I still the Iblis? I hadn't seen that fucking sword since Alaska. It was the symbol of the office, but even with it gone, I still *felt* like the Iblis. The responsibility sat like a weight on my shoulders, and I wasn't sure if it was official or self–imposed. Either way, greedy imp that I was, I wouldn't let go of the title without a fight.

"Yes, I'm the Iblis, but you may call me Sam."

I don't know why I gave him the human name I'd assumed so long ago instead of one of my demon names and titles. It just seemed to fit. More and more I was identifying with the humans.

"Normally I would not meet with a demon on such short notice, or in their territory, but I've heard intriguing things about you."

Intriguing things? "That Feille tried to hire me to hunt you down?"

"More that you exploded the top of his throne with some magical device and overpowered his restraining net. I've also heard that you managed to attack and kill one of his sorcerers from a dungeon, and that you have some rather prominent connections in the demon hierarchy."

Ahriman. The guy's name did open doors. I had no doubt my contract with the ancient demon weighed more in my favor than any of my alleged antics with the elves.

"I've heard things about you, too. You've taken out every demon sent to bring you in, made a home for yourself among us. And the reason you ran from Feille? Could it have been a special project through the gates that involved tearing demons into little bits for angels and stashing away their energy to super–power spells."

Gareth caught his breath, a shimmer of gold rising around his body in protection.

"It's not that I have any issue with that special project. I had planned to leave long before then, and the proposed project expedited my departure."

"And you have had dealings with Ahriman in the past? Could it be that he assisted you in your escape?"

The sorcerer's eyes narrowed. "I thought you were his consort. Wouldn't you know that sort of thing?"

I smiled, trying to appear sly. "Even the closest of demons have their secrets. I'm trying to gauge your loyalty."

There were a few tense seconds while Gareth dissected me with his eyes. Finally, the gold protective shield around him vanished.

"The ancient one requested a specific magical item from me that required over twenty years of research to produce and perfect. In return, I was given protection and guaranteed a certain amount of contracted commerce. That affiliation is one of the main reasons I agreed to see you."

I nodded, forcing a pleased smile. "I hope to make a similar arrangement with other humans currently under elven rule."

His eyes lit up at the suggestion. I felt his loneliness, his longing for human companionship beyond his apprentice. The ground seemed to tilt slightly, to shift, and I saw lines of this man's future before me. One path to leadership and greatness, another short path to a gruesome death. *Mine.* Suddenly I wanted to do everything in my power to make sure the first path was the one that saw the light of day.

"Why did you want to leave Feille and the kingdom of Wythyn? His sorcerers achieve remarkable things. It must have been difficult to give that sort of research opportunity up to live among the demons and produce vast quantities of transport buttons and fireball launchers."

He grimaced, relaxing his wary posture slightly. "Although the opportunity to learn, the investment in spell components and research was appealing, Wythyn is not conducive to a long life. The project in question was ...intriguing, but there was a significant amount of personal risk, and Feille is not known for providing back–up when things go bad."

I nodded. "Understood. His whole team is gone. That Pash guy, his two mages and apprentice. All dead."

Gareth paled. "Well, that's what happens when humans get between demons and angels. Add elves into the mix and we'll most likely wind up dead. It's better to pick a side that will shelter you under their wing, so to speak."

And which side would Gareth pick? He clearly wasn't in favor of elves, and few humans had dealings with angels that they were aware of. He'd managed to make a life for himself in demons lands. I was banking that his loyalty was with us.

"I have a proposal," I watched for his reaction. "But I don't want to run afoul of any prior commitment you might have with another demon. I need to ask — are you part of Ahriman's household?"

The sorcerer recoiled in revulsion. "No! I do service for different demons on a freelance basis. Ahriman is a client that receives priority attention, but my earlier project with him satisfied any debt. I don't need to belong to a demon household in order to survive in their lands."

"Yet...." I let the word hang in the air between us, watching Gareth's increased rate of breathing. "Eventually you'll get caught in the middle, just like Pash. Wouldn't it be better if the humans had their own space? Freedom from the elves, protection in return for a tax in addition to the protection of a powerful demon?"

Gareth spat and gave a wave of his hand. "The elves would never let us go, and for the demons to shelter us, give us land ...well, the price would be far too high. I was lucky that an ancient saw my talent and had a need. I was even luckier that he followed through and didn't betray me. Most demons can't be trusted. I took a horrible risk, but I didn't have much of an alternative."

"What if the humans *did* have freedom and their own lands?" I smiled a secret smile. He was intrigued. "Times, they are a–changing. And I intend to rush the whole thing along a bit."

We studied each other in silence. Gareth trying to determine if he could trust me, gauge how much of my words were truth and lie. I wondered how I could possibly gain his support without revealing information about Taullian's impending attack. Gareth seemed to have broken all ties with Feille, but if the price was right, I couldn't discount the chance he'd sell me out.

"I need five potions of non–detection, twelve snare–nets, twenty vials of paralyzation, forty slippery–skin amulets, and a phantom–hands garrote. Oh, and a chicken wand. I need a chicken wand. Within the next seven days."

Gareth stared, his mouth open. He had nice teeth for an old guy. Elves might be assholes but they seemed to have decent dentistry services.

"What do you think I am, a magic factory?" he sputtered. "It's not like I have a warehouse full of items, ready to go. Each one of those will take days to make. Some have to be created under specific astrological conditions. I can't make all that in seven days."

I shrugged. "Then steal it."

His mouth opened even more. I could see tonsils. It wasn't a pretty sight. "Steal it how? Waltz into the citadel in Wythyn, fill up a bag and waltz right out? You're insane."

"Feille can't manage six kingdoms. Everything is on the edge of chaos right now — the elves are panicked, the humans are panicked. Skilled mages would happily fill up a bag and waltz right out the door if they had a safe place to go."

His mouth snapped shut and a shrewd look crossed his face. "How would I contact them? And how could I guarantee they'd get safe passage out of their respective elven kingdoms?"

I threw up my hands. "You're a fucking sorcerer. I'm sure you have some way to message each other without physically traveling the distance. Crystal balls, a mirror, a cell phone. As for the safe passage, it shouldn't be a problem.

Don't mess with Cyelle. Taullian still has a decent handle on his kingdom through some treaty with Feille. Target Tonlielle, Klee, and Li. Their high lords are either dead or imprisoned in Wythyn, and Feille is spread really thin in management."

Gareth tapped his finger against his chin. "Give me forty–eight hours, and I'll let you know what I can get."

I swallowed hard. Now came the hard part. "What's your fee?"

He quoted a number and I felt the room spin. Fuck. How much was I willing to pay for this gamble? Because it was a gamble. If we didn't win, Taullian wouldn't honor his deal concerning the humans and I'd be out for everything. Even if he did win, I'd be out for everything. It's not like I could collect any kind of recompense from a group of ex–slaves, or claim restitution from Feille's coffers. I'd be destitute. Destitute and dependent on Ahriman with the burden of a household of forty demons to support. I owed them too. I'd promised them protection and support. How the fuck could I possibly afford this?

"Done".

We shook hands, and I caught that rare smile from Gareth. "So what other human customs can you show me?"

"Hot wings, chilled vodka, fast cars and projectile weapons, heated swimming pools, friendship, loyalty, and love." I thought about Wyatt and all my friends back home — my other home. Warmth filled my chest. "If things work out, I'll get you passage through the gates and you can visit me and my earthly household. You might just decide to stay."

He smiled, like he didn't quite believe me. "But Hel is my home. What would I possibly do there? What kind of life could I have among people I don't even know?"

"A wonderful life," I said, thinking of Nyalla. "Better than you could ever imagine."

"I'm not interested in imagining it. You do realize I was brought here as an infant sixty–four years ago? I know no one on the other side of the gates. I don't know their languages, their customs, or their jobs. This is my home, and I'm not leaving."

He and so many other humans felt the same. Not just the older ones brought in as babies. How many had been here five or ten years and would be reluctant to go back to a world that changed without them? We demons were different. We'd spend decades, centuries even, in Hel before popping across the gates for fun. It was disorienting, and we had so much to learn each trip. That was part of the fun for us, the rush of not knowing what to expect once we'd crossed over and evaded the gate guardian. Humans, as demon–like as they were, valued security and stability far more than we did.

Gareth left and I once again thought about what I needed to do. Kill Feille before he could move against the demons. Help Taullian win and stabilize six kingdoms so he'd grant the humans freedom and the beginnings of a new life. That was the big heartburn on my to–do list. I had a household of forty. I'd need all of the magical items I'd asked Gareth for to make it seem like that forty was four hundred, and to ensure their safety. In addition to winning this fight, I had to make Taullian think I was a mighty force so he wouldn't weasel out of our deal. If we impressed him enough in battle, if Leethu and Dar were instrumental in stabilizing the kingdoms, he'd *have* to honor our agreement.

And then there was Ahriman. I'd hoped to keep all this from him, but each day that passed lessened the chance that he'd be unaware of my actions. When all was said and done, I'd probably have to come crawling to him and beg forgiveness. I don't do crawling, and I got the idea that Ahriman didn't do forgiving. He'd begin our thousand–year contract pissed at me, only to become more enraged when he found out how terribly damaged I was. If I then went on to refuse him the devouring pattern for his offspring, who knew what he'd do to me? I'd survived meeting an angel, battling a vengeful demon, exploding, and imprisonment by the elves, and, hopefully, a hand–to–hand fight with Feille, but this might be the end of the line for me. I'd need to take satisfaction with all I'd accomplished in my short life. That would give me comfort when Ahriman tore me to pieces in a rage.

~21~

A door opened, and I halted my nervous pacing to watch Leethu cautiously peek around the door. "Is he gone? Did the meeting go well, Ni–ni?"

"Yeah. I gave him a shopping list. He's supposed to get back to me in a few days."

I motioned her in, admiring the way light reflected off her tiny golden scales, the smooth and sensuous way she moved across the floor. I searched her features, her mannerisms, trying to see some hint of Amber in her, but there was none. Beyond the pheromones, and Amber's explosive temper, she seemed far removed from her daughter.

"Have you heard from Irix at all? Was he able to help Amber?" I had a vision of her booting him out the door within an hour of our last conversation. Amber had the Lowry stubborn streak, even without the genetic link.

The succubus laughed. "He's still there. Which amazes me given the amount of complaining he's done. My daughter is not an ideal pupil. She's obstinate, willful, foul–mouthed, and argues constantly. I have no idea why he's remained."

Leethu sounded rather proud of her progeny, which surprised me. None of those were traits valued by succubi or incubi. They weren't elven traits either. What exactly had Leethu planned when she'd formed Amber?

"How ...how well do you know this Irix? Do you trust him?" I was worried for both my girls. Nyalla was learning to navigate the human world, and she had Wyatt there to help her, but Amber was a young woman on the edge. She was afraid she'd be discovered for what she was; she feared her powers; she feared not having her powers. She was volatile and impulsive. It wasn't that I thought Irix would betray her — I just needed her to be in good hands. I needed her to be with someone who would care enough about her to guide her through this tough period, not an incubus who thought she was a spoiled pain in the ass.

Leethu's shrewd eyes dissected my thoughts. "Irix only complains like this when he likes someone," she reassured me. "He'll stay and watch out for her. You can be assured that he'll care for her."

I felt weak with relief. I'd been in Hel for months, having no contact with my humans beyond my daily calls with Wyatt. I worried about them.

"Thanks, Leethu." I hugged her, and she took the opportunity to squeeze my rear end. "I owe you."

"No, Ni–ni, I owe you." Her hand caressed its way up my back. "I know it is strange for me to care for my offspring, but I am so proud of this child of mine. I want to ensure she is safe, that she lives to grow strong and powerful, that she sets the world on fire."

I thought of Amber with her elven looks and cool reserve, all hiding a volcano of demon emotion. So young. Who knows what she'd be in a few centuries?

Leethu dipped her head down to kiss me, and I lost myself in the softness of her lips, the smooth feel of her scaled skin against mine. She wasn't Wyatt, wasn't Gregory, but I loved my succubus foster sister, and this affection, so rare from another demon, filled an emptiness inside me.

"Can I join in?"

I tilted my head to better see, although I recognized Dar's voice. He was peering in around the door in a re–run of Leethu's entrance, his furred snout twitching, eyes glowing in the dim, indoor light. I closed my eyes, immersing myself in

Leethu's embrace for a few precious moments. My hand was warm against the cool scales of her arm. They were jagged as I rubbed them the wrong way, moving my palm up to rest on her shoulder. The succubus shuddered, enjoying the discomfort, and clasped me close, rubbing her naked, scaled front along my equally naked body.

"Please, Ni–ni?" Her voice was soft against my lips. "Let me show you my loyalty, my devotion. I will not tie you to me, I promise."

"Another time." I spoke louder than her, to include Dar in my answer. Dar and Leethu had frolicked together many times, but I needed to restrain myself. I loved Leethu, but she lied. The succubus would never be able to resist the opportunity to tie me to her, and I didn't want to spend all eternity pining for her touch. She was hard enough to deny as it was.

In consolation, I caressed her face with my hand, pinching hard at an earlobe as she closed her eyes in ecstasy. "I need to speak to both of you about our upcoming battle strategy. Dar, will you join us?"

I heard a spray of air and spit that could only be Dar's amusement. He strode through the door, his body rounded and full, covered in sparse gray hair, his long, naked, pink tail twitching behind him.

"Strategy? We're demons, Mal. Any strategy you're thinking better not be longer than three seconds."

I pulled away from Leethu, immediately missing her coolness, and picked up an iron poker from the fireplace.

"Here's Wythyn," I drew in the dusty floor with the poker. I really needed to get someone to clean this fucking place. Who the hell was in charge of housekeeping, anyway? "Four main cities — the capital, Chime, then Rush, and Sweep. I haven't heard from Taullian, and he's probably not going to reveal his exact plans, but I'm assuming he'll use the relays to transport troops within the capital. It will cause a huge disruption, and the element of surprise will be on his side."

Dar pointed a clawed digit toward the dots on the dusty map. "If he's got a brain in his head, he'll gate some troops into these cities too. It will cause a distraction, and he'll quickly take the small number of fighters there in a show of power across a broad geography."

I nodded. "How can we best support his efforts, then? I've requested a wide variety of magical weaponry from Gareth for our household. Where should I place them?"

Dar locked his little red eyes onto mine. "Magical weaponry? Mal, what exactly did you buy?"

I squirmed. Dar might be under my household, but I always considered him a peer — more, actually, since he was a few decades older than me and was the only demon who had ever been able to sway my decisions on a regular basis.

"Just a few things. Some non–detection spells, snare nets, paralyzation potions, slippery skin amulets, a phantom–hands garrote scroll. Oh, and a chicken wand. I couldn't resist that one."

Dar's eyes glowed, his whiskers vibrating at the speed of light. "Mal. You. Are. Fucking. Joking. Me. Where? How? Money?" he sputtered.

I shrugged with a deceptively casual mien. "Don't worry about that. We need to make forty demons seem like an army, and I don't want to risk my household against skilled elves without some kind of advantage on our side. I want to try to get everyone out of this alive. They're my household, my responsibility."

Dar blew out a huge breath and clasped his furred cheeks with clawed hands. "Mal, they're demons. They'll risk themselves because it's fun and exciting, and probably half of them will die. That's the way things are here in Hel. Have you forgotten? There's no need to bankrupt yourself to save a bunch of Lows and demons that you've adopted from dead masters."

I pulled myself up to full height, staring him down. I hadn't forgotten, but that didn't mean I had to play by the old rules. I wasn't that demon anymore, and I refused to backslide just because I was in Hel again.

"This is my money, Dar. My trust fund, my spoils from Haagenti's blood feud. If I choose to use it to protect Lows and my adoptive households, as well as your and Leethu's households that I folded in under my own, that is my decision."

His eyes wavered, and he finally dropped his gaze, covering the submission by pretending he was looking at the map in front of him.

"What shall I do, Ni–ni?" Leethu moved to stand beside me in support. Dar glared at her under bushy eyebrows.

"Each member of my household should have a slippery skin amulet, to protect against both the elven nets and the restraint collars. Your household is the most sneaky, and I'd like to use all five of them for one specific purpose."

Leethu glowed at the compliment. Sneaky was a trait all demons aspired to, and she was proud of her small, handpicked household. "We will give our lives in your service, Ni–ni"

I hoped not. "Your five will have the non–detection spells. I need them to enter the capital and disburse the vials of paralyzation potion in the food, wine, water supply — whatever would be best. Timing is critical. The effects last for a month and wear off very slowly, but a sudden onset would tip off the elves and they'd be on the alert for the attack. I need them to time their poisoning so the maximum amount of debilitation takes place as close to Taullian's arrival as possible."

She nodded. Of all the demons, Leethu's household was the one most likely to follow direction to the letter.

"Here," Dar said, his voice grumpy as he pointed toward an area to the east of the capital city. "Here, and here. These areas are just outside the major barracks. We can create a diversion in the woods, lure the elven soldiers in then snare them in the nets. I hope you asked for the bladed ones. It would simplify the whole affair."

I knelt, looking at my makeshift map. Dar's plan would split the troop numbers, greatly lessening what Taullian would be facing.

"Timing would be critical here, too," I said. "If you wait until Taullian is in, none of the elves will be fooled. If you go too early...."

"There is no 'too early'," Dar contradicted. "We're just demons. Pesky demons who have caused a riot in the woods. The elves will come out to deal with the minor inconvenience, and no one will come back. By the time they figure out something is wrong, Taullian is in and their attention is on him. We can jump the gun by twelve hours and still be effective."

I looked up at him, noting the eager bead of sweat along the fur of his upper lip. Dar always loved a good fight, but he especially loved the planning. "As long as no one gets away. That's critical, Dar."

He shrugged and licked his lower lip with a long pink tongue. "Not really. Feille might suspect you're behind it, but he'd never believe Taullian was coordinating an attack with demons, or that demons would ever work with elves in organized warfare."

He was right. Dar was so fucking smart. I had no idea why he'd put up with me all these centuries. "You stupid fucking dick–for–brains. This better work, or I'll rip the fur from your balls with duct tape."

He grinned, his teeth sharp as knives. "Promises, promises."

I grinned back. "Okay. Everyone gets a slippery skin amulet. Dar gets the snare nets. Leethu gets the non–detection spells and the paralyzation potions. I want Leethu to have the phantom hands garrote, also."

Her dark, chocolate–colored eyes widened in surprise, and her mouth opened in a lovely 'O'. It was a lavish gift, but of all my household, she was the least skilled in combat. She was a diplomat, a manipulator of great skill, but I was worried that even her expertise wouldn't keep her safe in a violent encounter against elves. They'd always seemed immune to her charms, and I didn't want to find her dead in the forest. Dar was brutal, a fierce fighter, a survivor, but Leethu.... I feared for her, and I'd never forgive myself if anything happened to her. Amber would never forgive me either. An orphan. I couldn't do that to her.

"What about the chicken wand?" Dar asked, his chest quivering with amusement. He didn't seem envious of my extravagant gift to Leethu, in fact, he seemed to approve.

"That's mine." I was defensive. It was a stupid waste of money. A chicken wand. What the fuck good would that do me? Still, it was one of the coolest things a sorcerer could create, and demons loved a good chicken wand. I'd never been able to justify the cost, and still couldn't, but if I didn't get one now, I'd probably never have the chance. Between this insane battle and my thousand years with Ahriman, I'd most likely not live to get another chance. Might as well seize the moment.

I took the poker and drew five squiggly shapes extending out either side from my map of Wythyn. "Okay. Post battle. How should we stabilize this mess?"

And a mess it was. The southern elven kingdoms were basically in a line, east to west, separating the stretch of demon lands from the mountains to the north. Li was the furthest to the west and the most diverse in terms of topography — rivers, marshlands, peaks that divided them from the northern elven kingdoms, along with the dwarven lands on their western border. Cyelle nestled against them to the east and slightly south, a forest of autumn color no matter the season. Tonlielle was along their northeast edge, miles of grassy plains broken by ancient foothills. Wythyn the next, a floral forest in palest green, then Allwin, the most eclectic with its mix of mountains, forests, and plains. At the east end, Kllee stood, the northernmost elven kingdom. Kllee was smack in the middle of steep mountains with dangerous precipices, unstable outcroppings, and towns perched on cliff edges.

We stared down at my makeshift map, each of our faces registering despair.

"There aren't enough of us," Dar said mournfully. "Unless Taullian has a few key people, we've got six kingdoms and three to act as diplomats. And with Cyelle and Wythyn right in the middle, it will be a logistical nightmare to handle two kingdoms. They'll go through a truck–load of elf buttons just getting us around in time."

"Well, Cyelle should run just fine with a proxy." I checked that squiggle off with a sweep of my poker. "Which one of these is going to be the biggest pain–in–the–ass? What kind of approach would work best with each kingdom?"

Leethu stepped forward, gently pulling the poker from my hand. "Let me, Ni–ni. I am familiar with all of the northern and southern elven kingdoms."

She flipped the poker, tapping the sharp edge against her lips. We all watched as she contemplated the crude map. Leethu got around, and not just in the carnal sense either. Unlike most demons, succubi and incubi were skilled at following social conventions. They could make small talk, entertain listeners with lively, audience–appropriate, stories. They knew which fork to use, and actually used it. As long as one could resist the overwhelming sexual lure, they were the ideal party guests. Leethu made the rounds. Demons, elves, dwarves, goblins, orcs, trolls, it didn't matter. She always received a second invitation, and she often got lucky. Of all the beings in Hel, Leethu was the most able to negotiate the convoluted culture and conventions of elven society.

"I think...." She tapped the poker again on her lip before reversing it to smack the floor. "There. Taullian should take Cyelle and Tonlielle. They have the most similar government structure, and they've been very intimate with each other during the last two hundred years."

I pursed my lips in thought. I remember I'd had no problem passing through Tonlielle when I was working for Taullian this past winter. I'd got the feeling they were allies.

"Lady Moria was having a clandestine affair with Taullian. They tried to keep it quiet, but the gossip was on the streets. Neither kingdom seemed to be displeased by the rumors, either. I think she was paving the way towards a more permanent joining, of both their kingdoms and their personal futures. He can frame this as revenge for his lover's death and the elves will eat it up."

It was true. For all their stuffiness, elves loved a good romance — especially one that ended in poignant tragedy. Tonlielle would welcome him with open arms for avenging their beloved Moria's murder.

"Wythyn is the obvious problem," she continued, smacking the poker over the appropriate squiggle. "They will chafe under another kingdom's rule, even those who despise Feille. Taullian will not be able to initially have a self–governance model with them. It will be too dangerous. He'll need his strongest people in that kingdom for a few centuries before he can ever trust them."

I snorted. "Taullian may be a good bureaucrat, but he's weak. They'll eat him alive in Wythyn. He should get the heck out of Dodge after he wins the battle and leave the bloody work to someone who doesn't mind getting his hands dirty."

"That would be me." Dar raised his hand like an eager schoolboy. "I'll whip those fuckers into shape. They'll be begging for Taullian to waltz in with his festivals and forest preservations after a month, guaranteed."

Leethu shot him an admiring glance. "I think I need to take Kllee," she said with another whack of the poker. I feared for the condition of my floor — not that it didn't have plenty of dents and gouges in it already.

"Kllee?" Dar leaned over the map as if it would miraculously reveal information. "I don't know anything about that kingdom. Aren't they reclusive?"

"Which is why I need to be there. I've visited them a few times, so they know and trust me more than they would elves from other kingdoms. They're the most likely to give Taullian the finger and go off on their own. They're isolationists. Feille claims he's conquered them, but they're a very painful thorn in his side. They'll never submit."

Leethu had a look on her face I could only describe as rapture. She clearly knew something about the Kllee elves that no one else did.

"Okay, slutty–girl, spill it," I encouraged.

"Have you noticed they appear rather ...diverse for elves who avoid associating with other kingdoms?"

I hated it when Leethu teased. Well, I loved it, but not this kind of teasing. I'd never seen an elf from Kllee. I'd never been within a mile of their border. Their lands were not the easiest to navigate, and they trapped all mountain passes with an intense paranoia.

Dar waved a sharp–clawed digit at the succubus. "I've only met two, but they had smaller ears and were shorter with a more muscular build then other elves. They also appeared rather dark for southern elves. Are they breeding with their northern cousins?"

Northern elves were more commonly called the 'dark elves', which mean their skin tone ranged from latte to the deepest midnight. Their hair tended toward black and mahogany, although some kingdoms had a genetic streak that delivered an odd, colorless, white hair. It was shockingly attractive, especially combined with a dusky skin–tone.

I gasped, more for effect than because I was truly shocked. After all, I was a demon and very little actually shocked us. "But Eresh separates them from the closest northern kingdom. That's pretty far to go for a quickie."

Leethu shook her head, practically exploding with her secret. "Noooo. Guess again!"

Arrrgh! "Leethu, I'm going to make the next hour very unpleasant for you if you don't spill it!" She grinned, knowing it was an empty threat.

"Where is their gate? The elven trap?" she prompted.

Dar and I looked at each other, both lost. Where the fuck was she going with this?

"Uh, about fifty years ago it was Cairo, but they usually move them every decade or so and I haven't kept up. It's not like I'd ever be seven–thousand feet up on a mountain in the middle of a remote elven kingdom to use the fucking thing anyway."

Leethu waved her hand at Dar. "Winner, winner, chicken dinner," she shouted. She'd stayed at my house far too long this winter and had picked up some unfortunate human colloquialisms. "Cairo, then Dar es Salaam, then Harare, and now it's Lagos. It's been there for the last two decades. They've always favored locations on that particular human continent."

Lagos. I wracked my brain with earth geography until I settled on Nigeria. I hadn't been in that part of the world for at least a century, but had fond memories. Who knew that those fat hippos could tear the shit out of a demon? I'd bet on one of them against an angel any day of the week. Those fuckers could fight.

"They've been secretly mating with their humans." Leethu whispered as she leaned in, only to pull back with a mischievous look on her face.

Dar stared, uncomprehending while I sputtered in outrage. "Leethu, that's racist. Just because they look different than their neighbors, doesn't mean they've been forcing the humans to have their offspring!"

"Not forcing." Leethu looked smug. "It's all very hush–hush, but humans there have *rights*. They hold property. They earn wages. And, most importantly, they are not sterilized. They are allowed to form long–term partnerships with each other and some are in consensual relationships with elves. It's not common, but they are allowed to intermarry. They no longer do changeling exchanges, and they've even taken to returning humans that fall through their trap and choose not to remain."

Dar and I could have caught an entire summer's field full of flies with our mouths. No shit. Was this part of the reason they were so reclusive? No other elven kingdom would remotely approve of that sort of thing.

"This might go easier with them than you think," I told Leethu. "If Taullian is able to unite the kingdoms, the humans will have the peninsula of Cyelle as their own. It opens the door to the practices in Kllee being acceptable."

Leethu raised a sexy eyebrow. "Freedom for humans is one thing, Ni–ni, but allowing sexual relationships with them and treating them as the equivalent of consort is another. Plus, Kllee will resist the closing of their gate."

I sighed. Yet another hurdle to overcome. Why were these elves such pains in my ass? "Okay. You get Klee."

She rapped the poker back and forth between two squiggles separated by three shapes. "That leaves Li at the west, and Allwin. Which shall you take, Ni–ni?"

An awkward silence fell, and Dar looked at me with sympathy and sorrow.

"I won't be able to help with this, Leethu. I have another commitment."

I felt the temperature drop at least twenty degrees. Odd. I hadn't known Leethu could do that sort of thing. Slowly, her dark eyes rose to meet mine, full of an unfamiliar anger.

"Ahriman." It felt as if her voice seared through my veins with ice. It made me realize there was far more to Leethu than I ever realized. She raised the poker and smacked it down again near my feet, edging closer to me, one menacing step at a time. It was not an appropriate way to treat the head of her household.

"You're sending us away. What have you done, Ni–ni? What have you done?"

Dar, that unhelpful bastard, jumped in before I could even open my mouth.

"He's not even remotely supportive of this project. She used his name and his influence in this whole elven thing. He's going to be livid when he finds out. She's sending us away to be safe, so he doesn't punish her by hurting those she loves."

Leethu grabbed my face, her eyes meeting mine. Deep in their brown depths, I could see her pride that I cared so much for her and Dar that I could not hide it, and anger that I was choosing to face this alone.

"Ni–ni, he might kill you. What will become of us if you die? You are our anchor." She placed her forehead against mine, and I closed my eyes, feeling her cool scales against my skin. "I did not frivolously pledge my loyalty and my household to you — and neither did Dar. Let us all face this together, and we will be stronger."

I shook my head, feeling the prickle of her little gold scales along my forehead. "There are changes in Hel that I need to assist. I feel that I'm a catalyst, a spark to tinder. If I burn, then so be it. That's my choice. But I will not take you and Dar with me. I'll survive. I'll endure, as long as I know you both are safe."

The succubus released me, blowing an exasperated puff of air into my face. "Can you talk some sense into her, Dar?"

"Nope." He stroked a whisker, a faint smile hovering around his thin lips. "Can't talk sense into an imbecile."

"Good. Glad that's settled." I pulled the poker away from Leethu and walked back to my map in the dust, drawing another set of squiggles in the dirty floor. "The relay device that's keyed to mine is supposed to put me in Feille's private, royal chambers. Now, I've never had the honor of being there, so I don't have any fucking idea how many rooms there are, or what the layout will be. My strategy right now is to pop into some unknown room, then race around like a total idiot until I can find the fucker. Leethu? Any ideas?"

Leethu growled and snatched the poker out of my hand. I was beginning to think that Amber's aggressive tendencies came honestly.

"I've never been in the royal chambers, but most elven high lords have an entire wing warded for their private use." She drew more geometry into the floor, and I saw a faint curl of smoke rise from the poker. Leethu was pissed. It warmed my heart. "There's always a bedchamber with a salon for entertainment, a dressing room full of mirrors and various tables and chairs. A wardrobe is usually attached to the bedroom. I'd suspect there's also a private armory, perhaps a private art collection area, a serenity room for meditation and contemplation. Most high lords have a safe room. He may not be in his private rooms when you arrive, so you'll need to determine which room he uses the most and hope there's an adequate hiding place to ambush him. Always know the location of the safe room. If you're too late, and Taullian attacks, he'll head there."

Leethu was right. Feille was too much of a coward to risk himself in battle. He'd be behind eight circles and wards the moment the first arrow let loose.

"Hopefully Taullian's intelligence will provide his spies with the optimal place to put the relay," I commented. "Otherwise, it's going to be a race against time."

Leethu nodded, putting an arm on my shoulder and sliding her hand down to grip my elbow. "You're lucky, Ni–ni. Always so lucky. The great creator smiles upon you."

I jolted in surprise. I'd never heard any demon refer to a higher power. That was an angel thing. We demons tended to throw our lot in with a more fickle fate than any kind of universal creation power.

"Perhaps it is the great destroyer who favors me," I teased her.

She smiled, a strange knowing smile. "Oh most definitely, but I think the great creator has an affection for you as well."

Hopefully some higher power would send a bit of divine assistance my way because I wasn't sure how I was going to pull any of this off.

~22~

This whole situation kept getting worse and worse. He should be up in Aaru, meditating, trying to center himself and increase his vibration level. Instead, he was here in northern Washington State, seagulls diving all around him in search of bits the fishermen had left behind when they cleaned their catch on the pier. The tang of salt and decay filled his nose. The ocean, her power subdued in this calm inlet, still called to him, making him wish they'd chosen a water creature to bestow the gifts of Aaru upon instead of the humans.

Oak Island — gone, allegedly by a meteor strike. Or a nuclear facility destabilized. He wasn't ruling either one out. It wouldn't be the first time the humans had covered up an alarming disaster by falsifying records and claiming it was a natural occurrence. It was a clandestine nuclear facility that went up, or a campsite taken down by an astrological event. Either way, several humans with magic had died along with the angel. Why Furlac had been there at all was Gabriel's primary concern. Hopefully there would be something, some clue toward Furlac's purpose, his cause of death, and what linked him to Vaol.

Gabriel frowned, squinting up at the heavy clouds. He'd never been quite as good as Uriel in knowing the movements of the universe, but he was fairly certain no meteor, however small, had been on a trajectory with earth during that time period. There were always little bits of things pelting the planet, but nothing large enough to make it through the atmosphere to impact within the last few months, and certainly nothing big enough to destroy an island. Cloaking himself, he unfurled his wings and took to the skies.

The angel left the harbor, heading along the channel and toward the islands ahead, the city of Bellingham at his back. Hugging the edges of the bay, he veered south around the tip of Lumm Island before flying north into the Strait of Georgia. After passing several islands, he dove down, circling where the report had indicated Oak Island had been. It had been a small island, only about half a mile long and a quarter of a mile wide by the report. A lighthouse blinked from the nearest island two miles away, in the early evening light.

Now there was nothing except small waves. No debris, no sediment clouded the water. The dark sea should have been greenish brown in the area, but there was nothing to indicate that an island had ever been there. Gabriel circled around, dropping low to land, his feet skimming the water. Slowing, he pulled his wings in tight. A shaft of sunlight pierced the cloud cover and reflected off their pure white with blinding intensity. The angel paced about on the surface of the sea, trying to find any indication of the small half–mile land mass that had once occupied this space.

Gabriel had a special affinity for water in all its forms. Extending his spirit being, he divided, allowing a second aspect of himself to merge with the water below. Only he and his eldest brother could manage this, a testament to how far their vibration level had progressed.

The seawater welcomed him like an old friend. It teemed with life and death, a complex mixture of mineral and algae swirling in a dance with bacteria and microscopic creatures. Becoming the sea was the closest Gabriel had ever come to divinity, to holding the entire universe in his soul. He'd missed this, forgotten how centering it was. Meditation in Aaru suddenly felt cold and sterile by comparison.

Carefully he examined the water where the island once was and found miniscule bits of debris — sediment, tree bark, rock, and various metals. The quantity was not what he would have expected from a normal explosion, let alone a meteor strike. Reaching further, he tried to piece together a history of the event. The sea had a memory, open to an angel who had the patience and skill to coax it from the depths. It told a perplexing story. There should have been trace elements of iron–nickel alloy, of iridium. Searching deep to the channel floor, he found none of the bits that should have lodged there. Meteors were heavy, most of them over ninety percent iron in an interlocking crystalline structure. One big enough to completely take out an island of this size should have left remains.

And it should have left other damage. The lighthouse two miles away blinked, unharmed. Another nearby island appeared untouched. This was no meteor. The same factors also brought him to doubt a human explosion on the island. He'd seen firsthand how sloppy the human destructive techniques were. The damage to the gate at Novaya Zemlya had been horrific, but the explosion two and a half miles in the air still devastated the island below. Any bomb or blast big enough to reduce an island to bits of dirt would have cracked the lighthouse foundations through and blown the foliage off every tree on neighboring islands. Nothing. They were pristine, yet this island was gone. Which left only one option to consider. Demons.

Gabriel reluctantly left the sea and consolidated his aspect back into human form. There was a reason his eldest brother was so well suited as head Grigori — he was the bearer of the sword. Guardians and enforcers could handle almost every demon that came through the gates, but every now and then a powerful one made the trip. They were generally easy to sense, energy spilling everywhere, destruction and death in their wake. They weren't so easy to kill. And when they died, the raw energy they'd stored within them to fuel their evil burst into being, exploding like a mini nuclear blast. But a localized blast, with strange clear–cut borders. An angel could survive a small blast, but an explosion big enough to take out this island would have easily killed an angel of Furlac's level.

So what was a non–enforcer doing sneaking down from Aaru? Why would he have been at a human research facility, or even a rural campground? He could have been indulging in sinful contact with a human, but Gabriel suspected it was something else. But what? The humans had hundreds of thousands of scientific endeavors. Demons often busied themselves in all types of nefarious industries. Could this have been one? Maybe Furlac's connection with Vaol had been innocent, and by coincidence he had found himself in a deadly fight with a demon right after his friend had lost his life to another.

Spreading his snowy wings, Gabriel once again rose to the air and headed back to the port, determined to find some answers. He just didn't have an adequate level of knowledge concerning human businesses. For the information he needed, he'd have to converse with them. He shuddered. Humans. He'd spent hundreds of years avoiding contact with them, but he had no choice if he wanted to get to the bottom of this. Still cloaked, the angel circled about the pier, dropping down next to a building that separated the dock area from the parking lot. Huge glass windows overlooked the bobbing boats in their slips, and a large man, shirt straining at the buttons, sat inside, appearing bored as he leafed through magazines and cast occasional glances up at a television.

Taking a deep breath, Gabriel extended himself further into his corporeal form, feeling the overwhelming pain of sensation flood through him. The smells of the seaport town increased a million fold; the colors became blindingly brilliant, the sounds deafening. It took him a moment to process it all and regain control. Staggering from the onslaught, he put his hand against the metal railing, only to recoil from the touch — cold metal, chips of bright green paint covering the gray. He'd have to remember to try not to touch anything ...or anyone. That sensation — skin on skin, was the most difficult of all to handle.

Walking slowly, he made his way to the marina office, wincing at the merry jingle of the bell over the door as he entered. The man at the counter looked up, a smile on his round face.

"Can I help you?"

Gabriel relaxed, walking toward the man. He hadn't lost his touch. It had been so long since he'd made himself visible to the humans. Centuries ago he had walked among them, indistinguishable from any other human. His siblings stood out, but Gabriel had been able to blend in, communicating without the adoring reaction the other angels caused. It had been a source of pride — something normally only the Angels of Chaos could do. But it had been so long. He had hoped to never do this again, but he couldn't just let two angels die under mysterious circumstances without doing all within his power to investigate. That was his responsibility as a member of the Ruling Council, as an Angel of Order.

"I've got a question about the island that exploded. Oak Island, I believe it was called?"

The man shook his head, jowls swaying, eyes grieving. "Shame that was. Nice little island. One of the smaller ones and not as popular as the others. Never thought it would have gotten taken out by a meteor. Thing sent waves flooding all across the area. They felt it all the way up in Ketchikan."

Meteor. A millennium ago and they would have blamed it on some vengeful god. Not that they would have been far off, if the cause of the explosion was what he suspected.

"Did the scientists see the meteor coming?"

Again the jowls swung from side to side, the man's bulldog eyes widening with the seriousness of the topic. "Nope. Took everyone by surprise. Course, some are thinking it wasn't a meteor after all but some secret underground government facility that exploded."

"Either way, it's rather frightening that that sort of thing would happen with no advanced warning at all. The loss of life must have been terrible."

The man's head tilted, his mouth pursed. "Well, no, unless you count a few campers. Not many people normally there."

Gabriel frowned in confusion. His brother had said that there had been two dozen humans present as well as the angel when the catastrophe had occurred.

"Skip really lucked out. He usually takes those corporate folks out there for their team building retreats." The man's sour face clearly indicated his feelings for said "team building" exercises. "There hadn't been any for a week or so. Last trip he made out was with that woman a few days before the whole thing blew."

Maybe instead of a hidden nuclear facility, it *had* just been a campground rented out to a human company for their summer group sessions. Lesser demons did like to terrorize campers. Perhaps a major one had decided to get in on the fun and had been caught in the act by an angel who hadn't, in good conscience, been able to turn his back on the slaughter of innocents.

Gabriel turned to leave, but the man continued on, clearly desperate for any kind of conversation, no matter how one–sided.

"That woman was really eager to get out there. Had some plane to catch and was trying to get someone to take her out right away — just an out and back. Told her everyone was done for the night, but that Skip could run her out in the morning. Was really surprised when he said she was staying. She didn't have any camping equipment or nothing. Thought she was eager to get home. Sad. She's dead now. Blowed up along with the island."

The angel shook his head. It was folly to keep pursuing this. It was a demon. An angel had come down, probably tempted into a sinful activity, and had died killing a demon.

Regardless of his sin, his noble death would wash that clean. He'd move on to the thousands of other reports and matters awaiting his attention. He had other things to do.

But he couldn't let it go. There was too much "what if", too much unknown and he'd never be able to find his center with these questions unanswered.

"Is Skip around?" He interrupted the man, who was going on about the other islands and their superiority in camping facilities to the ill–fated Oak Island.

"Yeah. Third pier, fourth boat on the right."

Skip was relaxing on his boat drinking a beer. He pulled his mirrored shades off and got to his feet as Gabriel approached.

"What can you tell me about Oak Island? The man in that office said you were ferrying groups for a corporate retreat? That you took a woman out a few days before it exploded?"

Skip shifted his feet and carefully put his sunglasses back on. "Yep. Shame. I made a lot of money taking those folks out. They were camping and stuff."

"But the woman had no gear, and she went out alone. Was she the only one on the island that you were aware of?"

It was a warm day, but not warm enough for the beads of sweat forming on the man's forehead.

"Think she met someone there. I'm not the only one who hires out for these kinds of things. Might have been a group there. I don't know."

He was lying. It spiraled from him like fog, dimming his aura. He'd tried to cover it up with an answer that wasn't quite an answer, but the lie clung to him, thick and dark.

"Was she with any other person either on or off the boat?"

Skip fiddled with his beer bottle, taking a quick sip. "I took two other guys out with her, and they all stayed," he admitted.

"When were you supposed to pick them up? How long did these groups usually stay?"

Again Skip raised the beer bottle to his lips, only to find it empty. "I don't bring em back. I never do. Figure someone else does that."

Gabriel watched Skip toss the empty into a bucket and pull another beer from a cooler. He declined when the man offered one. Reading thoughts wasn't one of his strengths, but he could often gather bits and pieces if a human was particularly emotional. Skip was extremely emotional. He felt uncomfortable about what these corporate groups were doing on the island. It wasn't any of his business, but it seemed kind of cult–like and kinky. He knew all the boaters in this area and no one was bringing these people back. Gabriel had a sudden flash of vision from Skip's mind, a mass grave, bodies on the ground. It wasn't his business. None of his business.

So not a research facility, nor a corporate teambuilding retreat either. Some kind of weird death cult. Gabriel again felt a wave of revulsion. Just the sort of thing a demon would do. But this man was almost as bad, turning a blind eye on the whole thing. The angel let a bit of his human mask slip, let his spirit shine out toward the man and filled his words with compulsion.

"It was your business. Tell me the truth of what happened."

Skip dropped his full bottle of beer to the deck of the boat and shook with fear. "Charters are down and it was good money. I didn't suspect anything at first, just thought it was some weird religious group, but the woman ...I left her there. Left her."

He paused for a moment, trying to get himself under control, and Gabriel eyed him with loathing. This man's sins were not his to forgive. Humans were horrible creatures. Every second he spent among them confirmed it.

"She didn't go quiet. All the others were subdued and kind of obedient, but when we got to the island, they slapped one of those collars on her and she went crazy. Sucker punched the one guy, fought like she was possessed. Never seen a woman fight quite like that. Like she didn't care if she got hurt, like she enjoyed it."

"And you left her there. You didn't help her defend herself, didn't call the authorities. You just left her there."

Skip winced. "She took off into the woods, and they ran after her. I got the heck outa there. I was scared. I didn't want them to do that to me. Two days later the whole place blows sky high. I haven't seen those guys since, so I'm guessing they went up with the island. Good thing I wasn't there when that meteor hit."

Yes, good thing indeed, Gabriel thought, a feeling of revulsion rolling through him. This man turned a blind eye to dozens of people possibly meeting their doom on this island. That was bad enough, but here he walked away from a woman, assaulted and running for her life. He never even reported it to the police. Gabriel looked into the man's heart, and what he saw disgusted him even more. Beyond his fear of being punished, Skip felt little remorse. He'd not lost any sleep over a woman who may have been raped and murdered while he just turned his boat around and left. At that moment, he wished he were a demon so he could curse the man, but instead he could only walk away and trust in a just universe to provide a measure of karma. Where was the Iblis when he needed her? This was her job, four–nine–five report notwithstanding.

"Her car's over there. The rental place from the airport in Seattle still hasn't come to pick it up. It's been months. You'd think they'd want it back."

"Which one," Gabriel asked. He might as well see if there was something to indicate who the woman had been. Perhaps he could make some token gesture to her loved ones, ease their pain like he used to so long ago.

"The red Focus. It's locked, though."

Gabriel left the dock and strode toward the car, surprised to see an angel waiting for him at the end of the dock. She stood patiently, wings hidden, her golden–brown hair blown about by the sea breeze. She clenched her hands before her and dropped briefly in respect, waiting to be addressed.

"Asta. Is there a problem? I had not expected to see you again so soon."

She lifted her eyes to his and he saw the indecision there.

"Ancient One, I have a moral dilemma concerning the task you have assigned to me."

Gabriel waited while the younger angel gathered her courage. A moral dilemma? Had there been conflicting orders between him and his brother?

"The demon essence I delivered …it's not what I thought. I can tell, and these aren't small donated portions — they are entire demons, chopped up and stuffed into vials." Her words choked, her voice full of disgust.

Gabriel curled his lip. Demons were a violent bunch. It was horrific that they would slaughter one another for monetary gain, but that's how they were.

"Demons kill each other all the time," he told her gently. "I was informed the supply was a donation, but I'm not surprised those creatures would do such a thing. What happens beyond the gates to Hel is not something we can control."

She shook her head. "I've seen the worst demons can do, but this turns my stomach. It's wrong for us to profit from their evil. Wrong."

He couldn't force her to do something she found morally repugnant. Gabriel would never do that to one of his angels. "Asta, I appreciate you bringing this to my attention. Don't worry about continuing with the project. I understand your feelings on the matter."

Her shoulders sagged with relief, and she looked back up at him. "There's more. I had some conversation with the gate guardian in Seattle where I picked up the supply. Before I was assigned to this task, Furlac was the angel acting as an intermediary."

Furlac. He did seem to get around. Before his death, that was. Gabriel frowned.

Asta continued. "And he wasn't couriering little vials either. The gate guardian spied on him once and saw what he was doing. He allowed groups of demons to come through the gate. They'd go off with one demon, and he would stay behind to speak with the other before leaving." Asta waved her hands in agitation. "They were bringing the demons across the gates, participating in the harvesting of their spirit–selves right here among the humans. The killings may fall under a gray area of the law, as the demons were this side of the gates in violation of the treaty, but Furlac *assisted* their crossing!"

"That is troublesome indeed," Gabriel said when she paused, obviously wanting some confirmation on his part that he, too, found this shocking and reprehensible.

"Contracting for another to commit a crime is still a crime," she insisted, her voice strong. "The slaughter of demons aside, their organizing and facilitating a crossing of the gates is a direct violation of the treaty on our part."

She was right, and Gabriel felt a chill snake through him. If Tura's organization was capable of this, what other unsavory things, what other violations of angelic law was he unaware of?

"I dread asking you this, Asta. Can you manage to continue with this project of mine? If your moral sensibilities will not allow it, I'll understand. I would appreciate any intelligence your sharp eyes can find."

She swallowed hard and nodded. "I will continue, my Sovereign."

He thanked her then turned his attention to the dusty, red Ford Focus as she vanished. The car looked like it had been sitting for more than a few months. Gabriel brushed the grime from the handle and easily unlocked to door to examine the interior.

Inside, the car smelled of heat, vinyl, and lemon air freshener. There was nothing on the seats that would reveal anything about the woman who rented it, nor was there anything in the small trunk beyond some neatly boxed repair tools. Gabriel was about to lock the door and move on when he felt the pull of something under one of the seats. It tingled of electricity with a strange, fresh note he hadn't felt in hundreds of years. Magic. Elven magic with that odd twist that humans gave to it. The angel bent down and ran his hand under the seat, pulling out a notebook, a folded leather square, and a ring.

Putting the other objects on the seat, he examined the source of magic — the ring. It was gold alloy with an inscribed onyx stone. The stone itself was the source of the power, the gold just a setting for ease of transport on a human finger. The inscribed "X" and inverted triangle sealed the magic, holding it at bay until the wearer activated it in some fashion. Next, he picked up the notebook, paging through the columns of numbers and notations. He paused in surprise to see two angelic sigils. Furlac and Vaol. Anger built deep inside him as he saw other pages, clearly marked with unknown demon sigils. Tura might be dealing with elves and humans, but if Asta were correct, he and his group had dealt directly with demons. He waved a hand and carefully stored both the ring and log book before picking up the folded leather square.

It held human money, some square plastic cards with a magnetized strip, and an identification card. Gabriel turned it over, mildly interested to see who this woman was that had been in possession of a magical ring and damning evidence of angel and demon collusion. Familiar brown eyes met his from the picture and he nearly dropped the small rectangle. The picture seemed to be of an attractive human woman, but he knew this was no human. It was the Iblis.

~23~

There was a storm brewing, and that sort of synergy always made me nervous.

I would leave at dawn. Dar and thirty two of my household had already started toward the Wythyn border. We'd debated the visibility of a large group of demons tromping across the desert and through Dis verses the questionable wisdom of splitting into smaller groups. I had no stable leader besides Dar. With smaller groups, there was a strong possibility over half of them would get sidetracked and never make it to their destination. We wound up choosing the big–group approach, hoping anyone who saw would just assume they were a rowdy band of partiers, working their way through the demon cities in search of fun.

Leethu had left too, with her five handpicked assistants. I'd barely recognized her. She Owned no elves, but had somehow managed to pull off a very convincing young male. The five demons posed as her human servants. Only dignitaries traveled with that many servants, and they would have had to be a highborn clan to afford to send them out with a single elf. The succubus had the whole thing worked out, including somehow securing a party invitation to Feille's palace. I would have fucked the whole thing up within five minutes of walking through the gate, but Leethu lived for this sort of thing. Her eyes sparkled with anticipation as she carefully hid the potions.

"You'd make a good drug mule," I had told her. She would too. I was amazed she could squeeze that many vials into various orifices. I hoped they didn't break in transit.

Gareth hadn't been able to procure everything I wanted. Thankfully I had all five non–detection spells, since Leethu's assistants weren't as skilled as she was in hiding their demon natures. The phantom hands garrote was within Leethu's elven man–bag, and I had my chicken wand strapped to my leg, hidden by my pants.

The rest concerned me. Six instead of twelve snare nets, only three of them bladed, which meant we might not be able to capture and kill all the elves chasing Dar's team. Ten paralyzation potions meant we had to concentrate it in specific foods and drinks instead of a widespread application in the water supply. That also ratcheted up the danger for Leethu's team, who would need to manage to slip them into beverages and foods practically under the nose of the intended victims.

Worse yet, we only had thirty slippery skin amulets for forty demons. I declined one, as did Leethu and Dar. Leethu felt her team wouldn't need them as much as Dar's, but it still left thirty amulets for thirty–two demons. They drew straws, and I felt sick thinking of the two demons, both Low, who got the short straws. The amulets wouldn't protect against everything, but they would help the demons shrug off nets and numbing arrows. A good blow with a bladed weapon, or head shot with an arrow, and the amulets wouldn't do any good at all. Still, it was like going into a sword fight naked instead of in light leather. I rubbed my chest, worry over my household threatening to overwhelm me.

Storm or not, I needed to get out. I was in an empty house, every creak from the wind reminded me I was here alone, reminded me I'd sent those I was supposed to protect off to their possible deaths.

Wind buffeted my house, unsheltered by any trees. To the north lay the end of the Western Red Forest. To the east, a four–hour hike to Patchine. South, the landscape flattened to sandy plains before merging with the huge desert that encompassed the entire lower third of the landmass. My eyes turned to the west, the place of my childhood. It was still a two-hour hike — maybe longer having to skirt the swamplands, but I could get there before the slow-moving storm hit.

I ended up having to hustle, to turn farther north since my human form didn't navigate the terrain as well as some of my demon ones. If only I could change to my first form and fly, or at least manifest wings on this human one, I could beat the storm, but I was afraid any major form change would land me back into pond scum. I couldn't assassinate Feille as pond scum.

Fat drops of rain had begun to fall, the increased wind threatening a deluge, when I arrived and knocked on the little wooden door. It opened a crack, and a wrinkled face peered out. She'd always reminded me of an apple left in the sun too long.

"Who is it?"

Oh, for fuck sake! It's not like she hadn't sensed me coming. She'd probably known three days ago from her tea leaves or something. Ridiculous old woman.

"It's Niyaz, Oma. May I come in and shelter from the storm?"

The old woman clucked, and the disapproving noise sounded oddly amused. "Don't you dare think such impolite thoughts about me, little dragon. Did your foster parents not teach you manners?"

Warmth bloomed inside me, and I felt at home before I even crossed the threshold. Nothing had changed in over nine-hundred years. The elderly dwarf had the same red-brown, lined face, the same twinkle in her stern gray eyes. Her long, silver braids nearly brushed the floor. Oma always had the most beautiful hair — thick and full. I sighed, looking about the small room, seeing a roaring fire in the stove, table and chairs in the center, and a metal-tipped staff a quick grab away by the door. That thing hurt like fuck. I was convinced she had some kind of spell on it for it to hurt so much. Oma had always insisted on manners and respect and wasn't shy about discipline when it came to the young demons that followed her around as if she were the Pied Piper. I'd been her most devoted shadow for hundreds of years.

"Sit," she ordered, pointing to the table. I noticed one thing had changed. A carved stone ring, which practically covered the joint of her thumb with its width.

"Oma!" I squealed, impulsively hugging the dwarf. "You have wed. Who is he? A younger dwarf? You scoundrel, you."

I felt her cheeks heat up as she pummeled me with her fists, trying to disengage from the inappropriate contact. "His name is Khoar. He's five thousand years old. Now let me go and sit down so I can stir my soup."

Cradle robber. Oma was thirteen thousand. Not that age really mattered to dwarves. Love was love.

The dwarf turned her back on me to stir a bubbling pot, and I sat at the table, in the same spot I'd always chosen as a little imp. The table was scarred from years of carvings and attempts to "fix" the damage by inexperienced, young demons. Oma always left it that way. I got the feeling it was the same thing as hanging children's drawings on a refrigerator door for her.

"Sooo, will this hot young man of yours be home soon? I'd like to meet him."

Oma turned her head and glared at me from under bushy, silver eyebrows. "He won't be above ground for another week. Some of us actually have gainful employment. And I sincerely hope you're not staying long enough to meet him."

Mining involved long stretches of time away. No, Oma would definitely not want me around for that reunion. Even if she'd married a century ago, they'd still be newlyweds, bonking every chance they got.

I watched her ladle soup into a huge stoneware crock and again ran my fingers over the scars on the table. I'd made these so long ago that it felt like a different person had done so. Was that me? It seemed I'd lived several lives since then.

"Eat," Oma commanded, sitting the bowl of soup forcefully on the table and pushing it toward me. It sloshed over the rim, thick and steaming.

Eat me. Her word triggered the memory of Gregory's command. I'd forgotten to try, in all the frenzy of the last two weeks.

"Thanks," I said, picking up a spoon.

She eyed me with upraised eyebrows, surprised at the courteous word from a demon. I took a sip, feeling the liquid burn its way down my throat. It was so much better than the elven food, much better than the food my household had been serving. Spicy. It had a vinegar bite and bits of root vegetables with tiny shreds of meat. Dwarven cooking ruled, and Oma was the best. No wonder she'd scored some boy—toy hottie as a husband.

Oma made a disgruntled sound and turned back to her stove, but I could see her faint smile of pleasure at my eager consumption of the soup. I emptied the bowl, and with a surreptitious look at the dwarf's back, I reached down into my spirit self to explore the red purple of Gregory's energy. It had always been separate and unyielding, resisting any attempts to combine it or remove it from my system. Wrapping myself around it, I let loose the hunger and turned it in upon myself, targeting the angel's spirit that I'd stolen.

Nothing. It was like gnawing on a smooth piece of granite. I didn't even scratch the surface. Once again, I tried to shift the energy, move his spirit and perhaps consolidate it into a more manageable, edible chunk. Unsuccessfully, I once again tried to "eat" the red—purple, to devour it, but the angel essence resisted my efforts.

"Niyaz, what are you doing?" Oma's stern voice jolted me back to reality.

"Uhh, nothing." Fuck this was embarrassing. It was like being caught masturbating by my grandmother.

"You are too old to be playing with yourself. You're not a baby anymore. You've eaten, now get out there and go home. You've got things to do beyond hiding out in an old woman's house, eating her dinner."

"But the storm...." I protested, sounding like a much younger version of myself.

"There's always a storm around you, Niyaz. I would have thought you'd be used to it by now."

I hesitated, looking at the door then at the dwarf. It wasn't just the storm, I needed guidance, and who was more knowledgeable than a thirteen thousand year old dwarf?

"Oma, I don't know what to do. I'm broken and damaged; I've made a commitment to a high level demon that I regret, and I can no longer meet my end of the contract. I've put my entire household at risk to protect demons who'd just as soon see me dead as thank me, and to provide freedom for a bunch of slaves that may not even want it."

She nodded, waving her spoon in a circular motion. "And?"

"And I have deep feelings for a household of humans and werewolves on the other side of the gates. I worry about their safety and wellbeing in my absence, and I fear I'll never see them again with their short lifetimes. And ...and ...and I'm in love with an angel."

The spoon hit the ground. Oma stared in amazement. Finally, after nearly one thousand years, I'd managed to surprise her.

"I know! An angel. He was going to kill me, but he bound me and things heated up from there. We're not bound anymore, but I miss him."

Oma picked up her spoon and composed herself. "Niyaz, of all your sibling group, you were my favorite. Even more than that little rat friend of yours. Ask. You didn't come here to admire your childish artwork and eat my soup. Ask."

"How can I succeed at all this? I'm broken, facing tasks far beyond my skills and abilities. I humbly ask for your help, Oma."

Dwarven assistance could come in many shapes and forms. Sometimes it was advice, sometimes it was a tool or item, sometimes a gift of skill or physical assistance in a task. More often than not, a request for help was refused. Dwarves were big on self–determination — they didn't often provide assistance and never offered.

Oma walked to the table and picked up my bowl, peering nearsightedly into the bottom. With a horrible noise deep in her throat, the dwarf spat into the bowl, holding it away from her face to observe the new contents. I held back a gag of revulsion. I might be a demon, but that was just gross.

The expressions dancing their way across Oma's face were amazing. She frowned, pursed her lips, barked out a laugh then paled in concern.

"What? What?" I urged, dying to know what she was divining in her loogy.

"Hush." She waggled her eyebrows, shoving her face even nearer the bowl's center. I had a sudden gruesome vision of her eating the contents. I'd hurl if she did that. Fuck, I was ready to hurl just thinking about it.

"Be an imp," she announced, turning around to set the bowl into a washbasin.

That was it? 'Be an imp?' What the fuck did that mean? "Oma, I am very grateful for your guidance, but can you be more specific?"

She spun about, clearly irritated that I was still in the room. "Niyaz, because I am entertained by the visions of your future antics, I'll tell you more. Your household is bigger than you think. Cultivate the angelic virtues of trust and patience. But most importantly, be an imp."

Walking to the door, she grabbed the metal–tipped staff with one hand and flung open the door with the other. "Now, get out of here before I beat you."

Wind tore through the door, the first big drops of rain blowing in over the threshold. I smiled and darted through to the night, avoiding the swing of Oma's staff. Just like old times.

~24~

The cold bore through clothing and flesh down to bone. It wasn't as frigid here as in some places since there was a rather limited range to earth's surface temperatures at the moment. Sill, a human physical body felt these things rather keenly, even if an angel held himself as distant as possible from the flesh. With a flash of guilt, Gabriel edged his spirit–being down farther into the nerve endings of his form to better experience the sharp ache. Yes, bone–chilling was an accurate term for this temperature.

Looking ahead he saw an angel's wings, blending in with white snow, except for the pattern of gray scarring, like a starburst along their width. There had always been gray along the tips, darkest at the long flight feathers, but it was the scarring that stood out. Gabriel looked down at his own stark, white wings, invisible against the landscape, and felt a wash of remorse. He'd always been a messenger, not a fighter, but his brother's injuries when compared to his lack always filled him with a sense of regret. If he'd been there, would things have been different? Would Samael and the other angels have remained in Aaru?

The other angel shifted on his perch and the three sets of wings parted, revealing a vaguely human form with dark, reddish–brown curls. The warmth of his brother's power hit Gabriel like a thousand suns, making him smile with remembrance. He'd always been a spirit of water, of ice, but even here, surrounded by his favorite element, he was outclassed.

Gabriel glided toward him, leaving no footprints in the white. Halting before the still seated angel, he snatched a large, bound document out of the ether and presented it to him.

"Close the gates. The major seven and all minor ones. Close them all."

His brother chose to ignore the dramatic statement, words that had not been spoken since the creation of the passageways nearly three million years ago. Instead, he frowned at the document in his hands, turning it over to examine it from all sides.

"A four–nine–five report? Surely you must have retrieved the incorrect form. I've not had the pleasure of seeing one of these from you in a millennia or more."

"It was an accident," Gabriel lied. "The human man was drunk, fell off his boat and drowned. I neglected to save him."

The older angel looked up from the report, his eyebrows raised in skeptical amusement. "Always such a stickler for the rules, Gabriel. Other angels would not feel the need to complete a report under circumstances such as you described. Are you sure you didn't push him? Perhaps spike his beverage with something sleep–inducing?"

Gabriel waved the question away, irritation like a burr in his mid–section. No one knew how to annoy him like this brother. At least, no one since Samael had left.

"This human is of no matter. Close the gates."

"Oh, I beg to differ. Just look at this impact study, which is very thorough, by the way. I commend you on the level of detail here. This report warrants additional analysis, perhaps a secondary level, just to ensure we're not missing anything here."

"Forget about the stupid human," Gabriel exploded. "You need to close the gates."

A burst of flame hit the younger angel, but he held fast, neutralizing it with his opposing element. He'd not be able to hold out against a serious attack from his brother, but these little reminders of their respective positions were easy to shrug off.

"I *need* to do nothing," the older angel replied, sweeping his lower wings along the snow in an "S". "And I will not forget about the 'stupid human'. You will subject this report to the same process and procedure as all other four–nine–five reports. The man's soul cries out for fairness in judgment."

Normally Gabriel *was* a stickler for the rules. The irony of having his brother be the one insisting on due process wasn't lost on him. Process and procedure were there to ensure fairness and balance, but in a time of crisis, all that could wait.

"He's dead. It's not our job to weigh his soul. If the Ruling Council as a whole wants more detail, then I'll deliver more detail. Until then, we have more pressing matters at hand."

The cream–colored wings with their spiderwebs of gray whispered against the ground as they traced patterns in the snow. "Dearest brother, please enlighten me as to these pressing matters that require me to close the gates to Hel — something that has never before been done."

Gabriel felt everything inside himself ice over. This was the only brother that could make him feel small with one look, with a handful of words. An ancient, powerful archangel, a member of the Ruling Council, and he was instantly reduced to a small boy who could do nothing right, who lacked the speed and strength in his ice–white wings to keep up with the older two, but who was too old for the baby games of Rafi and Sam. An angel in the middle.

"There is a group of angels that have devised a method to bring about creation without unholy contact with demons, but they sin greatly and break the terms of our treaty with the demons."

Gabriel waited, but his brother didn't seem particularly surprised, let alone alarmed. Fury boiled inside him at the unemotional response.

"Furlac and Vaol, they were involved in this. If you had bothered to do a decent investigation, you would have known. If your Grigori had been doing what they were supposed to be doing, then these unforgivable violations of angelic law would never have occurred."

"I know."

He knew? He knew? Why in all of creation hadn't he put it in the reports? Why? The fury spilled over, and Gabriel saw red. His brother had never had his degree of moral certainty, but this was unforgivable. So Gabriel did what he always did, struck where it would hurt the most.

With a flick of his hand he tossed a small plastic card to the ground. It slid across the snow. His brother tensed as he looked down at the picture on the license.

"She was there. That's why she was injured so badly. She killed Furlac, killed an angel, and nearly died in the process."

The elder angel seemed not to hear him as he picked up the card and looked longingly at the picture. "Yes. She and I tracked down the devouring spirit and killed him, but she felt there was more to the situation."

Gabriel watched his brother carefully. "What did you think?"

He shrugged. "Some vigilante angel tangled with the wrong demon and was devoured. At the time, I didn't connect what happened there to any larger plot."

"They sinned, Furlac and Vaol. They were aiding demons to break the treaty and cross the gates. They were killing them and parting them out to use in procreation research. They involved humans in this unlawful plot. *Humans.* Once again, we contributed to the downfall of a species we sought to enlighten."

His brother nodded, running a gentle finger over the license. "Uriel confided in me. She still mourns, my brother, and had hoped Furlac could ease the pain she and so many others suffer. She is repentant. Furlac is dead, and with him the entire scheme. The matter is closed, unless you wish to indict the Iblis in the murder of an angel."

Gabriel winced at his brother's tone. He had no doubt that his pursuit of the matter would widen the chasm between them to unforgivable proportions. "I don't fault the Iblis for her actions. She has a responsibility to ensure the safety of her people, and Furlac broke the law. But the matter is far from closed. You must shut down the gates."

"I appreciate your leniency in regards to my Cockroach's murder of an angel," his brother commented wryly. "But I will not be closing those gates. Now run on back to Aaru to increase your purity and let me deal with all these messy human things."

Gabriel's anger bubbled to the surface. He was nearly four billion years old, and still his brother treated him like a newly formed angel.

"Your inattention to duty nearly cost you the life of your imp. How many more will die while you sulk in grief and ignore the betrayal that occurs right in front of your face?"

He was prepared this time for the explosion of heat that came his way but still struggled to protect both himself and the pristine environment around them from damage.

"You dare to bring her into this? I am fully aware of my failings, as well as the existence of rebellion in my midst. Angels were making deals with demons and elves, involving humans in their treachery, but the matter is over. Furlac is dead, their facility destroyed. Leave this alone and go back to Aaru."

"This goes deeper than Furlac, you thick—headed idiot. You sit here and grieve, and, in the meantime, they continue."

And now he had his brother's interest. The elder angel jerked to face him, his black eyes furious, his corporeal form shimmering with anger. "What do you mean? I've watched carefully, and there are no more large groups of Low demons brought through. I've imposed added scrutiny on any angel outside Aaru who isn't Grigori."

Gabriel winced. No wonder Tura had asked him for assistance in transferring the vials. He felt a wave of guilt that he'd involved Asta. If he hadn't asked her, maybe the project would have died. Or maybe Tura would have found another patron to help him, one with fewer morals than Asta. The information she'd gathered may have never come to light.

"They may no longer be bringing demons through the gates, but they are still bartering for their chopped–up bits and transporting them to Aaru. They are colluding with demons who are selling out their own kind and subjecting them to an unmerciful death. No matter what you do, they'll still find a way around it. You have to shut down the gates."

His brother frowned up at him, perplexed. "Why do you care? They're demons. Don't you wish them all dead? And this is by their own hands, even. I'd think you would find it rather poetic."

Gabriel didn't want them all dead. He thought of Samael, poised on the rim of an active volcano, his wings reddish–orange in the reflected light, daring them to swim in the molten lava. He didn't want them all dead, because somewhere deep inside, he still had hope of a different future than the grim one outlined in that horrible treaty.

"It's wrong. Morally and ethically wrong, whether it's angels doing the slaughter or demons. We cannot sully our wings with such sin. I beg of you, as head of the Grigori, to close the gates. Shut down the gates. Shut off their supply, then find and punish everyone involved."

"And how am I to find them if I close the gates and tip them off?" He waved his hand in emphasis, the heat still flowing from him like a noonday sun. "They will scurry like rodents into little cracks and crevices the moment the light comes on. Temporarily, we will stop them, but the moment the gates are re–opened they will continue."

Gabriel smiled. "I already know who one is. He approached me for assistance in setting up a presentation before the Ruling Council. They are ready to announce their procreation method."

His brother stood, towering over the younger angel. "You're an unlikely ally in this particular project, Gabriel. Since when have you ever been inclined toward creation? Are you sure there isn't some other motive for why they approached you? Something else behind this scheme of theirs?"

Gabriel thought for a moment, taking the questions seriously. He'd put out the word he might be interested through Sidriel, but why had the Ruling Council member even brought the subject up with him? He *was* an unlikely ally in this matter. Had he once again allowed zeal to overshadow common sense? "We should be cautious. Do you believe this project is a front for some other activity?"

"I think they need to bring proof to this meeting. I want to see their creation mechanisms, including how they manage to overcome the problem of formation. We'll address the ethical issues then. And we should hold this meeting here, among the humans. They will be more vulnerable if they plan to attack."

Now that was more like the brother Gabriel knew before the war. "I will let them believe our meeting will be in Aaru until the last moment. Should we use the same place we have held the last few meetings?"

The older angel shook his head. "Another location as an added precaution. Normally I would arrange for some Grigori to be close by, but I honesty am not sure which of them to trust at this point. Circumstances lead me to believe quite a few may have conflicting loyalties."

Gabriel squirmed, unsure whether that last remark was directed at him or not. "There will be the six most powerful angels in all of Aaru in attendance. I think we can do without additional protection."

His brother nodded, a faint smile quirking up one side of his mouth. "Agreed. But if they show up with a large wooden horse, shoot first and ask questions later."

How a large wooden horse could be a threat was beyond Gabriel, but he would defer to his brother's superior knowledge of the modern human world on this point. "Then you agree to close the gates to Hel?"

The elder angel sighed, looking off into the distance. "I can't. Just in case...."

Gabriel reached an awkward hand toward his brother, pulling it back at the last moment. He knew there was another reason the elder angel did not want the gates closed.

"What if she doesn't live?" he asked as gently as he could. "You would risk the lives of so many, allow this monstrous violation of all that is right and good on the slim chance that she survived, that the demons didn't tear her to shreds the moment her damaged body was discovered?"

"She does live," the older angel insisted. "She has contacted her human, and although she is still injured, she will survive."

"Even if she does live, how could she ever use the gates again? Didn't you banish her?"

The older angel sighed, his wings drooping further onto the ground. "I hope that she somehow overcomes that. She's not like the other demons. Perhaps she can travel through the gates again, even banished. It's not like she hasn't done other, very unexpected, things."

Gabriel winced, remembering that the Iblis devoured. His brother had surely lost his mind, loving a demon that would probably cause the end of all creation.

"What will she think of you if she learns you did nothing to protect her people, made no move to avenge the wrongs against her person? They nearly killed her. My brother, the Angel of Justice, can you ever face her if you let this continue?"

The elder turned a wry smile to his brother. "I think that title has shifted to your shoulders. I'd like the Vengeance one instead."

Gabriel couldn't help the snort that escaped him. "Good luck getting rid of any of your titles. You know you'll just wind up with Vengeance as an addition."

Reddish curls swayed as the angel shook his head. "What's one more? I've already got ...fifty? Or is it sixty?"

"I lost count. Don't ask me to name them, either. I had to write them down on notecards last time."

His brother laughed, a hint of real amusement behind the bitterness. "All right, Gabriel. I will lock down the gates to Hel. All but one. We can surely safeguard one gate, and I need to leave her an option — just in case."

Gabriel stood for a moment, watching his eldest sibling. "I hope . . I hope she finds a way back to you, my brother."

He turned to leave, pausing when his brother spoke. "Thank you, Gabe."

Gabe. It brought back a flood of childhood memories, of when they fought and played together, closer than any five angels could be, a time before they were saddled with titles, before envy, pride, and greed scarred their love for each other and wrenched them apart. Back then, he was just Gabe.

He turned and met his brother's black eyes, feeling the love and admiration he'd once had when he was young. "You're welcome, Micha."

~25~

The elves had planned to attack at breakfast. It was a clever strategy. Most of their stealth attacks happened in the dark of night, which was an odd choice given their amazing night vision. Coordinated battles — usually feuds and large-scale settling of disagreements — happened during the day. Feille would realize the instability of his new kingdoms and the inevitable resistance. He'd be braced for battle at dark and dawn especially, but not in the middle of the morning meal. Elves were creatures of habit, and respect for dining hours, holy moments, and festivals was ingrained into their culture. Attacking a kingdom as they ate muffins and dried fruit was unthinkable.

So I had from dawn until breakfast to make my move. It was a tight window. Feille would have the utmost security about his person as he slept, but as all elves, he would be up with the sun. That's when I needed to find him, somewhere between bed and royal breakfast room. I patted down my various weapons, so unusual for a demon to be carrying, and contemplated my list of likely spots to find my victim. Bath? Wardrobe? Contemplation room? Or maybe he was an early morning, wake-up sex kinda guy.

Letting out a breath, I looked at the twig I held in my hand. At the other end would be the relay, an exact replica of this twig with opposing spell components burned unnoticeably into the end during a complicated incantation. I had no idea how Kirby had managed to do this to his marble, but it was impressive. I ran my finger along the twig and felt nothing. Even to a demon, it appeared to be just a small stick. I hoped the elves hadn't found it and tossed it out into the woods or I'd be in deep shit.

Ly—swiciall.

Unlike the elven buttons, this transportation gave me the same vertigo I got when Gregory moved me from place to place. Blinking to clear my eyes of swirls and stars, I felt myself on my side, laying on a cold, hard surface. As I went to sit up, I smacked my head on something and heard a bump and crash — so much for stealth.

The room swam into view. I'd transported myself to a hallway, underneath a table. The crash was some kind of pottery item that now lay in tiny pieces all over a shiny marble floor. Frantic, I looked around for somewhere to hide, diving through the nearest door as I heard footsteps from the hall.

The footsteps quickened. Whoever it was, they must have seen the broken vase, lamp, or whatever the fuck was on the floor. They halted, and I heard a gasp. It must have been one hell of a gasp because I was in a tiny closet–sized room that was stuffed full of hanging fabric things. Draperies? Tapestries? They smelled clean but old, and I was getting hot, wedged in among them.

"Oh no, oh no," a voice cried. "His Lordship will be furious."

Hopefully his lordship would be dead in an hour, so any fury would be short lived.

I heard clinking sounds, and a brushing noise, presumably this servant cleaning up the broken stuff. It better not take long. It would really suck if I was still trapped in a closet, hiding, when Taullian attacked. I'd never be able to find Feille in time. The soft sound of crying reached my ears and I couldn't help myself. I opened the door just a crack and looked out to see a boy, barely ten, on his hands and knees sweeping the broken bits into a piece of cloth. Judging by his naked chest, I assumed it was his shirt. A tear slid down his nose and onto the floor.

"Hey, it's okay. Don't worry." Stupid, I know, but I couldn't help myself from reassuring the poor child.

He jumped, cutting off his scream with a palm to his mouth. "Was it you that broke the urn?" he whispered through his fingers.

He clearly thought me one of the human servants. I was wearing a Wythyn style outfit and was relieved to know I could at least still fool the humans into thinking I was one of them.

"Yes," I whispered, coming out of the closet. "Don't cry. You won't be blamed for it."

"But I will." He shuddered. "Why would you take the blame? You'll be killed."

I thought fast. "I've got a secret. Can you keep a secret?"

He nodded, and I pulled the wand from beneath my pant leg. His eyes grew huge when he saw it, and he began to slowly back away.

"Don't worry. It's not one of *those* wands." I swept the birch stick in a series of arcs, ending with something that looked like an exclamation mark.

"Bwak."

The boy grinned at my chicken noise then gasped as a spray of white feathers burst from the end of the wand to land squawking on the floor.

"Run and tell the housekeeper that some idiot has let a chicken in and it's trashing this room." He nodded and began to leave. "Wait. Where is his lordship's royal chambers? I'm ...a bit lost."

He gave me a puzzled look. "Down that hall, through the third archway. But he's not there. He skipped his devotionals and went to pay a surprise visit to the guards. Well, it was supposed to be a surprise, but everyone knew it was coming."

Fuck! Double fuck! I could hardly assassinate him surrounded by his troops, and now Taullian would face an army alert and ready due to Feille's paranoia. On the other hand, although I didn't know much about elven religion, skipping morning prayers couldn't be a good thing. Hopefully his goddess would turn her smile on some other, more deserving elf today.

The boy raced off. The chicken strutted around, occasionally pecking the marble floor, and I sped down a long hallway, counting archways as I went. My hope now was to find Feille's safe room and lay in wait for him. I hoped my assessment of his character ran true, and that at the first sign of battle, he took off for shelter, leaving his sorcerers and generals to do his dirty work. Otherwise, I would have risked the lives of my entire household for nothing.

I slid as I ran on the marble floors. They were polished to high gloss, golden brown, with cream and black inlaid patterns. The walls served as a backdrop — a lighter brown with faint fleckings of gold. Artificial skylights and windows lit the room, focusing all attention onto the beautiful floors. It was an odd arrangement for an elf to have in his palace. Usually all the attention was directed upward, toward the light, intricate foliage, sculpture, or artwork. This drawing of the eye toward the floor and the encouraged appreciation for the stone below gave me the idea that the designer had been a dwarf. Not what I'd expected of Feille. Perhaps one of his ancestors had commissioned this design, and he'd not had the time or inclination to change it.

It took a while to get to the third archway. This had to have been the longest hallway in all the elven kingdoms. Wondering how close to the breakfast hour we were, I dashed through the archway and down another length of hall — this one more in keeping with elven tastes. Thick vines covered the walls, giving the impression of being in a secret garden. Morning glories of white and blue were open, along with orange trumpet flowers, giving me hope that I still had a few moments until Taullian's attack. The hallway stretched nearly fifty yards, yet when I skidded to a stop at the end, I hadn't seen even one door. Had the little boy led me astray? How could there be such a long hallway with a dead end? There had to be a secret door somewhere. Fucking elves. I had no time for this bullshit.

I was ripping out vines and patting the walls behind them when to my left, an elf materialized from the wall. An illusion. I would have spent half the day looking for the thing if he hadn't appeared. Of course, now that he had appeared, I was totally busted.

"What in the name of the Goddess are you doing?" he barked, striding over to me and grabbing me by the ear.

I squealed like a human and cowered. "Sorry! Sorry! They told me there was a chicken up here, and I needed to get it."

His eyes bugged out. "In the vines? What would a chicken be doing in the vines, or in the palace at all? You stupid, incompetent, worthless human. I'll have your ears removed for this. I'll have you whipped at the stake and left in the sun for two days. I'll have you buried in a hole in the forest."

As a demon, that all sounded mighty fun, but for a human, the threat would be terrifying. Anger surged up inside me, furious that they would do this sort of thing as punishment for such a paltry mistake. I wanted to tear the ribs from this elf one at a time as he screamed in pain, pull chunks of his brain out his nose, tie him in the desert for the sand snakes to slowly devour, but that wouldn't help me kill Feille, and it sure as fuck wouldn't help the humans.

"Sorry! So sorry!" I wailed. The elf drew back a fist to punch me but paused as the sound of frantic squawking and flapping came from behind him. He turned to look down the hall and saw a blur of white feathers being chased by two elves through the doorway.

"By the Lady, what is that doing in here?" he shouted, letting go of my ear and racing down the hallway. I could almost hear his thoughts: Feille would string them all up to find a chicken running around his personal quarters.

I took advantage of the distraction and slipped through the shimmering illusion of vine and flowers that led to Feille's chambers. A lavish greeting room met me — plush couches, waterfalls and fountains with aquatic plants floating in them. A flash from the iridescent scales of brightly colored fish and birdsong from the indoor trees completed the vision. It was an idyllic reproduction of a forest retreat, complete with mossy benches and soft grasses underfoot. I raced around the mini forest, desperately searching for a doorway to the private areas and very much aware that I was running out of time.

The sound of alarms echoed through the palace, and I panicked. I'd run out of time. Who knows how many entrances Taullian would have to his safe room. If I didn't find it right now, he'd be behind a dozen salted circles while I was still racing around this damned fake forest.

Taking a deep breath, I closed my eyes and tried to block out the sound of sirens filling my ears. What would Gregory do? WWGD?

A calm filled my mind, the calm of six billion years. Where would Feille sit in this greeting room? The door would be behind him. The safety of his own quarters in his blind spot. Opening my eyes, I looked around and saw a mossy couch, higher than all the others and covered with purple flowers. Behind the couch was a large oak, gnarled and twisted as it rose toward the ceiling far above. As I reached out to touch the oak, it shimmered before my hand, revealing an opening, and beyond that opening, a room.

I raced through it, the sound of sirens pounding through my head. A reception room connected to a private entertainment area, which had both a wardrobe a bath, and a bedroom. The devotional area was off the bedroom, as well as the saferoom. Bingo.

I halted, my feet inches from the threshold, and looked down. A row of runes shimmered along the gilded trim, encircling the door. Carefully, I backtracked and grabbed a chair, throwing it through the doorway. Fifty arrows thudded into it. Then it caught fire. Thankfully, the runes around the doorway vanished in a puff of smoke, hopefully meaning this was a one–charge booby trap. I peeked my head in the door, tensing just in case more knives came my way. None did, but the whole room lit up in a swirling globe of runes. They hummed, rotating in opposing directions around an ornate throne. Idiot. Some fucking panic room this was. Where was the cooler full of beer? The twelve days of dried rations? The extensive library of reading materials? Feille must think whatever threat he would encounter would be over pretty fucking fast. I chuckled, imagining him sitting with his ass in the chair while his country exploded into months–long revolution. He'd be pretty damned hungry and bored by the time he felt safe enough to emerge from his hidey–hole. But where the fuck was he? He should have been here by now, with the chaos of the attack, the absence of a bunch of guards who were chasing demons in the forest, the incapacitation of most of his magical staff with a mysterious paralysis. He should be racing down the hallway right now in a hurry to get behind these runes.

Or not. Something tickled in the back of my mind that Feille would definitely want a saferoom close to his sleeping quarters, but he might be paranoid enough to want a second one closer to the main palace areas, or perhaps even outside. I tore back out into the reception room, frantically trying to think. Would Feille want several entrances to his quarters, or would this one room be it? I weighed the risks of having one escape versus having only one entrance to defend and decided that if there was another entrance, it would be a hidden one. But the silence of the whole area struck me. Feille didn't spend the day in his private quarters; he spent them out and about. At night, the room by his bedroom would suffice. During the day, he'd need something closer.

I smacked my head in frustration. I'd lost my chance. I should have gotten here earlier, before he awoke. I should have taken this fight to him when I realized he wasn't in his quarters, instead of trying to do some kind of wait and ambush. I'd failed. The battle had started, and I had no idea where Feille's other hidey—hole was. I'd lost all opportunity to take him out.

I may have missed my shot at the elven lord, but I sure as heck could make sure the battle turned the way I wanted it to. I raced out of the illusionary doorway and down into the main hall. Just as I rounded the corner, my feet flew out from under me, and I landed ass—hard onto the floor. What the fuck had I slipped on?

Chicken shit.

"Are you okay?"

I looked up from the floor to see the boy from before, a sponge in one hand, a bucket next to him. There was chicken excrement everywhere. Who knew that one chicken could have that much crap and manage to dump it out all over the glorious marble floors of this hallway before being caught.

"You're cleaning the floor while the city is under attack?"

It seemed an odd thing to be doing. He was human, and certainly not old enough to be fighting, but I'd assumed they would have had him caring for wounded, or hiding safely away somewhere.

He shrugged and knelt back down onto the floor, scrubbing the whitish poop around with his sponge. "They're not likely to come here. All the soldiers are outside, and his Lordship is in his sanctuary. Nobody's in here but servants. All the elves who aren't fighters ran and hid."

Leaving their humans behind like abandoned, heavy luggage. Fuckers.

"You wouldn't happen to know where Fe ...I mean, his high lordship's sanctuary is?"

He glanced up at me in curiosity before dropping his eyes back down to the task at hand. "Sure. It's under the gnarled feetig tree garden."

Well, that information was better than nothing, although I had no idea what a feetig tree looked like, where this garden was, or what exactly the boy meant by "under".

"So, like a subterranean room? Or is this a raised garden?"

He laughed, as though I was the stupidest adult he'd ever encountered. "The tunnels. Don't tell me they've never sent you down there? They're under the whole city."

My heart sank. Catacombs, no doubt with all sorts of magical and non–magical traps and many escapes — a labyrinth of underground tunnels. Feille was slyer than I'd ever given him credit for, although these tunnels may have predated his rule, or even his birth.

The boy shuddered. "The rats take over every few weeks, and we have to go down and run them out of their nests. I'm little, so they suit me up, give me a wand, and stuff me down a hole. They can't bite through the suit, but they try."

"Think you can show me this hole? Think I'll fit through it?"

He looked up in surprise, his gaze wandering over my human form. "Probably. Why would you want to go down there? And why would you want to go out of the palace in the middle of a fight?"

I thought of what I could offer the boy for his help, but I had nothing. This whole thing had impoverished me, and I couldn't even trade a favor. I had none of my demon abilities to deliver on it, and I wasn't sure Ahriman would allow me to honor my commitment. All I had was two knives strapped to my calves, hidden by my pants, and a chicken wand. I wasn't giving up my chicken wand.

"If you can show me the hole, tell me how to get through the catacombs to Feille's hiding place, I'll give you this knife."

He sucked in a breath as I pulled it from beneath my pants leg, his eyes growing round as saucers. "Dwarven made! With magical resistance!"

Yes. And I only had two. They were my hope for getting through any magical circles protecting Feille. I'd need multiple knives to pierce multiple circles, but if I couldn't find him, the knives wouldn't do me any good.

The boy jumped to his feet, knocking over the water bucket in his haste to reach for the knife. "Uh–uh," I told him, holding it up out of his reach. "Hole and directions first, then knife."

His eyes narrowed. "The entrance I know is by the kitchen, but the sanctuary is under the gnarled feetig tree garden. You'll need to keep heading west, but there are some places where you'll double back."

"Tell me as we head for the kitchen," I commanded, waving him on to lead. The boy took off, and I raced after him, slipping and sliding on the soiled floor.

"Take the first left, then go for about fifty feet taking the third right."

"Wait, the third right after fifty feet or the third right, which is about fifty feet from my first turn?" I sensed disaster. I sensed I'd be found two thousand years from now, pale and hunched over, my eyesight wasted from the darkness in the tunnels, my body emaciated from existing on bugs and rats for two millennia.

"Third right about fifty feet down the tunnel." He darted through a series of small rooms, and into an unadorned part of the palace, clearly designated for servant use. "You'll go uphill, and the tunnel will turn further right and narrow. There's a portion where you'll have to crawl."

Great. Just fucking great. Cause that's how I wanted to spend my morning, crawling through a dark muddy tunnel wondering where the rats were.

"There's a huge root that comes down, forking the tunnel in two. Take the left fork, then take the fifth left, the eighth right, and the second left."

What the hell? Where was this fucking sanctuary? In the next kingdom?

"You'll begin to see the walls change from dirt to wood. It's the roots from the gnarled feetig trees. They look like striped, glossy wood on the walls. The hallway will seem taller and lighter, with a paved stone floor. The sanctuary is straight ahead."

I frowned. There was no way Feille got there through the kitchens, crawling in the dirt. "There has to be another entrance."

"Well, sure. There are two directly into the sanctuary. There are hundreds into the catacombs."

We'd reached the kitchens, and the boy slowed, looking around in surprise. The kitchen was a huge, long room with two mammoth–sized fireplaces and four stoves. Pots dangled from the ceiling from one end of the room to the other. Three washbasins had an intricate series of tubes and hoses connected to them, and several wands sat alongside the stoves. One pot boiled furiously, another smoked, on the verge of burning. The only two humans in the room were sprawled on the floor, snoring. I hadn't given Leethu any sleep potions. What the heck had happened here?

"Where are the traps to the sanctuary?" I grabbed the nearest wand and turned off the magical fires under the two pots. Safety first. It would really suck to risk everything on freeing a bunch of humans, only to have hundreds of them die in a palace fire.

He grinned. "There are wire traps in the spot where you need to crawl, and spells in place once you get under the tree garden. I don't know what those do since I've always had an amulet on. I've never actually been in the sanctuary. Rats won't go within five feet of the place. Looks pretty though, with all the words on the walls and floor."

Lovely.

"Just how extensive are these catacombs?" I had a bad feeling about this whole thing.

"Huge. They network under the entire city and extend in long underground hallways into the forest. There are lots of entry points, but they're all hidden and magically shielded. Only the elves know where they are." The boy shrugged, his eyes far older than the age his body indicated. "Too well–hidden for a foreign force to use for invasion, but there for any Wythyn agents that need to enter the city unseen. Or leave it."

I took a deep breath. This didn't bode well for Taullian's occupation of Wythyn. It was a good thing Dar would oversee this kingdom instead of the elf lord. Dar was probably better at detecting and heading off any sneak attacks. But that didn't matter right now, because if I couldn't somehow manage to find Feille and end his life, this little rebellion was likely to be short–lived.

The boy went to a small iron door set in a stone wall. It had to have only been three feet high. With a creak, he wrestled it open, letting damp, cool air curl into the kitchen from below. Steps led down from the door into the dark, earthy–smelling world below.

"You'll see the hole. It's wide enough for you to squeeze through, and it's about a three foot drop into the catacombs."

"Thanks." I handed him the knife, grabbing a magical light globe from the shelf beside the door and murmuring the word to set it alight.

The boy snatched the knife from my hand. "Don't you want me to lead you there?"

I looked at him, so young with tangled brown hair in a messy braid at the nape of his neck. His face was still round with youth, his eyes full of curiosity and suspicion. As much as I needed a guide, he was too young to risk his life. It would be best for him to stay here, safe, while cleaning chicken shit off the floor.

"Nope. First left, third right, left at fork, fifth left, eighth right, second left and straight ahead. You find a safe place and stay there until this is all over."

He looked at me, the suspicion growing. "You've got a really good memory for a human."

I grinned, turning to descend the stairs. "That's because I'm not a human."

~26~

The door closed behind me, leaving me in darkness with the faint light of my globe to guide me. Thirty steps down, my feet hit level ground. I squeeze through the hole in the ground off to my left and dropped lightly down, landing easily on the floor. I held the globe up to see a low hallway stretch before me. It was so dark down here; I'd need to go slow, so as not to miss a hallway in my count. I could only see a maximum of five feet in front of me, the tunnel fading to gray as it extended out. I edged forward, seeing my first left.

At least there were no rocks or roots to trip me. The walls were damp packed dirt, with the floor a softer dust over clay. I paced out fifty feet, counting the tunnels to my right and turning on the third, hoping the boy hadn't miscounted, or been unable to tell his left from his right.

A faint, distant sound caught my ear; a soft scurry, and I once again thought of the boy's tale of rats in the tunnels. I had no problem with rats, but they could be a vicious bunch in a pack, and they were fiercely territorial. I didn't want to stumble upon a nest, so I kept my ears sharp for further sounds.

Ducking down to a crawl, I lifted myself carefully over the thin lines of wire that criss—crossed the tunnel every few feet. It took forever, and I was grateful it was only about fifty feet before I saw the fork in the path. The root that marked it seemed more like an underground tree. It was nearly three feet in diameter, its skin brown like peeling paper. I bore left, standing in the taller space. In spite of the spaciousness of this tunnel, I slowed down considerably, scanning the floor, walls, and roof for any additional wire traps.

The first one was ten feet from the fork, stretched a scant inch from the ground. I studied it carefully, now that I wasn't on my belly in a cramped space, and tried to figure out if it would set off any alarms if activated. I desperately wanted to see what it did so I could be better prepared for future ones, but, of course, didn't want to alert anyone that I was in the tunnels. After considering it for a few moments, I decided it best to leave it alone. I was guessing it was wire trigger for knives or arrows as the runes had in the bedroom safe–spot.

It was slow going. I could hear nothing of the battle above me, and I wondered if it still raged or if either side had won. It would suck to go through all this to find Feille had left his sanctuary to congratulate his troops, leaving me empty–handed below ground. I ducked to hands and knees for the length of the tunnel and counted five passageways, and over twenty wire traps, which I thankfully avoided, before I turned left again. The scurrying noise was more frequent, louder, and I had a long hallway with eight passageways to go before my next turn. My heart thudded. Whatever animal was in this tunnel, it sounded solo. Hopefully it was small and weak.

One, two, three, four, five. I saw a shadow dart across my dim beam of light, and I started, jumping instinctively to the right to hug the wall. My foot hit resistance then slid forward. A thwang sounded and I felt a brush of air before pain soared through my backside.

"Ow, motherfucker." I choked the curse out as quietly as I could, managing to retain a grip on the light globe as my other hand reached around behind to feel the arrow shaft protruding from my ass. At least it wasn't poisoned, although I did feel a rather unpleasant burning sensation along with a searing throb.

"Mal? Shit, you sound like a fucking herd of elephants. It's a wonder half the elven troops aren't down here after you."

Dar. He was a great one to talk. I'd heard his shuffling around long before he'd heard me. I yanked on the arrow. It tore painfully, and I was unable to remove it.

"Give me a hand here. I've got an arrow in my ass."

Dar snickered, turning me around to face the wall and bracing himself with a foot on my back. He pulled. My vision went white as the arrow came out.

"Ah, that hurts like a son–of–a–bitch," I whispered.

Dar patted my rear, sending a fresh wave of pain through me. "You'll live. Lucky for you it wasn't barbed, or you'd have half your butt cheek torn out."

I tested to see how well I could walk with my new wound. I could fix it, but it would take me a few hours. Pitiful. "What the fuck are you doing down here? You're supposed to be managing the forest ambush."

"Which was wrapped up hours ago." His tone added the "duh" to the end of his words. "And what the fuck are you doing down here? Did you manage to kill Feille?"

"I'm working on it." Asshole. We stood and stared at each other in the dim light, shifting awkwardly, neither wanting to explain.

"I came to find you," Dar finally admitted, his voice gruff. "I thought you'd be out by now, and when I didn't see you, I worried."

His words sat heavy in the tunnel, the only other sounds our breath against the dirt.

"Feille left his rooms before I got there. He's already holed up in another safe house, under the garden at the end of the tunnels," I admitted, feeling a wash of shame at my failure. "I'm trying to find him and hopefully finish the job before he escapes."

Dar tilted his head to the side, his eyes a bright red in the dark. "The warded room under the gnarled feetig tree garden? You missed the turn about ten feet back."

I sucked in a deep breath and let it out again, but the frustration remained. "I counted. I've got five more hallways to go before tuning right."

Dar brushed passed me, fur against my arm. "Well, yeah if you want to have your head taken off by magical tree roots. Since I doubt you have time for that sort of fun activity, let's take the back way instead."

I followed him, watching the swish of his tail in the faint light of my globe. "How do you know? Did you get a map or something?"

The demon came to an abrupt halt, and I nearly plowed into his back. His nose twitched, and I saw the sheen of his eyes as he cocked his head to the side. "I played in these catacombs growing up. You had your swamps; I had my tunnels. I know them like the back of my paw — all their entrances and exits. I've expanded on the elven tunnels with some of my own. It's how I planned to get into the palace undetected and look for you."

I eyed Dar, a surge of respect and admiration roaring through me. "You rock."

His chest puffed out, his snout lifting slightly. "Damned straight."

And off he ran, me scrambling to keep up with his pace. His eyesight was keen in the dark, and I stumbled around, trying not to lose him and not to fall flat on my face.

"For fuck sake, Mal," he hissed. "Could you try to be a bit quieter? And you stink. When was the last time you bathed? You smell like chicken shit."

I bit back the retort and tried to blindly run through the narrow dirt passageways with greater stealth, my ass throbbing in pain. We took a complicated series of turns, and I was grateful that I had Dar to lead me, otherwise I'd never find my way out of this labyrinth. After a scant few minutes, the tunnel lightened, and I saw a glow from the edge of the hall before us. Dar halted and held out a hand for me to do the same.

"The light is the passageway to the sanctuary," he whispered. "There's always a set of mechanical as well as magical traps along the hallway, in addition to the ones in the rooms. Because of the battle, there are likely to be elven troops posted there."

I grimaced. I had little more than human strength and ability right now — a slightly enhanced human with a dwarven knife and a chicken wand. "Can you scout for me?" I asked Dar.

He wiggled his eyebrows, casting me a playful look before condensing into a small, furred shape. Dar had always been able to convert his form to this particular shape without a lot of show. He stood up on hind legs, twitching whiskers at me before darting down into the lighted hallway.

An alarm sounded. I heard a shout, followed by a relieved, somewhat disgusted noise.

"Rat. Stupid things keep setting off the alarms. I thought the humans cleansed these tunnels last week."

"They did. Disguising things keep coming back quicker and quicker each time. Nothing we do seems to keep them out."

I pressed sideways against the dirt wall and slowly looked around it. Two elves, armed with small swords, stood near a doorway filled with light. They had their backs turned to me, trying to skewer Dar with the tips of the swords. I held back a laugh. Dar was fast. There was no way they were going to get him.

Normally I would have taken advantage of their inattention and blown their heads off, but I lacked my demon powers. All I had to fight these two armed elves was a small dwarven knife and a chicken wand. It wasn't just their swords against my puny knife that concerned me; it was their elven magic too. As a human, I was helpless.

But I was an imp.

Holding the chicken wand in one hand, and the knife in the other, I contemplated my options. The dwarven knife would not only cause a physical wound but would disrupt any magical ability they had for a short period. I doubted I could stab both of them before someone ran me through like a shishkabob, though. Actually, I doubted I could stab one before someone ran me through like a shiskabob, even with the element of surprise on my side. So I slid the knife back into its sheath under my pant leg, and whispered the sound to activate the wand.

I had to stifle a laugh as the elves whirled around, astonished to see three clucking chickens strutting around the subterranean tunnel. The birds paused, jerking their heads from side to side as they contemplated the elves.

"His Lordship! Don't let him see them," one gasped.

They both took off, chasing the chickens around and down the hallway, out of sight. Dar loped past me, transforming to his larger, more upright size as he watched them head further away.

"I'll go take care of those guys. You get Feille."

And how, exactly, was I supposed to do that, I wondered as I looked toward the bright light. I had an arrow wound in my ass, and Feille was most likely in a room surrounded by a rotating globe of runes, if this safe spot was anything like the one in his bedroom.

"There's another entrance to the room," I told Dar. "Can you take care of the guards, find a quick way out and circle around to guard the other door? I wouldn't put it past him to try and bolt."

Dar rolled his beady red eyes. "What am I, fucking Superman? Faster than a speeding bullet, able to kill guards and race through miles of tunnels in seconds?"

I blinked at him, waiting.

"For fuck's sake, Mal. You owe me for this."

"I love you, Dar," I teased as he ran down the hallway, grumbling under his breath.

Then I walked toward the light, wondering in the back of my mind why my chicken trick had worked so well that both guards had abandoned their posts to chase them.

The entrance to the sanctuary was an archway, runes flaring as I drew near. I contemplated using my knife to enter versus using it on the multiple protective circles that I knew surrounded Feille. The circles were the bigger obstacle, but if I couldn't get in the damned room, I'd never even get the chance. I pulled the knife out of the sheath and reversed my grip in a Hollywood–worthy spin.

"I'm coming for you, Feille, you dickless fairy," I proclaimed, plunging the knife into the doorway.

Dwarves have a special skill that makes them ideal foster parents for young demons. They are tough and hardy, difficult to wound or kill ...and they are practically immune to magic. They imbue their weaponry, their dwellings, and their artwork with the same immunity. The silver light from the runes flew toward the knife then fled like children from a plate of mashed turnips. Rather than the dramatic explosion that occurred when demons countered elven magic, the runes withered, shrinking and twisting into faint traces in the wood grain of the doorframe.

I strode into the room and saw Feille, standing majestically before an ornate throne, in the middle of a globe of rotating runes. A salt ring encircled him, three feet from the throne, and he held a jeweled dagger that glowed silver in my presence. He'd covered all his bases.

"Coward," I taunted. "Safe here while your troops are slaughtered."

He lifted his other hand, and a translucent globe appeared. "I am seeing the opposite. Seems your demons have lost the advantage and are being picked off one by one. My troops from Allwin are arriving as we speak. That weak fairy, Taullian, will lose."

"At least that weak fairy is leading his own army. You're hiding in here like a sniveling coward. What do you think your troops think about that?"

He waved a hand and the ball projected an image large enough for me to see. Feille, fighting right alongside his elves. The fucker had some kind of doppelganger to take his place. That was some serious magic, and I hoped it had weakened him a bit. I remembered Feille killing the guard in his dungeons, him causing the magical vines to sprout from the stone floor. No, I really didn't want to meet Feille when he was at full power.

"Doesn't matter. You'll die out there, and you'll die in here."

And hopefully if his doppelganger died, it would weaken him further. I'd take any advantage I could get at this point.

He looked around at the runes and laughed. "And just how are you going to get past this magic, Az? Where is your exploding stick? Has it left you? Found a demon worthier of the title 'Iblis'?"

My breath locked inside my chest, head pounding at his words. I'd never wanted the damned thing, but the thought that it had tossed me aside the moment the going got rough, abandoning me for someone else, sent a wave of fury through me. I was the Iblis. Me.

"I don't need it to take you down." I waved the knife at him, knowing full well that after dismantling the doorway protection, it would never withstand the humming might of magic before me.

"Pig sticker." He shrugged, sitting down in his throne with a dismissive slump. "Fully charged, it might get you past the first layer, but no more. Unless you happen to have a few hundred of those knives glued to your person."

Only one way to find out. I stabbed the knife into the silver swirl and felt a vibration that numbed my arm to the shoulder. The knife sizzled and melted from the tip upward, hitting the ground in a puddle as I dropped it before my hand suffered the same fate. The high lord laughed.

"What now, Az? Can I convince you to throw yourself into the circle? I'd love to watch you burn."

As a demon, I might have attempted it, but with my compromised repair skills, and fragile human form, I wasn't about to risk it. I might be able to live inside a corpse, but a melted blob was probably beyond my skills at the moment. I stalked around the circle, looking for a weak point while Feille continued to mock me. Nothing. He wouldn't have been safer in Fort Knox. He wouldn't have been safer in Aaru.

Be an imp.

Oma's vision. Her words came back to me. Demons might not be able to penetrate a circle, but non–sentient things could. The protective barrier around Wyatt's house last fall had kept out demons and angels, but Haagenti's hit men had been able to throw rocks through it, fling fire through it, and even lightning. Elven circles would resist any demon energy, any attack directly from me, but not things of this world, or the magic of elves. I could spit on him. I could throw bits of dirt and roots at him. And I could lob chickens at him.

The wand was smooth in my hands, a light birch with carvings stained red. A round, black–veined jasper was embedded at the tip. I wasn't sure how many charges it had, but I was about to find out.

Feille jumped to his feet as the first white bird materialized. "What are you doing?"

I threw it through the circle, amused to see it pass unharmed to land gracefully near the throne. Feille jumped on top of his ornate chair as if he'd seen a mouse, and I created another, again launching it into the circle.

"What are you doing?"

The air filled with the soft clucking of contented birds. They seemed happy within the circle, nodding their heads as they strutted about, occasionally pecking at the ground.

"What are you doing? Get them out! Get them away from me!" Feille screamed, standing on his throne and waving his knife at them. He seemed unwilling to get close enough to the fowl to kill them with his knife, and his panic over the harmless, feathered things amused me. No wonder the boy in the palace, and the guards, had been so nervous when they'd seen my chickens. Their high lord had a phobia.

Fifteen birds, and still more came from the wand. Things were getting really cozy within Feille's protected area. The chickens squeezed together, voicing displeasure over the reduced space and rising a few feet above the ground as they squawked and pecked at one another.

Feille shrieked and swung his knife. Blood flew and the chickens panicked, flying about in a calliope of feathered sound. Twenty–five birds. The runes shuddered, the revolving globe of silver slowing, evidently unable to protect so many within their embrace.

"Stupid, worthless slug of a demon," Feille shrieked, killing chickens as fast as I could toss them in. I'd taken to throwing them directly at the high elf, trying desperately to nail him in the head with one.

"Come out and fight, asshole," I shouted, lobbing another bird at his ducking head. "You'll never escape my killer chickens."

Escape. Feille jumped off the throne into two feet of feathered chaos, slashing with his knife as he cleared a path. I dashed around the edge of the protective globe, but weak as it was, it still held solid against me. There was a trap door, and Feille reached it as I stood helpless, fenced from him by a swirling band of silver. Swinging the knife, he launched a bloody chicken at me and laughed as he vanished through the door, safe.

"Son of a bitch," I shouted, spearing the silver globe of runes with the jasper end of the wand. Everything exploded in a flash of silver and I felt myself thrown backwards, rocks and roots creating new injuries adding to my arrow wound. I hit the root—covered wall behind me, shielding my face with my arm as a shower of blood, feather, and bone pummeled against me. By the time I opened my eyes, the room was clear of magic, my wand and the rune circle destroyed, and all the chickens were reduced to a spray of gore.

I raced for the trap door, yanking it open and diving through. The escape hatch was built into the floor of the room, so I'd expected to drop into another underground chamber, but, instead, I found myself stumbling in the sunlight, plowing face first into a gigantic oak tree. The door was a cleverly disguised portal — but to where? I heard the distant sounds of battle and wondered just how far away the escape hatch had put me.

Feille. I looked around, not seeing the high lord. I sucked at tracking. I had no sense of smell beyond that of an allergy—ridden human and had no sixth sense when it came to elven prey. Demons, angels — I could feel their spirit—selves, their leak of energy, even within this human form, but I lacked the skill to do that with elves.

I spun around, looking frantically for some clues. Where would he run? Not toward the battle. Not toward the huge open clearing to my left. There was a massive briar thicket in one direction, which left one logical path. Into the woods, but with a path that would facilitate a run to safety, and no one could run like an elf. I sprinted like the hounds of hell were after me, hoping that fate would smile upon me and let me catch him. Maybe a tree would fall on him, or a landslide, because otherwise, I'd never catch the fucker.

Ahead, I heard a crash, the sound of several explosions, and shouting. In vain, I tried to access my small stash of energy to propel my human legs faster, but it just sputtered around me in useless fits and starts, like a lighter that refused to spark into flame. The explosions increased in volume, drowning out the shouting, then silence. My heart and the crashing of my feet through the underbrush were the only sounds I could hear as I kept running.

I didn't pause at the first body, even though I recognized one of my own household. After the fifth, my anger was a living thing, coiling around me like a snake. Digging deep into my spirit being, I found the small, fragile, scarred part and pulled, demanding it come to life. Faster. Something tore inside me, freeing up. With a burst of energy, I went faster, racing through the forest with a speed an elf would envy.

Another explosion, another shout; this time closer. I ran faster, branches smacking me in the face like whips, briars leaving stripes of red through torn clothing. This time I saw several dead elves next to the dead demons, and I also saw Feille ahead of me, slowing down as he watched cautiously for the enemy. Pulling up every bit of anger and frustration, I launched everything I had at him, searing the forest with a ball of fire.

He felt the heat and dodged, avoiding a direct strike. Still, his embroidered coat caught, and he halted, taking time to rip the burning jacket off. I put on an extra burst of speed and launched myself at him, tackling him with the finesse of a linebacker just as he turned to dash off. I was lucky. A fraction of a second later, and he would have been gone. Elves were all about speed and agility.

I thought the high lord would scream and taunt me, struggle against me as he'd done before, but instead, he raised a hand to my side and whispered a soft word.

Everything seized up inside me. My heart froze; breath in my lungs left in a rush as they collapsed inward. I felt a moment of panic in the face of my death, and as my vision blurred, I saw Feille's triumphant smile. It had to have taken every last bit of magic he had to perform the death spell. That kind of spell didn't come cheap.

"I'd planned to let you suffer, Az, but you've forced my hand. Die knowing that I've won and that I'll see everything you love in ashes if it's the last thing I do."

I was going to die, and although I could live inside a corpse, I wouldn't do much good just lying there, rotting in the forest grass. Some of my conversion skills had returned, and I had no doubt that eventually I'd be able to form a living body again, but it might take days. By then Feille would be long gone.

Keeping my spirit–self distant from the dying flesh, I felt the elf begin to pry my hands from his neck. He laughed, mocking my plight, his eyes a maniacal orange in the reflected light of the fire that leapt from tree to tree.

Fire. My angel's favorite element. I felt the red–purple of his spirit–self within me and remembered the pair of us playing in the forest blaze, creating fireworks, existing inside a flame. I left my body behind, and in that moment of glorious free–fall, where my spirit–self existed in its pure form, I felt as though I had the power of the universe at my fingertips. As if taking a deep breath, I gathered the thick, sweet energy that flowed all around me in Hel, and I created.

Feille shrieked and tossed aside my dead body, frantically rolling as he tried to put out the flame that appeared from nowhere to consume his clothing and blister his skin. I wasn't an ordinary fire, though, and refused to be smothered. As I clung to him, I thought of all the humans he'd killed, callously tortured, murdered; crushing their spirits as he crushed the bodies. Mine. They were mine, and he couldn't have them.

It didn't take long. I lingered against his charred remains, the more traditional flames licking through the trees around me. Feille was dead, but how many of my household still lived? Had Dar made it out of the tunnels? Was Leethu safe within the palace? How many of my Lows had met their end?

"Who the fuck lit off a fireball?"

Dar's voice sounded annoyed. There weren't many demons that could produce the element, and without a launcher, a fireball wouldn't go far. I concentrated, again pulling from the energy around me as I desperately tried to create my human form. It was agonizingly slow. The newly repaired sections of my spirit–self stretched painfully as I demanded far more than they were prepared to give. I felt a shape form, a structure of bone, a branching of nerves and vessels, threads of muscles and skin, and the shock of cold water against my naked body. I was wet — drenching, soaking, near–drowning wet.

"Dar, you ass," I sputtered, spitting water from my mouth and nose, brushing soaked hair from my face to glare at my brother.

"Mal?" He jumped backward, his hands coming up defensively before dropping when he recognized me. "Are you snuggling with an incinerated elven corpse? I'm impressed. That's the sickest thing I've ever seen, even for you."

I scooted off the unrecognizable, blackened body of Feille and motioned toward him. "Got the fucker — no thanks to you. Where were you? So much for my back–up at the escape door."

Dar glared and parted the fur on his arms, showing a mess of bloody scrapes and tiny stab wounds. "The elves were nothing compared to those damned chickens. Meanest motherfuckers I've ever seen in my life. I barely got away with my life."

I laughed. It was a giddy, high–pitched laugh that people get when they're at breaking point, on the edge of insanity. Dar, nearly taken down by a pair of chickens. No wonder Feille had been so afraid of them. But whatever humor the moment provided, it was chased out of my mind as I remembered there were insurmountable tasks ahead of me. Were the elves still fighting? How many of my household remained alive? Would Taullian honor his promise? And just how pissed was Ahriman going to be if he found out?

Dar reached out with furred paws to shake my bare shoulders. "Focus, Mal. We've got bigger problems. Taullian's elves are within the palace gates, but your household has gone mad with blood lust. They're storming the city walls, killing everyone they see, no matter which side they're on."

I pushed his hands away and looked around, trying to judge the direction of the city. "Dar, you ass. You were supposed to be in charge, to keep this from happening. How could you leave your post like this?"

His face tightened, eyes shadowed as he looked at me. I knew my words hurt. Dar took his responsibilities very seriously.

"Mal, you are a broken demon, going up against a powerful elven high lord. The others seemed to be okay. I thought you needed my help more."

We'd always been close. We'd always been there for each other, sometimes causing more harm than good. But as much as I loved my brother and cherished his loyalty, I was beginning to wonder if his protectiveness hid something else.

I sighed, rubbing the end of his damp nose with my knuckles. "Let's go rein them in before they massacre the entire town."

It didn't take long since only six of Dar's troops remained alive of the thirty–two he'd brought in. I felt a wave of nausea course through me at the losses and hoped that Leethu and her five were safely hidden in the depths of the palace. If they'd made it through all this alive, I would have gone from a household of forty to fourteen in one day. My dangerously low funds would still be a problem, but at least I could feed this reduced staff and provide for them a few years before I became destitute. Hopefully, that would give them enough time to find other, more well–funded households.

We'd no sooner corralled my depleted household than an elven officer appeared at the wall, a sorcerer at his side.

"His Lordship, Taullian of Cyelle and the United Elven Kingdoms wishes to speak with the leader of the demon mob, to negotiation their peaceful retreat from the Wythyn lands."

What. The. Fuck. Had we been betrayed? I could see Taullian doing something like this to me, especially after our misunderstanding over the elf/demon hybrid contract, but I couldn't believe he'd pull this crap when he thought I was working on behalf of Ahriman. There was no way he was arrogant and stupid enough to think he could double–cross one of the highest demons in all of Hel.

Unless he had taken it upon himself to contact Ahriman directly. My blood ran cold at the thought. If so, he'd know that Ahriman had not sanctioned this little activity of mine. Ahriman would know that I'd committed him to this mad plan, exceeding the reach of my authority as consort as well as directly going against his orders. Taullian would realize I was acting alone, and that he could fuck me over however he wished. My hopes of covering this up before word got to Ahriman, of minimizing the whole affair, vanished. I wouldn't have to worry about a thousand years under the demon's cruel claw, because I'd be dead. He'd never forgive such an insult.

I exchanged a quick, anxious glance with Dar and stepped forward. "I'll speak with his Lordship."

The gate creaked open, and a guard beckoned me forward. Normally I'd insist on a neutral meeting place, but I figured nothing he could do to me would be worse than what Ahriman was going to do.

"I'll come with you," Dar whispered, stepping to my side. "Who knows what that jerk has in mind. He'll have one of his sorcerers with him; you should be allowed one of your own too."

Dar had a good point, but looking at the eager, barely restrained, six demons around us, I shook my head. "I need you here more. If they all start up again, any negotiations I'm doing will fall apart, and we'll both find ourselves dismembered and up to our ears in burning ash."

My brother glared at the city wall. "I'll stay, but one shout from you and I'm storming the castle."

I left him as he tried to find interesting entertainment to occupy the six demons while they waited. I walked to the gate, which the elven guard had opened barely wide enough for me to squeeze my naked body through. Elves had no problems with visible body parts, human or otherwise, and no one batted an eye at my nudity.

A makeshift reception area had been set up in the courtyard. I recognized the ornate, jeweled throne Taullian sat in, his expression smug. A sorcerer stood beside him, and the look he sent me seemed downright sympathetic. The guard escorting me paused, motioning me to continue through the ring of elven fighters, arrows notched and swords ready. They surrounded Taullian, far enough away that soft conversation would be inaudible, even to sensitive elven ears.

"Az," Taullian addressed me in ringing tones by my more common name, rather than the childhood one he usually used. "I understand your feud with Wythyn and their previous lord, and am willing to overlook the trespass and attack, in spite of our prior issues, as long as you and your demons leave immediately and never return."

I looked at the sorcerer. His shoulders slumped; his eyes had a glazed, defeated expression, and I knew then that Taullian didn't intend to keep his end of the bargain. Somehow I needed to turn things in my favor, and fast. Once Ahriman got his hands on me, I'd either be dead, or powerless to demand so much as a glass of water.

"Where's Leethu? Where are my five other demons?"

He shifted in his chair and I realized that he had no idea where my household members were beyond the rowdy ones outside the gate.

"I am here, Ni–ni." Leethu came forward, her young, elven male appearance exploding in a pop as she resumed her scaled, humanoid form. The crowd gasped, and the elven soldiers vacillated between keeping their sights on me, and covering this new threat.

The succubus pushed passed them, hips swaying, pheromones snaking out in seductive curls. I was amused to see the elves' eyes drop to run along her graceful figure, the bows in their hands trembling slightly. Leethu was a force to be reckoned with.

"Your lordship," her voice rang out like a delicate chime. "I have five demons hidden here among the Wythyn citizens, just as undetectable as I was. I suggest you re–think your offer to the head of my household."

The elves and humans looked around nervously, trying to determine who among their neighbors may be an enemy. The circle around Taullian hummed with speculation and accusations as some turned their arrows on each other.

"Quiet!" the high elf boomed. Silence fell, and once again, he turned to me. "What do you wish, Az? I cannot give you the previous lord of this kingdom. I refuse to turn an elf over to the demons, no matter what his crimes. That justice belongs to us."

The crowd murmured in admiration, while I rolled my eyes. Taullian had already begun his elitist, benevolent, high lord act for his new empire, but it didn't mean shit to me. He'd paid me to kill the elf; he'd been happy to agree to just about anything to sit on that throne. The elf might think he held all the cards, but his position wasn't as solid as he thought.

"I've already killed Feille." Once again, a gasp arose. "Over where the fire is, you'll find his body. Better take a sorcerer to identify it — he's pretty charred."

I let the image soak into the imaginations of all who heard and took a few steps toward the throne as the elves once again turned their arrows to me.

"You know what I want, Taullian. And you best give it to me, unless you intend to be the shortest–lived ruler in all elven history."

The high elf drew himself up taller on his throne, squaring his shoulders in defiance, but I saw the flash of unease in his eyes.

"You dare threaten me, Az? Once again you bluff. You've gambled it all on a lie, but you've been exposed. There's nothing left for you to leverage, imp. No household, no powerful supporters. Nothing. Go home, and if Ahriman lets you live, you can take your place among the Low."

He was right. I was powerless and alone, my household decimated. I didn't even have my chicken wand anymore. I saw the threads of my possible futures before me, and they all were bleak and short. Leethu and Dar would survive if they quickly distanced themselves from my sinking ship, but the rest of us were at a dead end.

"Perhaps you should re–think your definition of power, Lord Taullian," a seductive voice sang from beside me.

Leethu's eyes glowed as gold as her scales, the pheromones flowing in a wave from her swaying form. Several guards dropped to their knees, swords and bows clattering on the flagstone; others gasped, shaking as they tried to fight the power of her call. I felt a surge of love, appreciation for the loyalty of my sister, but I didn't want to see her sacrifice herself for a lost cause, and no matter how powerful a succubus she was, she'd never prevail against an entire army, against a high elf, with only the intoxication of her sexual lures.

A soft word escaped her lips, and I saw her hands fist, pulling a small string taut between them. Instantly Taullian's hands went to his throat, a line of red appearing just below his chin.

The high lord made a choking sound, his hands scrabbling to pull away a cord that wasn't there. The sorcerer beside him paled.

"Phantom hands garrote," he breathed, frantically attempting to break the spell with various incantations.

Leethu held the noose steady — tight enough to turn the high elf's face red, but not enough to kill him. The guards who remained free of her pheromones hesitantly pointed their arrows at her. They could kill her, but one twitch of the hand and Taullian's head would be rolling across the floor — Elves were a sturdy race, and high lords were powerful enough to survive some pretty drastic physical wounds, but decapitation wasn't one of them.

"Since you seem to be incapable of speech, let me do the talking for you," Leethu said, her light tone more suitable to socializing at a luncheon than threatening a powerful ruler. "As formerly agreed upon, we will assist you in stabilizing the newly created Southern Alliance of Elves, and in return, you will grant the humans in all six kingdoms their freedom anytime they desire such, along with the peninsula as their own land. The elven traps will be closed, and no longer will humans be taken from their homeland without their permission."

Taullian made a choking noise, and I was sure it wasn't just from the magical cord squeezing the breath from his throat. The courtyard erupted into chaos. Elves and humans exclaimed their shock and surprise over the unheard–of deal this elven lord had allegedly agreed to.

Leethu relaxed her hands slightly, and Taullian drew in a series of ragged breaths, continuing to reflexed clutch his throat. The sorcerer discontinued his efforts and looked wary, taking two very small steps in my direction. I got the feeling he would break and run, given the slightest opportunity. I felt for him. He was clearly torn between the dream of freedom, and the safety and security he held as one of the highest humans in elven society.

"Lies," Taullian choked, his voice raspy. "I do not make deals with demons."

I held out a hand to stay Leethu. "Fine. We'll leave. But will you ever be safe? Demons can clearly come and go undetected among you. We know your hidden catacombs like the back of our claws; we know your forests and your mountains. We can poison your waters, your foods. Who will you trust?"

The elves looked about them, uneasy, but I wasn't through.

"You can't trust us. You can't trust the other elves, who may decide they would rather boot your ass from their kingdom and go back to the way things were. You certainly can't trust the humans. Already a sorcerer and his apprentice live free within the demon lands, secretly trading among your own magic users and selling their skills for great profit. Others will join them: magic users, skilled humans. Can you ever trust them not to slit your throat in your sleep? Not to rise against you in a show of magical power?"

I walked closer to him, interested to see that no one tried to stop me. "Best keep your end of the bargain, Taullian, and go down in history as a progressive leader, one who took risks to benefit all of elven kind. Or die and be remembered as the king who betrayed those who put the crown on his head, whose maggot–filled body dangled for centuries from a demon's parapet."

I took another step, and the sorcerer moved aside to make way for me. My eyes met his, and I saw within them a mute appeal. He'd join Gareth in a heartbeat, and others with him. Soon Cyelle would be empty of magic users.

Taullian's eyes narrowed, glancing around at the crowd awaiting his response. With an audience, he'd be unable to back down on his word. Elven society demanded truth and the honoring of commitments. It was one thing to lie in the middle of a forest with only a human sorcerer to overhear; it would be disastrous to lie now. Reputation, in life as well as in death, meant everything to an elf.

I saw his indecision. "No" would support the current elven culture and practice, preserve his link with tradition, but he'd face rebellion in each kingdom and by the end of the season wind up holding only Cyelle, if that. Human runaways would increase a hundred–fold, and he'd risk constant guerrilla warfare from both the demons and the escaped humans. "Yes" would secure his kingdoms, but at the price of traditional elven support. History was not always kind to the change–agents, but the winners wrote history, and he could have a glorious legacy, if he could secure his win.

Silence stretched out, the tension as tight as the phantom hands garrote cord in Leethu's delicate hands.

"Deal."

The humans shouted, tossing bits of cloth, spoons, rakes, and baskets into the air. Celebration rained down upon the ground in the form of household items, while the elves stood frozen in shock, their entire world rocked to the core. I almost felt sorry for them. Almost.

Leethu let loose the garrote string, and Taullian gasped in relief. I moved a few steps closer, so I could speak without the entire courtyard hearing.

"You obviously have Cyelle under control, so you can oversee the entire united kingdoms in general and take Tonlielle. Dar is best suited to handle Wythyn and Allwin. Leethu will secure Kllee, as she has a history of friendly relations with their kingdom.

I'd assigned Dar an extra kingdom, hoping to keep him busy. Today had clearly shown me he would abandon his post in a heartbeat to protect me, and I wanted him too busy to even think about what might be happening to me in Ahriman's hands. But what to do with the kingdom of Li at the far west of the continent?

"Radl will assist with Li." It was an insane idea. Radl was a Low, the Low who had been trapped at Columbia Mall, unable to activate the gate back to Hel. I'd let him through and marked him as part of my household. He might be a Low, but he was sly and observant, adaptable to a variety of social situations. And he was pretty much all I had left.

Taullian smiled. "And how will you help, Az?"

His tone was mocking. He knew exactly what I'd be doing, and I had no doubt that if Ahriman killed me, he'd find a way to go back on everything we'd agreed upon. It was vitally important that I stay alive, that I hold his feet to the fire and keep him from reneging on our deal.

"I will be busy fulfilling my duties as consort to Ahriman."

It wasn't really a lie. The crowd murmured, surprised at the revelation that I'd managed to land, what amounted to, the match of the millennium.

Taullian's eyes narrowed, his expression calculating. "Happy nuptials, Az. May your partnership prosper."

I felt a chill. He knew. And Ahriman knew. This elf lord would be watching, and the moment I ceased to be a threat, he'd find a way to backtrack on everything.

Leethu and I put on our best poker faces as we exited through the gates, leaving her five demons behind undercover, to gather intelligence and assist in the transition of the most dangerous of the elven kingdoms. Once outside the walls of the city, the succubus let out a whoosh of air, her shoulders slumping in relief.

"That was a close one, Ni–ni. I thought for sure our goose was cooked."

"Me too," I replied, my mouth watering at the thought of roasted goose. Would I ever get to eat again? I could see starvation as something Ahriman would enjoy inflicting, although he might not even let me live long enough for that. Would I die in his dungeon? Would I ever again see Wyatt, the girls, my angel?

I forced myself to grin at Dar as we approached, giving him a thumbs–up, as if all was completely okay.

"Sorry, dude, I've saddled you with an extra kingdom," I told him. "You've got Wythyn and Allwin."

"My five have remained here to assist you," Leethu added. "They are masquerading as humans and will be your eyes and ears, as well as undertaking communications back to Ni–ni."

The succubus turned her golden eyes on me with sorrow. "We will let you know what happens, and how things are going. If you can, please keep us updated on your ...status."

Status. That would be whether I was alive or not. I'd try, but for their safety, it would be best for me to remain out of contact with any of my former household.

I turned to look at my five remaining household members. "Thank you for your wonderful service in my household. If any of you wish to stay and help Dar, you are welcome to. If not, I release you from any obligations you hold to me. You are free to pursue membership in another household."

My words were greeted with stunned silence. I'd never truly bound any of my household, just marked them as members. They were always free to come and go, but it was a brutal world out there for an unaffiliated demon.

"But Mistress, you are Ahriman's consort. Why would we want to leave such a high level household?"

It was one of my Lows, the stooped, color–changing one. My heart ached for him, ached for all of them. I took a steadying breath, trying to figure out how to tell them. They'd been elated at the meteoric rise in status we'd all had, and now it was all gone. My fault. I'd ruined it all to save a bunch of enslaved humans, and it was a long shot if I'd even achieve that goal. My only consolation was that they'd be safe from Feille's plans. Taullian may be an ass, but he had no aspirations to rule all of Hel.

"I'm afraid Ahriman is very displeased with me. If he kills me, you would be better off unaffiliated with my household. If he lets me live, he will have no compunction about killing any of you on a whim. I want this to be your choice."

They murmured among themselves, uncertain. Life as a demon was a risky thing, and they'd known they could be killed by anyone stronger, at any time, for no reason at all. I could see them weighing the possibility of my continuance as consort, even besmirched, against the risk to their persons.

"Radl," I called out. The Low demon jumped forward, eyes respectfully lowered as he bowed before me. "I have a special proposal for you. Dar and Leethu will each assist in the integration of one of the elven kingdoms. I would like you to be our representative assisting the Cyelle elves in bringing Li into the fold. Could you do this?"

His eyes rose to meet mine, shock and surprise overcoming his usually excellent manners. "Consort, I would be honored. A Low has never been so favored. Others choose as they may, but I will remain in your service until my death."

His pronouncement was contagious, and the other four jumped to pledge their loyalty.

"I'll take Snip, Rot, and Pustule," Dar announced. "Hack, you go with Radl. He's your superior for the time being, so I don't want to hear any shit about refusing orders or backstabbing. Got it?"

"Got it," Hack squeaked, saluting Dar with a ragged wing.

I smiled at Dar in gratitude. I knew it wouldn't be easy for him to handle two fractious elven kingdoms as well as keeping tabs on three rowdy demons. I knew he'd also be overseeing Radl and Hack as they worked in Li. All that should be enough to keep his mind busy, and away from imagining what Ahriman would be doing to me.

"Thank you all," I announced. "After the integration is complete, Dar will be the head of my household until the end of my contract as Consort. I hope to see you all then."

Hope. Depression edged its way onto the edges of my mind like a shadow, but I pushed it back. I had to stay alive — for my remaining household members, for the humans I'd worked so hard to free, for Wyatt and my friends, and for my angel. Most of all, for my angel.

~27~

"Why here? I thought the Ruling Council met in Aaru," Tura asked, looking uncomfortable as he gazed around the room.

Besides Gabriel, the only others present were humans, setting up coffee, donuts, and flip charts. The angels would arrive fashionably late, making an entrance and giving their guest plenty of time to squirm with building anxiety.

"We began meeting outside of Aaru to accommodate the Iblis." Gabriel fought to keep his attention on the other angel and not the tray of pastries next to the coffee urns. Ruling Council meetings weren't nearly as much fun without the imp's disruptive presence.

"Will she be here, too?" Tura picked up a coffee cup and casually filled it with the dark liquid.

It would be just like her to show up unexpected, crashing through the door half naked with a fist full of lightning bolts. A part of Gabriel wished she would. "No. She is attending to urgent business in Hel at the moment."

Tura nodded, a look of relief in his eyes as he turned toward the chairs before halting abruptly. Gabriel knew right away what he was thinking. There were seven chairs around the huge table, and even with the absence of the Iblis, it was quite clear that Tura was meant to stand. As if on cue, the other angels arrived and promptly took their respective seats.

"There is some business we need to attend to first. I'm sure you understand," Gabriel told the angel beside him. "I'll introduce you when we're ready."

It was all part of the elaborate ritual to make it quite clear to Tura where he stood in relation to the other angels in the room, that no matter how important he felt his project was, it ranked somewhere below determining process steps for grade secession candidates. This was a dance Gabriel had done his entire life, yet he suddenly felt irritated with the delay. Impatient. *Let's just get this over with.*

Of course they would not discuss anything of significance with a non–member in attendance. Four hours were filled with inane discussion and obscure diagrams while Tura stood, remarkably composed, fingering the cup holding cold coffee.

Finally Gabriel nodded Tura forward, and he approached without introduction. In spite of the fact that all this was meant to rattle him, the angel appeared confident; the picture of balance and order.

"For too long, Aaru has suffered from lack of creation. I present to you a way to bring new life to the angelic host. Using donated demon essence brokered through the humans and elves, we can invigorate our homeland and once again enjoy positive evolution and increased vibration."

With a wave of his hand, six tubes of swirling green arched through the air. As if synchronized, the seated angels each reached up to catch one. It was a bold move. One broken tube, demon essence all over the floor, and Tura would look like a cocky fool.

"These are samples, to show you that this isn't just a theory. We are ready to begin today. With the Ruling Council's approval, of course."

The angels studied the green tubes and silence stretched on. Gabriel watched their faces intently for reaction. Was this truly as Tura had said, or was there more to his sin than violations of the treaty?"

"Plague and warmongering," Uriel finally spoke, her brow creased with a frown. "These are not exactly traits I would wish in an offspring, although the contributing demon is of a suitably high level."

Gabriel winced. Contributing demon. More like butchered victim.

"Ancient Revered One, Angel of Prophecy, plague traits are also healing ones, and warmongering is a mirror to peace. With the appropriate contribution of Order, these undesirable qualities will be transformed."

"Or hidden." They all turned toward the eldest among them. "How many times have we declared an Angel of Order, only to realize our error a century later? It's only through trust in our breeding partners that we achieve the results we *both* truly desire."

"But we're not here to discuss breeding partners." Baradel chimed in. "That is forever lost to us. This may be a dim shadow of what we used to have, but it's worth considering."

"We have to do something," Raphael added. "Uriel may be the Angel of Prophecies, but I see an Aaru rotting from the inside out, and I fear for our future. This may seem cold and sterile, but I agree that it's worth consideration."

"The process is unconventional," Tura chimed in. "But the result will be the same as we had before the war — creation. New angels will bring vitality back to Aaru. There will be no violation of our treaty, no sinful contact, and our offspring will be identical to those created through conventional breeding."

There was silence as the angels examined the tubes. Gabriel sat his down on the table, unable to stand holding it any longer. Let the future of Aaru be what it may, he couldn't give his vote to such a project.

Uriel caressed the tube of green, a look of longing in her eyes. "I vote we approve the premise and proceed to discussions of the methods of collection and formation."

Baradel, Sidriel, and Raphael nodded, and the eldest shrugged. "I'll reserve judgment until I know more."

Tura waved a hand and a stack of papers appeared before each angel. "These detail the collection process and the formation process at a high level. There is also a proposed screening document for applicants as well as a list of testing mechanisms to ensure the resulting offspring are suitable in quality and type."

Raphael stabbed a finger on one of the pages. "The flow chart that shows the acquisition process for the demon essence is rather lengthy. Is there a chain of custody procedure to guarantee nothing has been tampered with? Can you illustrate the quality control and security at each hand–off point?"

"The appendix, page six–hundred–and–twenty–three through nine–hundred–and–fifty outlines those details."

They all flipped to the back pages, quickly scanning the dense text and diagrams.

"The formation section is unacceptably vague," the eldest noted. Gabriel bit back a smile, realizing his brother had echoed his own words.

Tura smiled serenely, a small, clear box appearing in his hands. "If you wish to study the mechanism for formation, you are welcome to do so. It is a product of sorcery — elven and human magic combined. I documented the basic workings of the item, but due to its magical nature, there are some functions not easily explained."

Uriel reached for the box, examining it with eager hands while her older brother scowled.

"What happens if the offspring is defective in some way? With traditional breeding, that was never a possibility, but a magical device lacks sentience. What shall we do with unanticipated results?"

Tura looked wary. "There will be no broken angels. The magic is of the highest quality and level. Errors are not possible."

"But what about Angels of Chaos," Rafael broke in, giving the box a hopeful look. "That's one factor that's always been up to fate. Under the rules of the treaty, we cannot allow an Angel of Chaos in Aaru, but I would damn myself to Hel before I tossed away a helpless, newly formed angel."

"There will only be Angels of Order produced," Tura assured confidently. "Guaranteed."

"There are no guarantees," the eldest interjected. "I've seen many Angels of Order with chaos traits, and those close to the median are most likely to straddle both worlds. If Raphael would sooner die than throw away a newly formed angel, think how he would feel after a hundred years when hidden traits manifest? Think how any angel would feel."

"We could make provisions for that unlikely scenario," Tura said. "At one hundred, they could live elsewhere, protected and sheltered until they were able to live in Hel like they are meant to."

Baradel and Sidriel nodded. Uriel did nothing but stare at the vial of green before her and the plain, crystal box.

"I'm *not* casting my children into Hel," Raphael snapped. "How can we possibly sit here as angels, supposedly the most enlightened and balanced of all beings, and even consider such a thing?"

"Of course not!" Tura said indignantly. "There are other realms. We can have dwarves brought over to assist in their development; we can journey there to visit. It would be a neutral territory, outside the confines of the treaty. And all this is merely conjecture — the box is guaranteed to only produce Angels of Order."

Perhaps he would make a good Ruling Council candidate, Gabriel thought. They all had their skeletons. If they excluded every angel who had plotted and schemed, who had bent or broken the rules, there would be no one left on the Council. With some minor rehabilitation, perhaps this angel would make a good addition.

Or not.

"No," the eldest said, tossing the vial of green back to Tura. "There is too much chance for corruption and evil actions couched under benign motives from beginning to end. This project ends now."

"No!" Uriel's voice was shrill. "We can make it work. We'll form a committee to explore options, investigate a way to structure acceptable procedures."

"I think we should at least look into it further," Baradel agreed.

"Although I am sympathetic to your views, dear brother," Raphael interjected. "You are only one member of this council. We should put this to a vote."

"Vote away. This project will never see the light of day."

"Too late." Everyone turned in surprise to Tura. "So convenient that you chose to have your meeting here among the humans. While you all nattered on about how many of us could fit on the head of a pin, my colleagues were announcing the availability of our services. Right now, Aaru is a seething mess of violence and anarchy as every angel tries to claw their way up to the top of our 'list'."

The eldest glowed in fury. "I'll have your wings for this, Tura."

The other angel smiled. "I think I'll have yours instead."

A light strong enough to penetrate his subdued visual senses blinded Gabriel, and he suddenly felt the presence of many angels. The room erupted into action.

Raphael stood and launched the huge conference table on its side as a makeshift shield, nearly crushing Gabriel on the other side. He dropped and rolled, pummeled by the bound reports and the vials of demon essence. Two broke, filling the room with a green haze. It was nearly impossible to see with human vision, so Gabriel reached out with angelic senses to perceive what was happening.

Bolts of white energy flew about the room as Tura's angels and the Council battled. Rising, Gabriel was again knocked to the floor as the conference table exploded into flying debris. What the heck was he doing in the middle of this? He was a messenger, the Angel of Truth, not a warrior.

Staggering to his feet, Gabriel saw how outnumbered they were with nearly a hundred of Tura's angels crammed into the small room. Normally it would take an army to go against the strongest angels in Aaru, but here, among the humans, they were vulnerable in their corporeal forms. Tura's forces were hampered by the close confines of the conference room, but they were also prepared with physical weapons.

An explosion filled the room, and the walls around them vanished, allowing for greater maneuverability for both sides. Gabriel ran for the action, trying to determine who was friend or foe in the blinding light and dust. A blaze of white scored his side. He tripped, landing face down on a human. He stared into dead, shocked eyes then looked down to see the lower half of the man was nothing but a pile of sand. Once again they'd brought their problems into the human world. When would this stop? Filled with anger, Gabriel blindly shot out at everything around him. It didn't matter. *They* were the horrors in this world. There was no good, only evil as far as their impact on the humans. He'd wanted to wash the world clean of humans, but it was the angels who had brought this to their doorstep. Samael had been right, but what was done was done. Gabriel couldn't change the past, but he could change himself, and, hopefully, the future.

He dove at the nearest angel, taking him by surprise. The angel blocked Gabriel's blast, and jammed cold steel against his chest, firing off ten rounds from the human weapon. The impact drove Gabriel backwards a step into the sharp edge of a table, but he managed to keep a firm hold on the angel, wrestling to grip his spirit self. The angel twisted to get loose, hammering Gabriel with both his fist and bolts of energy. He might not be a fighter, but Gabriel was old, and he was strong. He put a hand back on the table to stabilize his physical form as he fought the angel for control, and felt something soft and sticky under his palm.

A pastry.

His hand curled around it, digging through the icing shell, the sweet caramel center, and the roped bands of bread. Grain, strands of delicate gluten, dairy fat, and sugar. Far more sugar than any human should ever consume. Raising his hand, Gabriel crammed the pastry into the angel's face, crushing it deeply into his eyes and nostrils. The angel sputtered, hesitating in his surprise and giving Gabriel the opening he needed. He seized hold of the angel's spirit–self and tore through it, blasting it directly. His opponent realized the danger and struggled, hitting Gabriel repeatedly in the face with the metal human weapon. Gabriel grunted in pain, ignoring the tickle of blood running down his face, and the burning agony in his chest. He shook the angel like a terrier with a rat, letting go as the last bit of flesh and spirit dissolved into sand.

One down, one hundred or so to go.

Without pausing to heal his wounds, Gabriel looked around for the area of greatest need — Uriel frantically battled two angels, hampered by the crystal box clutched in her arms. Raphael was gleefully whacking angels with chairs, blasting them as he knocked them to the ground. Baradel had crawled behind the table, desperately healing his tattered flesh.

Gabriel saw a flash of light and turned to see his eldest brother, sword blazing as he single–handedly fought nearly the entire rebel force. Of course they would target him, the one who had always been the strongest, their leader in spite of the alleged equality of the Ruling Council. Take out the eldest, and the rest of them would be scrambling for power. Anyone with enough force could take Aaru with the strongest angel gone. Gabriel paused. How many times had he wondered what life would be like without him? How many times had he been ridiculed, humiliated, mocked? Perhaps Aaru would be a better place without him.

Then he thought of his brother's expression as he looked at the Iblis, his pain and sorrow as he'd held her broken in his arms. Suddenly Gabriel saw a whole different view of his childhood than the bitter one he'd clung to all these eons. He remembered feeling protected. He remembered Micha encouraging him as he pulled the seas into his embrace, creating intricate globes of water and ice. Most of all, he remembered his brother's empathy during his own darkest moment. It had been too late when he'd realized how much he'd loved Samael. There was no way he was going to let that happen again.

Angels crowded close. The swinging sword slowed, unable to gain advantage in close fighting. Gabriel saw Tura and ran toward him even as he felt the sizzle of human magic from a device in the angel's hand. A light shot from Tura's hand, and Gabriel slammed into him, knocking him to the floor. As Tura fell, the beam of light glanced off its intended victim and cut in a wild arc across the room, instantly dusting a dozen rebel angels and disintegrating the back half of the hotel. Tura snarled and twisted, swinging the weapon toward Gabriel. It seared along his left wing, the smell of melted feathers filling the air, but it was the agonizing pain as sections of his spirit being burned away that occupied Gabriel's mind.

I'm dead, he thought, realizing the trajectory of the magic would slice him in two.

"Four!"

A wooden chair leg smashed into Tura's hand, and the light spun away, sputtering out as a small metal object flew from his hand and bounced across the room. Gabriel had only a moment to look into Raphael's gleeful face before Tura threw him aside to land painfully on his damaged wing.

"I'm benching you for the quarter."

Gabriel felt his younger brother's hand on his arm, dragging him to a spot next to Baradel behind a sofa. He took one look at the other angel, still trying to heal his physical wounds, and pulled himself upright. He'd held back two and a half million years ago, but there was no way he was going to let his brothers and sister fight this one alone.

But by the time he'd managed to make it to the center of the room, the fight was over. Bodies and piles of sand littered the floor — most of them angels, but quite a few of them human. There were too many to count, but Gabriel quickly realized that many angels, including Tura, had escaped. Five angels stood around him, all bloodied and damaged. Uriel put the crystal box gently on one of the unbroken chairs, and went to Gabriel, hovering a hand over his mess of a wing.

"You're hurt," she said.

"We're all hurt," he answered. "And we're going to face even worse back in Aaru. But the big question on my mind is how did Tura know where we were meeting? He had to have known beforehand to plan an ambush like this. No communication came or went from this room once I gated him in. Someone tipped him off."

They all took a step back, looking at each other with suspicion.

"It has to have been one of us," Raphael said. "We are the only ones who knew, and we were all aware of how confidential this was. We have a traitor in our midst."

"Tura is in Uriel's choir," Baradel noted, edging away from the angel. "She was clearly in favor of this project — perhaps she tipped him off to gain advantage in his presentation."

Gabriel felt the sharp scrape of Uriel's power. "Plus Furlac was also in Uriel's household, and he was working with Tura when he was killed."

Uriel spun around, glaring at each of them in turn. "The other angel involved, Vaol, was in Raphael's choir and you're not accusing him. You all saw the rebel angels that attacked us today — there were members of every choir involved in this."

"But Tura was clearly the leader," Baradel continued. "I wonder if you weren't behind this entire breeding project from the start. It wouldn't surprise me."

Uriel's gaze drifted to the box of crystal.

"You had been supporting this project through Furlac," Gabriel said. "You had to have known about Tura's involvement. How deep is your connection in this, Uriel?"

"I'll admit to supporting and funding the project secretly," she said, looking toward Gabriel in appeal. "I contributed whatever resources to it I could, but it was Tura that approached me, not the other way around. And I was absolutely *not* behind the coup attempt or the rebellion going on in Aaru. I only wanted to see creation in Aaru once again."

"At all costs?" Sidriel chimed in. He'd been oddly silent throughout the entire meeting, his obsequious behavior absent. Gabriel frowned, remembering something.

"Tura wasn't always in Uriel's choir. He used to be in yours, Sidriel."

Sidriel shrugged. "He was angling for a Ruling Council spot and felt it would better serve him to change choirs. It's not uncommon."

"Vaol was also in your choir before moving to mine," Raphael noted. "As was Furlac before going to Uriel's."

"And you were the one who enlightened me about this little project," Gabriel said, moving closer to the angel. "You were the one who had the 'connections' to put me in touch with the angels in charge. Why me? I've never expressed any burning desire to create, and Uriel was already a strong supporter. Could it be that you felt I'd be supportive of your other 'project'? The one to take our eldest brother out of the picture and completely re–arrange the power structure in Aaru?"

Sidriel remained silent, but his aura shifted, twisting with black hate. Gabriel reached out, but his younger brother was quicker, snatching the angel's arm.

"Let me, brother," Raphael grinned. "You've only got one and a half wings right now. I'm in better shape to make sure our friend enters his rehabilitation with a calm and centered demeanor."

The pair vanished in a flash and Gabriel turned to his eldest brother. "Aaru. We need to get there."

"Not yet." The sword vanished from his hand, and the ancient angel turned to face the small crystal box on the striped cushion of a chair.

"No!" Uriel shrieked, throwing herself over it protectively. "You can't. Micha, don't do it!"

"It's not right, Uri. You know it's not," he said gently, crouching down to look directly into her face.

She sobbed. "You don't know. Every waking moment I see the look on Marax's face as I left him. I turned my back on my life partner, on my child, and for what? Empty, meaningless rules, and philosophies I never fully believed in. I walked away from the most important parts of my life, too afraid to stand alone as an Angel of Order in favor of the rebels."

She looked up at them all, very human tears streaming down her face. "I know you all think I desperately want a child to replace Haka, but this box isn't for me, it's for Aaru. I want every angel in Aaru to feel the joy I once had. I made a terrible choice and lost all I held dear. This box can heal Aaru and maybe allow me to finally forgive myself."

The eldest cupped Uriel's cheek, his eyes full of sympathy. "I recognize the hand that went into the making of this box, and I can assure you that every being it creates will be a twisted monster. Maybe not at first, but it will happen. I agree that things must change in Aaru, but this isn't the way to do it. There will be no quick fix for our problems, and no easy redemption for you, Uri. You are the Angel of Prophecies. Surely you see this yourself?"

She nodded, and with one last glance, handed the box over with shaking hands. "I request pilgrimage, my brother."

Gregory crushed the box, raining a cascade of sand upon the bloodstained carpet. "First, we must bring peace to Aaru, my sister, and then you shall be granted your pilgrimage."

~28~

G one. It was all gone.

I'd managed to sneak through the demon lands using the edges of the elven forests as cover as I made my way home, but there was no more home. For nearly seven–hundred years I'd owned this dwelling, and now all that remained was a smoldering pile of wood, melted metal, and rock. Portions were so hot that they were pools of lava, bubbling red with a cooling, blackened crust. I could feel the fury in the destruction, and my stomach lurched. Where could I hide? There had to be somewhere to hide.

There was nowhere to hide. Nowhere that he couldn't find me. The longer I drew this out, avoided him, the worse it would be. If I had any hope of staying alive, I needed to go to him and beg for forgiveness. I needed to hope that the devouring ability he so desperately wanted would cool his anger and stay his hand, even though I had no intention of allowing him to breed the monster he wanted to create. If I survived the next few days, the next thousand years would take every bit of passive aggressive skill I had.

I turned and began my long walk toward Ahriman's nearest house. I hadn't gone far before I saw them. Ghostly shadows, like red chiffon in the wind. The Wisps rolled in from the east, separating as they spied me, each taking a strategic route to surround me for capture. I stood still, head lowered in submission as I tensed, waiting.

"I'm on my way to him now," I called out. "I was given two weeks to put my affairs in order, and I'm ready to begin my contract."

The Wisps swirled in close, blistering my skin where they brushed against me. They never spoke, communicating only through touch and mindspeak. These refused to do even that, taunting me with the threat of their nearness, leaving me wondering if I'd even make it to Ahriman alive. I gritted my teeth at the welts and blisters their touch caused, reluctant to fix the wounds with my limited abilities. It would be best to save my meager powers for the coming confrontation.

Prepare for transport, one of the Wisps said.

They all circled me, pressing close until I gasped with pain from their stinging touch. In a disorienting jolt, I found myself in a cold, dark room. The smell of mildew and damp decay filled my nose, and I squinted, trying to adjust my human eyes to the dim light.

The Wisps vanished, and I stood as still as possible. I wanted to assess my surroundings without alerting any potential other resident to my presence. Normally I would welcome a fight with another demon, but I wasn't exactly sturdy in this human form. Dripping echoed from behind me, accompanied by a shuffling sound, as if something were dragging itself along the hard floor. I tensed, judging by the sound that the moving creature was a safe distance away.

Slowly the room came into focus. Stone and dirt walls with brown and red slime interspersed with black mildew. The room was about thirty–by–fifty, with several dark passageways on both my left and right. As silently as possible, I turned around to see the room open up far behind me in a hallway. It was dark and extended beyond the limits of my eyesight. I smelled oil and soot, rotting flesh and burned hair and knew he was near, watching me, even if I could not see his form. How could he do that? How could he exist in a spirit form within Hel, survive without a corporeal shape to house his being? Or was he possibly within the very molecules of air itself? I held my breath, suddenly afraid of where the inevitable blow would come from.

A shape materialized in front of me, sliding across the ground to rest by my feet. I jumped, letting my breath out in a rush and stared at it, alarmed. A blackened, charred husk, a torso with burned sticks for extremities lay before me. I recognized it.

The only reason I did not let the Wisps have you is that I am intrigued by this latest kill of yours.

Ahriman, his mindspeech like a whip in my thoughts. And the body before me was the high elf, formerly known as Feille. I hoped the demon didn't recognize him. He didn't look much like an elf right now. He didn't look much like anything right now.

"The torture," I stuttered. "I told you I had an enemy I was torturing. Well, this was him. I'm here now, ready to start our contract."

You flout my authority, use my name without permission, commit me to actions I do not support. You disobey my orders, kill a man who served my needs. Your actions have not only brought me embarrassment, but they have caused delays in a project near to my heart.

"He stole my possessions, had his scouts hunt me down and drag me to him like an animal. I was locked in his dungeon, subjected to humiliating actions by his sorcerers, then sold to my enemy. It was a blood feud."

My only hope was to find some reason for my actions that he would accept. Revenge, torture, a feud. Surely he would mitigate my punishment for such understandable motives.

Still Ahriman did not appear, his voice in my mind the only indication of his presence. *Although I admire such a dedication to vengeance, I cannot allow your disrespectful actions to go unpunished.*

My heart raced. I was absolutely aware of how close to death I was. "I know why you want my devouring ability, and

I'm honored to be able to contribute to such a project. I will proudly take my punishment and only hope that you still consider my skills worthy of your offspring."

I felt him hesitate, actually felt a slight shift in his anger. *What do you know about my intentions, imp?*

I knew my next words would mean the difference between life and death. Pride. The whole war with the angels had been over stubborn pride. Not just on our part either. The angels had more than their fair share of that sin. I may not have much pride, but the ancients all seemed to. I just needed to stir it up within Ahriman, to direct his anger and murderous impulses to something other than me.

"You are ancient and powerful. You could have all of Hel with the wave of a talon, but you don't want that. Vengeance is what you want. We are not so different in our passions. I destroy an elf lord who insulted me, and you seek to destroy the angels that took away everything you held dear, who cast you into Hel to rot for all eternity. Fuck them. As I said, I'm proud to contribute to anything that causes the angels pain and suffering. Let me live, and I'll help you create the offspring you desire."

He needed me. He needed my devouring ability. I'd deal with the fact that I had no intention of giving it to him later. Right now, I just wanted to live through the night.

You assume I cannot replace you? Millions of years I have waited. A few hundred thousand more are of no consequence.

But they were. I knew he was impatient, that he'd waited long enough. Each century that went by saw him falling further from the angel he used to be. It had to eat away at his soul to know what banishment had done to him.

"I know, Ancient One. I only hope you find enough value in what I have to offer that you will allow me to make up for my disobedient behavior."

Black smoke billowed before me, inches from my body. Shit, shit, shit. Was he about to kill me? I had no idea his intent, but this manifestation of his physical form couldn't be a good thing. I held still, trying to show no fear. Demons like Ahriman lived on other's terror. One taste and he'd lose his tightly held control, satiating his desires in my nightmares for as long as he could draw them out. Slowly a curl of smoke reached toward me, a talon materializing to rake down my cheek. Another tendril snaked through my flesh to my spirit–self, taking unmentionable liberties. I clenched my jaw and tried to calm my racing heart.

Your fear is like the honey of Aaru. I long to indulge my passions, but I do not want to wait thousands of years for another such as you. I need what you have, Az, and that will keep you alive for a while, in spite of your disobedience. Perhaps you'll live through the entire contract period, if you prove worthy of my affection, that is.

His spirit–self plundered mine, and I allowed him as many intimacies as I could tolerate, trying to keep the extent of my damage from him as well as the red–purple of Gregory's spirit. I needed to stay alive —permitting this assault while deceiving him as to the extent of my usefulness seemed a good plan for now. I wasn't sure how long it would stall the demon, but it was all I had.

You have much to recommend you, Az, Ahriman continued as he stroked along my spirit–self. I tried to ignore him, tried to keep down the bile that rose in my throat.

I am dismayed at Feille's untimely death, but admire the painful revenge you enacted on his person. Time and time again I see you in this weak, vulnerable human form, covered in wounds you do not repair. Your obvious enjoyment of suffering, of agony, further endears you to me. In spite of your defiant, disobedient nature, could you possibly be the partner I have longed for in my exile? A mirror to myself, one to enjoy the pain I so love to give.

I could not keep the shudder from rolling through my body. Shit. He thought I was allowing these blisters, these burns, on purpose, that I kept to this form because I was some kind of demon masochist. We all loved a degree of pain.

Sensation was appreciated whether it was pleasure or torment, but some things were beyond the bounds of reasonable enjoyment. Ahriman seemed to feel I had transcended these limits. I wavered in indecision. If I let him know the truth, he'd realize how broken I was, as well as my inability to fulfill the terms of my contract. If I let him believe I was open to the sort of torture he wanted, I'd spend the next thousand years in non–stop agony.

I took a deep breath and caressed him back, wincing at his enthusiastic response.

"You should punish me. Prove to me you are worthy of my respect, force me to obey."

I didn't have to ask twice. The demon coalesced into a more solid shape, gripping the edge of my spirit–self with his own. With claws, he raked my physical being, tearing strips of skin until they hung in tatters from my arms and chest. The blisters and burns from the Wisps sizzled with acid from his touch, and I felt every coherent thought sink under a drowning wall of pain. All the while, he gripped my spirit being, holding me as if he owned me. He might think so, think the contract gave my body and soul to him, but there would always be a secret part he could never touch. I hid a portion of myself safely away along with the angel spirit networked though me. He could have the rest, but never this tiny bit, and never my angel. I clung to that part of Gregory, taking comfort in memories, in the knowledge of his strength and skill. I could survive this, I could endure, and the thought of my angel would be my rock to keep me steady throughout it all.

By the time Ahriman was finished with his fun, half my skin lay shredded on the floor, blood falling in rivulets from the torn flesh. I panted in agony, uncertain how I'd managed to stay upright throughout the entire experience.

Yes, Az, I think I will keep you alive and by my side. You'll be a lovely addition to my household — my new favorite toy. It seems there are many more benefits to this contract than I ever would have thought.

He vanished in a slick puff of smoke. I collapsed to the dirty floor, holding as still as I could in the pool of my own flesh and blood. Reaching deep inside myself to the broken sections, I pulled on the thick energy that surrounded me and tried to convert my form, to recreate my entire body anew. I'd been doing this since I was a mere century old — it was like breathing to me — but my broken spirit rebelled, sending a very different spear of pain through me.

Come on, come on, I urged myself. I'd managed to convert into flame to kill Feille, created this human form afterward. Why could I not do it now? Had I re–injured the healing portions of myself when I'd turned to flame in the forest? Was I just not sufficiently angry or desperate to force my damaged powers into action? Or perhaps the waves of pain tearing through me were too much of a distraction.

Unable to recreate my form, I set about repairing my injuries. It was a slow process, but I was pleased to feel blood vessels knit together, new pink skin creep along the open wounds. I was grateful that this skill had returned, that at least I no longer had to exist with wounds for days or weeks at a time and worry that they'd never close or heal. If I could just stall Ahriman, hold off any attempts at breeding by steering him to other, more enjoyable, activities, then maybe by the time he got around to it I'd be recovered enough to give him some of the traits he wanted. I just needed to hang on.

~29~

I'd never make it. Two weeks in Ahriman's dungeon, enduring his "affections," and my repair abilities were at full. All this non–stop fixing of my physical form had accelerated the recovery of those skills. I still had a long way to go, though. I was able to convert small sections of myself, but I could not hold more than a moderate amount of energy, and I was afraid to shift from this fragile human form. It had its flaws, but it was my connection to those I loved, and it was preferable to pond scum or a lizard.

Ahriman delighted in his new toy, visiting me as often as three times a day. The flaying of my skin had progressed to broken bones, removal of extremities, and now evisceration. For the second time in a matter of hours, I lay twisted unnaturally on dirt wet with my own fluids, a rope of intestine inches from my face. I'd never make it. At this rate, I wouldn't keep my sanity for more than a few more days.

At first there had been breaks between his visits, time to explore the windowless connecting rooms I called my dungeon. I wasn't restrained, wasn't locked in, but I could never seem to find my way out of the labyrinth of moldy dirt and stone. I would walk for hours, trying to map out the rooms in my head, but beyond all laws of physics, I always returned here. The whole place was like an Escher print, up and down, left or right, I always came back to the same room.

There had been others down here. I'd found the source of the shuffling sound — a demon so damaged he was unable to speak, crawling in mindless circles on the floor. The next day he was gone, replaced with another in even worse condition. I was the healthiest being here, and that wasn't saying much.

Drawing a ragged breath into repaired lungs, I grabbed the dried, dirty chunks of my guts spread out before me and stuffed them back in, forcing myself to create an entirely new midsection and digestive tract. There were some things I didn't want to risk fixing, and torn colon sections were one of them.

I'd had a visit from one of my household earlier in the week and forced myself to appear healthy and sane as I spoke with Snip. I couldn't have Dar and Leethu know the extent of what I was going through. I needed them where they were, doing what they were doing, and I didn't want to risk them in Ahriman's presence. I'd been worried about Snip the entire time he was in the dungeon, afraid that he'd be torn apart in front of me in some new game of Ahriman's, but the demon seemed to realize this was business and did no more than watch my Low with covetous eyes, occasionally sending a black smear of oily smoke along the lesser demon's exoskeleton.

Snip had treated the ancient demon with nervous respect, understanding the need for careful speech and guarded information—sharing in his presence. From what I'd gleaned, Leethu had quickly brought Kllee onboard to the elven alliance. They'd already shut their trap—gate, and some of their humans were planning to resettle to the new territories, while the rest were happily remaining free in their current kingdom. Allwin was following suit. Dar struggled with Wythyn, having to employ considerable force in his diplomatic relations. It didn't help that Taullian kept sticking his nose in the kingdom's business, counteracting any progress my brother had made. Radl was making a horrible mess of Li, but that was to be expected. Ah well, two out of four fractious elven kingdoms was more than a little imp could hope for.

I struggled to my feet, continuing to fix various small but serious wounds I'd missed while repairing my destroyed midsection. I'd been naked when I assumed this form after killing Feille and had lost every possession including clothing when Ahriman's demons burned my house to the ground. He'd not supplied me with any covering since my arrival. I found myself constantly fixing various scrapes and pressure wounds. I'd never make it.

The odor of charred flesh, of burnt, oily smoke filled my senses, and I couldn't help but whirl around in a panic, looking for him. I constantly thought I smelled him, heard him coming. I couldn't sleep without the remembrance of his speech in my head. I could never escape him. Insanity advanced from the edges of my mind a little more each day. I'd survived torture before, but this was more than physical pain. Ahriman constantly groped my spirit–self, and I knew one day he would want more. I felt ill at the thought. Would I let him? How could I stop him?

The physical damage was nothing to make light of. I couldn't relieve the torment by fixing the injuries instantly, and the human form wasn't as sturdy and pain–resistant as my other traditional demon shapes. I'd been able to use enough of my demon abilities to keep myself from starving or dehydrating to a dangerous point, but food would help. Food. A soft bed. A gentle touch. I closed my eyes, shivering in the dark chill of the dungeon, and imagined Wyatt's warm hands on me, the smell of him as I nuzzled his naked chest, the way his sun–kissed blond hair felt as my fingers roamed through it. I saw his kind blue eyes in my memory, concerned, full of love and care.

And my angel. He'd be furious over this mess I'd gotten myself into. Absolutely livid. I imagined him shaking me, smacking my back against some hard surface as he always did. Then he'd crush me to him, soothing my ragged spirit–self with his own. His power would burn against me in welcome warmth, reminding me of how very ancient he was, how very strong. I was safe with him, the other half of my whole. He'd merge himself slightly with me, teasing and tempting, maybe kissing me as he'd done only twice before, his teeth sharp points of pleasure on my lips and tongue.

I can't do this. Can't.

I needed to get out of here, get some kind of break from the nonstop agony, from the despair and dread I felt every time Ahriman touched me. At the thought of him, I shuddered, every inch of skin rising in goosebumps. Again that too–familiar odor filled my nose, dark and slick, burning and rotting. I gagged, collapsing in dry heaves as I saw a curl of black smoke rise from the floor to fill the space a few feet from where I wretched.

Was he really here? He'd just left, and I was exhausted from his recent affections, worn and sore from fixing injuries that grew worse each time he visited. It was hard for me to tell if he'd come back for more, or if I was once again hallucinating. I constantly smelled him, felt him, even when he wasn't near. *Please let it be my imagination; please let this just be a nightmare I can wake from.*

The black smoke formed an upright shape, eyes glowing like coals. Again I tried to empty the nonexistent contents of my stomach. I saw the slash of a mouth on his face twist up with a glint of yellowed fangs just as his foot hit my midsection, flipping me over onto my belly. At least I'd stopped gagging.

I tried to curl tight into a defensive ball, to protect the core of my body that I'd just repaired. The demon countered by kicking my back repeatedly, one impact cracking my tailbone.

Az, I find I cannot stay away. My favorite toy, my consort. You constantly occupy my thoughts. I am only at peace when I am with you.

His words burned through my pain, and I realized in horror that this would only get worse. How much more could I take? Would it become non–stop, so that I would be unable to even have the time to fix myself? I envisioned endless torture. One thousand years of suffering with no respite.

Ahriman tired of kicking me and picked me up by my hair, one hand going to my neck as he held me upright, my feet dangling above the ground. Maybe he'd kill me in his enthusiasm. The prospect was beginning to sound very appealing.

Blood ran down my neck from his sharp talons. His breath smelled like a rotted corpse as he pulled me close to bite down on my shoulder. My collarbone snapped, and he chewed, gnawing muscle and tendon and bone. I couldn't feel that arm. I wanted to fight him off, to kick and punch him, but it was all I could do to fend off his assault upon my spirit being, trying to frantically to keep my secrets from him.

I can't. I can't do this.

I hadn't realized I'd said the words out loud until I saw Ahriman raise his head from my shoulder, orange–red eyes inches from my own.

What can you not do, my darling?

I froze. Anything I said would just make it worse. As if sensing my indecision, the demon pushed himself slightly into my spirit being, joining in a line of white. I recoiled, feeling none of the ecstasy I'd felt when Gregory had done the same.

"Stop that." I don't know where I got the strength, but I pushed him back. "You can feel me up all you want, but that's as far as it goes."

How could my voice be so strong and steady when all I wanted to do was curl into a ball and disappear, to cry away every memory of this horror.

Ahriman chuckled, and pushed in again, holding me firmly in place. He was the stronger demon, and all my panicked attempts to expel him were ineffective.

But I want so much more than just to feel you up, more than to bring sweet torment to the flesh you wear. You are my consort, Az, and I find I must re–negotiate our contract.

His spirit–self had pinned me, holding me immobile, so I did the only thing I could. I slugged him in the face with the one functioning arm. The demon wasn't completely solid, and my knuckles sank slightly into the clingy smoke before crunching against something hard. My fist exploded in pain, and I knew I'd broken my hand as surely as I'd broke whatever passed for a face on this demon.

He laughed, diving deeper into my spirit–self before halting abruptly.

You're broken.

His words were furious, and I felt an icy chill seep through me. We all had scars, and the fact that mine were extensive and recent shouldn't normally give him any cause for concern, but he'd discovered the missing sections I'd tried so desperately to hide from him.

"I'm repairing myself. It won't take long. I've already regained much of my skills." I tried to steady my voice, realizing that my life was on the line.

His spirit–self was frigid as it dug through me, cataloging what I'd lost and regained while I desperately tried to hide the red–purple of Gregory's energy from him.

You can barely hold any energy. Your storage has dwindled to almost nothing, and your ability to convert is severely compromised. It will take centuries for those skill to re–direct elsewhere. Centuries that I will be unable to recognize any gain from our contract.

Tearing my body to bits for the last few weeks wasn't gain? Groping me beyond what any consort would expect wasn't gain? I could understand being upset over the delay in breeding, but he'd entered into a thousand–year contract — he surely wouldn't be expecting the offspring of his dreams right out of the gate.

"I still devour." My voice was beginning to take on a desperate quality. "That's what you really wanted, isn't it? You can contribute storage capacity and conversion from your end in the first few attempts, and I'll supply the devouring."

I wouldn't, but I'd say anything to delay my execution. I winced as he merged slightly with my spirit–self, tearing his claws into the abdomen I'd just repaired. The physical I could withstand, but this rape of my soul both terrified and infuriated me. I'd never survive this demon, no matter his decision. I needed to get out. I needed Gregory. If I could just get back to him somehow, I know he'd move heaven and earth to try to help me out of this mess.

I find myself enjoying you too much to kill you. I will wait until you repair before I make my decision, and in the meantime you will be my favorite toy in all ways — physically and otherwise.

My mind whirred with thoughts of how I might escape, might find a way to the safety of my angel. Even if I got a message to him, he'd not be able to save me from Hel. I'd need to cross the gates before I could rest easy in his protection. I'd need to do it in a way that didn't set off Ahriman's suspicions otherwise he'd kill Leethu, Dar, and the remnants of my household.

I took a deep breath and reciprocated Ahriman's caress, cringing as I merged his sooty spirit with mine. He shuddered in delight, and I choked back the vomit that rose in my throat.

"I ...I'd like a vacation with the humans, please," I begged, my voice as seductive as I could make it given the circumstances.

No. You just got back, and with your inability to store energy, you'd surely die. I find I do not want you to die, Az. Not yet.

I clenched my jaw and stroked against him. "I can devour. Gain my energy reserves that way. It will help me recover faster."

He paused, and I realized there was some truth to what I'd thought were lies. *An excellent idea, my imp. But you can devour here in Hel and be safe. No, you shall not go.*

I pulled against his spirit–self, drawing him further in. I swear his orange eyes rolled slightly backward in his head. "I will give you a breeding occurrence now if you let me go. Just a brief vacation to spread an Ebola virus variant, grab my hellhound and hybrid horse, and I'll be back."

He panted, fetid breath against my cheek. *Ebola is a particular favorite of mine. I will grant you this trip in exchange for a breeding occurrence, but you must return in one week. If you do not, you'll spend the rest of your contract chained to a wall. Do you understand, Az?*

"Yes." One week. Fuck. And how I'd manage to pull off this breeding occurrence was beyond me. There was no way I was giving him the devouring skills, but I had nothing else he wanted.

Ahriman continued to partially join with me, careful to mostly remain inside his corporeal form. Once again I felt my intestines spill from a searing tear in my belly. It seemed an eternity before he'd satisfied his needs and left me bleeding on the dungeon floor. Tears pricked the back of my eyes as I began the painful process of fixing my physical form, well aware that nothing would wash away the filth that coated my spirit–self.

~30~

Although I was unable to accurately track time, it seemed to be a few days before the demon returned. I tensed as I saw black smoke seeping through cracks in the walls, leaving a greasy stain behind.

Let us see what you can contribute to our offspring, my consort.

I took a deep breath, pulling together the courage for the ordeal ahead. "Can we do this in a more comfortable setting? I don't mean to complain, but I've been down here for ages with no food or drink."

He tilted his head and regarded me with those orange eyes. *You are broken, and the need to combat starvation and dehydration has taken a toll on your strength. How rude of me to have forgotten.*

He wrapped me in darkness, transporting me with a disorienting jerk to another room. This one was warm, with a fire in a central hearth. A variety of plush seats were scattered about the room, designed to accommodate an assortment of demon forms. A tray of meats, vegetables, and breads stood by a sofa, and a glass decanter full of red liquid and two glasses sat nearby.

I dove at the tray, cramming food and drink into my mouth as fast as I could. The repast was in the elven style, and for once I didn't bemoan the blandness. Giving up on the glass, I chugged the red liquid, which turned out to be wine. My head buzzed, and I hoped the alcohol would make what was to come less painful. Ahriman watched. I didn't care. I was so relieved to be out of that horrible dungeon, even if only for a few moments.

Are you ready, Az? I'd finished every bite of food on the platter and drained the decanter dry. My stomach bulged out uncomfortably, but I felt the happy sleepiness that came from a meal after so long without.

"Yes." I approached the demon and stood before him, reaching into my spirit self to section off the portions I'd offer him. I'd thought long and hard about what to give, knowing I'd need to include some of my devouring skills to pull this whole thing off.

Ahriman reached inside me, extending only a small amount of himself to receive — so much for Plan A. I'd hoped he'd risk enough contact to attempt to seize and devour him, but even when he was joining his spirit–self with mine, he'd always been careful to hold the majority of himself a safe distance away. If he'd been weak, I could have spooled him in with a touch, but an ancient demon like Ahriman wouldn't devour easily. I'd need to be able to grab and hold at least seventy percent of his spirit–self to have a chance at taking him in.

I held forth my contribution, and he took it, retracting fully into his corporeal form as I tried to appear relaxed and casual. I'd never procreated before, my one practice attempt resulting in the death of my tutor. What happened now?

"Can I go?"

His semi–solid shape pulsed, sending out a puff of gray. *Yes. One week, Az*

I couldn't help but bolt for the door, slowing to a more respectable pace as I reached a series of hallways leading out of the building. The sunshine blinded me, hitting eyes so used to the dark, and I realized that I was in Eresh, close to the angelic gate that linked Hel with Seattle.

I picked up my pace, panic creeping along the edge of my mind. How long would it take Ahriman to realize I'd given him crap, that his formation wouldn't be able to devour so much as a bacterium? I saw the gate ahead and couldn't stop myself from breaking into a run. Just a few more yards.

Shaking as I reached the passageway, I reached out a hand to activate the gate I'd used several times before. My hand hit the shimmering rift and passed right through. What the fuck? I tried my other hand, a foot. I threw myself through the gate, only to land flat on the gravel just beyond it. I couldn't go through, couldn't activate it. I'd been able to activate gates since I was a few centuries old — what had happened?

Frantic, I looked around, trying to find another demon to open it.

"You! Yeah, you with the slime–covered legs. Can you activate the gate?"

The demon slid over to me, leaving a trail of green behind him.

"Of course I can. Are you a Low or something?"

I winced. Imp wasn't an especially high demon, and this wasn't the first time I'd been mistaken for a Low, but it still stung. I clamped my arm to my side to hide Ahriman's consort mark and nodded.

"You're lucky." The demon swiveled a many–eyed face toward the shimmer. "This is the only one still open. All the other gates are closed."

No, it couldn't be. For two and a half million years the gates had never been closed. Had Gregory gotten my message? What was going on in Aaru? I felt even more anxious to get back, especially since this gate might not remain open much longer.

"I can pay you. I'll owe you a favor."

The demon's seeping eyes swept down my naked human form. "Okay. Who are you?"

"Zalanes." He'd be pissed that I'd used his name, but since he was an imp too, it was somewhat believable. I'd have to remember to make it up to him sometime.

The round shape before me extended a damp protuberance toward the gate, and it glowed, opening to reveal the Seattle street. Relief flooded me, and my limbs felt weak. One step, and I'd be safe. Then I'd have one week to figure out what to do.

I walked forward and smashed against a hard surface, bouncing back to sprawl on the rock pathway. The slime demon burbled out what must have been laughter.

"You've been banished. Sucks to be you. And you still owe me a favor."

He slid away, and I stared up at the sky in shock. Banished. I hadn't realized the full implications of what I'd asked Gregory to do when he'd broken our binding and sent me to Hel. It wasn't that I couldn't activate the gates — I couldn't use them at all. I was stuck here. Damned to Hel forever.

Numb, I stood and brushed the gravel dust from my skin. There was nowhere I could go that Ahriman wouldn't find me. No elf would risk his kingdom to protect me, and other ancient demons wouldn't care. I was his toy to do with whatever he wanted for a thousand years. And once he figured out I wasn't going to give him the devouring skill he wanted, I'd be dead.

As if on cue, I smelled the thick, oily scent of burning flesh. I closed my eyes, unwilling to see what was about to form before me. Even if I did give in and let Ahriman have the devouring skills he wanted, he'd kill me. As soon as he achieved his desired offspring, and tired of playing with me, I'd be dead. And I was willing to bet it would be far sooner than in one thousand years.

I felt the air chill with a sharp bite of frost, the smell of burning flesh intensifying. I was dead either way. The best I could do at this point was ensure that Aaru was safe from his plans for the time being, and that my household was safely out of his grasp. The thick smoke choked me, burning through my lungs as I breathed. Wyatt. Amber. Nyalla. Candy. Michelle. Boomer, Diablo, Piper, and Vegas. Dar and Leethu. And Gregory. *I love you all.*

Claws brushed against my arms and something sharp pierced my side. I bit my tongue, trying not to cry out in pain. *Az, you are an imp of disobedience and trickery. Shall we go home and try this again? Otherwise there will be no vacations for you.*

I had no idea why he was so restrained. I'd expected violence, fury, my body a smear across the pavement of Eresh. Instead, he was giving me a chance to try again. I steeled my resolve. I'd give him nothing more.

"Yes. I will try again." It would only delay the inevitable, but I found I really didn't want to die, and another hour was better than nothing.

He gathered me in a suffocating embrace of black. I opened my eyes to the dark damp of the dungeon. This wasn't my home. It would never be my home, although it was likely to be my grave.

~31~

For some odd reason, it took Ahriman a few days before he approached me to "try again". I wasn't sure if he needed a recovery period, or there was other business he needed to attend to. During that time, I paced the damp dungeon, practicing holding energy within me and converting my form. I *was* recovering my abilities. Too bad I wouldn't have the time to fully regain them.

I cringed when I smelled Ahriman's familiar smell, watching his smoke form coalesce in the dim light. Just as he became vaguely solid, a furred lump crashed from his arms to the floor. I stared into Dar's one red eye, the other swollen shut, his snout covered in blood.

I would have had the succubus join us, but she is well protected at the moment.

"Fucking Wythyn elves." Dar's voice was slurred, but the one good eye was fierce with anger.

Yes. Shame their leader is dead. He had his uses.

It was then I noticed the silver collar around Dar's neck. No wonder he was so physically damaged. He wasn't able to fix any injuries with that damned thing on him.

"Let him go." I strode toward Ahriman, clenching my fists. "We had a deal. You don't touch my household. Any discipline of them goes through me."

We did have a deal, Az. But you neglected to disclose your damaged state, and you've been duplicitous in our very first breeding attempt. Breach of contract, my dear. All bets are off.

I halted, staring down at Dar as my blood ran cold. "I'll give you want you want."

I'd risked Dar's life enough — all for demons, humans and angels he didn't care about. Gregory refused to kill me up on Devil's Paw, but he wouldn't hesitate to take out the monster I'd be forced to create. Would he and the other angels prevail? They were ancient and powerful, but so was Ahriman, and if he had not just one, but a small army of devouring spirits, Aaru would fall. But with my brother before me, I couldn't choose otherwise, even with the entirety of creation at stake.

"Don't you dare give this fucker anything!" Dar snarled.

Ahriman kicked him in the side, launching him to land at my feet. He coughed, and chunks of bloody flesh sprayed my legs.

"There are things in life worth dying for," he whispered, blood bubbling from his mouth. "Make me proud, Mal. Be the demon I would follow through hell and back."

My eyes stung, Dar blurring as I looked down at him. We were going to die. We were both going to die.

"Fuck you, Ahriman. I won't give you shit."

In a flash I was pinned against the damp wall, glowing silver restraints pinning my wrists to the stone. I didn't have much energy, but I'd be unable to get free, unable to fix any of the damage Ahriman was sure to inflict.

Then I will just take what I want.

Ahriman dove his spirit–self into mine, easily resisting my attempts to expel him. I began a series of futile evasion tactics, trying to hide my devouring ability from him while knowing full well it was just a matter of time before he gathered whatever he wanted and ripped it from me. It didn't take long before he'd cornered me. He reached for my devouring abilities. I closed my eyes and felt the red–purple within me, the angel–spirit I'd stolen from Gregory, leap forward, blocking him. Ahriman screamed and yanked clear of me, nearly tearing me in half in his haste to retreat.

An angel! You have part of an angel. And not just any angel, one of ancients — the Dragon Slayer, the Prince of the Presence.

I opened my eyes and saw Ahriman inches from me, his orange eyes calculating as they swept me.

You will give me what I desire. Give it to me!

We'd gone from "I'll take it" to "give it to me". I realized that the angel–spirit would keep Ahriman from snatching my devouring ability. His increased eagerness was easy to understand. I'd managed to tear away part of a powerful angel — probably the most powerful angel in Aaru. That kind of skill was what he so desperately needed. Too bad.

I spat at Ahriman. He grinned, before turning to Dar. I looked at my brother in apology, and saw the angry resolve in his eye. It gave me strength.

I will drive him to the point of death, and you will have a few brief moments to change your mind before he is gone forever. Just give me what I want, Az, and I will raise you to the highest state. You'll be my equal, walk by my side as I crush Aaru under my heel. I'll even let you finish eating that sanctimonious bastard of an angel.

I kept my eyes on Dar, drew from his strength. "I'd much rather angel–fuck that sanctimonious bastard than eat him. Rot in Hel, Ahriman."

The demon sprouted vicious claws on his feet and began to kick Dar, tearing sections of his abdomen with each blow. When Dar became a bloody mess of fur and flesh on the stone floor, Ahriman turned to me.

It was my turn, and it wouldn't be quick. I thought of Gregory and realized that we'd never have our eternity of sin together. He'd mourn, but I knew in my heart he'd be proud of my decision. Would he ever know my sacrifice? Would he ever realize I'd died doing the right thing?

The right thing. *This is my parting gift to you, my angel*, I thought, and I opened up the place in me where all my Owned beings resided. I flew wide the doors to my soul and felt a rush as they exited. Ahriman laughed and gnashed his yellow teeth, slowly approaching.

You too, I told Samantha Martin. *End of the line, girlfriend*. She hesitated a moment, and just as the demon reached for me, she left, sweeping out of my spirit–being into her afterlife.

Teeth tore into my neck. I felt the muscles tear, the blood pour down into my lungs and out along my skin. I looked death in the eye and felt oddly light. Something bright and shining swam through me, like a river of fire. A river of smokeless fire. As I danced on the knife's edge between life and death, the red–purple of Gregory's spirit–self erupted within me, suffusing my being with a burning heat of power.

The dungeon exploded in light. I heard Ahriman scream, felt him slap against me as he pushed himself backward. The restraints that held my arms melted, dripping on the floor to smoke like white acid. I felt oddly unbalanced, as if something unfamiliar and heavy rested against my back. But it didn't matter, because I was free, and even if I died, I was going down fighting.

I dove for Ahriman, but my physical attack was wasted on a semi–solid demon. His black surrounded me, seeping into my pores and through to my spirit–self where he hit me with a massive surge of energy. It should have split me in half. It should have killed me. It certainly hurt like fuck, but I wasn't dead. I blasted him back, realizing my efforts were in vain. I just couldn't pull as much energy as I used to, and Ahriman was ancient.

He swarmed me, and his oily, black essence was doing something to me that his energy attack couldn't. I felt my skin sizzle as if he were acid, and where he touched my spirit–self, I burned. The pain overwhelmed me and I gave up my attack, swatting frantically at his black smoke with both arms. I heard his high–pitched scream, saw slashes of light appear in the darkness and realized that something was in my right hand. A sword.

Fucking piece of shit. Where had it been? I'd needed it desperately, and it had refused to come. But I wasn't about to refuse to use it in a fit of pique. I'd use the damned thing now, and yell at it later.

I hacked at Ahriman like a woman possessed. He pulled back, his oily smoke swirling into a column. My downward stroke tore a line of white through him. I reversed my grip to hit him on a backstroke, and his coal–black hand grabbed the hilt just above my fingers, nearly wrenching my shoulder from its socket.

Ahriman pulled. I pulled. We danced around the dungeon in a deadly tug–of–war. He was winning. What would happen if I lost my grip? Would the sword abandon me as before? Would it betray me and go to him? Fury coursed through me as I thought of my fickle artifact, and I yanked with all my might. Ahriman held firm, and my grip slipped. He pulled. The sword slid from my grasp. By some odd turn of fate, he had unbalanced himself, expecting me to hold firm. He staggered backwards, his heels hitting something large as he tumbled onto the damp dirt floor.

Dar. The sword vanished. I hesitated a split second, looking at my brother as he lay on the floor in a pool of blood. He was going into convulsions. With no time left, I needed to give this everything I had if I had any hope of saving Dar.

I leapt onto Ahriman and straddled him as he bounced against the floor in a puff of oily, black smoke. White streamed from me into the demon, and I frowned. What the fuck was up with that? Whatever it was, it seemed to be working. Ahriman thrashed and screamed under me, pieces of him shattering into frozen chunks. His smoke held motionless for a second in the air before it dropped to the floor in tiny grains. Sand.

His orange eyes met mine, full of hatred. *Angel–loving bitch.*

"Damned straight."

I threw everything at him, and he erupted in a sandstorm of particles, blasting the dungeon walls. I stared down at the gritty floor, at the golden dust coating my hands. Holy shit on a stick, what had I done? I'd somehow managed to take down an ancient demon, one of the strongest in all of Hel.

But there was no time to contemplate my strange new powers. I crawled through the sand and grabbed Dar, sending my spirit–self into his body.

He wasn't there.

Fuck. Fuck! I expanded, frantically searching while keeping myself anchored to my physical form. It seemed like hours that I searched, panicking. He couldn't be gone, couldn't be dead. Not Dar. No.

I felt a feathery wisp of his spirit–being and pulled, spooling him to safety inside my form, holding him as Gregory had done to me in the fire. He shuddered in pain, and I ran myself over and through him, hoping he'd excuse my intimate familiarity. After an exhaustive search, I finally relaxed. All the damage was on the surface. Nothing significant had been lost. I had gotten to him just in time. One more second and he would have been in the same shape I'd been, or perhaps worse.

If I let you go, can you create a corporeal form?

I felt his confusion. He'd never done this sort of thing before, never been without a body. Sharing mine, he wasn't sure how to separate and create his own. We do this upon birth, but it's not a skill we practice afterwards.

Stay here. Hold onto me.

I felt him cling, and I reached down to his dead body, brushing the grains of sand from it, melting the silver collar like warm butter in my hands. Dar's form had been ripped to shreds by Ahriman's claws. He'd quickly bled out. I couldn't put him back inside a dead body — he'd not learned to live inside one as I had. I reached down and ran my hands over the gray fur, staring as the flesh knitted beneath my fingers. This was a day of surprises. I'd somehow gained the power to dust ancient demons, and now I could heal. The rat–like snout of Dar's body grimaced up at me, a variety of unsavory fluid coating the lips. This was totally gross, but it was how the angels did it. I shuddered in revulsion then leaned down to place my mouth against his.

Golden light spilled from me. The body shimmered, lungs inflating and heart pounding.

In you go, I told Dar, snatching him and tossing him into the body. I sensed his panic, and then he grabbed hold, clinging to his rat form with all his might. I pulled my mouth away, spitting in an attempt to rid my mouth of the horrible taste, and I watched. And hoped.

"Come on, Dar. I can't lose my favorite brother."

Red beady eyes opened a fraction, then wider. He bit me, jumping as far as he could and baring his teeth.

"Son of a bitch!" I swore, clutching my arm. "Dar, you bastard! What the fuck is wrong with you?"

His jaw dropped. "Mal? Mal? What happened? What did that shit–for–brains Ahriman do to you?"

What was he talking about? For the first time, I became aware of my surroundings. I'd noticed the sand grains that had once been Ahriman spread across the floor, but the whole thing seemed abnormally lit up, as if someone had finally found the light switch to the dungeon. The light wasn't coming from any fixtures, though: it was coming from me. I looked down and saw myself, a vaguely humanoid form, shimmering indistinctly with a golden light.

And I panicked. Holy fuck, would I always look like this? I'd let all my Owned souls go; would I have the ability to recreate anything beyond this weird, alien–looking silhouette? I tried to calm myself, to steady my breathing and assume a shape, any shape — my first form, Samantha Martin, an insect, anything. The light dimmed, and I saw my hands become flesh. I breathed easy, realizing I'd created the human form I'd worn for over forty years. I had no idea how accurate it was, but anything was better than glowing, gold alien.

"I don't know what happened. Do I look all right now?"

Dar's eyes went from my face to something off to my left. I heard a rustle, felt a shiver of something beyond my back and looked in that direction, dreading what I might see.

"Mal, you have wings," he whispered, as if afraid someone might overhear him.

I did. And they weren't the leathery kind I usually created. Black feathers covered my wings — light–devouring matte–black that absorbed the dim light of the dungeon. It was noticeably darker for a few feet around the wings. I caught my breath, and they shivered in response. They were so sensitive, and I was aware of every particle of air against them.

"You're an angel."

I'll be damned. "I am *not* a fucking angel. I'm a demon, an imp."

"If you say so." Dar's eyes drifted to the black–feathered protuberances.

I scowled and concentrated, trying to dissolve them as I would my leathery ones. Nothing happened. I tried a few more times, then attempted to make them smaller, change them into leathery ones, hide them from view. Nothing I did altered the huge black–feathered appendages attached to my back. If I changed my form would they remain? I had a feeling the answer was yes, and the mental vision of myself as pond scum with huge black wings was disconcerting. They were impossible to ignore. I could feel their weight and sensitivity, like extra limbs.

"Dar, they won't go away. I can't make them go away." My voice rose dramatically, ending with me nearly hyperventilating.

My brother reached out a paw and awkwardly patted my knee. "Calm down. I'm sure they'll eventually go away. Or maybe we can cut them off. There's got to be a sword somewhere, or a chainsaw."

"No! Don't touch them, don't even breathe on them."

I panicked at the thought of slicing them from my body. Demons have a huge tolerance for pain, but I wasn't sure I could survive their removal. I felt every barb, every hook of each feather. My spirit–self was driven down deep into their structure, and unlike the rest of my form, I couldn't seem to distance myself from the appendages.

Dar expelled a breath. "Well they're kinda pretty, in an angel sort of way."

They were, but that didn't mean I had to like them. And how the fuck was I supposed to walk around with big–ass angel wings sticking out of my back? I'd cause a panic, a riot in the streets. Other demons would either flee at the sight of me, or try to kill me. I pulled the wings in tight against my back and tried to make them look as small as possible. They were massive, either sticking out far above my head, or out to the side. I couldn't seem to adjust them so they'd be hidden by my body from the front.

"Maybe if I wrap a large blanket or carpet around myself, they won't show. I'll just look like I have a big hump or something."

Dar snorted a laugh. "You'll look like you're smuggling a small dragon on your back. They wiggle around a lot. Can't you hold them still?"

"No." The wings twitched, as if they had a life of their own. "I'll just have to hope no one rips the carpet off my back. The fewer people that see these things the better."

Dar nodded. "There's got to be some way to dissolve or hide them. Other angels aren't prancing around with their wings out all the time."

"I'm not an angel!" I protested hotly. "Not!"

It was a good idea, though. I needed to find another way to contact Wyatt since my mirror had been destroyed with my residence. Once I did, I'd ask him to check with Gregory. Homesickness washed through me at the thought of both of them. I was free of Ahriman, but I was still banished. How would I ever manage to get home?

"Sooo, carpet it is then." Dar looked around. "I'm not seeing any down here, but I'm sure Ahriman has some in the more comfortable sections of his house."

Probably. I thought I saw some tapestries when we were in the room we'd used for breeding. "You wouldn't have any idea how to get out of this dungeon, would you?" I asked.

Dar shook his head. "The guy teleported me in. If there's a door here, I'll find it."

I watched him scurry around, his nose twitching and paws scrabbling along the walls. My heart warmed. I was so happy he was alive. A paw paused, hovering. There was a click and the wall moved, revealing a staircase. I eyed Dar in admiration.

"You rock! I've been down here for weeks and couldn't find that thing."

He smirked as well as a giant rat could and raced up the stairs. I hurried after him, slowing the moment I tried to wedge my huge wings through the doorway.

"Dar! Hold up."

He waited impatiently while I adjusted and shifted, finally managing to negotiate the narrow stairway by shuffling sideways at a squat. I was never so happy as the moment I saw the warm, dry room through the doorway at the top of the stairs, sunlight streaming through colored windows.

"Consort?" One of Ahriman's servants squeaked in surprise, eyes traveling from Dar to me. I halted at the threshold, hoping my wings weren't visible in the dim light of the stairway. The demon didn't run away in fear, but tilted his head, as if he expected to see another coming behind me. "Is our master still in residence?"

I couldn't envision Ahriman taking the stairs anywhere. He'd always done his smoke—entrance thing and teleported everywhere. I hesitated, not sure what tactic to take. Would the demon's household attack me if they found out about their master's death? And what would they do if they caught sight of the huge feathered things permanently attached to my back? Guess it was time to find out. Ahriman was dead, and I couldn't hang out in this stairway forever.

"Nope. I'm afraid there's been an early termination of the contract. Ahriman and I have parted ways."

I stepped into the open and felt my wings spread out to their full length, flexing after the cramped confines of the passageway.

The demon clutched his chest and let out a scream that shook the windows. Before I could say a word, he'd turned to bolt toward the door. Dar got there first.

"Oh no you don't."

The demon skidded to a halt, his eyes darting between my brother and myself.

"I don't want to hurt you. I know I look terrifying right now, but I really don't want to hurt any of you. I've killed Ahriman, but I have nothing against any of the members of his household."

The demon shuddered as he glanced at my wings, then his eyes traveled to my hair. I reached up, feeling the familiar tingle of a feathered barrette. No fucking way. After all I'd been through, all the times I'd needed this thing and it had refused to appear? Now it shows up, after I've been through some of the most painful, gut—wrenching moments of my short life. Now it shows up.

I ripped the barrette out of my hair and threw it against the wall where it stuck like a ninja star. It hadn't been there when I'd needed it, and now wanted back in my life like some dickhead boyfriend crawling back with apologies?

"Go fuck yourself," I shouted at the thing. Ahriman's servant stared at me with shocked eyes, no doubt thinking my words were meant for him. "Not you. You're fine, it's the sword I'm pissed at."

Dar raised an eyebrow. I knew I sounded like I'd gone over the edge, cursing an inanimate object. I didn't care.

"Iblis," the servant squeaked. "I humbly beg that you accept us into your household. We can promise you loyalty as well as all the talents and skills we possess."

Shit. Ahriman had to have nearly two thousand in his household, what with all his residences and alliances. How the fuck was I supposed to afford to keep them all? I couldn't pitch them out on the streets. Probably thirty percent would quickly find a new household, but the others wouldn't live past the end of the week. There's no way I could provide for them, though. My home was a melted blob, and I was broke.

Or was I? I looked around at the ornate chairs, the bone and flesh dé cor, the elven tapestries on the walls, embellished with blood stains. I wasn't broke; I was rich. Filthy, stinking, rich.

"Petition either my steward or my second," I indicated Dar. "I don't want to just go accepting any old demon into my household. They can decide which of you are worthy. I have more important things to do."

Dar choked back a laugh. He knew I was a complete pushover when it came to household petitions. Every one of them would make the cut, even the lowest of Lows.

The servant bowed and I waved him off with instructions to compile and present me with an inventory of all my new properties and items. I knew half of it would be stolen before it ever hit the balance sheet. That's just how things happened in Hel.

"Nice save, Mal," Dar commented, examining a crystal bowl filled with wood chips. "Hey, check this out. They're chopped up bits of an Ent."

I looked into the bowl with morbid curiosity. Ents were tree creatures not native to Hel. Ahriman got around, and he seemed to have a fascination with saving body parts of his victims. I was just glad I hadn't wound up as chair upholstery or part of a staircase banister. But I could contemplate psychotic decorating ideas later, right now there were more pressing things on my mind.

"So, I'm assuming things aren't going well in Wythyn if they bundled you up and sold you out to Ahriman."

Dar grimaced, turning reluctantly away from the bowl of Ent. "Wythyn still rebels. Kllee will agree to the alliance as long as everyone leaves them alone. Cyelle and Tonlielle are besties — practically one kingdom at this point. Allwin wants some assurances of military protection since they suffered the most in the war with Wythyn and don't trust them to hold to any sort of peace."

"What about Li?"

Dar compressed his lips and shook his head. "They ran Radl out on a pike after twelve hours. I sent him back in with some reinforcements and he's still there. Last I heard, he was desecrating their holy statues with added, inappropriately placed genitals, and demanding all their songs feature the mighty hero Radl the Repulsive."

Better news than I had thought, given Radl's questionable skills. "I heard Kllee was on board with the humans gaining their freedom. Has there been any significant resistance from the other elves?"

Dar looked grim. "I was saving the worst for last. Taullian has gone back on his word to free the humans. Once he realized how powerless you were under Ahriman's thumb, he changed his mind. The elven gates are all closed, but the peninsula remains a part of Cyelle, and no humans have been allowed to leave their masters. All the kingdoms except Kllee are happy to follow Taullian's lead."

I felt the wings at my back snap outward in fury. "Well then, I think it's time we paid the ruler of the United Elven Kingdoms a visit."

~32~

I flew under the cover of a rare moonless night on the long trip to Dis, worried that my interesting new wings would cause a commotion that would end with me shot out of the sky. It was an exhilarating trip. As much as having them bothered me, these things were fast, and the feeling of wind through my feathers was pretty damned close to sex. I hadn't taken into consideration my increased speed and arrived pre–dawn, forcing me to wait around for a respectable time to pay a call to Gareth.

The sorcerer greeted me informally in a workshop full of magical supplies. Bundled tree limbs and sticks were propped against the wall, jars of herbs and various liquids neatly shelved in rows. His smile faltered when he saw me, eyes widening.

"Yeah. I know. I can't figure out how to get rid of them."

"When? When?"

I shrugged. "Sometime between me turning Ahriman into a pile of lifeless sand and stuffing a dying demon back into his newly healed body."

Gareth made a choking noise. "You killed Ahriman?"

I heard the unspoken question — an imp killed an ancient demon that ranked at the very top of the hierarchy?

"And the high elf up in Wythyn, and Haagenti, a few sorcerers, and a real asshole of an angel." And a whole lot of others that I wasn't so proud of. But my past was my past, and my future was hopefully before me. It was time to make my mark — both here and in Aaru, if I could ever manage to get out of Hel, that is.

"I heard about what you tried to do for us humans. I appreciate your efforts, although they don't seem to have made any difference in the end." Gareth approached to shake my hand with his left, his eyes darting occasionally to my wings, as if he couldn't help himself. His right hand was bandaged, half hidden beneath a long sleeve. I was surprised he remembered the handshake I'd taught him.

"Don't you worry. I'm not through with those elves yet."

His eyes swept my naked, human form with unconcealed doubt. "I can't see how an imp could be of any further help."

I grinned. "You should never underestimate an imp."

The sorcerer nodded, clearly not believing me, and ran a tired hand over his stubbled chin.

"What did you do to your hand?" I gestured toward the bandages.

He held up the hand and carefully unwrapped it to reveal blackened, twisted fingers. "Ammonia nitrate and puffwretch sap." I grimaced in sympathy. "Wish I had a curative scroll, but they're pretty scarce right now, with the war and all. Times like this I wouldn't mind having an elf around."

Or an angel. Before he could protest, I reached out to grab the mangled hand, a stream of gold light pouring from me. His hand lit up in a blazing glow while he watched, perplexed. After a few seconds, I retracted the energy and was pleased to see his hand strong and tan, the skin smooth and free of age spots. Crap. I'd probably need to do the other one or he'd look strangely lopsided: an old man with one wrinkled hand and one young one.

He stared at the hand in amazement, then up at me, new respect in his eyes. "Demons don't heal."

"This one does." I didn't want to say the word. I wasn't an angel, just some weird mutated demon. Yeah, that was it.

"A sorcerer with one hand is a sorcerer without a career," he said slowly. "Please tell me how I can repay this gift."

I got right to the point. "I need an elf button, something to get me in front of Taullian without having to fight my way past hundreds of elves."

A look of regret came over his face. "The city and palace are warded, locked down tight. Taullian is not about to be surprised at breakfast — he's learnt from what he did to Feille."

Damn. "A relay device?" I asked hopefully.

He shook his head. "That's not Wythyn magic, and I haven't had time to attempt a copy."

There had to be some way. I couldn't fly in without setting off all sorts of alarms, and I didn't want Taullian to go into hiding while his elves slowed me down with an endless stream of attacks.

"Wait, I've got an idea." The sorcerer walked through a door at the rear of the room, partially hidden behind a tower of baskets. He was gone only a few moments before he returned, thrusting an amulet into one hand and a bundle of fabric into another.

"Clothes," he said, pointing to the bundle. "As delectable as that human body is, you should probably cover at least a portion of it."

Dirty old man. I grinned, and his eyes twinkled in response. He was right, and I was getting a bit tired of being naked all the time. Human flesh was susceptible to nicks, cuts, and bruises unless protected. The elves wouldn't care, but I'd have more of a commanding presence if I were clothed.

"This," he indicated the amulet, "allows for an hour of enhanced non–detection."

"Invisibility?" I turned the amulet over in my hand to admire the glyphs engraved on the back.

"No, enhanced non–detection. It's not the normal 'look away' or 'no–see' spell, and it does more than hide you from sight. It allows you to travel in an inter–dimensional rift. No one can see you, smell you, or sense you in anyway. Magical detection spells don't register it either."

That was huge. Some of the sneakiest magic leaked enough of its own special energy signature and set off alarms. "The flight wards?"

"You can fly in undetected, but you only have an hour. It may not be enough."

It would be, if one had the wings of an angel.

"It's my most precious item." He looked at the amulet fondly. "Almost a decade of my time went into its making. It took me almost as long to perfect as the item I made for Ahriman."

I weighed it in my hand, realizing the significance of the gift. This was worth far more than the healing of his hand warranted. In spite of his doubts, he dreamed of freedom for humans and was willing to give his most valued creation for the cause. I liked this guy.

"What did you make for Ahriman?" I was curious what magical item would have taken two decades to make and would have been considered valuable enough for the ancient demon to offer a lengthy period of protection.

"I called it a breeding box. It does the forming process when two demons procreate. Just add the portions of each spirit–being, and it acts as a catalyst. I'm not sure why he wanted it. I just assumed he had some sort of fertility issue he wanted to overcome."

I frowned. Ahriman hadn't seemed to have any difficulties breeding. Suddenly I remembered his anger over Feille's death, how he mentioned he needed the elf for some project, and all the pieces fit together. The forming magic that the angel on Oak Island had boasted of, how they could now breed again without needing us at all. But why would Ahriman want to assist the hated angels to procreate?

"Ahriman gave me all the specifications for the device. He was very adamant that it only produce a demon with certain traits," Gareth continued.

"What traits?"

The sorcerer ticked the traits off on his newly healed fingers. "Warmongering, avarice, anger, envy, and devouring, all hidden until the offspring reached the age of one hundred. Oh, and all offspring would turn into demons at that point, which I truly didn't understand. Why would they be anything but demons?"

Because they might be angels — Angels of Order, and that just wouldn't do if an ancient demon wanted to eat up Aaru from the inside. It wasn't just a coup facilitated through devouring spirits under his control that Ahriman planned; it was more. Desperate angels would create monsters that would crack the virtues of Aaru and turn heaven in upon itself. Another war. More death. But Feille was dead, Ahriman was dead, and I could only hope that Wyatt managed to get my message to Gregory, that he ended this twisted plan before it could begin.

"Thank you," I told Gareth, turning the amulet over in my hand. Saving Aaru was momentarily out of my hands. My immediate task would be to ensure the humans in Hel actually had an opportunity for a decent future.

"Thank you." Gareth wiggled his healed fingers toward me. "Please let me know if there's anything else you need."

"You wouldn't happen to have any more of those chicken wands, would you?" I hoped so, because that thing had been amazing. Maybe Taullian was just as terrified of chickens as Feille had been. Maybe it was an elf thing.

Gareth smiled. "If you pull this off, I'll ensure you have a steady supply of chicken wands as long as I live."

I slipped my bundle under one arm and gave him a quick salute, tucking my wings in tight to my body. "Consider it done."

~33~

I stood outside the Western Red Forest at its narrowest point, feeling an odd sense of homesickness. I'd played in these woods as a child, eaten grubs and hidden from cruel siblings. That imp seemed like a different demon from who I was now. I wasn't even a thousand years old, yet I felt like I had lived several lifetimes. Did Gregory feel the same when he thought back on his past? At over six billion, he must feel as if he'd been through a kaleidoscope of lives. What would he make of me now, standing in the humid summer heat, insect song surrounding me, fifty feet of feathered wings arched to soak in the warmth of the sun?

He'd wanted my redemption, wanted me to take responsibility, but what if the changes he longed for turned me into a creature he could no longer love? He'd fallen for an imp, not ...whatever I was right now. I glanced sideways at the black wings. I refused to be an angel. Refused.

Closing my eyes, I breathed in the thick damp air. The humans were mine. *Mine.* The word reverberated with purpose, with intent. It was time to be more than an imp. I slid the amulet over my head and said the activation words.

The air shimmered, thinned, and I felt as if I were standing inside a long tunnel of a gate. There was no time to explore the odd sensation. I had only one hour to travel nearly four hundred miles. Hoping the passageway was wide enough to accommodate a fifty–foot wingspan, I took to the air. If not, the elves would see an odd image of black wingtips against the sky. Which would probably just look like a bird if I stayed high enough.

The incredible power of my new wings propelled me forward faster than I'd ever flown. I'd loved the demon ones I used to form, but these.... It was like driving a Formula One racecar after thinking your suped–up Charger rocked the world.

The cold air bit at my sensitive feathers, tearing my eyes and stinging exposed skin, the heat of summer falling before the chill of speed. Trees far beneath blurred, but even with my odd new abilities, I still worried my time would run out.

The air began to shimmer and thicken as I dove for the center of Cyelle's capital, near the palace gates. A crowd was gathered there, and I hesitated a fraction of a second, realizing I'd probably be detected by the time I landed, destroying any chance at surprise. Sure enough, I felt the protection of the amulet give way just as I raced in for landing, trying desperately to hit the ground with enough time to hide before I was truly visible.

No such luck.

The wards shrieked when I was ten feet from the ground. Worse, my hot approach was completely beyond my ability to control. I'd only had these wings a few days, and I hadn't quite figured them out yet, especially under speed.

The crowd screamed and scattered as I slammed into the ground, tumbling and digging a trench in the cobblestone street before I came to a stop by crashing into a fruit vendor's cart. Yep, no matter what had happened, I was still an imp. I scrambled to my feet, shoving apples aside and shaking grapes from my huge wings. The guards surrounding me with nocked arrows lowered their bows to look at me, mouths agape.

"Where's Taullian," I demanded.

The guards continued to stare. I heard the clink of arrows hitting the ground, a murmur from the crowd. A young elf reached out his hand toward one of my wings, and his mother yanked it back with a quick whisper about manners.

Did they know? How could they know? Surely these elves had seen winged demons before. Some of us did feathers, although it was always considered a weak affectation. Yeah, they were big, and they were black, but it's not like I was an....

"Angel."

I really wished people would stop calling me that. Just as I was beginning to ask them in simple tones to take me to their leader, I heard him. I heard the stomp of the guards, saw the crowd parting to let them through, heard his ringing, scornful tones.

"So the imp has slipped her leash. Shall I call the pound?"

The guards that arrived first through the crowd came to an abrupt halt as they saw me, causing a mini traffic jam behind them that must have irritated Taullian to no end.

"You think to invade my kingdom, to deliver more threats? You have no leverage, imp. You're not the Iblis, not a demon of any stature. You're just a plaything of the powerful, a Low with no household to speak of, no money, no property. You're ...."

He'd pushed his way past the shocked guards to see me.

"Say it, you pansy–ass elf boy."

He didn't. Instead, he took off at a run, and I sprinted after him. Everyone parted to make way for me, some of them bowing as if I were royalty, others dropping to their knees. Running with huge wings isn't easy. I pulled them tight against my back, trying to streamline my profile and reduce the wind resistance as I ran.

Taullian was fast, as all elves were, but the crowd didn't part for him, and he found himself shoving people aside to make his way, slowing him down considerably. Everyone was too busy staring at me to exercise any respect for their ruler. He could run, but he couldn't hide, and eventually I'd find him. With the crowds, the elf couldn't find a decent exit, and I finally cornered him, the stone palace wall at his back and sides, a large market table in front of him.

"Ahriman is going to kill you for this." His voice was high and thin with desperation. I jumped with both feet to land on the table, crouched like a gargoyle with my wings trailing behind. Taullian trembled, meeting my eyes, and once again I wondered what exactly I looked like. I'd need to find a mirror and figure out why everyone was suddenly so shocked with my appearance. It couldn't just be the wings, could it? They were just big—feathered things sticking out of my back. There had to be something else about me that was different.

"Not unless he can return from the dead. Now, I'm not ruling it out — he was a pretty powerful demon. But I'm thinking it's not going to happen." I jumped off the other side of the table and slowly edged toward the high elf, stalking him like the predator I was. At least that hadn't changed.

I halted a few feet from Taullian and stared him down. To his credit, he lifted his chin, and in spite of his trembling, managed a fairly good sneer.

Showtime. I'd killed Ahriman. Everyone was staring at me as if I were the baddest thing to walk the surface of Hel. Time to live up to my very recently acquired reputation.

I leaned toward Taullian and let anger take over. I let myself glow and smiled at him with as much cruelty as I could muster. "The humans belong to me. All of them. They are mine, and you will let them go."

He swallowed, eyes darting around to the elves and humans hanging on my every word.

"You rule these kingdoms because I allow it. If you betray me again, you will find yourself in exile, and it will be you who will be a demon's plaything."

His eyes widened, recognizing the truth in my words.

"Not my toy either. No, I will not give you such an honor. You'll serve the Lows, entertaining them with your pain. Do I make myself clear?"

He nodded, the movement full of fear, his eyes shifting from mine to the wings visible on either side of me.

"Hel is *mine*. I grant both the peninsula and the adjoining hundred miles that extends into the Western Red Forest to the humans. And if I find that you've hindered them, mistreated them in any way, I will carve off more and more of the elven lands until you find yourself ruling over a cesspit at the edge of the swamp."

"No!" He clamped a hand over his mouth. The Western Red Forest was sacred, and it would pain them terribly to give away a third of it to another species. Too fucking bad. I ramped up the wattage, and Taullian's eyes watered, squinting in my light.

"I question your ability to rule, but in the spirit of mercy toward my elven citizens, I will give you another chance to prove your value to me. Don't fail."

"Yes." It was a whispered word. I raised my eyebrows and cupped an ear. "I will do as you say." His voice rang out that time, loud enough for the crowd to hear.

"I'll be watching. In the dark of the night, hidden in the shadows of the day, I'll be watching. This is your last chance, elf."

I spun about, not caring that my wing knocked him to the ground as I extended them for balance and vaulted the table. The crowd parted for me, and I took to the air, once again setting off alarms as I rose through the wards of the city. I'd have to keep a close watch on things here, returning often to Hel to make sure the humans were truly free.

Returning. What was I thinking? I was stuck here. My heart was like a stone in my chest. Feille was dead, the humans were free, and I had escaped Ahriman's deadly clutches. But I was still damned to Hel.

343

~34~

I flew low over the forests of Cyelle, confident the elves wouldn't attack me. I wasn't so sure about the demons, so I landed at the southern edge of the Western Red Forest, just inside the neutral zone, and walked out to sit on a rock by a mess of trumpet reeds to wait for Dar.

I saw him from nearly a mile away — on four legs so he could move with greater speed. He had some kind of pack strapped to his back and was running in a strange leaping hop which popped him above the tall grass at regular intervals. He slowed at fifty yards, walking upright the remaining distance before depositing himself beside me on the rock.

"I haven't run this much since I was a nestling," he puffed, rubbing a hand over his round belly. "I'm gonna lose my figure if I keep this up."

"What's in the bag?" I gestured to his back.

He yanked it off, grinning, and began to dig through it. "Check it out. I found all kinds of stuff at Ahriman's house. I had to hide a bunch of it since I couldn't carry it all. And some things were too big to sneak out easily."

I watched with amazement as Dar pulled goblets, bones, candles, a timepiece, and a gaudy hat from the bag. He was such a packrat. I should be pissed. These weren't Ahriman's things anymore — they were mine, but I wouldn't begrudge my brother his trinkets.

"I call dibs on any shoes." Okay, maybe he wasn't the only packrat in Hel.

He shot me a quick smile and a thumbs–up. "I'll keep my eyes open. How did things go with Taullian and the other elven assholes?"

"Everyone freaked at my wings. They all think the apocalypse is at hand."

I refused to say the A–word. Angels, not apocalypse. The former was far more terrifying.

My brother sighed, putting his treasure carefully back in the bag. "So, I guess it's back to Wythyn for me?"

I shook my head. "Let Taullian deal with them. I really don't care about elven politics anymore. As long as they free the humans and let them live peacefully in their own lands, they can do whatever they want to each other."

Dar raised a shaggy eyebrow. "And if they don't?"

I stood up to face him, snapping my wings to their full span. Golden light hummed from me, and I leaned close to Dar. "I'll be watching. In the dark of the night, hidden in the shadows of the day, I'll be watching."

Dar made a strangled noise. "I think I just shit my fur. Damn, Mal, you are one scary mother–fucker."

"Pretty cool, huh?" I folded my wings and returned to what I hoped looked like a normal human.

"I'll say. So what's your game plan, besides bullying the elves? Rolling in Ahriman's riches? Scaring the piss out of demons with your angel–in–Hel routine? Are you heading back to Wyatt and your life there?"

Remembrance crashed through me. I was damned.

"I can't cross the gates, Dar. Can't activate them, can't go through them at all. Gregory had to banish me, and now I'm trapped here."

Dar's red eyes searched my face. "The elf gates are closed, but they could make another."

I snorted. The elves weren't exactly my friends right now, even with the influence of my big–ass wings, and gates weren't something sorcerers could do. An idea wormed its way into my mind. "I need a marble, like Kirby has."

"Or a pair of ruby slippers."

I caught my breath, looking down at my filthy bare feet. I was an ang ...no, I was a *special* demon. With skills we'd lost nearly three–million years ago, with wings we'd lost when we were kicked out of Aaru. Maybe I had other talents as well.

"Promise you won't make fun of me if this doesn't work?" I asked Dar as I got to my feet to stand in front of him.

He snorted. "Yeah, right."

How did Gregory do this? He didn't make any hand movements like the elves did when they transported themselves from spot to spot. He just pulled me close and off we went.

Home. I closed my eyes and thought of my kitchen, and the smell of coffee. I thought of the sun warming my skin as I sprawled by my pool, the feel of wingless flight as I jumped fences on my horse, the way Wyatt stroked the inside of my thighs, the feel of Boomer's velvety ears. Home.

I peeked open an eye and saw Dar before me, eyebrows raised. Pushing down the sick feeling that rolled through me, I squeezed my eyes shut and thought again. Wyatt, his blue eyes laughing, sharing some joke as we sat on his ratty, chip–encrusted couch. Gregory making me coffee, teaching me, sharing his form in a spray of fireworks. Gregory kissing me in Juneau, holding me during my 'punishment', saving me when I thought all was lost. My angel. My nemesis and my savior all rolled into one. I just wanted to see him again, to see everyone I loved. I wanted to go home. The longing ached like no pain I'd felt before. Home.

My stomach twisted, every cell compressing painfully as if I'd been squeezed in a vise. It only took a second, then everything released. I staggered with vertigo and opened my eyes.

This wasn't home. It was a place filled with nothing: a wall of white where none of my human senses worked. My skin itched. Aaru. What a complete fuck—up.

I felt a presence near me — multiple presences. No one addressed me, but their hostile intent felt like a lit match in my head. I wasn't supposed to be here. Aside from the punishments, when Gregory had snatched me from the jaws of death, and the times I'd done a quick ring—and—run into his circle from the gate in Sharpsburg, I'd never been. I wasn't allowed.

I felt them move closer. The only thing saving me was probably their uncertainty in attacking me. Where was Gregory? I couldn't feel him without our bond, and I knew he couldn't feel me either. Would these angels tear me to bits before he realized I was here?

A streak of white came toward me, and instinctively I raised my arm, deflecting the blast with a sword that appeared from nowhere in my hand. The angels retreated, and I felt a sense of confusion mixed with anger and loathing. As much as I hated this sword, at least it had come to me now, and it was probably the only thing keeping these angels from killing me.

"Stay back," I ordered, trying to keep the fear from my voice. My wings flared, and I did a quick sweep with the sword. I wasn't the least bit skilled in fighting with this weapon, but I figured I could hack down a few angels if I needed to. They jumped back as one, giving me space. I felt them murmur, like a thousand voices at once, and knew I didn't have much time. Where was the exit? There had to be a way out somewhere?

"I want to see...." My voice trailed off as I realized I had no idea what Gregory's real name was. He'd never told me. I'd never asked. He was always just Gregory to me. Or Asshole.

"I want to see my angel." Which sounded an awful lot like "I want to see my Mommy." Fuck. I was so dead. Their murmurs increased, and I felt them edging forward, testing me. They surrounded me, and I spun around like a top, keeping my sword in front and pointed to where I sensed one coming closer than the rest of the group.

The crowd parted like water, and one came forward, shimmering into corporeal form as he approached. Gregory, with all of his wings revealed and open. I felt a wave of relief, even if he did have his sword in hand, but as he approached, I saw beneath his corporeal form, to the battered spirit inside.

"What the fuck happened to you? Shit, you look worse than I do."

He ignored my questions, his eyes moving from the Sword of the Iblis up to my face where his gaze halted as he searched my eyes with his. Didn't he recognize me? How could he not recognize me? I looked the same, looked like Samantha Martin, didn't I?

He frowned and shifted, relaxing his grip on the sword, then something caught his attention off to the side of my body, and his eyes opened wide.

"Is it ...you?" he asked, as though he were afraid to say my name, the name he'd given me.

"Yes." My wings shivered, extending slightly as if they had a will of their own. Again his eyes were drawn to them.

"You're an angel."

I couldn't tell if that was a good or bad thing from his tone. Not that it mattered — I *wasn't* an angel.

"No, absolutely not. I'm a mutated demon. That's what I am."

His lips twitched into a smile, his eyes growing warm. I could tell he was going to humor me in my delusions — at least for now.

"Are you going to use that sword? If not, I'd suggest you put it away."

I looked around at the non–corporeal angels still surrounding us, then down at the sword still in his hand. "You first."

The sword vanished, and once again his eyes were drawn to my wings. He frowned, and fear lanced through me.

"It's me," I whispered. "I'm not an angel, I'm not. I'm still me. I'm still your Cockroach."

I was going to break inside, shatter into a million pieces if he didn't say something, do something. All my doubts flooded me. What if he didn't love me anymore? I'd become something else — a *special* demon. Maybe that was too far removed from the imp he'd fallen in love with.

His gaze returned to my face, warm and sympathetic. "You will always be my Cockroach."

Then he held his arms wide and I ran, tossing my sword aside as I dove into his embrace. I buried my face into his polo shirt and clung to him with all my might. His hand stroked my hair, his spirit–self gently examining the edges of mine.

"You're an angel." I felt the breath of his voice on my hair, his chest reverberating against my cheek.

"No. A mutated demon. I am not an angel. Don't you dare call me that!"

He chuckled. "An Angel of Chaos. My choir was shocked senseless. One hasn't been seen in Aaru for two and a half million years. One hasn't been seen *anywhere* in two and a half million years. What happened?"

I leaned back so I could see his face. "I let all my Owned souls go. And ...I know you said to eat you, so I hope it's okay that somehow I kinda did."

He examined my spirit–being further. "This wasn't what I thought would happen. I expected it would enable you to repair your lost functions quicker, not turn you into an angel."

"I'm not an angel," I protested hotly.

His eyes traveled to my side. "I like your wings."

It sounded sexual, like he was saying I had a nice rack or a hot ass.

"How can I hide them, like you do? It's not exactly convenient walking around with a fifty–foot wingspan. How am I supposed to get in my car? Or sleep on my side? Fuck, I can't even manage to squeeze through half the doorways."

He smiled, and my heart lurched at the sight. "I'll show you how to do it. But they'll always be visible to other angels. As they should be."

I glanced and clearly saw his — the six wings, cream with a spider–web pattern and tips of gray. Mine shivered in response, and his eyes again darted to them, something akin to lust sparking in their black depths. Dragging his gaze to my face, he ran a hand through my hair, picking up a strand to rub it between his thumb and forefinger. It was such a familiar gesture that I nearly cried. I thought I'd never see him again, that I'd never leave Hel alive.

"You came to me," his voice was husky. "Here in my very own fourth circle of Aaru. Home."

Home. I'd wanted to go home. But it wasn't Aaru that drew me, that signified home in my heart, it was this angel. Home would always be wherever he was.

"Wyatt is distraught over your absence, as are all the humans and other creatures that follow you. We should go to them and celebrate your return."

We. I smiled up at him, skimming my hands down his waist to touch the skin under his huge polo shirt. "Can you give me a lift? I'm not very good at this yet and I don't want to wind up in Siberia by accident."

He drew me in close, and I felt that familiar, disorienting sensation as he transported us. I was an angel, no, a *special* demon. Everything had changed except the things that really mattered, like the feel of being in my angel's arms. Whatever the future held — Wyatt and my human friends, the elves, the humans in Hel, my demon household, the Ruling Council, none of that worried me as long as I had my angel by my side.

About the Author

Debra Dunbar primarily writes dark fantasy, but has been known to put her pen to paranormal romance, young adult fiction, and urban fantasy on occasion. She lives on a farm in the northeast section of the United States with her husband, three boys, and a Noah's ark of four legged family members. When she can sneak out, she likes to jog and ride her horse, Treasure. Treasure, on the other hand, would prefer Debra stay on the ground and feed him apples.

Connect with Debra Dunbar on Facebook at DebraDunbarAuthor, on Twitter @Debra_Dunbar, or at her website http://debradunbar.com/.

Sign up for New Release Alerts:
http://debradunbar.com/subscribe-to-release-announcements/

Feeling impish? Join Debra's Demons at http://debradunbar.com/subscribe-to-release-announcements/, get cool swag, inside info, and special excerpts. I promise not to get you killed fighting a war against the elves.

Thank you for your purchase of this book. If you enjoyed it, please leave a review on Goodreads, or at the e-retailer site from which you purchased it. Readers and authors both rely on fair and honest reviews.

Books in the Imp Series:

The Imp Series
A DEMON BOUND (Book 1)
SATAN'S SWORD (Book 2)
ELVEN BLOOD (Book 3)
DEVIL'S PAW (Book 4)
IMP FORSAKEN (Book 5)
ANGEL OF CHAOS (Book 6)
IMP (prequel novella)
KINGDOM OF LIES (Book 7) Fall, 2015 release

Books in the Imp World
NO MAN'S LAND
STOLEN SOULS
THREE WISHES

Half-Breed Series
DEMONS OF DESIRE (Book 1)
SINS OF THE FLESH (Book 2) Summer, 2015 release
UNHOLY PLEASURES (Book 3)Spring, 2016 release

Other titles in the *Paths for the 21st Century* series
edited by Marcus Raskin

The Business of America: How Consumers Have Replaced Citizens and How We Can Reverse the Trend
Saul Landau

THE
American
Ideology

A CRITIQUE

ANDREW LEVINE

FOREWORD BY MARCUS RASKIN

ROUTLEDGE
NEW YORK AND LONDON

Published in 2004 by
Routledge
29 West 35th Street
New York, NY 10001
www.routledge-ny.com

Published in Great Britain by
Routledge
11 New Fetter Lane
London EC4P 4EE
www.routledge.co.uk

Printed in the United Stated of America on acid-free paper.
Typesetting: BookType

10 9 8 7 6 5 4 3 2 1

Library of Congress Cataloging-in-Publication Data

Levine, Andrew, 1944-
  The American ideology : a critique / Andrew Levine.
      p.   cm. — (Paths for the 21st century)
  ISBN 0-415-94549-6 (hardcover)
  1. Political science—United States—History. 2. United States—Politics and government.
  3. Political culture—United States. 4. Ideology—United States. 5. Social values—United
States. I. Title. II. Series.
  JA84.U5L54 2004
  320.5'0973—dc22

                                                                                    2003025686

Contents

Series Editor's Preface

The aim of the Paths for the 21st Century series is to encourage new ways of looking at problems, to foster practical approaches to longstanding problems, and to promote the knowledge capable of positively influencing people's everyday lives. The books in this series are intended to give the powerless a greater role in the discourse that strengthens communities without creating barriers between these communities. To these ends the "Paths Project" seeks out new ways for future generations to evade the pitfalls of the twentieth century while fostering a spirit of liberation that focuses on dignity and decency for all people.

The Paths Project acknowledges three contending approaches to the use and function of knowledge. The first views knowledge and inquiry as primarily in the service of domination, control and the manipulation of others. This form of knowledge most often results in a blind, unquestioning, and dogmatic faith. The second approach focuses on knowledge as merely utilitarian with an ever increasing focus on technical specializations and sub-specialization. It assumes a specific cause and solution to a given problem, and pays insufficient attention to the aims and values to which knowledge is ultimately subservient.

It is the third approach which I take as the basis for the Paths Projects. This approach assumes that knowledge and inquiry are directed toward liberation rather than control, seeking to understand the relationships between institutions, systems, problems and, most importantly, values. This approach ultimately fosters greater democratic discourse and a more progressive social reconstruction. The Paths Project presumes that this third approach affords us the insight and wisdom necessary for creating the conditions of dignity and equality and for ending the exploitation of one group over another.

Paths for the 21st Century seeks to draw together scholars and activists to create an invisible college, working together and trading ideas to stimulate thinking and discussion about issues affecting us domestically and internationally. It will present radical alternatives concerning what should be changed, and how these changes can be accomplished. In the end, the aim of the Paths Project is to lay the foundation for a new progressivism chastened by the lessons of the twentieth century and reconstructed for the twenty-first century. This is no small goal which, ultimately, in a democracy, can only be achieved through discussion and a community of inquiry and deliberation. It is my hope that the books in this series will help to begin and contribute to that dialogue without which social justice, personal freedom, and a progressive twenty-first century will never come about.

Marcus Raskin
Institute for Policy Studies

Foreword

Marcus Raskin

" . . . Philosophy is an activity that responds to situations that rational beings, or at least beings who are aware of their own rational capacities, sometimes confront, and cannot evade. Seen this way, philosophy is not exactly a body of doctrines or set of beliefs. Rather, it is a way of addressing a kind of puzzlement, one that is mainly conceptual in nature—in the course of which doctrines and beliefs will typically, but not necessarily, emerge. Perhaps no idea fits this description better than the idea of Reason."

—Andrew Levine

The question in politics is *whose* rationality?

By the mid-1970s, Watergate and the end of the Indo-China war had changed politics and intellectual fashions. The system worked, the war ended, and the time was ripe to get these nightmares behind us. But emphasis on alternatives and new social structures flagged. For liberals, progressives, and radicals, it was a time to find the mainstream in politics. A constricted view of Adam Smith became popular as neoliberalism. Selfishness grew through an unfettered market which was supposed to result in a common good and individual betterment. Nevertheless, the idea that profit could be taken out of the society by a few for their sole benefit seemed like a quaint concept.

There had been more palatable ideas which found support and expression from New Deal and post–New Deal liberals, especially those who had struggled for a measure of economic justice. But first they had to confront the concept of the free market—a system whose reality was tangential to the workings of American capitalism—except in one important case. Equity and efficiency in capitalist economics are often contradictory. Andrew Levine correctly states the problem for democracy: "It is always an open question just how much efficiency one would be willing to trade off for the sake of equity or other non-efficiency concerns. Presumably, in a democracy, this is a question for the political process to decide. In the American case, to a degree seldom rivaled in other developed countries, equity considerations have never been vigorously pursued. At present, with free market fundamentalism the order of the day, equity concerns have fallen even further into disregard."

The alternative capitalist model does not shirk the free market ideology. It merely civilizes its excesses. It is more realistic and more in keeping with American dreams. The new meritocratic and entrepreneurial class of whites and blacks embraced equality of opportunity in the economic and social spheres. Because equality of opportunity allowed—and even implicitly encouraged—inequality, a major political question arose. How can this system be rationalized without change in the fundamental distributions of power? The answer supplied by liberalism was that there must be opportunity for the individual and that existing government programs must have individual opportunity as their goal. In this sense, equality of opportunity acted as an ideological and political safe haven. In practice, equal opportunity encouraged and accepted inequality in an economic sphere that did not touch the operations of political democracy.

Bill Clinton was for more "millionaires and more billionaires." Everyone would partake of the growth pie and the employed would get something too if they acquired skills, and were self-motivated and capable of following orders. Clinton's American ideology was a win-win situation where each received according to his ability but not necessarily his need.

No one could deny that there were a number of examples reinforcing the system as it was. In fact the examples proved the utility of American ideology. No doubt some of the formerly impoverished could become multimillionaires, such as those who found oil on their farms, or organized the work of others or who had mastered the intricacies of financial capital. There was no question that people formerly denied entrance to universities for reasons of race, religion or ethnicity were able to climb the ladder given to the deserving. Government interventions were more helpful than the marketplace. Thus, for example, the GI Bill, which probably saved the United States from economic depression and intense violent struggle.

Imagine 16 million GIs returning from World War II with no economic and educational prospects. The United States would have faced the kind of catastrophic situation that had occurred in Germany after World War I where returned veterans took up arms and were critical in bringing down the Weimar Republic. Unfortunately, the United States by 1949 linked itself to war and war preparation as the means to promote stability. For 40 years after World War II military Keynesianism served as the instrument of economic growth, individual opportunity, and subsidization of private corporations. This project has meant "guns before butter."

The Left, however, could not find the coherence and political agency necessary for a political project. Liberal realists believed major changes were unnecessary, utopian and doomed to failure. The plea to rethink American values along Martin Luther King's vision of economic and social justice, antimilitarism, anti war, and racial equality had no place in the official American ideology.

The lingering question is: What political strategy makes sense for the 21st century where illusions multiply and wars are there as natural as the weather? It is daunting to think there is any ideology, American or otherwise, which can uplift the billions of people racked with disease and hunger.

Reform is never, as Levine would say, enough if it merely restates the status quo, and revolution is unsatisfactory if it is just another form of violence. American pragmatism sought another way. The purpose of the great pragmatists—John Dewey and William James—was a political one in its widest meaning. Perhaps because the United States was a frontier society, they believed that America could remake human nature. This was also the claim of most Marxists. In 19th and 20th centuries, America had groups struggling for perfection and survival. So it was hardly surprising that pragmatists would see American society always in the act of becoming.

Pragmatism, beyond being an analytic tool, retains the Aristotelian notion of the good end. On the other hand, pragmatism never loses its skepticism. This keeps advocates and analysts honest. Neither pragmatism nor reconstruction are exercises in metaphysics. They are attempts at finding alternatives to mounting crises. Happiness may be the result from time to time. But the search for it must continue and cannot be at odds with rationality. It is, of course, a curious search in a time when our awareness of human disaster and frailty are greatly expanded. The crisis is now multiple and interconnected, demanding a very different set of capitalist definitions for such root terms as the concept of efficiency.

The Cold War masked the meaning of efficiency for both the US and the Soviet Union. Bureaucrats and policy makers from opposing camps played from the same rulebook and often with the same habits of mind. The Cold War demanded that the American ideology live up to its stated ideals of justice and human rights. Progress in women's and blacks' rights went on unabated, voting was expanded to 18 year olds, and blacks voted without interference. As the Cold War drew to a close, new realities appeared in the United States. There was no need for the Right to continue the pretense of advocating economic and social justice. Indeed, the reverse was true. Now was the time to march back to the good times of the 1920s.

After 1990, claims against the Left by the Right became more strident. Efficiency meant narrowing public expenditures, and privatization meant public planning by the private sector.

America has a tradition of pluralism and a philosophy of reasonableness. In answer to Rodney King's question "Can't we all get along?" John Rawls would probably have said we can have boundaries to encourage mutual toleration, but we don't have to be friends. He and his philosophic colleagues might say that we can have a fair and disinterested judicial system. They might say that in the context of democratic ideals we can have an economic system that manages minimums and maximums of wealth so that the spread between the two is not so great. Under this system, those who share the same nation and geographic space won't destroy each other in civil war out of need or envy. But political philosophy is more than a neutral observation post above the fray of everyday life. Thus, Levine's political philosophy—after examining neutral, disinterested approaches, and the limits of efficiency as defined through the market— elides into public policy. The starting point for public policy/political philosophy is the social problematic and the person inside of it. People are born on a moving train running on tracks that may be corroded and dangerous. From birth they learn through others, from their own experience, and from the experience of institutions, what to know and what to discard. They also learn what helps them redefine the values of the future. If I am black and live near a toxic waste dump, I need to know the dangers why the decisions of others have resulted in a personal crisis for me. If our food is tainted, I need to know what to do. Obviously these examples can be multiplied a thousand-fold. The question for political philosophy and a public policy of reconstruction is whether its advocates can construct action projects that will alleviate even these multifarious conditions. Some of them are caused by the present organization of capital.

That is, certain contradictions become evident between capitalism and the common good, especially where equality is not held in high regard. Liberal reformers have tried to finesse the problem of inequality through ideas of economic growth and the ideology of equality and opportunity. These ideas mask disparity because each class gets more, especially those at the top of the pyramid. As a result, their political and social power grows exponentially.

But can political philosophy do more than elaborate the status quo? And can political philosophy relate to strategic social action as Dewey, Marx and others have argued? Not all political philosophy is linked to strategic action, although action may take on new meaning as concepts are rethought and constitutions are redrafted. Constitutions may or may not be strategies for action once they are put in place. They may be boundary-driven systems of thought encouraging changes made by those with the power of implementation.

Perhaps the most prominent aspect of reconstructive empiricism is that its roots are in dialogue rather than statistics. Reconstructive empiricism is meant to look inside to see who is served by facts; what the values inside the facts are; and who decides how and where the camera of research for facts is pointed. What is the nature of power and what knowledge sustains that power? The dialogue is the path to a different society and while words may be deficient, dialogue remains our primary tool for understanding and social change.

Democracy is a challenge to a written constitution because democracies are protean in character and constitutions are sets of rules that are very seldom open to change. Constitutions, the rule of law, and other such concepts are supposedly guarantees of predictability as automatic as a clock that is wound up once and then tells time forever. The irony is that socialist governments such as Allende's Chile believed in the constitution and its constraints. This was not true of the opposition that overthrew Allende and the constitution through a bloody coup.

As Levine has pointed out, liberalism has not shifted economic power and political power towards equality. This claimed goal of democracy is illusory given the impediments of class and contradictory reforms offering equality of opportunity as the endpoint for society.

Rawls's political philosophy for democracy, much praised in the academy, is linked to social agreement. It requires listening to what the other says and coming to a consensus which allows the adversaries to continue living with each other on the same planet or in the same town, or boat depending on what the political boundaries might be. The practical problem is the relationship between hierarchy and equality as they relate to the distribution of power and resources. Rawls's notion is not meant to surrender equality, and certainly not equity, but the idea is weak in practical terms. A political philosophy espousing just distribution misses the realities required to bring about this condition, or anything like it. Imagine the number of changes necessary for democratic participation in corporate capitalism that might yield elements of equality. Imagine the structural changes in voting procedures and the constitution needed to approach political democracy. It would be necessary to radically change the political, economic and social world to bring Rawls's thought to life. Levine, while appreciative of Rawls is well aware of Rawls's deficits. What is left out of Rawls's position is a strategy of social change. There is no motion or dynamic in Rawls's position. If one is uncomfortable with our present situation, Rawls is of little help.

Marx, on the other hand, believed in double truth. As a scientist, he expected that his facts would be accepted as the facts of the situation. In Marx's mind he was continuing the work of Charles Darwin to whom he dedicated *Capital*. Where Darwin undertook a confrontation with religion through the science of empiricism and conjecture, Marx sought to use empirical science and economics as an attack on capitalism. At the very least a working class coming to consciousness about its own condition would be awakened. Marx would use evidence gleaned from the workers' struggles. The second meaning to Marxist thought was that the struggle for freedom could only be understood in material terms, and with this understanding, human liberation was possible. The time would come that freedom would yield a situation not tied to the search for necessities. While this moment of utopia might come, it was not guaranteed. Historical progress was not automatic. It required a shove from time to time.

Marx and King were practical prophets who realized that struggle produced change and one must be involved in existential struggles. Thus, Marx had his Workingman's Association and King formed the Southern Christian Leadership Conference. It is not clear whether Marx knew what the program of a post revolutionary society would be. It might have to be resolved through continuous struggle. Note that the American constitution also assumes struggle in its recognition that conflict is inherent in human endeavor, but cooperation is possible even where there is disagreement with the rules. For American thinkers and activists the good end was reached through practical results which could be measured qualitatively and quantitatively in terms of their consequences.

In such a democracy it is not the sovereign who has the conscience for the rest of us. It is the collective that is burdened with mediating social roles through individual conscience. All good leaders know they must touch an individual's moral sense to goad him into transcending his social role. It is with the help of our moral sense and the capacities for it that we are able to determine the validity of particular consequences.

At different points in history this moral sense is written into law, which establishes boundaries of behavior—even over leaders and sovereigns. Its weakness is that vengeance degrades the moral sense. Social justice can become a collective monster operating from economic and military exigency.

When the guidance is coercion or the elimination of alternatives, guarantees of choice become hollow. Levine understands that social systems may guide people in one direction or another.

Levine's philosophic direction is clear and unassailable: Recognition of one's humanity was the purpose of political struggle. How must that humanity manifest itself and how far must it extend to achieve the dignity of freedom and equality? King's last demonstration in Memphis, Tennessee for black sanitation workers, featured a sign which said: "I am a Man;" a slogan which resonated among all who cared to look directly at the nature of work, exploitation, necessity and economic justice in America. Philosophy, science, economics, and religion came together in this plea for simple dignity. Was their "demand" nothing more than incrementalism? Hardly. Ultimately this slogan came to mean equality for women as well.

Seemingly simple incrementalist activities around civil rights fell into several categories. The first was what we might term *incrementalism of the particular*. This encompassed the right not to step off the sidewalk to make way for a white person; the right to shop and eat in desegregated public places; and the right to swim at public beaches. But incrementalism of this kind redefined the terms "private" and "public," creating privilege and private law for a few insiders.

The second category was *civil society desegregation* marking the end of property segregation on the basis of race, and the formal acceptance of blacks in predominantly white universities. Over time the black experience was incorporated into the curriculum and a certain amount of integration of economic class occurred. As a result, businesses and the military had to integrate to function. A third, more complex category might be termed *incrementalism of citizenship*. This refers to the extension of the right to vote, protection of that right through legislation and the courts, and access to capital and public resources. These rights represented real

xvi   The American Ideology

gains in a predominantly apartheid society. But these advances did not overturn inequality and injustice. For this one would have had to progress far more broadly in a society which believes only technology should be revolutionary. However, it should be noted that changes and choices in one area open up changes elsewhere, and privileges held by one group invariably open up the question of privileges or rights for the society as a whole. Social change can mutate as it is extended to other groups. For example, when the phrase "life, liberty, and the pursuit of happiness" was coined, blacks and women were not included. But the phrase itself became a sword in the hands of those who pointed out its contradiction with their lives. Can such contradictions and some such as economic disparities reinvigorate instruments for social change?

Levine does not hold much hope for the two party system moving the society to democratic equality. He presents with great force the idea that America's core ideology is mistaken. He is contemptuous of movements of thought and practice which minimize rationality. But how integral to rationality and reason are facts? In every fact there is the brooding presence of fact or value which requires constant re-examination.

Dewey argued that facts were to be derived in a disinterested way but always using the expansive principles of inclusiveness and equality. Dewey's position on reconstruction was to proceed experimentally. But this is a difficult concept to put into practice. In social policy people are not passive commodities. They are not atoms of nature without their own animating force or agency who can be controlled by rulers and hierarchies. In practical terms, especially in a democracy, social policy is not a one-way street. It is a mistake to assume that statistics of double blind experiments are the way to proceed, as scientists might do in the natural sciences.

"The democratic impulse is not so easily put down," Levine says. "The burdens of life under the aegis of the American ideology generate discontents that even a full-fledged ideological assault cannot permanently quash."

Levine has done us a great intellectual service for he has cleared away the underbrush from the ground upon which American ideology stands, and from that dream which hems us and enables too many of us, including educators, to escape reality. As Philip Roth once said: "Now we begin."

Levine has made it possible to move to the tasks of repairing and rebuilding.

Introduction

NOTHING appears more surprising to those, who consider human affairs with a philosophical eye, than the easiness with which the many are governed by the few; and the implicit submission, with which men resign their own sentiments and passions to those of their rulers. When we enquire by what means this wonder is effected, we shall find, that, as FORCE is always on the side of the governed, the governors have nothing to support them but OPINION. It is therefore, on opinion only that government is founded; and this maxim extends to the most despotic and most military governments, as well as to the most free and most popular.

—David Hume, "On the First Principles of Government" (1742)

Because it is "on opinion only that government is founded," empires need to justify themselves to themselves and to others, beneficiaries and victims alike. The American empire is no exception. Now that it has taken it upon itself to exercise its economic and military power with hardly any restraint, the need is all the greater. It is therefore unsurprising that a certain constellation of philosophical doctrines has come to fill the required role. They comprise an ideology; one that it is fair to call American, because of the service it performs for American elites, the principal beneficiaries of the one empire left standing in the aftermath of the Soviet Union's demise.

In the chapters that follow, I will identify and assess some of the most important constituents of this American ideology. I will also broach a grander topic. Because the ideas that comprise the American ideology

only make sense in light of some historically particular and highly attenuated understandings of what a rational society can be, the role of Reason
in society will be at issue throughout. I will suggest that the American
ideology's purchase on this core philosophical question is inadequate and
shallow. But I will not have much to say in support of more robust understandings. My subject is the American ideology, not Reason in society—
except insofar as it is necessary to identify particular ways of thinking
about what a rational society is in order to investigate the ideas that
constitute that ideological configuration.

Visions of rational societies have fired the imagination of political
thinkers from the time that philosophers in ancient Greece first forged
the idea of Reason itself. In modern times, this aspiration was actively
promoted by important sectors of the political Left. By that route, what
was once only a philosopher's dream became an objective that resonates—
sometimes more, sometimes less—in real-world political life. But, like
other ideas of political consequence, conceptions of rational societies are
transitory and vague. They therefore belie efforts to find real definitions
of the sort that Socrates made it the business of philosophy to discover.
This is why I will not even try to define the notion here. There are,
however, historical linkages joining conceptions of Reason in society to
one other and conceptual affinities as well. There is therefore a long and
complex story to tell. However, my focus here will be limited to what is
assumed in the American ideology. My concern will be to analyze and
assess the content of the particular conceptions presupposed there and
the positions they undergird. I will also remark on some of the connections joining these conceptions to their ancestor notions. A combined
analytical and genealogical approach of this sort is appropriate for
revealing the considerable merits and not insignificant shortcomings of
the constituents of the American ideology. It is also indispensable for
explaining their susceptibility to ideological appropriation in our time
and place and for suggesting how we can move beyond them.

Readers will notice that, in occasional references to ways of thinking
that fall outside the purview of the American ideology, I evince more
sympathy for views of Reason in society associated with old-fashioned
socialism than for the conceptions presupposed in the views I will
examine. This impression is correct. However, I will not defend my
sympathies here, at least not directly; neither will I fault the American
ideology from a socialist (or any other) vantage point. I will instead
examine its component parts from *within* their own conceptual horizons.
Because the positions I will investigate are, to a considerable degree,

cogent and defensible, they are worth being taken seriously on their own terms. At issue are good, though not irreproachable, ideas gone bad—thanks to the real-world circumstances in which they operate. According them the attention they deserve is the most expeditious way to identify what is sound and therefore salvageable in them and what must be discarded.

Left, Right, and Center

The designation Left has been in general use since the early days of the French Revolution when the more radical delegates to the National Assembly seated themselves to the left of the presiding officer. It is a fortunate description—not only because enduring political orientations require a name, but also because this particular name introduces a useful ambiguity into descriptions of political positions. Left—like its antonym, right—is a relational concept; left is defined in contrast to right and vice versa. Strictly speaking, then, these terms have no fixed meaning. Political parties and social movements that everyone understands to be on the Left have their own left and right wings, as do parties and movements of the Right. Nevertheless, it has been and continues to be commonplace to use the word Left to designate a position on an idealized political spectrum, approximated in varying degrees in most political cultures and in the collective consciousness of nearly everyone who has thought about political affairs in the years since the term came into use. It is this *notional* Left that is committed to continuing the commitment to liberty, equality, and fraternity that emerged in the French Revolution, even at the expense, if need be, of other values—such as tradition, authority, and order. Those are the values dear to the notional Right. Because the traditions and authority relations that sustain order in real-world conditions have little to do with conceptions of Reason in society, the Right has never been friendly to the idea, though it has seldom been overtly hostile. The Left, on the other hand, has made a rational or, at least, a less irrational society a preeminent objective.

The term Center is similarly ambiguous. It designates both positions within political parties and social movements and a notional position on an idealized political spectrum. However, in both senses, the description can be misleading. The center is almost never a midpoint between the Left and the Right. And it is emphatically not an Aristotelian intermediary or mean—a position that is, by definition, appropriate to prevailing circumstances. Centrist views are those of the political mainstream. Thus their content varies with time and place. Typically, the Center is at some remove from both real-world and notional Lefts and Rights. However, in periods of instability or upheaval, political formations organized around what had been centrist convictions will sometimes fail to hold. Then the population radicalizes—usually siding with the tendency that wins the day. This is the exception that proves the rule. In the real world of politics, the Center is where it is in consequence of the balance of forces between the Left and the Right. Until recently, centrist political groupings usually sided more with the notional Left than the notional Right on the question of a rational society. But with the rightward drift of mainstream politics, this is no longer generally the case. Even in left-leaning periods, however, political Centers seldom make the rationalization of society a goal. This is why it is fair to say that, although the Left has no exclusive title to it, the idea of a rational society has been, in the main, a left-wing idea.

As the American ideology has gained ground, a real-world political convergence is underway that has diminished the impact of ideas associated with the notional—and historical—Left. Groupings still identified with the Left have come to adopt positions long associated with the Center and Right. Indeed, genuine continuators of the historical Left have all but vanished from the scene and, along with them, the visions of a rational society that the historical Left once promoted. In their place, stands the vision implicit in the American ideology. Despite its ancestry, this is a pale approximation of the notional Left's ideal. Thus, in practice, the conviction that Reason ought to rule human affairs has fallen into desuetude, giving way to more modest, though still related, objectives. Many would argue that this is a welcome change. This assessment is not without merit. But, as we will see, it can and should be resisted; not least because relinquishing more robust visions of Reason in society works to the detriment of the objectives around which the notional Left is organized: liberty, equality, and fraternity.

There are many reasons why the historical Left declined as precipitously as it did. The most obvious, the global implosion of communism, is probably not the most important; it may even be more an effect than a cause. However, this question, important as it is, has little to do with analyzing the American ideology or tracing its origins. I will therefore have little to say about it here. I would speculate, though, that the Left's apparent demise is only a temporary phenomenon. Political thinking reflects political life; in the real world of politics, the pendulum is sure to swing back. Liberty, equality, and fraternity appeal nowadays as much as they ever did and the conditions that joined visions of a rational society implied by the values endorsed in that slogan remain very much in force. If anything, the needs that engendered the Left and that sustained it are now more urgent than at any time since the French Revolution. Today, the entire world stands on the brink of devastation—whether through imperial overreach and war, environmental degradation, the consequences of ever-widening inequalities, or all together. As long as this is the case, there is always a place in the political culture for a genuine Left. However much the old, historical Left may be discredited, however much it may have brought discredit upon itself, there is every reason to think that its place will not remain vacant for long. There are signs of renewal everywhere. Perhaps, before long, it will seem, in retrospect, that the first years of the new millennium was a time when the Left's long march forward resumed— with a vigor and rectitude unknown for generations. Even so, there are still the remains of the present and recent past to deal with—the consequences of two decades or more in which Left ideas were in plain retreat.

It is widely thought nowadays that Left understandings of Reason in society played a role in the Left's undoing. It is said that the lure of a rational society underwrites a dangerously utopian politics; one that subordinates peoples' present needs and interests—including their interests in leading good and decent lives, free from degradation and fear—to the struggle to build a future that is impossible to achieve. It has even been claimed, by figures no less eminent than Isaiah Berlin and Karl Popper, among others, that the notion leads to totalitarianism. Until recently, it was mainly anti-Communists who advanced this view. Now that communism is defunct, it has become the conventional wisdom. Conventional wisdom holds too that neoclassical economic theory and liberal social philosophy have finally set these matters right; that economists and philosophers have developed much deflated, but genuinely defensible, views of the role of Reason in society. It bears repeating that this contention is not easily dismissed. But it should be also emphasized, with even greater force, that these conclusions are flawed and that, in present-day circumstances, they have become the core of an ideological configuration that puts liberty, equality, and fraternity in jeopardy.

The American Ideology

Unlike rationality, ideology has no pedigree reaching back into antiquity. The idea is a creature of nineteenth- and twentieth-century social theory— taken up mainly by the political Left. Even so, it is a disputed notion. I will have more to say about ideology presently (Chapter 2); though, in this case too, I will avoid the temptation to propose a real definition covering all the term's customary uses. For now, I will just say that my use of the term is a standard one. What I take ideology to designate is a body of doctrine, more or less comprehensive, that, deliberately or not, systematically serves particular interests at the same time that it purports to represent the world as it really is or, what often is equivalent, to articulate values from a standpoint beyond particular interests. Typically, the interests ideologies serve are the interests of elites. This is emphatically true of the American ideology. However, this fact does not entail that the claims it makes are false. It only implies that what sustains its contentions, along with the view of the world they promote, is not their truth value, but their social function. To say that the ideas in contention constitute an ideology is to underscore this fact about them.

To investigate the American ideology philosophically and historically is necessarily to engage recent and ongoing academic discussions, some of which are, unfortunately, rather arcane. But, even as the discussions that follow veer off into precincts remote from real-world politics, it is crucial not to lose sight of the social and political consequences of the ideas in question. These consequences are anything but academic. They affect how people everywhere live and they condition the prospects for changing life for the better.

Social elites are seldom of one mind on questions of public policy. However, in recent years, in the United States, a rough consensus has coalesced around a strategy of globalization. Free trade and the free flow of capital and, along with it, privatization and deregulation have become the order of the day. Policies consistent with this strategy are supported, with varying degrees of enthusiasm, by most elite strata and by nearly the entire political class, Democrat as well as Republican. Even more recently, the Bush administration has exploited the tragedies of September 11, 2001, to advance a blatantly imperialist agenda: projecting American military power globally, with a view to installing neocolonial regimes, wherever possible, in economically significant areas. It has done so in the face of enormous worldwide and domestic opposition, but with the abject compliance of all but the most marginalized sectors of the Democratic Party. Thus, globalization has taken on a military dimension as well. When I speak of *the American ideology*, it is not this specific configuration of policy positions that I have in mind. Instead, I will use the term to refer to the underlying philosophical and economic doctrines to which its defenders appeal. One reason why this is the appropriate level to target in ideological criticism is just that policy is intrinsically unstable; changing along with changing circumstances and changing political leadership. There are other, more trenchant, reasons that will become apparent later, especially in Chapter 2. However, it will seldom be necessary to probe very deeply into the foundations of policy debates. I will therefore have very little to say about the most basic philosophical issues raised by the doctrines that comprise the American ideology. Ideological criticism is generally most useful when it targets what I would call middle-range theories—not those that address fundamental questions of meaning and value, but theories that articulate the general philosophical orientation that contending parties in policy debates assume.

So understood, the American ideology comprises two constituent parts. One is mainly the province of economists and political scientists who think like economists, though its roots are in the utilitarian tradition in moral philosophy. Its core value is efficiency, a notion closely connected to a conception of practical reason developed, implicitly but trenchantly, by Hobbes more than three centuries ago. It is this component of the American ideology that is most often enlisted in defense of market arrangements, private property and, lately, globalization. The other component is especially evident in Rawls's political philosophy and in the work of philosophers influenced by him, but it is not an invention of Rawls's. Among their many achievements, Rawls and his cothinkers give theoretical expression to a way of thinking implicit in American political practice. "Political liberalism," Rawls's name for his account of political legitimacy, is, in effect, a theory of this practice. Its core concept is reasonableness; a notion that, in Rawls's hands, joins older notions of Reason in society with modern understandings of the requirements of justice. The discussions that follow are organized, in part, around these concepts—the efficient and the reasonable. My concern is not limited to these ideas. To grasp the character of the American ideology, it is also necessary to engage some of the many notions that cluster around them.

Economists' accounts of efficiency have come to influence public policy directly and profoundly. Political liberalism, on the other hand, has had little immediate impact on real-world politics. But, the ideas and practices to which political liberalism gives expression nevertheless comprise part of the American ideology; there is, in fact, no more perspicuous treatment of these ideas than this body of theory. Therefore, in this case unlike the other, it is not the theory itself so much as the ideas it articulates that drives opinion. If the concern here were to investigate the actual operation

of ideas within our body politic—the political sociology, as it were, of the
American ideology—this difference would matter. However, it is of little
consequence insofar as the aim is to investigate this ideological configuration philosophically. This is why it is appropriate, for our purposes, to
think of efficiency-driven economic doctrines and political liberalism as
coequal components of a single ideological formation.

There is some irony in the fact that the two components of the
American ideology function ideologically in the ways that they do. Political liberalism articulates Left positions, especially with respect to equality.
In this sense, it runs against the current of the American ideology.
Although it is less evident nowadays, much the same is true of economic
doctrines that accord preeminence to efficiency. But, again, the ensuing
analytical and genealogical account of ways of thinking that cluster
around these notions will focus mainly on their susceptibility to ideological appropriation. On a strictly theoretical plane, both components of
the American ideology not only have progressive aspects; they are each,
on balance, progressive theories. But, in the world as it is, they are
disposed to change their valance. The task is to denounce this state of
affairs and, so far as possible, to rectify it.

I will suggest, from time to time, that the culprit is capitalism. But this
too is a theme that I will not pursue very far. It does bear repeating,
however, that it is the global preeminence of American capitalism in the
present period, not the provenance of the ideas that comprise it, that
makes the American ideology *American*. Political liberalism is American
in origin. But, the economic doctrines that are also central to the American
ideology are not. They descend from English political and moral philosophy and continental economic theory. These foreign ways of thinking are
now thoroughly assimilated. However, it is not for this reason that the
ideology they constitute is American. Circumstances turn ideas into ideological weapons. Circumstances condition the character of ideologies too.
It is the unchallenged cultural, military, and political dominance of the
United States in the world arena and the fierce determination of its
governing class to establish an unabashedly imperial order that has
pressed this complex of ideas into service in behalf of American interests. This is why the ideology they comprise is distinctively, though of
course not exclusively, American.

With the Left in eclipse, much of the opposition to the American
ideology nowadays is reactionary, spurred by a politically untenable,
historically inaccurate, and culturally retrograde nostalgia for premodern,

theocratic ways of life. It would be better, by far, to acquiesce in our unhappy present, than to succumb to such a future! Thankfully, this is not the choice we face. Despite everything, Left opposition persists. Even as the Left nearly disappeared organizationally in the final years of the twentieth century, Left sensibilities are everywhere on the rise. Thus, the vision the American ideology promotes has more detractors, and potential opponents, than one might suppose. It is therefore vulnerable to efforts to change it for the better. It is urgent that these efforts not dissipate or otherwise become ineffective. For the danger of reaction is real. The harms imperialism causes generate support for change, any change, among the ever-growing multitudes of the truly desperate. At the same time, they fuel the passions of religious zealots and political entrepreneurs who seek to mobilize them for reactionary ends. Meanwhile, the absence of an organized Left alternative has created a vacuum for religious obscurantism and clerical fascism to fill. A Left revival can undo the appeal of these noxious doctrines, just as the historical Left did in decades past. Of far greater importance is the degree to which a revived Left succeeds in its mission to replace the practices and institutions underwritten by the American ideology with alternatives that genuinely do implement liberty, equality, and fraternity and, ultimately, democracy itself. To the degree it does, the conditions that make desperation a factor in real-world politics and reaction a threatening prospect will themselves fade away.

Because, in the present political climate, even tepid liberalism is not to be despised, Left opponents of the American ideology today are, for the most part, wittingly or not, of the impression that what is harmful in it is only its first component. Thus, they target the support that efficiency considerations lend to neoliberal economic policies. This is why progressive, secular opposition to the American ideology has been directed mainly at globalization or, more precisely, at the extension of market arrangements and trade under the aegis of institutions that work to advance the interests of large, international (mainly American) corporations. The incontrovertible contention is that this economic regime gives rise to increasingly unequal exchanges—within sovereign states and, especially, at the global level—that generate brutal, destabilizing inequalities. This is true, but it is not the whole story. Neoliberalism and political liberalism—or, more precisely, the ideas political liberalism articulates—operate together as complementary components of a single ideology. To challenge the American ideology with a view to moving beyond it, it is necessary to take on this comparatively benign doctrine too.

A Democratic Alternative

I will argue that, singly and together, the constituent parts of the American ideology militate *against* democracy or, more precisely, against the further democratization of our not very democratic regime. It is widely acknowledged that, in comparison with other so-called Western democracies, American political institutions are unusually prone to privatize and therefore depoliticize political questions. The American way is to appeal to the marketplace, not the forum and then, in the forum, to treat many ostensibly legislative matters as constitutional disputes to be settled juridically. By these means, prevailing practices restrict the scope of collective deliberation and social choice, and therefore of popular empowerment, to a degree that is not only uncommon, but also unnecessary. The American ideology functions to sustain this practice and to expand its scope, domestically and internationally.

In practice, this has not been an altogether bad thing. Institutional arrangements that depoliticize public life, whether by substituting the Invisible Hand of the market for democratic collective choice or by transforming questions that invite democratic deliberation into legal problems calling for adjudication, have yielded mixed results. The nearly consensus view nowadays is that markets do a better job of delivering the goods than state bureaucracies can. Also, there are many who believe that courts generally make wiser decisions than legislatures are likely to contrive. In the world as it is this sense of how institutions work is plausible, unfortunately—even in a period like our own, when the American judiciary has largely resumed the reactionary role it abandoned in the glory days of the Warren Court.[1] But existing institutional arrangements are hardly congenial to democratic aspirations. Even when good outcomes result from their operation, the practices the American ideology helps to sustain remain obstacles in the way of extending the depth and range of democratic governance. For partisans of liberty, equality, and fraternity, this is reason enough to find it wanting.

To fault a complex of ideas for their ideological consequences is, inevitably, to raise the question of alternatives. Ideas associated with the historical Left—in particular, with European socialism—are an obvious place to begin the search. However, it is not only by looking abroad that we Americans can find ways of thinking that challenge the American ideology. For this, we should be grateful. The problem is not so much that socialist ideas are inapt. Quite the contrary. The problem instead is that a sense of American exceptionalism colors the American political culture—as much today as in the past, despite the global dominance of the United States and the ascendance everywhere of the American ideology. This sensibility has always worked to impede the acceptance of socialist theory on American soil. Today, with the historical Left everywhere in retreat, the likelihood that socialist ideas can finally take root and flourish here is especially dim. But, there are native alternatives at hand, connected genetically, so to speak, with European socialism, but evolved in conformity with local conditions. One strain of thought in particular warrants attention: the kind of democratic theory developed by American social critics and philosophers in the first few decades of the twentieth century. This theory promoted the notion that democracy is a form of civilization, not just of governance, and emphasized, in Dewey's words, the roles of intelligence and problem solving in the collective life of progressive, democratizing communities. By way of conclusion (Chapter 8), I will return briefly to this rival, emphatically American, perspective on social and political life.

About this Book

This book is intended mainly for a general audience. I have therefore tried to write it in a way that is concise, accessible, and comprehensive. That theories that privilege efficiency and reasonableness operate ideologically and that, in today's world, they comprise an American ideology, in the sense I've just explained, is plain enough. Yet, somehow, it eludes notice. My aim is to call attention to this fact—to specialists working in the disciplines on which the American ideology draws, to readers interested generally in political philosophy, economic theory, public affairs, and, above all, to militants and potential militants struggling to advance the ideals the historical Left made its own.

The first two chapters are introductory. In Chapter 1, I offer some thoughts on Reason in general. In Chapter 2, I investigate the notion of ideology. These are very large topics and I will only say enough about them to prepare the way for the discussions that follow. Chapter 3, Chapter 4, and Chapter 5 focus on efficiency and related matters. Chapter 3 explores the conception of rationality that underlies contemporary forms of thinking that accord efficiency pride of place. Chapter 4 explores the rationale that proponents of the American ideology invoke when they promote reliance on impersonal market mechanisms. Chapter 5 explores the susceptibility of this way of thinking to ideological appropriation, not just in the American ideology, but in some influential strains of socialist thought as well. Chapter 6 and Chapter 7 focus on the reasonable; that is to say, on ways of thinking associated with Rawls's moral and political philosophy. Chapter 6, on political liberalism, addresses the topic directly. Chapter 7, on the theory of deliberative democracy, deals with its extensions into the realm of democratic theory. The objective, again, is to investigate the ideas that comprise the American ideology philosophically and genealogically—to reveal their vulnerabilities along with their merits. In Chapter 8, where I broach the prospect of constructing a democratic civilization of the sort envisioned by Dewey and his cothinkers, I will venture some thoughts on how elements of the American ideology might, finally, be wrested away from their present ideological function and enlisted unambivalently into the service of liberty, equality, and fraternity.

1

Reason

Conceptions of rational societies, and of Reason itself, at most, share only family resemblances. It is therefore pointless to try to define these terms. It will suffice, instead, to provide some conceptual bearings. To that end, after venturing a few remarks on Reason in general and on the kinds of things that can be rational or irrational, I will reflect on what is, in effect, the founding myth of Western philosophy: Plato's account of the death of Socrates. The main contours of the idea of Reason, as it will figure in the discussions that follow, are portrayed in that story.

In recent years, it is curious that Reason has come under attack in quarters identified with the Left. The claim sometimes heard is that the idea works to the detriment of subordinate groups—largely, though not entirely, because it arose when, where, and how it did. I will not have much to say about this contention; it is not worth taking seriously. But, in today's political climate, the possibility that Reason is somehow bad for the oppressed cannot be ignored altogether. Because its proponents represent this charge as a left-wing claim, and because there is just a sliver of truth in this self-representation, this currently fashionable notion, if uncontested, could threaten efforts to renew the project the historical Left made its own. Not unrelatedly, the claim that Reason itself is oppressive, if taken to heart, could impede the development of richer notions of Reason in society than the American ideology assumes; notions that could prove indispensable for changing society radically for the better. This is why, at the end of this chapter, I will offer a few thoughts on this most implausible of charges.

The Idea of Reason

Like morality, rationality is a normative standard—an account of what one ought to do.[1] It is therefore also a standard for assessing what is. For beings moved by it, rational beings, it has imperatival force. Those who find it compelling are motivated (to some degree, at least) to do what it prescribes. Since Aristotle's time, it has been customary to distinguish theoretical from practical applications of this standard. Practical, in this context, means having to do with action, with doing—where action contrasts with contemplation and doing contrasts with knowing. Theoretical reason therefore has to do with the conditions under which rational beings ought to assent to knowledge claims; practical reason with what rational agents ought to do. It is mainly practical reason that will concern us in the chapters that follow. It is uncontroversial that this standard, in all of the various ways it has been understood, applies to individuals' actions. Everyone agrees that actions can be rational or irrational and that (human) agents can be motivated by rational considerations. It is more controversial whether and how similar considerations apply to entire societies.

Key to understanding what rationality is, in both its theoretical and practical senses, is recognizing the fact that rational beings are capable not just of having a first-order mental life, of thinking, believing, feeling, and desiring, but also of having thoughts, beliefs, feelings, and desires about their own and each others' mental lives. In other words, rational beings have second-order thoughts, beliefs, feelings, and desires. This capacity makes us rational or, in other words, makes rationality a standard for us. Rationality governs our reflections on first-order mental states. Thus, it applies to rational beings in general and, in its practical applications, to rational agents—to beings that can and do act for reasons.

Rationality is not the only notion bearing on belief and action that derives from the idea of Reason. There is also reasonableness. The term reasonable is used in a variety of related, but distinct, ways. For instance, it can mean cooperative, willing to go along. Thus, when we say, "be reasonable," we may only mean cooperate! In legal contexts, the term has a quasi-technical meaning—as in the expression "beyond a reasonable doubt" or in the call to judge what a reasonable person would do or think. The governing idea, in these and other instances, appears to be that what is reasonable is what is appropriate. In a similar vein, but in an expressly theoretical context, reasonable can mean plausible. Then the connection to the idea of Reason is plain. The demand for plausibility entails that beliefs be supported by reasons or, at least, that they not be refuted by reasons that rational persons would be obliged to accept.

It is best that beliefs be supported, not just not refuted, by compelling reasons. But, this standard can seldom be met. This is partly because, given the way the world is and given the nature of our cognitive capacities, we are almost never up to the task. It is also partly because all of the people some of the time and some (indeed, most) of the people all of the time have other things to do than endeavor to implement the requirements of Reason even to the limits of their capabilities, and because they are sometimes impeded from doing so by psychological, political, or ideological factors. Because these "burdens of judgment," as Rawls called them, are a fact of human life, a convergence of reasonable (that is, plausible) opinions is unlikely in most domains. In practice, a range of views would then have to count as reasonable in the sense in question. How wide that range is is subject to debate. One could hold that, where general bodies of doctrine are concerned, whatever is not blatantly delusional is reasonable. This was Rawls's position, as we will see. He maintained that nearly all extant "comprehensive doctrines" or general conceptions of the world and our place in it, including those implicit in the major world religions, are reasonable. On the other hand, it may be that, in order to mark off a position or course of action as reasonable, a higher standard should be set. But on even the most demanding interpretation, reasonableness is a less stringent requirement than rationality. Most, perhaps all, reasonable views in one or another domain may be false. A position that satisfies the standard of rationality cannot be false; at least not if it satisfies the standard perfectly. To say that a view is rationally compelling is to say that it can be known to be true.

It is our rational capacities, our ability to reflect on first-order mental states, that distinguishes the mentality of human beings from the minds of other (higher) animals. No doubt, dogs and cats also think, feel, experience, and desire. Like us, they have first-order mental lives, but they almost certainly do not have thoughts about their thoughts or about the thoughts of others. Neither, in the practical sphere, do they have desires about their desires or, more generally, about their dispositions to act. Dogs or cats can be friendly; but they cannot endeavor to be more or less friendly or even to conceive of this objective. This is why, unlike us, they are not rational beings. We human beings probably became rational at an early stage of our evolutionary history. However, an awareness of this aspect of our mentality, an idea of Reason, was a philosophical discovery. Its entry into human consciousness was philosophy's founding event. This epochal moment occurred in Athens in the fourth century BC. It was the signal achievement of the so-called pre-Socratics and then of Socrates himself.

The Death of Socrates

From the first, the idea of Reason was intimately connected with a certain, previously unknown, notion of justification. No doubt, from time immemorial, human beings everywhere used arguments to influence others. In Greece, by the fourth century BC, efforts to persuade with arguments had developed into a recognized form of art—rhetoric. This art was susceptible to evaluation according to more or less explicit standards. Rhetoric was assessed not only by looking at the consequences of particular rhetorical exercises, at whether or not they succeeded in persuading others, but also by examining their internal properties. In this respect, rhetoric is like music. In music, one can evaluate the quality of compositions or performances, regardless of their effects on audiences. Even if the purpose of music is somehow to communicate with others or to move them in particular ways, music can fail in this purpose and still exhibit musical excellence. Thus Socrates' speech in Plato's dialogue *The Apology*—in which he endeavored to persuade an Athenian court not to convict him of impiety and then, when that effort came to naught, not to sentence him to death—was considered a masterpiece of rhetorical art in the ancient world. It failed in its intended purpose; Socrates was convicted and sentenced to die. But by common consensus, Socrates' rhetoric was beyond reproach.

It was in Socrates' reflections on what to do in the wake of this death sentence, recounted in Plato's dialogue *The Crito*, that a radically new way of arguing arose—a departure in the technique of persuasion so far reaching as to amount to the inauguration of a new standard altogether. According to Plato's report, Socrates' friends and disciples gathered together in his prison cell to persuade him to escape. Their claim, never rebutted, was that escape was not only possible but also honorable according to prevailing expectations. In response, Socrates—or, rather, "the Laws of Athens" speaking through Socrates—made a different sort of case. The speech of the Laws is more notable for what it attempted than for what it achieved. The case it presented was hardly one that rational beings are obliged to accept, but that is not the point. Socrates broke new ground because he appealed to rational standards, not communal expectations or internalized norms of honor. The conclusion he reached is that he should accept the court's legally rendered sentence of death, even though he was not guilty of the charge. This is what he did. His acceptance of death—on the strength of an argument that aims to appeal to reasons rational beings must accept—is an allegorical statement of the goal of philosophy itself. It dramatizes the philosophical project then in the process of being born. The aim of philosophy, and of the separate sciences that philosophy would eventually spin off, can be put succinctly: it is to put Reason in control.

Why this new standard? As with any truly momentous development, no one can say entirely. But at least part of the answer has to do with the fact that philosophy, as it then emerged, is an activity that responds to situations that rational beings, or at least beings who are aware of their own rational capacities, sometimes confront and cannot evade. Seen this way, philosophy is not exactly a body of doctrines or set of beliefs. It is a way of addressing a kind of puzzlement, one that is mainly conceptual in nature—in the course of which doctrines and beliefs will typically, but not necessarily, emerge. Challenges to received ways of understanding our being in the world and our relations to others, along with other far-reaching changes in traditional patterns of life, upset received ways of thinking. They call for a fundamental rethinking of the conceptual moorings through which beings equipped with rational capacities endeavor to make sense of their situations and, in light of their understandings, to negotiate their ways through life. Challenges of this sort have arisen mainly in response to the development of new ways of knowing. In the Western philosophical tradition, science has taken the lead. In Greek antiquity, at the moment of philosophy's birth, it was mathematical science that called for a philosophical response. In mathematics, a new way of establishing claims emerged. Self-evident first principles—axioms—and self-justifying rules of inference—laws of logic—lead to conclusions that rational beings must either accept or else run afoul of the normative standard that governs belief acceptance. Deduction, as this method came to be called, discovers truths—something other forms of argumentation, including those that pass muster as rhetoric, cannot be counted on to do. Thus, the idea of a logos, a theory or account appealing to Reason alone, was born along with logic, an account of the formal structure of arguments suitable to this task. Logic too persuades; it leads individuals to conclude whatever can be inferred from the premises they accept. In this respect, it is like rhetoric. However, its goals and methods are enough unlike other efforts at persuasion through words and symbols that, from the moment of its inception, it was rightly thought to be a new discipline entirely.

Unlike Socrates' speech in the *Apology* or his friends' and disciples' speeches in the *Crito,* persuasion through logic does not depend on cajoling or flattering or otherwise appealing to particular characteristics of persons—except to their rational capacities. Deductions appeal to principles that are accessible to rational beings as such, irrespective of the non- or extrarational factors that distinguish them from one another. For this reason, they are universal and according to one standard sense of the term, objective. The speech of the Laws of Athens, spoken through Socrates, represents an effort to export the goal, if not the form, of this type of argument outside the realms in which it had already been deployed to use it to determine what Socrates ought to do. No matter that it falls short of a full-fledged mathematical or logical demonstration; what counts is that its aim was to present a case that holds objectively, from any and all standpoints—in just the way that conclusions of mathematical or logical arguments do.[2] Standard rhetorical arguments, even when they aim at the Truth, as Socrates' speech before the Athenian court did, assume particular vantage points. They are directed to particular persons or types of persons, not to rational agents as such. Rational beings can therefore fail to assent to their conclusions. On the other hand, anyone who understands a sound argument, one that proceeds from rationally compelling first principles by means of valid inferences, is obliged to assent to its conclusion on pain of offending the standard of rationality itself. Were the speech of the Laws of Athens as sound as Socrates believed, its conclusion would be unavoidable. Were he to reject it nevertheless, he would be irrational. This is as grave a charge as can be leveled against any rational agent. Socrates went to his death to avoid it.

In time, with the progress of science and especially after the rise of the new sciences of nature in the modern period, other ways of making objective cases, ways that appeal to evidential support, came to stand alongside the deductive model. But, these ways are less compelling than deductions; therefore their conclusions are less secure than those reached in the way that mathematics pioneered and that logic made its own. To this day, our first way of discovering truths remains the gold standard.

The problem is that, outside formal contexts, the deductive model is almost never adequate to the task at hand. Therefore, puzzlements that call for philosophical responses can almost never be relieved in the way that mathematical problems can be solved. What mathematics provides is an ideal, not a method. It is a fact of our condition that this ideal can seldom be realized completely, especially in practical deliberations, as when Socrates had to decide whether to accept his death sentence or to escape. Following Socrates' lead, one can make this objective one's own. One can endeavor to marshal arguments in an effort to arrive at conclusions that are rationally required.

To anyone with modern, democratic sensibilities, the particular argument that led Socrates to his death is not only contestable; it is repellent. Socrates' reflections and the Laws of Athens speech taken together imply that while no one is obligated to do what is wrong because political authorities command it, no one has a right to resist their authority when they do. Socrates was commanded in proper legal fashion to desist from engaging in philosophical investigations of the kind that led to his conviction on the charge of impiety. But Socrates tells us, he was commanded by the gods to do what he was condemned for doing. Plato's account of the story assumes that he was right, that Socrates was required to do that for which he was sentenced to death. Therefore, Socrates was not obligated to stop doing philosophy as the authorities commanded. Were he to have done so, he would genuinely have been guilty of impiety—guilty, in other words, of that for which he was wrongly convicted. Because it is also wrong to do anything that challenges the legitimacy of those who ordered him to desist, Socrates had no choice but to accept their punishment. Thus, he became a martyr in philosophy's cause.[3]

Hardly anyone today, Left, Right, or Center, would maintain that Socrates bequeathed posterity a satisfactory, let alone a rationally compelling, account of what individuals owe the political communities to which they belong. However, nearly everyone would agree that in his life and, more so in his death, he bequeathed an aspiration that has inspired the human imagination ever since. After Socrates, it became a goal of reflective persons everywhere to act on principles that are binding on all rational agents. It is profoundly ironic that his way of setting forth this objective was to set out a theory of the duties of citizenship that is repugnant not only to the Left, as it would emerge more than two millennia later, but to all significant political tendencies of the modern era.

Is Reason Bad for the Oppressed?

In recent years, with the Left in retreat, a variety of theoretical tendencies identified by the prefix post (postmodern, poststructuralist, post-Marxist, and so on), have emerged. As remarked, some of their practitioners claim the designation "left" for themselves. It is not uncommon, in these circles, to condemn anything that smacks of Eurocentrism—typically because a focus on things European demeans persons not of (exclusively) European ancestry or otherwise detracts from diversity.[4] One would imagine that there would be little sympathy from this quarter for an aspiration that traces back to the birth of philosophy in ancient Greece. This expectation is seldom disappointed. From these quarters too, rationality is sometimes deemed arbitrary and therefore dispensable. It is even argued that the real-world impact of this standard is detrimental to the interests of subordinate groups; indeed, that it somehow contributes to their oppression. This way of thinking has little appeal outside a few academic redoubts, but its indirect influence is more extensive. As right-wing critics of an allegedly left-leaning academic and media culture in the United States and elsewhere tirelessly observe, the various post-isms have trickled out into mainstream thinking giving rise to political correctness and related follies. What these critics disparage has little to do with the Left, in the historical or notional senses of the term; and the idea that American universities and the mainstream media in the United States lean to the left borders on the delusional. But it is true that, for reasons both historical and philosophical, the Left has also always sided with "the wretched of the earth;"[5] and it is also true that, nowadays, more than in times past, the interests of the victims of the system in place do include demands for the recognition of racial, ethnic, and gender differences. It is also true that, for the remnants of the historical Left, including the New Left, support for the victims of extra-economic forms of oppression has remained a steadfast commitment. Thus there is some truth, after all, in the charges leveled by the Right and in the self-representations of adherents of the various post-isms. It would be a gross and misleading exaggeration to claim that the mantle of the historical Left has passed to those who would disparage Reason for the sake of a politics of difference. However, there is just enough merit in this contention not to dismiss it out of hand. What, then, should we make of the charge of Eurocentrism and of the more general contention that rationality itself is a pernicious ideal?

Of the former complaint, the answer is nothing. It is true that the idea of Reason first appeared in ancient Greece; in other words, at the time and place where, on the usual account, Western civilization began.[6] But should this be a cause for concern for the wretched of the earth or their allies? Surely not. What occasioned the discovery of Reason was the emergence of mathematical science and the philosophical response it elicited.

None of this had anything to do with modern notions of ethnicity or group identity. The idea of Reason was born when and where it was in consequence of the disruption of deeply entrenched traditional patterns of thought brought on by a new way of knowing. No doubt, similar puzzlements can and have arisen elsewhere. No doubt, other traditions too have discovered Reason, in their own way. But, the Greek case was the most definitive, the most influential, and, most likely, the first.

From the beginning, the Greeks' discovery resonated well beyond the frontiers of the so-called West. It has been central to the intellectual life of the Middle East and its extensions into the Indian subcontinent almost from the time of its inception. The military and then cultural expansion eastward of Greek civilization during the Hellenistic and Roman periods and then the Arab invasions centuries later made this the case. Contrary to what the anti-Eurocentrists suppose, ideas stand or fall on their merits, not their ancestry; once established, they are there for everyone to make their own. This is as much the case for the idea of Reason as for the principles of arithmetic—an invention not of the West, but of India and the Middle East.

The other contention, that Reason, viewed as a timeless normative standard, somehow harms the oppressed is even more ill-conceived. Because its proponents are disinclined to make their case clear, their position is difficult to engage. But, at least some of the self-described theorists who disparage Reason for its purported role in maintaining oppression do appear to endorse a position that can be briefly sketched and summarily dismissed. Their case derives from a skewed reading of the philosopher Friedrich Nietzsche, filtered through the prism of Michel Foucault's forays into philosophy and intellectual history. Key to understanding the thought that underlies their view is Nietzsche's observation that rationality, particularly in its practical applications, involves principles and therefore categorization and the erasure of differences between particulars. Nietzsche inveighed against this way of thinking because the differences universal principles obliterate are precisely those that matter—differences in natural merit. He seems to have believed that these differences were, in turn, functions of the degree and authenticity of what he called "the will to power." Adopting Arthur Schopenhauer's account of the connection between volition or willing and ideas or mental representations, Nietzsche maintained that the will to power is the stuff of the world. He insisted too that its quantity and perhaps its quality differ from person to person. To subsume particulars under general categories is therefore to deny this reality. It is also to level down the top and thereby to implement that "slave revolt of the spirit" that, according to Nietzsche, defined Judeo-Christian civilization from its inception. This reprehensible because inauthentic condition, based on resentment, arrives at its ultimate realization in a distinctively modern scourge—democracy. To confer equal rights and, worse still, to empower the demos, the popular masses, is to turn society itself—or, at least, its governing structures—over to the slaves.

Post-ism theorists mask the antidemocratic implications of Nietzsche's position by invoking the Left's, especially the Marxist Left's, skepticism toward universalism. Strictly speaking, Marx never faulted the universalist ideal. However, he did maintain that it is seldom, if ever, realizable in class-divided societies. It was Marx's view that professions of universalism are usually ideologically self-serving. Marxists were therefore disposed to look for differential power relations masked in (ostensibly) universal declarations. By a dialectical turn insusceptible of cogent reconstruction, Foucault and the others conflated this skepticism with the doctrine of the will to power. They and their followers then concluded that there is nothing more to the adoption of universal principles—and, more generally, to the notion of objective truth—than the subordination (and oppression) of some groups by others. By this route, they arrive at a thoroughgoing relativism, according to which there is nothing true nor false outside systems of power relations constituted by ways of speaking and acting or, as they say, "discourses." None of these ways is or can be authoritative in an extradiscursive sense. Contrary, then, to what everyone has supposed since antiquity, there is no Truth to be discovered, understood, and, as the Left would have it, put to use in the service of human emancipation. Power is all there is.

An obvious problem with so sweeping a relativism is that it puts the status of its own contentions in peril. This difficulty is hardly mitigated by contending, as some philosophically astute exponents of these positions do, that arguments advanced in support of global relativism should be understood ironically, not metaphysically. In other words, that, despite what appears, defenders of these views do not actually assert what they claim but rather, in setting out their views, somehow deny the legitimacy of any and all assertions, including their own, that purport to declare what is really the case.[7] Here, we are on the threshold of a conceptual tangle about which I will have little more to say. Perhaps global relativism somehow is coherent. The problem, as even its proponents must concede, is that it is impossible in principle to say how.

It is plain too that anyone who accedes to the relativism practitioners of the post-isms endorse, while also purporting to advance the interests of "the wretched of the earth," falls prey to a disabling problem. Because Reason is a universal standard, one that holds objectively, what it requires holds equally for everyone. As Nietzsche realized, this fact about it works to the advantage of subordinate individuals and groups. Therefore, were the oppressed and their allies to fall under the sway of global relativism, they would effectively deny themselves the use of this means of deliverance. Then, according to the Foucauldians' own account, they would have nothing but their own power upon which to rely. But by hypothesis, it is their lack of power that renders them oppressed. Without even the possibility of deploying Reason in their own behalf, their situation would be grim indeed. The choice of academic theorists and others to stand with them would be not only unwise, but arbitrary.

In any case, the relativism that the Right inveighs against and that the post-ism theorists promote is not part of the American ideology. This is reason enough to say no more about it. There is a deeper reason as well. It is a reason that, so to speak, stands Nietzsche on his head. Much as Nietzsche wanted his readers to turn away from expressions of that slave mentality that allegedly riddles modern science and politics, in order that their susceptibility to his vision not be swamped by the weight of humanity's long detour from authentic norms of action and belief, defenders of Reason would do well not to become distracted by atavistic revivals of positions Socrates defeated long ago. Or, in terms the post-ism theorists themselves invoke against discourses that still (naively, in their view) accord Reason the preeminence it has enjoyed for so long, it is best simply to avoid the conversation the Foucauldians have started. It is a diversion, of doubtful cogency, leading nowhere.

2

Ideology

Ideology too is a concept that it would be pointless to try to define by supplying necessary and sufficient conditions. But it is feasible to illustrate the general features of the conception of ideology that I have in mind when I speak of *the American ideology*. To this end, I will briefly refer to Darwin's theory of evolution by natural selection and then, at greater length, to Max Weber's *The Protestant Ethic and the Spirit of Capitalism*.[1] It may surprise some readers to see Weber's work invoked for this purpose. The concept of ideology has come to be associated with Marxism and Weber's account of the Protestant ethic is widely thought to oppose Marx's celebrated contention, stated first in *The German Ideology,* that "consciousness arises out of life," not vice versa. Put crudely, Marxists are supposed to believe that capitalism somehow explains Protestantism. Put even more crudely, Weber is supposed to have argued that Protestantism explains capitalism. These understandings are misleading at best. But, since it is ideology, not Weber or Marx, that is of concern here, I will not attempt directly to dispel these mistaken interpretations of their views. There is a sense, though, in which what I will say about the Protestant ethic does indirectly rebut at least part of the conventional wisdom, the part that pertains to Weber.[2]

What is plain, in any case, is that, despite what is widely believed about the differences between Weber's and Marx's views on the relation between consciousness and life, Weber provided an especially perspicacious illustration of what an ideology is. In doing so, he pioneered the philosophical and genealogical investigation of systems of ideas that work, in particular circumstances, to further the interests of economic elites. Ironically, *The Protestant Ethic* provides a better model for the kind of investigation I will undertake here than Marx's writings do.

Natural Selection

Within biological populations, individual organisms will differ in a variety of ways. Darwin assumed that these variations have causes and that these causes are knowable in principle. But, from the standpoint of the evolutionary theory he developed, they are random in the sense that the theory itself has nothing to say about their causes. What evolutionary theory does maintain is that variations that enhance reproductive fitness—the ability of organisms to produce offspring that are themselves able to reproduce—are selected by nature. In other words, organisms that have these traits will come to predominate in the general population as time unfolds. This is so because individuals with fitness-enhancing traits are better able than those without them to pass on all their traits, including the ones that enhance fitness, to succeeding generations.

Whether or not a trait is fitness-enhancing depends on local conditions. In bucolic environments, there may be no advantage (or some disadvantage) for squirrels to have, say, darkly colored fur. However, introduce factory soot into the countryside and the situation changes. Lighter fur colorations that previously conferred an evolutionary advantage, in these new circumstances, might make squirrels more visible to predators and therefore less likely to survive and reproduce. In these conditions, dark fur becomes advantageous. Evolutionary theory then predicts that after a number of reproductive cycles, dark fur will become the rule in the squirrel population—provided that it first somehow (randomly) appears there. Natural selection works on what is at hand. From within that range of possibilities, it selects those traits that are fittest in particular environmental niches.

Natural selection contrasts with artificial selection. Artificial selection is commonplace wherever human beings control reproduction in plant or animal species. Then they can breed for the traits they want—again, assuming that these traits already exist thanks to random variation. Until quite recently, the science behind selective breeding was poorly understood. In fact, it was not until Darwin discovered natural selection, that "artificial selection" entered the biologist's lexicon, but the technique has been in use for millennia. All domesticated plants and animals differ from their wild, undomesticated ancestors in consequence of deliberate human interventions.

Ideas that operate ideologically, in the sense in question here, are selected mainly by blind mechanisms, more akin to natural than artificial selection. Seldom are they deliberately contrived to serve particular interests. Certainly, the ideas that comprise the American ideology were not—even if political considerations, broadly construed, did sometimes shape the way these ideas were developed. Seldom if ever are available ideas selected deliberately to foster beliefs or practices deemed desirable by interested parties. For many decades, in all liberal democracies, but particularly in the United States, a propaganda apparatus, comprised of public relations and media agencies working to manufacture consent, has been an important factor in public life.[3] The influence of these agencies has grown enormously, especially in recent years. However powerful these artificial selectors of ideas may be, the mechanisms that cause ideas to become predominant in the intellectual culture go far beyond deliberately contrived propaganda ventures. Today, as throughout human history, ideas are less easily controlled than captive biological populations. In the intellectual and cultural realm, analogues to artificial selection are therefore of less importance than structural factors analogous to natural selection. This is one of the principal lessons of *The Protestant Ethic*.

The Spirit of Capitalism

What Weber wanted to explain, in the first instance, is why—in the period in question, from roughly the seventeenth to the early twentieth century—capitalism flourished more in Protestant than in Catholic sections of Europe; especially in areas of central Europe, like Germany, that were otherwise similar in relevant respects. Thus, his aim was not to account for the rise of capitalism, but for what he called its spirit—the mentality or cast of mind that makes it work well. His assumption, which he never directly defended, was that differences in spirit that account for differences in capitalist flourishing.

Weber observed that the spirit of capitalism was stronger in Protestant than in Catholic Europe. Therefore, his working hypothesis became that Protestantism accounts for this difference. He observed too that the spirit of capitalism is an anomaly in human history; that it is at odds with all forms of traditionalism—in other words, with the mentalities of pre- and noncapitalist peoples. In traditional societies, people toil as they must to obtain means of subsistence. Beyond that point, they seldom work

voluntarily; if they do, they almost never work regularly and methodically. This is why economically dominant classes in precapitalist societies
found it necessary to coerce direct producers, slaves, and serfs to obtain
labor inputs from them.

Traditionalism, Weber pointed out, is a liability in capitalist economies.
For capitalism to flourish capitalists must want to invest rather than
consume; and workers must be disposed to supply labor inputs without
capitalists having to waste resources coercing them. These conditions are
approximated when capitalists and workers embody an ascetic and
methodical cast of mind that leads them to reject spontaneous enjoyment
and everything else that stands in the way of the pursuit of the tasks the
economic system assigns them. This disposition is the spirit of capitalism.
Where it reigns, activities that traditional peoples undertook only because
they were required to do so, by others or by force of circumstance, are
undertaken voluntarily. Individuals set about their tasks with no other
end in view than doing their work well. It is for this reason that Weber
called the spirit of capitalism irrational. It is at odds with human nature
or, more precisely, with the disposition to enjoy life to the greatest extent
possible and therefore to toil only when there is effectively no other
choice.

The spirit of capitalism was anticipated in medieval monasticism, but
the lives of the religious in monastic orders were directed toward spiritual,
otherworldly pursuits. The spirit of capitalism is this-worldly. However,
it is no less rigorous on this account. Good capitalists and good workers
work unrelentingly, deferring gratification indefinitely. The ideal can never
be implemented perfectly; one can only oppose human nature so far. In
practice, workers imbued with the spirit of capitalism do endeavor to
enjoy life to some extent. So too do capitalists who also consume at levels
workers can barely imagine. But, even as they do, they consume a much
smaller proportion of the surplus they appropriate than did members of
economically dominant classes in precapitalist societies.[4] In this sense,
even the most spendthrift capitalists are worldly ascetics too—accumu-
lating wealth not to enjoy it, but because this is the role the economic
system prescribes for them.[5]

The Protestant Ethic

Weber's central claim was that Protestantism, as it emerged in the teach-
ings of the magisterial Reformers, Martin Luther and John Calvin and
their successors, explains the spirit of capitalism; that Protestant theology

engendered a distinctive ethic or guide to living, a Protestant ethic, which, in turn, promoted an ascetic and methodical mentality conducive to capitalist flourishing. Two venerable theological doctrines, taken up and transformed by Protestant thinkers, figure prominently in the formation of this ethic: the idea of a calling and the doctrine of salvation through unmerited grace. According to Weber's account, Protestantism recast the notion of a calling from otherworldly vocations to ordinary occupations. Even more tellingly, it pressed the doctrine of salvation through unmerited grace to its limit, where, as often happens in extremis, it effectively turned into its opposite. In Weber's narrative, the figure who brought the idea of a calling to the fore and then transformed it into the notion the Protestant ethic assumed was Luther. The Reformer who did the most to develop the this-worldly implications of salvation through unmerited grace was Calvin. Of the two, Calvin was the more important figure in the emergence of the Protestant ethic. Thus, Weber argued that Lutheranism after Luther fell increasingly under the sway of Calvinist ideas, and that, in the decades after Calvin's death, even Calvinist denominations became ever more radically Calvinist.

The idea that some individuals are called to religious vocations was a mainstay of Catholic Christianity. But, according to Weber, the notion of a secular life project or plan of life was unknown to Catholic peoples. It was not until Luther transformed the idea that the notion of a secular calling (*Beruf*) emerged. Thus, it is to Luther that we owe the modern conception of a life or, rather, a life's work as a career. Before him, it was only in monastic orders that individuals had coherent life plans. Protestant theology extended this idea into the world beyond the cloister's walls. After Luther, living acceptably to God became a matter of fulfilling the obligations imposed on persons by their positions in the world. It should be noted that, despite its ancestry, this idea had antimonastic implications.[6] For it conflicts with the notion that one should, if called, strive to surpass the things of this world by removing oneself from earthly endeavors. Lutheran Protestantism taught otherwise. For the first time in the history of Christianity, it maintained that the way to answer a calling is to do one's worldly duty—not more and certainly not less.

Neither Luther nor Calvin in any way renounced the fundamental Christian belief in Original Sin, nor did they deny what it implies about the ultimate futility of human pursuits. They both therefore adamantly opposed the doctrine of salvation through works. Their rationale was the traditional one—that sinful human beings are incapable of doing anything that might justify their being saved. Salvation can therefore only come from a merciful Creator, through unmerited grace. But with their focus on worldly callings, the way that Protestants came to regard the connection between salvation and the things of this world changed significantly. Once doing one's earthly duty was held to matter theologically, in ways that it never had before for proponents of the doctrine of salvation through unmerited grace, succeeding in earthly endeavors came to be seen in a new light.

Blaise Pascal famously remarked that any position, pushed to its extreme, turns into its opposite—"too much light," he wrote, "blinds us." Calvin's purchase on the doctrine of salvation through unmerited grace illustrates this point exceptionally well. Calvin realized that the doctrine of Original Sin, in conjunction with the equally venerable Christian notion of Redemption through Christ, implied predestination. Individuals' eternal destinies must be sealed even before they are conceived. This implication led to a train of thought that, as if to vindicate Pascal's thought, effectively brought works back in.

If salvation can only come from unmerited grace, it follows that nothing people do can affect the likelihood that, at the Final Judgment, they will find themselves among those souls elected for salvation. Catholic Christianity, even as it maintained this doctrine, nevertheless held that it was necessary for salvation—though not sufficient—that individuals receive the sacraments of the Church. Calvin and his followers detected the self-serving disingenuity of this insistence, at the same time that they distrusted the Church's reliance on rituals and, more generally, on anything that smacked of magical ways of manipulating or eluding predestined outcomes. They therefore abandoned the idea of sacraments. This was just the beginning. In time, the more radical Calvinists came to value plainness and to eschew ceremony altogether. The most extreme of them even rejected the very notion of a Church—that is, of a structured, ecclesiastical institution. Anything more universal (Catholic) than self-governing congregations smacked too much of Rome. Still, there were aspects of Catholic thought that even the most radical Calvinists could not do without.

Within the monastic tradition, it had always been acknowledged that there were, as Calvin put it, "outward signs of inward grace." For those monastics and priests who pursued otherworldly goals, ascetically and methodically, doing well in their sacred duties was a sign—not an infallible indicator, but a sign nevertheless—of having genuinely been called. It was only natural, then, that Protestants would carry this understanding over to worldly affairs. Thus, within the Calvinist fold, success at one's *Beruf* came to be seen as a sign that one was saved.

Prosperity therefore became invested with theological significance. This is not to say that Calvin or his followers regarded wealth per se as an indicator of salvation. In capitalist economies, only capitalists are able to amass large fortunes. Most people are not, and cannot be, capitalists. Therefore, worldly success cannot be gauged by determining how much wealth an economic agent has accrued. What matters is how well one discharges one's worldly duties, whatever they happen to be. Since success in one's calling does normally issue in prosperity—or, more precisely, in a level of prosperity commensurate with one's station in life—wealth is a kind of indicator after all. The inference is irresistible—successful capitalists and diligent, prosperous workers are very likely manifesting inner grace. Becoming rich, relative to one's station, does not cause anyone to be saved; nothing can do that. However, it is a (fallible) sign that one is predestined to that condition.

Because doing well economically is a symptom, not a cause, Calvinists adhere strictly to the traditional Christian doctrine of salvation through unmerited grace, according to which Fallen Man can do nothing to ensure a place in the City of God. But from a psychological point of view, the effect is similar to what it would be if they had, instead, advanced the rival view, the doctrine of salvation through works. If earthly success is a sign of being saved, people will be disposed to try to alter the symptom. They will therefore work at their appointed tasks in ways that will increase their likelihood of manifesting outward signs of inward grace. Ironically, Calvinism inclines people who take the doctrine of salvation through unmerited grace seriously to devote themselves—methodically and ascetically—to the tasks the economy assigns them. In this way, Calvinism engendered and subsequently promoted the spirit of capitalism.

An Optimal Ethic

Western Christianity, at the time of the emergence of the Protestant ethic, was a mansion with many chambers. Like other great religions capable of surviving in a variety of circumstances and through changing times, it had a host of theoretical resources at its disposal—some ready made, others awaiting development. Some of the theological positions available to Protestants, like the doctrine of salvation through unmerited grace, lent themselves readily to the spirit of capitalism. Others were less useful. A problem Weber's work raises is to account for how those parts of the received theology that foster the spirit of capitalism came to predominate. Darwin faced a similar problem, but he had an answer. Natural selection, operating on random variations, explains changes in biological populations—by selecting traits that are optimal; traits that maximize reproductive fitness in particular circumstances. Is there a parallel mechanism in the world of ideas?

It is important to note that if Weber's account is generally on track, as it surely is, it was theological, not economic, exigencies that explain the theological turns that gave rise to the Protestant ethic. The question, then, for anyone who would understand their ideological operation, is not why these doctrines arose—for that, there are theological explanations—but why they become as influential as they did; and, in particular, why they took hold of the popular imagination. Religious fervor alone cannot explain this outcome. In fact, according to Weber's account, the Protestant ethic did not really come into its own until religious fervor subsided in the aftermath of early modern Europe's wars of religion. Thus some of the most prominent exemplars and exponents of the Protestant ethic— Benjamin Franklin is an example Weber cited often—would not have endorsed any of the defining tenets of the Calvinist faith. Franklin was a deist; therefore, strictly speaking, not even a Christian. In the story that *The Protestant Ethic* recounts, it is as if Protestantism set a train of events in motion and then turned away—just as deists, like Franklin, thought God Himself did for all of His creation.

The theology that had so powerful an impact was not invented to serve capitalists' interests. Quite the contrary. The doctrine of salvation through unmerited grace had achieved orthodox status in the Roman Church more than a millennium before capitalism emerged. Although, many capitalists contributed in various ways to the dissemination of Protestant theology and gave generously to Protestant institutions, no one set out to promote Protestantism because it was, so to speak, good for business. Nevertheless, it is because it was good for business—good, that is, for that sector of the population that was coming increasingly to organize economic life—that it took hold as profoundly and extensively as it did. It is for sociologists and historians to explain how this state of affairs came about. Unlike in the biological case, there is almost certainly not a single mechanism, analogous to natural selection, that explains all (or many) of the relevant changes. But at a sufficiently high level of abstraction, it is not necessary to have a fine grained account of antecedent causes. The general process is clear enough. Darwin's notion of evolution through natural selection exemplifies the process. So too do more mundane examples of functional relations.

Where there is a functional relation between X and Y, X and Y causally affect one another. But, there is an explanatory asymmetry. Consider, for example, causal interactions between a furnace and the ambient temperature in a room heated by the furnace and regulated by a thermostat. Thanks to the thermostat, the ambient temperature causally affects the operation of the furnace and the operation of the furnace causally affects the ambient temperature of the room. However, it is the function of the furnace to regulate the room temperature; it is not the function of the room temperature to regulate the firing of the furnace. A similar relation holds in Darwin's account of evolutionary change. Natural selection operates like a thermostat. It explains why, for example, giraffes have long necks. The explanation is roughly that within the population of giraffe ancestors, those individuals who had longer necks, thanks to random variations in neck size, did better than individuals with shorter necks because they were more successful at obtaining nourishment from leaves that grow on tall trees and therefore had a better chance of surviving to reproductive age. Thus, they produced more offspring and so their descendants, rather than the descendants of shorter-necked giraffes, came to prevail in later giraffe generations. If this explanation is correct, there is a causal interaction between the long necks of giraffes and the trees whose leaves giraffes eat. But, again, there is an explanatory asymmetry. The function of giraffes' long necks is to obtain the leaves that grow on tall trees; it is not the function of the trees or their leaves to lengthen giraffes' necks.

For X to stand in a functional relation to Y, it is not enough that X benefits Y. There must be a causal interaction: a feedback loop of the kind that thermostats or natural selection exemplify. Where none exist, the fact that X benefits Y may be of considerable intellectual interest or practical importance, but it is not explanatory. Weber was plainly interested in explaining the emergence and reproduction of the spirit of capitalism, not just in describing how the Protestant ethic was beneficial for it. But in *The Protestant Ethic*, he never identified causal mechanisms through which properly functional relations were achieved. His account of the Protestant ethic and of its connections with the spirit of capitalism was therefore incomplete. Weber was clear enough about how Protestantism benefited capitalism. But, he never explained how this beneficial relation took hold or how it was maintained. Thus, his account of capitalist flourishing is less complete than Darwin's account of evolutionary change. But this shortcoming in no way renders his view of the relation between the Protestant ethic and the spirit of capitalism—or what he assumes about the connection between the spirit of capitalism and capitalist flourishing—false. Before Darwin, people could truthfully say that giraffes have long necks because long necks help them obtain food. They could even say, plausibly, that the length of giraffes' necks is in some vague, but not entirely unspecified, sense optimal. But, they either had no idea how this outcome came about or else they had a false idea; they believed, for example, that God designed giraffes' necks to enable them to eat leaves that grow on tall trees. Because he had hardly anything to say about how the functional relation he identified was sustained, Weber's account of the connection between the Protestant ethic and the spirit of capitalism is similarly deficient. It is pre-Darwinian.

Weber's Lead

Despite this theoretical deficit, *The Protestant Ethic* remains a model worth following—especially where the American ideology is concerned. The American ideology is more like the Protestant ethic than first appears. In its case too, there is almost certainly no single mechanism, like natural selection, that explains how the ideas that cluster around its notions of efficiency and reasonableness operate ideologically. This is why, for the American ideology as much as for the Protestant ethic, an exhaustive ideological critique cannot remain forever fixed on the analysis and genealogy of ideas, why there is no substitute for concrete sociological and historical investigations of the real-world functioning of the ideas in question. Nevertheless, as Weber's work shows, much can be learned about ideologies without undertaking a protracted inquiry of this sort. It is also plain, following Weber's lead, that it is not necessary, in this instance, to squander effort establishing the fact that these ideas actually do serve the interests of prevailing elites. It is obvious that they do, just as it was obvious to Weber and to his readers that the spirit of capitalism fostered capitalist flourishing. My focus, in the chapters that follow, will therefore center on the ideas themselves, much as Weber focused on the theological roots of the ethic he described. The difference is that these ideas are not just historical artifacts, but living presences in our political culture.

Weber's work calls attention to a point, anticipated in the Introduction, that will be assumed in the pages that follow: that philosophical—

or, in the case of the Protestant ethic, theological—doctrines underdetermine policy prescriptions. Luther and Calvin and their successors advanced views on many matters of sectarian relevance. Their arguments in behalf of their respective positions were, for the most part, continuous with the underlying theological doctrines on which they relied. However, the theological tenets that grounded their conclusions—the idea that God bestows callings on some individuals, for example, or that He saves only some souls through the bestowal of unmerited grace, the rest being condemned to eternal torment—though suggestive of the conclusions they drew, hardly imply them. These doctrines had enjoyed orthodox status for more than a thousand years before the Protestant Reformation turned them to the service of capitalist flourishing. Even as the Reformation unfolded, the main opponent of all radical Protestants, the Roman Catholic Church, accepted these doctrines unequivocally. Arguably, Protestant thinkers, Calvin especially, developed the implications of these positions with a rigor that no one before him had. Weber thought so, but even he never suggested that, as a matter of logical inference, the radical Protestants were right and everyone else wrong. The underlying theology was too indeterminate to warrant such a conclusion. It supplied only the raw materials for the positions the Reformers advanced; it did not determine the finished product.

Similarly, the philosophical and economic doctrines that cluster around its notions of efficiency and reasonableness underdetermine the policy provisions that proponents of the American ideology nowadays advance. Privatization, deregulation, free trade, unrestricted movement of capital, and low tax rates for the rich, along with foreign policies directed toward projecting American military power throughout the world and imposing regimes friendly to the United States in economically strategic areas, are indeed supported by arguments that appeal to the core doctrines of the American ideology. But, these doctrines can also support different policy prescriptions; including some that, as we will see (in Chapter 5), transcend the frontiers of capitalism itself. As remarked, the fact that these ideas are currently invoked in support of neoliberal and imperialist policies explains why it is appropriate to call this ideological configuration American. However, what the name denotes are the ideas themselves, not the policy prescriptions that they presently support.

Weber's account of the Protestant ethic is exemplary in another respect—its focus on middle-range theories. In recounting what is distinctive in the theological underpinnings of the Protestant ethic, Weber concentrated on doctrines that presuppose deeper theological commitments. But these positions hardly figure in the story he tells. *The Protestant Ethic* includes no discussion, for example, of the bases (or lack of them) for believing in the existence of an omnipotent, omniscient, perfectly good God or of the grounds that distinguish Christian from other monotheistic conceptions of the divinity. Rationales for these and similarly foundational claims are of no consequence for marking off what distinguishes the theology that feeds the Protestant ethic from pertinent rival, mainly Catholic, views. Therefore, they are excluded from Weber's story. Similarly, it is not necessary to probe the deepest philosophical questions raised by the American ideology to submit it to ideological criticism. In its case too, it is best to aim at the middle-range—between basic philosophy and public policy.

Weber reproached the spirit of capitalism for its irrationality. However, he wrote as a social theorist and intellectual historian only. *The Protestant Ethic* was not intended as an anticapitalist, much less an anti-Protestant, tract and it is seldom read as one. The emphasis here will be different. I have many misgivings, of a philosophical nature, about the constituent parts of the American ideology, but I write to oppose it because I oppose the policy prescriptions it supports. Nevertheless, my target will be the body of theory that sustains these prescriptions, not the prescriptions themselves. I would hazard that had Weber assumed a more directly oppositional stance, he would have adopted a parallel focus. He would have taken aim at the Protestant ethic itself, not at this or that Protestant position (partially) derived from it. In any case, his example supports the idea that it is wise to undertake ideological criticism at this level, whether one's concerns are scholarly or political or both.

Protestant Ethic versus American Ideology

Despite the self-representations of the majority of its exponents, the American ideology works to quash democratic aspirations. Thus, for all their differences, there is a certain functional equivalence between the American ideology and the Protestant ethic. The Protestant ethic helped shape the capitalism of the period Weber's work covered. The American ideology plays a similar role today. Among other things, it works to immunize production, distribution, and exchange from political, and therefore democratic, control. Thus, it helps to sustain the ostensible independence of the economic structure. It is a sad reflection on our times that it discharges its mission in a far less ennobling way than the Protestant ethic did. It engenders no new spirit capable of motivating action for the sake of an ideal, not even an irrational one. Instead, the American ideology promotes acquiescence to the status quo. It reinforces the widespread disposition, encouraged by the depoliticizing and only minimally democratic institutions under which we live, not to try to change the world for the better. It does so by laying down what it claims are the limits of the possible—concluding that there is no feasible, genuinely democratic alternative that is more rational and therefore more desirable than what we already have. Left adherents of the American ideology—political liberals, for example—may suppose that we can improve our lot nevertheless by making policies and institutions conform better to what is estimable in the ideal the American ideology promotes. No doubt, we can. But even if all imaginable improvements were made, the ideal itself, however flawed, would remain secure—to the detriment, ultimately, of the values that anchor the (notional) Left. It is this profoundly debilitating state of mind, grounded in the conviction that we are locked into an unhappy but unavoidable condition, that ideological criticism can dispel.

3

Means-Ends Rationality

Aristotle distinguished theoretical from practical reason, a distinction that remains canonical to this day. There is therefore some irony in the fact that, in Aristotle's own philosophy, the idea of a rational society—of practical reason as a standard applicable to entire social orders—languished. His teacher, Plato, had made much of the idea—most conspicuously in *The Republic* and *The Laws*. The visions set out in those dialogues are mutually inconsistent and also, to modern, democratic sensibilities, unappealing. But they do articulate views of what Reason requires at the collective level. Yet Plato never developed an account of practical reason per se. He therefore never defended his visions of rational societies in terms that expressly distinguish doing from knowing. A rational society, in Plato's view, is one that accords with Justice or, what comes to roughly the same thing, that implements on earth the timeless, heavenly character of the idea (or form) of the Good.

Perhaps because this way of theorizing Reason in society was blatantly impracticable, and perhaps because Aristotle had other concerns, philosophical reflections on rational societies waned in the centuries that followed philosophy's birth. The idea lingered, however, to be revived from time to time—by the Stoics and then in late medieval political theory. By this route, it came to be everywhere assumed that Reason, in its practical applications, rules on the content of ends; that it commands certain ends and proscribes others. This understanding was central to Plato's thinking; it was less evident in Aristotle's, though it was never absent from it. Until the dawn of the modern era, it was a dogma of Western thought.

Even so, the tradition that Aristotle's work did so much to shape also inclined in another direction. What Aristotle focused on, much of the time, was not exactly the rationality of ends but their relation to means for realizing them. The most fundamental offense to practical reason, in his view, was to will an end, but not the means for obtaining it. Thus Aristotelian philosophy provided a source for what would emerge millennia later: a means-ends account of practical reason, according to which reason concerns only the adoption of means to ends, not the ends themselves.

Philosophy has its own internal dynamic, spurred on by the fact that, characteristically, philosophers engage each other's positions. However, philosophical ideas are never sealed off from the world around them. They arise in circumstances that, in any of a variety of ways, condition their character at the same time that these circumstances are affected by the ideas they help to fashion. This is plainly the case for means-ends or instrumental rationality. Far-reaching transformations in European social and political life in the seventeenth and eighteenth centuries—and comparable changes elsewhere in the world, as Europe expanded its influence globally—go a long way toward explaining why it was this aspect of Aristotle's understanding of practical reason that became so influential in the modern world.

I will not dwell on the causes of these transformations. No doubt, technological development, what Marx would call the development of "productive forces," and the emerging capitalist organization of European society, a phenomenon linked to the growth of productive forces, had much to do with them. So too, as readers of Weber would suspect, did the Protestant Reformation and the wars of religion that followed. But these larger historical themes only provide a background for the real-world transformations that propelled means-ends rationality into the forefront of social and political thought. It is their consequences that conditioned how practical reason came to be understood.

The Individual and Society

The emergence of the individual was one consequence. Needless to say, in all times and places, human beings, like other organisms, had distinct bodies and minds. Therefore, in a literal sense, the individual is plainly not an invention of the modern era. But in premodern societies, individuals, so conceived, were intimately joined, through relations of social solidarity, to other individuals—in families, clans, tribes, or other social groupings. In addition, the vast majority of the human race was tied by custom and law to the land on which people labored. This was as true in late European feudal societies as anywhere else. In consequence, everywhere before the modern era, people shared an understanding of their being in the world and their relations to one another that had little to do with the fact that they were separate bodies and minds. However differently their respective belief systems articulated the idea, they thought of themselves as constitutive parts of collective entities. This is why, in thinking about ideal social and political arrangements, it was collectivities, not the individuals who comprised them, that served as the starting points for reflection. To think about social and political arrangements from the standpoint of individuals, as we now do, would have been at odds with lived experience. The idea would doubtless have been comprehensible to premodern peoples. But, it would have seemed counterintuitive—in much the way that it would seem counterintuitive to us today, and to people everywhere throughout human history, to take, say, individuals' body parts as points of departure for reflecting on social and political life.

With the dissolution of feudal solidarities in late medieval Europe, the wearing away of the communal bonds that joined people together raised the salience of individuals' bodies and minds, at the same time that it diminished the perceived importance of the groups individuals comprised. Individuals were torn apart from each other and from the land they worked. Increasingly, their interactions came to be organized through their own (more or less voluntary) agreements—in other words, through market structures. This transformation was most evident in economic life, but it extended into the social sphere as well. Longstanding social solidarities gave way to ostensibly voluntary systems of bilateral exchange. Inevitably, this change in lived experience was reflected in social and political thought. The individual was born. In short order, the interests of individuals, conceived as entities in their own right, not as integral members of social groups, became the basis for political and social thought.

The same causes gave rise to society, as we now understand the idea. To this point, I have used the word anachronistically, effectively suggesting the modern notion and I will continue to do so. For most purposes, this anachronism is harmless. Still, it can be misleading and therefore ought to be pointed out. In premodern times, society, as we know it today, did not exist. The social order was composed of a loosely integrated agglomeration of collective entities—societies, as it were—organized internally through relations of social solidarity and joined to one another in hierarchical patterns. As these social units faded in importance, they were replaced, not entirely but nevertheless decisively, by an all-encompassing social whole, a society in the modern sense of the term, organized, for the first time in human history, through relations of exchange. Classical German sociology—the tradition of Weber, Georg Simmel, Ferdinand Tonnies, and others—famously characterized this difference when it distinguished *Gemeinschaft* from *Gesselschaft*. A "Gemeinschaft" is a society based on affective ties and entrenched social norms; a "Gesselschaft" is a market society based on the voluntary association of its members. This distinction has been a mainstay of social theory ever since.

Premodern notions of rational societies were nearly all, in one way or another, based on Plato's lead. But Plato, like everyone else who philosophized about politics in Greek antiquity, focused on the polis or city-state, the unit of Greek political life. By modern or even medieval standards, the territory encompassed by the polis was small and its population was composed of only a part, not even the major part, of the inhabitants of its territory. Women, slaves, resident aliens, and others—the vast majority of persons—were denied full membership. When philosophers reflected on what an ideal polis might be like, as Plato did in *The Republic*, most of its inhabitants, including those who were accorded a subordinate role in the existing social order, were placed toward the bottom of an even more rigidly hierarchical social structure than the one they endured in the real world. Thus, the polis was no *Gesselschaft*. Even so, to the degree that its full-fledged citizens ruled themselves, the Greeks did initiate forms of governance, including democratic procedures, inconsistent with the usual understandings of *Gemeinschaften*. It is therefore tempting to read back modern notions of society into premodern prescriptive accounts. However, this temptation should be resisted, not just because intellectual honesty requires that we understand philosophies in their historical context, but because ancient ideas ultimately resist application to modern conditions. This is why ancient political philosophy is of scant political, as distinct from philosophical, interest today. The world it theorized was at such remove from our own that the puzzlements it generated bear little resemblance to the puzzlements modern peoples confront.

The New Science

The emergence of the individual took place against the background of a far-reaching transformation in intellectual life inaugurated by the rise of the new sciences of nature and theorized in the writings of the first philosophers of the early modern period. For all their differences, these philosophers, and the scientific practices they endeavored to justify, agreed on a key point—that the Aristotelian account of explanation, the cornerstone of medieval science, was untenable. Above all, they rejected the Aristotelian conviction that one should inquire into the ends of phenomena. In their view, there are no ends to discover. Nature just is. To explain a phenomenon is to account for its facticity by identifying the causes that brought it into being. The aim of science, accordingly, is to discover the causal structure of the world. Aristotle distinguished four kinds of causes—material, formal, final (or teleological), and efficient. A material cause is the substratum or stuff of which a thing is made—the bronze of a statue. The formal cause is the thing's form—the statue's shape. Final causes are ends or purposes—that for the sake of which the statue was made. Efficient causes are whatever suffice to bring changes about. The first two of these causes had no explanatory role in the new sciences of nature. They were therefore quietly dropped. Final causes were less easily dismissed, because vestiges of medieval science lingered. However, it was deemed urgent by many that they, along with the understanding of nature they implied, be dispatched. To invoke final causes in explanations is not just to make an erroneous claim about ends or purposes. It is to imply that natural phenomena have meanings that can be specified in reference to their ends. This thought is foreign to modern science, as proponents of the new science realized from the beginning. This is why they took it upon themselves to excise this Aristotelian notion from philosophy. Thus the only one of Aristotle's four causes left standing, the only one that philosophers insisted mattered explanatorily, was efficient causality. The efficient cause of X is that which brings X into being. Notwithstanding the considerable attention that philosophers have lavished on the topics of causality and explanation in recent years, and the advances they have registered, the position early modern philosophers defended continues to be the operative view. To explain a phenomenon is to identify its efficient causes.

The philosopher of the early modern period most clearly identified with the elimination of final causes was Hobbes.[1] He was also the one who, more than any other, brought the notion of means-ends rationality to the fore. This was not an accident. It was because of the role efficient causes played in the new science, as he understood it, that Hobbes modeled political life in a way that led him to assume that (practical) reason is strictly instrumental.

Hobbesian Sovereignty

Consider Hobbes's account of sovereignty.[2] Where there is a sovereign, supreme political authority over a given territory or population is concentrated into a single institutional nexus; one that enjoys, as Weber put it, a "monopoly" of the (legitimate) means of violence.[3] Hobbes' account of sovereignty takes for granted the atomization of social relations that resulted from feudal disintegration. Thus, his point of departure was what might be called the atomic individual. To explain sovereignty, Hobbes imagined atomic individuals living outside political authority relations— in a "state of nature." He then set out to show how they might make themselves the efficient causes of the sovereign's authority. In other words, how starting from properly described initial conditions, atomic individuals, appropriately characterized, would concoct a form of political authority that is, at once, supreme and centralized in just the way that the real-world phenomenon he wanted to account for was.

The expression atomic individual is metaphorical. However, the idea behind it, like the metaphor itself, is motivated by Hobbes's larger philosophical project. Hobbes wanted to develop a political philosophy joined systematically to a metaphysics that reflects the findings of the new science. That science, Hobbes thought, vindicated a materialist metaphysics relevantly similar to that of ancient Greek and Roman atomism. For the atomists, atoms—indivisible units of matter—were both the fundamental constituents of material things and also radically independent entities. The second atomist tenet was as important to Hobbes as the first. Everything that is essential to a particular atom is, so to speak, in the atom itself. What an atom essentially is therefore has nothing to do with its relations with other atoms; it could be alone in the universe and still be the atom that it is. In nature, atoms do not stand alone; they exist in multitudes and enter into any of a variety of relations with one another. But, these relations are always external in the sense that they never affect an atom's identity conditions, the properties in virtue of which it is what it is. This was how Hobbes viewed the constituents of political communities.[4] The individuals who authorize a sovereign, the fundamental constituents of political communities, are radically independent entities. Driven by their own interests, they enter into external relations with one another—including some that render them subjects of a sovereign. Thus it was by his implicit use of this metaphor that Hobbes was among the first to accord paramount importance to individuals and their interests—something earlier thinkers, living in a world relevantly different from Hobbes's, would never have imagined doing.

Hobbes was not only an atomic individualist. He was a Galilean atomist, intent on incorporating Galileo's discovery—inertia—into the atomist picture, along with Galileo's understanding of absolute space. Because atomic individuals are inertial entities, they remain (metaphorically) in motion until the motion of other atomic individuals interferes with them. Because they inhabit an absolute space, a space whose coordinates are determined prior to and apart from the entities that occupy it, the position of each atomic individual is independent in principle of the positions of other atomic individuals. Thus, individuals are beings who pursue their ends independently and unrelentingly in a fixed, but confined area. Other individuals are either means for realizing their ends or obstacles in the way of pursuing them. Thus, what others do affects outcomes that matter to individuals. But others are, so to speak, of no intrinsic importance to individuals' wills. The wills of the inhabitants of a Hobbesian state of nature are radically unconnected; nothing, other than transitory desires, joins them together or holds them in line.

This condition militates against their well-being. Because they coexist in the same space, a territory they cannot exit, they will frequently collide with one another as they proceed along their self-directed paths. These metaphorical collisions are impediments to their natural motion. Less metaphorically, they are impediments to desire satisfaction, where desire, in the Hobbesian scheme, is the basis of value. Individuals therefore share an interest in regulating these (metaphorical) collisions to dissipate their ill effects. For their desires to be better satisfied than in a state of nature, they must coordinate their behaviors. It is this fact that motivates the institution of sovereignty.

It is useful to distinguish Hobbes's implicit, but plainly evident account of practical reason from his explicit account of human nature and human interests. In *The Leviathan,* where these ideas are set out, they are confounded. But, it is not difficult to disentangle them. Hobbes imputed certain character traits to individuals everywhere and at all times. Thus he maintained that individuals are always "diffident, competitive, and vainglorious"—in other words, that they are motivated by fear, especially the fear of violent death; that they seek to accumulate resources endlessly; and that they demand recognition from others and therefore seek to dominate others and not be dominated by them. From these claims about human psychology, Hobbes argued that, in conditions of relative scarcity, atomic individuals, being roughly equal in natural endowments and being obliged to interact with one another, will all share certain interests—in peace or order, in acquiring resources, and in esteem. Hobbes's account of sovereignty trades on this fact. But before it can be put to explanatory use, it must also be assumed that human beings are capable of acting on the interests they have. In elaborating on this idea, Hobbes pioneered an explanatory strategy that is widely deployed today—*rational choice theory*. In doing so, he effectively invented the notion of means-ends rationality—not from whole cloth, since Aristotle and his followers had already broached the idea, but decisively enough that it is fair to credit its creation to him.

What Hobbes maintained is that practical reason is instrumental, not substantive; that it concerns the adoption of means to ends, not ends themselves. Ends are therefore neither rational nor irrational; they just are what they are, thanks to the way human nature and the human condition happen to be. Were the facts different from what Hobbes thought they were—were it the case that human beings were by nature reckless even to the point of welcoming situations that increase their likelihood of coming to a violent end—it would not be rational to will peace. Peace is a rational end for the inhabitants of the state of nature and for us, because human beings' psychological dispositions require it. Reason itself is neutral on this and all other matters.

This is not to say that, as far as reason is concerned, the ends individuals will are beyond reproach. Means-ends rationality is a demanding standard. An individual can be instrumentally irrational in a variety of ways. There is, of course, the obvious one: willing an end but not the means to obtaining it. But, there are less obvious ways too. Individuals act irrationally when they act imprudently—when they fail to act in accord with their own best interests. Individuals act imprudently whenever they act on ends other than the ones they would have acted on, had they had full or at least adequate knowledge of the consequences of their actions, or when they fail to reflect adequately on the knowledge they have or they can act irrationally when they fail to do what they know to be best.[5] Also, consistency—a property of a set of agents' ends, rather than of the ends themselves—is a requirement of means-ends rationality. An individual who, for example, chooses A over B, B over C, and C over A chooses irrationally. Inconsistent choices are irrational because reason requires us to do what is individually best, given our interests as represented by our preferences for alternatives in contention. Individuals who choose inconsistently do not and cannot do what is individually best because their preferences and therefore their choices cycle. For them, there is no choice that is best. There is therefore no way for them to do what reason requires. Whatever they do is irrational.

Implicitly, Hobbes claimed both that human beings are instrumentally rational and that they have the interests he imputed to them. This is why it is irrational for an individual in a state of nature not to seek peace. The end, peace, is neither rational nor irrational in itself. But it would be irrational for such beings as we are, beings with psychological dispositions and therefore interests and therefore preferences like our own, not "to endeavor peace, as far as . . . [they] have hope of obtaining it." For the sake of peace, Hobbes argued, such beings will concoct a sovereign, if they are able to do so. He then set out to show how they could do precisely that. Thus, to his own satisfaction at least, he explained sovereignty.

Optimality

Hobbes's account of practical reason has had momentous consequences for shaping contemporary views about the prospects for making societies rational for a reason that was not readily apparent in Hobbes's day, but that has come to be appreciated in recent philosophical reflections on Hobbes's work. To draw out this reason, it will be instructive to reconstruct what Hobbes had in mind by using conceptual tools borrowed from the theory of games, the branch of mathematics that models (means-ends) rational choices in situations in which how well players in games do depends on what their opponents do. As a good first approximation, a Hobbesian state of nature can be thought of as a generalized Prisoners' Dilemma game. In a Prisoners' Dilemma, the unintended consequence of doing what is individually best is an outcome that is worse for each player than need be—not according to some external standard of better or worse, but according to the interests that motivate players to do what is individually best in the game. This is the case in a state of nature. It is because individuals, in the absence of a common power to hold them in awe, do what is individually best, given their interests, that they find themselves in a war of all against all—a situation worse, indeed much worse, than the peace they all desire.

The Prisoners' Dilemma is so named because of the story with which it has come to be associated. Suppose that two prisoners, Smith and Jones, have been arrested for a serious crime—armed robbery, for example. Suppose too that the prosecuting attorney has only enough evidence to convict each of them of a lesser crime—say, breaking and entering—unless one or the other confesses. The prosecutor therefore offers each prisoner a deal. She tells them both that if one confesses and the other does not, the one who confesses will go free, while the other must spend twenty years in prison. If both confess, she promises that they will each get no more than ten-year prison sentences. However, if neither prisoner confesses, she concedes that the most she can do is convict them of the lesser crime, for which they will each be confined in prison for three years. We can think of this story as a game in which there are two players— Smith and Jones—and two moves—confess or not confess. If we represent these outcomes in a payoff matrix, with the payoffs to Jones on the left and the payoffs to Smith on the right, then, pictorially:

		Smith	
		confess	not confess
Jones	confess	−10,-10	0,-20
	not confess	-20,0	-3,-3

Assuming that Smith and Jones are self-interested rational agents intent only on minimizing their own years in jail, it is clear what would happen. They would each confess. The payoff to each player depends on what the other player does. The opposing player can either confess or not confess. In either case, it is better to confess. If Jones confesses, Smith is better off confessing too, since he prefers ten years in prison to twenty. If Jones does not confess, Smith is still better off confessing, since he prefers zero years in jail to three. Since the payoff schedule is symmetrical, the same reasoning holds for Jones. Therefore, both will confess. Both will then get ten-year sentences. But, there is a better outcome for both of them—the one in which they are sentenced to three years in prison. However to arrive at that outcome, both Smith and Jones would have to forbear from doing what is individually best by not confessing. This would be irrational.

According to the way the term is standardly defined, an optimal outcome is one in which no individual can do better without another doing worse. We will consider the rationale for this definition presently. For now, what we should observe is that the unintended consequence of each player doing what is individually best in a Prisoners' Dilemma game is not optimal. We should also observe that there is an optimal outcome for this game—the one where both players choose not to confess. The optimal outcome is better for all the players. But, it does not obtain at equilibrium—that is, after the players have each made their individually best moves. In Prisoners' Dilemmas, the equilibrium solution is suboptimal in the sense that a better, outcome exists, one in which everybody would be better off. The problem is that self-interested, means-ends rational players cannot reach it.

Hobbes's solution to the problem he posed, his account of how relatively equal and rational atomic individuals with the dispositions he identified are able to contract together to authorize a sovereign to act in their behalf, need not detain us. What is important for us now in what Hobbes did and in subsequent philosophical elaborations of his core idea, has more to do with the problem he formulated than with his efforts to solve it. Hobbes focused attention on the unintended consequences at the macrolevel—in this case, the level of the whole society—of individually rational, microlevel choices. In doing so, he anticipated a notion of what a rational society would be like. That notion draws on the idea of optimality just defined. A rational society, on the view in question, is one that exhibits this structural property. As we will see, this property is invoked when economists and others, in formal contexts, speak of efficiency. For many political and social theorists nowadays, this is all the rationality one can or should expect at the societal level.

Utilitarianism

The concepts of optimality and suboptimality that Hobbes implicitly deployed were developed explicitly, nearly a century ago, in the work of the Italian-Swiss economist and social theorist Vilfredo Pareto. It is therefore to Pareto that we owe the notion of efficiency at work in the American ideology. However, the thinking behind Pareto's formulations only makes sense in light of the antecedent utilitarian tradition in philosophy and economics. Before turning to efficiency itself, then, it will be useful to look briefly at some of the fundamental doctrines of classical utilitarianism.

Utilitarians identify the good with well-being or welfare. These are placeholder terms, which may be used interchangeably. What well-being is is controversial. Thus utilitarians can and do disagree about the nature of the good. But, all utilitarians agree that well-being is a good for individuals and that it is something individuals have or possess, not something they do. All utilitarians agree too that, at the societal level, there ought to be as much of this good as possible; in other words, that the best outcome is the one that, of all the alternatives in contention, maximizes overall well-being. Utilitarians then go on to hold that what it is to maximize well-being overall, welfare at the societal level, is to maximize the logical sum of individual welfares. For a utilitarian, this is the only good that needs to be taken into account in normative deliberations. This is a strong claim, but it is not quite as strong as may at first appear. Utilitarians need not insist that welfare is the only good there is. They can acknowledge that there are goods that have to do with capabilities or functionings, with what individuals are able to do, or with what they actually do. They can even accept that there are goods that have nothing to do with individuals at all. They are only committed to the claim that nonwelfarist goods have no role to play in deliberating about what to do.

To maintain that welfare, at the societal level, ought to be maximized, utilitarians are obliged to hold that individual welfares are in principle quantifiable; in other words, that they can be compared along a single dimension. That dimension is utility. Utility measures welfare. Utilitarians therefore want to maximize utility. In practice, this usually means that they want to maximize the welfare of the entire society (in the sense of the term that has been assumed since Hobbes's time). In more formal terms, utilitarians want to maximize the value U_s, social or societal utility, where U_s is the logical sum of the utilities of each of the n individuals in the society, $U_1 + U_2 + \ldots + U_n$. For utilitarians, then, normative deliberations are about aggregating goodness or maximizing utility for the entire social group. The aim of a utilitarian deliberator is to amass the greatest quantity of goodness overall, subject only to the constraint that, as bearers of utility, all individuals count equally. What matters is how much goodness there is. Other concerns—say, about how utility (or anything else) is distributed—are subordinated to this imperative.

As an ethical theory, a theory of right action, the basic utilitarian claim is that an action is right if and only if, of all the actions the agent could perform, it has the consequence of generating the most utility overall. As a political principle, the corresponding idea is that institutional arrangements and social practices are justified if and only if, of all the alternatives in contention, they too generate the most overall utility. Thus, in both ethics and political philosophy, utilitarianism is a consequentialist theory. Only the consequences of actions or of institutional arrangements matter. Indeed, for utilitarians, only one kind of consequence matters—utility consequences, consequences for individuals' welfares.

Welfare, again, is a placeholder term. What its use implies is just that the good be a good for individuals. Many utilitarians identify welfare with pleasure or happiness. This was the view, for example, of the first generation of utilitarians, the generation of Jeremy Bentham, and it was what Pareto understood utilitarians to believe. It is also the position of many utilitarians today. But, utilitarians can and do identify welfare with desire or preference satisfaction. They can maintain, in other words, that individuals are well off to the degree that their desires or preferences are realized. Or, at greater remove from Bentham, they can hold that well-being consists in having obtained certain objective conditions; conditions that in principle have no direct connection to individuals' desires or conscious states. There have even been utilitarians, like G.E. Moore, who thought that welfare is a nonnatural property that individuals directly apprehend.[7] Utilitarians must have some view about what utility measures; otherwise, they would not know what to maximize. But, apart from the constraint that their view be welfarist, they can construe good-ness any way they like. What matters for making a theory utilitarian is not its account of what utility measures, but its determination to maximize utility, whatever one or another theory takes it to be.

Again, if U_s represents social utility, the utility of all individuals in the community, and U_1 represents the utility function for Individual 1, U_2, the utility function for Individual 2, and so on up to the nth individual, then what utilitarians want is to maximize the value of Us, where $U_s = U_1 + U_2 + \ldots\ldots + U_n$. This formulation supposes that there is a theoretically meaningful way to assign cardinal numbers $(1, 2, 3 \ldots)$ to welfare, however welfare is understood, so that individuals' welfares can be added together. Therefore, two measurement problems must be addressed:

1. How to measure utility intrapersonally or within the person
2. How to measure utility interpersonally or between persons

To measure utility intrapersonally, there must be a theoretically well moti-vated way to assign cardinal numbers to individuals' welfares, so as to measure not only how alternative states of the world can be ranked with respect to their welfare consequences, but also the degree of welfare differ-ences in alternative states of the world. To measure utility interperson-ally, there must be a way to meaningfully express these intrapersonal measurements in a common unit. Otherwise, it would not be possible to add them together, as utilitarianism requires. These measurement prob-lems have been addressed with considerable ingenuity over the past two centuries, especially by economists, and progress has been made on both fronts in measuring utility in highly restricted and stylized conditions. Still, the general problem remains.

Efficiency

Pareto was convinced, on the one hand, of the utilitarian conviction that social and political institutions are justified to the extent that they enhance overall well-being. But, he was also convinced of the impossibility of adding welfares together in the way that utilitarianism demanded. He was troubled, above all, by utilitarianism's dependence on interpersonal utility comparisons. His reasons were not so much technical as philosophical. He thought that the idea of interpersonal utility comparisons was incoherent. This is a more devastating complaint than the view, implied by it, that practical difficulties in the way of measuring utility are daunting and perhaps even intractable. That these practical difficulties exist is beyond dispute; the more far-reaching claim of Pareto's is another matter. This is not the place to take it on directly. But, I will indicate how dependent Pareto's position is on historically specific philosophical and scientific assumptions.

Pareto came to the position he held because he assumed that utilitarianism identifies the good with conscious states. But like so many others since the seventeenth century, he was persuaded by the arguments of René Descartes and philosophers after him that direct (noninferential) knowledge of other minds is impossible.[8] In Descartes' view, individuals, conceived as minds or unitary centers of consciousness, have access only to their own ideas or mental representations. It happens, of course, that minds are attached to particular bodies. Indeed, it is a fact that, as a "Cartesian ego" or self, I have one and only one body—my own, the one to which I am attached. I can feel pain only in that body. Even if, contrary to fact, I could feel pain in a body different from my own, it would still be my pain, part of my consciousness. It follows that I cannot even know directly that other minds exist. I can only surmise that they do by observing the behaviors of other bodies. Thus, I can infer that when another body behaves as mine would when, say, cut by a knife or hit with a hammer that the other body very probably, like my own, is attached to a mind that, like mine, experiences pain. But, I can never feel that pain. Therefore, even if I can know that others experience pain and pleasure, I cannot experience their pains or pleasures myself. As long as I lack access to their subjectivity, to the felt quality of their mental lives, I cannot compare my mental experiences with theirs. I cannot even be sure that their mental life is of the same nature as my own. A Cartesian, like Pareto, would have to concede that I can know that others see green because I can infer this fact from the way they react to green stimuli. I can observe that their behaviors, including their verbal behaviors, accord with my own. In a similar vein, I can perhaps know too that, when others and I see green, similar phenomena occur in our nervous systems. On these bases, I can infer that others, like me, know, for example, that grass is green. But, if Descartes was right, I can never know what anyone else's experience of green is like. Not just as a matter of fact but, in principle, I cannot know to what extent, if at all, it is like mine. Therefore, Pareto concluded, I can never meaningfully compare it with my own.

This is why Pareto maintained that it makes no sense to express the utilities of different individuals in a common unit. Even if, somehow, the intrapersonal utility measurement problem were solved—if we could meaningfully measure, say, individuals' degrees of pleasure—we could not add these measurements together in the way that utilitarianism requires. To determine their logical sum, utilities must be expressed in a common unit. In Pareto's view, this is impossible.

Cartesian philosophy was not the only source for this conclusion. By Pareto's time, early twentieth-century social science had already begun to take a behaviorist turn—focusing exclusively on observable behaviors and other measurable phenomena. It would remain locked into this paradigm for many decades, casting anything that smacked of the mental into disrepute. At the dawn of the behaviorist era, Pareto and his cothinkers wanted normative theory to be consistent with this emerging trend in descriptive social science. Economists and others who followed their lead therefore came to reject the mentalism of traditional utilitarianism almost reflexively. But some of them, like Pareto, were intent on retaining utilitarianism's ultimate aim. They wanted to maximize well-being.

What Pareto realized was that if we are to think about aggregating individuals' welfares in a way that does not offend Cartesian principles and behaviorist norms, it is necessary to change the way we represent welfare. The classical utilitarians wanted to represent welfare cardinally—by attaching cardinal numbers (1, 2, 3 . . .) to it.[9] They sought to represent information both about how alternatives are ranked relative to one another and about the degree of difference between items in the ranking. Thus, if welfare is identified with pleasure, cardinal representations of individuals' welfares would provide information about how different alternatives compare to one another with respect to how much pleasure they provide and, at the same time, about the degree of difference between alternatives in the ranking. It is information of the latter sort, about pleasure intensity, that runs afoul of Cartesian and behaviorist convictions. Pareto therefore reasoned that if we relinquish the goal of directly representing this information, we can go at least some of the way toward retrieving the utilitarian idea.

He therefore proposed that welfare be represented ordinally (using the ordinal numbers—1st, 2nd, 3rd . . .), not cardinally. Ordinal representations would capture information about preference rankings only. With this diminished but far from trivial information at hand, we can still make some welfare comparisons. We can say, for example, that state of affairs X is better in a welfarist sense than state of affairs Y, if all individuals rank X above Y in their orderings. When one state of the world is unanimously preferred to another, it is unambiguously better in the welfarist sense that classical utilitarianism intended. It is even possible to extend the range of application of this otherwise limited conclusion by maintaining, as economists after Pareto ingeniously did, that X is better in a welfarist sense than Y, even when it is not unanimously preferred, if the individuals who prefer X to Y can compensate the others, those who prefer Y to X, at least enough to bring them back up to their former welfare levels and still be better off.

An outcome is *Pareto superior* if everyone prefers it. It is *Pareto optimal* if any change, from the condition that actually obtains would make someone worse off. The rationale for this understanding is now apparent. Instrumentally rational agents, intent on maximizing their own welfares, would never want to move away from an existing situation if the change would diminish their welfare level. This fact about means-ends rational agents lends itself to ordinalist representations. It registers in the understanding that no one would choose an outcome that stands lower in his or her ranking of alternatives in contention.

In principle, there is any number of Pareto optimal outcomes. In this respect, Pareto optimality is unlike its ancestor notion, the utilitarian maximum. In the utilitarian view, there is only one best distributional outcome (or, in the case of ties, one set of outcomes that is best), the one that results in maximizing utility overall. In the Paretian scheme, there are infinitely many, because Pareto optimality is compatible with any pattern of resource distribution. More generally, since Paretian welfare analyses take existing distributions as their starting points or baselines, they are biased in favor of the status quo, whenever distributional questions arise. In this sense, Pareto optimality is a conservative standard, the utilitarian maximum is not.

Macrolevel Consequences of Microlevel Choices

Prisoners' Dilemmas lead to Pareto inferior outcomes. When each player does what is best, the outcome is worse than it could otherwise be for all players. This is a remarkable result. Indeed, it is remarkable that microlevel, individual maximizing choices can lead to outcomes at the macrolevel that exhibit any structural property whatsoever. It was therefore a major (though only implicit) discovery of Hobbes's that a state of nature has a Prisoners' Dilemma structure and therefore that, in consequence of choosing rationally, diffident, competitive, and vainglorious beings, interacting in state of nature conditions, would find themselves worse off than need be. What one would expect is that the macrolevel consequences of their microlevel choices would have no determinate structure at all. This is the case with most human interactions. As in the state of nature Hobbes described, what happens to us almost always depends, in part, on what other people do. However, there is usually nothing to say about what the outcomes of our interactions will be like. There is no structural pattern that we can plausibly impute to them. Once the notion of a Prisoners' Dilemma became available, it did become clear that, in many interactive contexts, we can indeed ascribe structural patterns to the outcomes means-ends rational agents will (unintentionally) produce, as they set about to do what is individually best. Thus, it became clear that there are many Prisoners' Dilemma situations in the real world[10] and that other real-world situations can be modeled by other games.[11] Nevertheless, the majority of human interactions resist this kind of representation. What happens at the macrolevel, when means-ends rational agents do their best in the conditions they confront, is simply indeterminate.

Intuitively, though, it does seem that macrolevel outcomes should be better when individuals do what is best for themselves than when they do not. It is therefore not surprising that, as the notion of means-ends rationality took hold, efforts were made to vindicate this intuition—to find situations for which it can be demonstrated that microlevel maximizing generates outcomes that exhibit desirable macrolevel properties. Until the middle of the twentieth century, these efforts were almost entirely speculative; hardly anything was actually proven. Smith's case for the workings of an Invisible Hand, turning individual greed into public benefits, is a case in point.[12]

Invisible Hand situations, as Smith envisioned them, are the obverse of Prisoners' Dilemmas. In a Prisoners' Dilemma, doing what is individually best leads to outcomes that are worse for everybody. Smith conjectured that in private property economies organized through markets, when agents do what is individually best, the outcome at the societal level will be as good as can be. Smith never quite explained what he meant. But twentieth-century economists and others, following Pareto's lead, did offer an interpretation. They understood his conjecture to mean that the resource allocation (ideal) markets generate will be efficient (Pareto optimal). This is surely a pale interpretation of Smith's claim. An allocation that is such that no one can be better off without someone else being worse off can be dismal indeed. At the limit, a world in which one individual has everything and everyone else has nothing is a world in which resources are distributed in a Pareto optimal way—because any change would make the individual who has everything worse off. It does not take much imagination to think of a better allocation (on any plausible understanding of "better"). Nevertheless, the interpretation that twentieth-century economists provided did at least make Smith's conjecture specific; and, in a highly attenuated sense, it made it provable.

Understanding the respects in which Smith was right is crucial for understanding how efficiency considerations operate in the American ideology. I will touch on the main points in Chapter 4 and Chapter 5. It will emerge that the American ideology is not the only site where efficiency, so conceived, has taken on an ideological aspect. For much of the last century, conventional wisdom held that there were two, and only two, ways of organizing social, political, and economic life—one capitalist, the other socialist. For the most part, proponents of one or the other of these economic systems were loathe to engage the justifying theories of the other, except to disparage them. Even so, an underground debate surfaced, from time to time, mainly in academic circles. Smith's conjecture played a role in these discussions. Both sides accepted its conclusions, even as they disagreed about its implications. This is one reason why many socialists in the middle and final decades of the twentieth century veered away from the more robust notions of Reason in society that had animated the socialist movement since its inception. It is also part of the explanation for the fact that socialism's most revolutionary idea—that there can be a more rational way to order societies than capitalism is capable of accommodating—became diluted and then enlisted in the service of entrenched elites in officially socialist countries and in political parties outside the socialist bloc that purported to carry forward the traditions of revolutionary socialism.

Reflecting on this irony is pertinent for thinking about what it would mean, in the present period, to restore the idea of a rational society to the forefront of the political agenda. Even before communism imploded, there was very nearly a consensus that an efficient (Pareto optimal) allocation of economic resources is, as it were, all the rationality there can be at the societal level. I will suggest that this claim is unwarranted. I will suggest too that it has been politically disabling—not just in the world that exists today, as (mainly) American elites endeavor to cement their dominance at a global level, but also in the bipolar world that preceded it.

4
The Invisible Hand

Smith was not the first to assert that "private vices," like greed, can be beneficial to the public at large. Long before *The Wealth of Nations* was published (in 1776), Bernard Mandeville had made that claim in *The Fable of the Bees* (1714, English edition, 1723). However, it was Smith who invented the metaphor of the Invisible Hand and it was he who applied Mandeville's thought to the economy—a notion first formulated, in its modern sense, in the eighteenth century. Smith declared that self-interested economic agents, interacting in laissez-faire market regimes with no deliberate regard for the common good, will produce outcomes that, at the societal level, are as good as can be given individuals' interests. In these circumstances, unlike in a Prisoners' Dilemma, the unintended consequence of doing what is individually best is an outcome that is socially best. Welfare, or at least those aspects of it that are affected by the economy, is maximized as if through the workings of an Invisible Hand.

Smith never proved this conjecture. Even so, in the years that followed, the Invisible Hand came to be a fixture of social and political thought. At first, it played a mainly anticonservative, especially antimercantilist, role in ongoing political debates. In time, it came to be invoked, with even greater enthusiasm, by liberal opponents of the emerging socialist movement. It assumed this function for historically contingent reasons. Until well into the 1930s, virtually all socialists opposed market arrangements. For the most part, their opposition, like the opposition voiced by conservative critics of capitalism, followed less from a commitment to an alternative economic doctrine than from a deep-seated hostility to market society; in other words, to the rise of the *Gesselschaft* form of social organization. Socialists endorsed new forms of community, not the old forms that market societies were replacing. Thus, from the outset, they differed from the conservatives, whose antipathy toward capitalism followed from a longing to restore the old *Gemeinschaften*. But, they and the conservatives were of one mind on this: that laissez-faire economies are devastating to communal values. Socialists also faulted market arrangements for the economic anarchy they encouraged, for the cycles of boom and bust endemic to nineteenth-century capitalist economies. This is why, when they speculated on the nature of economic institutions under socialism, they proposed more centralized—or more rational—ways of organizing economic life. This is why, in turn, they were unkindly disposed toward Smith's conjecture. To proclaim that market interactions, motivated by greed, produce public benefits superior to those that could be obtained by other, more rational, means—or, even worse, to claim that they, and they alone, make outcomes as good as can be—was to oppose an almost visceral conviction of the socialist movement as it existed at the time. Needless to say, this was not Smith's intention; socialism was not yet even conceived in 1776. Nevertheless, since the middle decades of the nineteenth century, Smith's conjecture and the metaphor associated with it have been enlisted into service by antisocialist, procapitalist ideologues. In this respect, the American ideology continues a long tradition.

Smith Was (Partly) Right

By the late nineteenth century, as the neoclassical paradigm in economic theory was being forged, the conjecture Smith advanced took on a new, more theoretical aspect, even as it continued to function ideologically in much the way it always had. In the body of theory begun by Léon Walras and others in the 1880s and 1890s and culminating in the mid-1950s with the work of Gérard Debreu and Kenneth Arrow, several startling results (partially) confirmed what Smith had claimed. Contrary to what procapitalist ideologues imply when they invoke the Invisible Hand, these results hardly apply to real-world capitalist economies. They apply unambiguously only to a highly stylized and abstract mathematical model of a market economy with private property.

In brief, the following two claims were demonstrated:

1. Provided certain background conditions are satisfied (see below and Chapter 5), it is possible for microlevel market choices to culminate unintentionally, as if by the workings of an Invisible Hand, in a general equilibrium, such that no demands go unfilled and no supplies of resources or commodities go unpurchased. This outcome results when there is a complete set of markets—in other words, when there is trading in everything that anyone is willing to purchase—when firms sell outputs in a profit-maximizing fashion subject to their technological constraints, when consumers purchase goods and supply labor and other resources to firms in ways that maximize their own utility subject to their budget constraints, and when market prices do not exceed the value of the resources and labor that economic agents are willing to sell. These are very demanding conditions. The fact that they must obtain for a general equilibrium bearing the mark of the Invisible Hand to exist forces a considerable degree of dissociation between real-world capitalist economies and the theory that purportedly describes and justifies them.

2. These equilibria are Pareto optimal. This is to say that, at equilibrium, when all markets clear—in other words, when there are no further gains from trade—the outcome is such that any change would make one or more economic agents worse off. Thus, if we take the prevailing distribution of resources and existing tastes (preferences for alternatives in contention) as given, if we hold production technologies constant, and if we exclude all other exogenous changes to the system, at equilibrium, the unintended consequence at the societal level of individuals executing their own maximizing choices in their market interactions will be a Pareto optimal allocation of resources.

As remarked in Chapter 3, this is what economists mean by efficiency. Or, rather, it is what they usually mean in technical contexts. Typically, economists use the term loosely. Like everyone else, they often use it in a way that is nearly synonymous with means-ends rationality. Presumably this is what people have in mind, when they say, for example, that a transport system is efficient if it fulfills its mission with a minimal waste of resources. Or, even more loosely, they may just mean that it works well, even if it could somehow operate more effectively. Too often in the economic literature and in the policy debates that economic reasoning informs, the looser and stricter senses of the term flow together. Too often, the luster that attaches to displays of formal pyrotechnics in mathematical models that employ the notion of Pareto optimality is invoked, wittingly or not, in policy arguments in which efficiency considerations are deployed unsystematically and in ways that trade on the term's vague, nontechnical senses.

The claim that, under the conditions specified, every competitive equilibrium is efficient (Pareto optimal) is standardly called *the first fundamental theorem of welfare economics*—where "welfare economics" designates that branch of economic theory that treats normative issues explicitly. A third result proven in (partial) vindication of Smith's conjecture is called *the second fundamental theorem of welfare economics*. It holds that any efficient allocation of resources can be obtained through market mechanisms. All that is necessary to arrive at any particular outcome is that the initial resource distribution be of the right sort; a condition that can always be implemented, in principle, through lump sum transfers carried out by the state. The second fundamental theorem enshrines the difference, noted in Chapter 3, between ordinalist welfare economics and classical utilitarianism. Both aim to enhance welfare to the greatest extent possible. But, unlike its predecessor and rival, ordinalist welfare economics dissociates this objective from distributional concerns. Utilitarian welfare economics favors that distribution which maximizes utility overall. Ordinalist welfare economics does not, it favors any distribution compatible with efficiency. The second fundamental theorem gives formal expression to this thought.

An implication of the second fundamental theorem is that considerations of justice or equity are distinct in principle from efficiency considerations. Thus, it came to be part of the common sense of the political culture—or rather of the policy-making part of it—that, in policy deliberations, there is generally a trade-off between these concerns. We will see presently how, in recent years, the second theorem, along with other components of the neoclassical or general equilibrium paradigm, has been superseded, in key respects. Even so, the idea that equity and efficiency are distinct and often opposed values persists.

Ironically, because it dissociates equity from efficiency in the way that it does, the second fundamental theorem makes it possible to disentangle Smith's (partially vindicated) Invisible Hand defense of market arrangements from Smith's and so many others' defense of private property. After the second theorem, defenders of capitalism, or rather of the distributions capitalist markets generate, cannot invoke efficiency considerations directly. The second theorem demonstrates that markets can be enlisted in behalf of any distributional objective. To defend the distributions capitalism generates on efficiency grounds, it is therefore necessary to resort to a more attenuated, ultimately psychological, justification—one that appeals to the incentive effects of (private) property arrangements. These, it is claimed, make market economies work well.[1] According to the usual view, it is the efficiency advantages that follow from the incentives that capitalist markets provide that may need to be traded off for equity reasons.

Defenders of capitalism have typically shown little interest in income or wealth equality. But states in capitalist societies can always implement egalitarian objectives through taxation and redistributive cash transfers. At the limit, the state could impose a 100% tax on market-generated income and on wealth, followed by a strictly egalitarian redistribution. But, the argument goes, there is an insurmountable obstacle in the way of such a program. Radical egalitarianism undoes the incentive structure that makes capitalist markets work. The same consideration applies, in diminishing degrees, to less radical redistributions. The idea, in all cases, is that departures from market-generated distributions undermine individuals' incentives to produce, causing overall production to decline. If the decline is steep enough, the market-generated distribution will be Pareto superior to the outcome obtained through redistribution. Then redistribution, whether it is warranted or not on equity grounds, would be inefficient in both the technical, Paretian sense and in many of the informal senses that cluster around that idea.

This is why, for those who take the neoclassical paradigm to heart, it is always an open question how much efficiency ought to be traded off for the sake of equity or other nonefficiency concerns. Presumably, this is an issue for the political process to decide. In the American case, to a degree seldom rivaled in other developed countries, equity considerations have never been vigorously pursued in the political arena. At present, with free market fundamentalism the order of the day, they have fallen even further into disregard.

Market Socialism

In contrast to procapitalists, who are not much in favor of income or wealth equality, socialists have always made equality along these dimensions a prime objective. What the second fundamental theorem of welfare economics shows is that income and wealth equality can be obtained, without detriment to efficiency, even with markets regulating economic life. All that is necessary is that the initial distribution of resources, the distribution prior to the time that self-interested, rational agents engage in trade, be such as to produce an egalitarian, but still efficient, allocation.[2] In principle, if property rights are arranged accordingly, markets can generate equal (or nearly equal) distributions without redistributive state interventions. Worries about incentive problems would, of course, remain. Because income and wealth inequality are indispensable for boosting overall productivity, the need to balance equity and efficiency concerns would continue. But with the right initial distribution of property rights in productive assets, the institutional context within which trade-offs would be struck would differ substantially from those with which we are familiar. In the view of some egalitarians, it should be possible, in these circumstances, to enhance equity through markets, with little or no state intervention, and without detriment to efficiency.

Very generally, property designates bundles of rights—to benefit from and to control economic assets. Economic systems, like capitalism and socialism, are distinguished by the forms of property they support. Because capitalism has existed for centuries, there is now a rather extensive and uncontroversial understanding of what capitalist property is. In contrast to the economic systems that preceded it and out of which it emerged, capitalism excludes property rights in other persons. No one owns anyone else, as they do, in varying degrees, in slave and feudal societies. However, there is private ownership of external things. In the extreme case, individuals have unlimited benefit and control rights over the things that they own. The only limit on private ownership in this case would be that individuals cannot rightfully use their property to harm others; a restriction that follows from a more general prohibition against harm.[3] But the extreme case is seldom the actual case—particularly with regard to ownership of things that, when used, affect nonowners in significant ways. Thus, capitalist societies permit private ownership of land, but they usually regulate land use. Similar restrictions apply in other domains. Therefore, in a vast array of cases, owners' rights to benefit from and to control the assets they own are not absolute, but the restrictions that the state places on ownership rights fall within well-prescribed limits. There is sometimes contestation around the edges. Laws are not always clear. Even so, there is no doubt about what capitalist property is. On the other hand, throughout the many decades in which procapitalists and prosocialists contended, it never became similarly clear what socialist property is. After the

Russian Revolution, it was widely assumed, by partisans on both sides, largely based on Soviet practice, that socialist property is state property. This was an unfortunate and unnecessary concession to historical contingencies, encouraged by significant gaps in socialist theory. State property is, at best, only one form of socialist property. However, to this day, there is only a vague apprehension of what other forms might be.

Nevertheless, thanks to the second fundamental theorem, the idea arose that, to achieve the distributional outcomes socialists want, it is possible—and might even be necessary, in practice—to reconstitute property rights in such a way and to such a degree that the boundaries of capitalist property, as they have come to be understood, would be exceeded. No one in the modern period favors reverting back to economic structures that permit ownership of other persons. Thus, the only relevant alternative to capitalism is some form of socialism; some economic system based on social ownership of external things. By demonstrating that any desirable final allocation of resources and commodities requires only a redistribution of ownership rights in the means of production and rights to the income from labor, the second fundamental theorem opened up the prospect of a socialism that relies on market mechanisms. (The Soviet model insisted instead on central planning.) Even in the absence of an adequately theorized account of socialist property relations, it put market socialism on the agenda.

From a theoretical point of view, this is how the idea that a rational society is nothing more than one with an efficient economy gained a foothold on the socialist side of the capitalism versus socialism debate. In an ironic twist that would have confounded older generations of socialists, it occurred to some in the socialist fold that the purported efficiency advantages of markets over plans no longer weighed exclusively in capitalism's favor. With the second fundamental theorem established, defenders of market arrangements could be socialists too. Both sides could invoke the blessings of the Invisible Hand.

*   *   *

However, market socialism, so conceived, like the capitalism defended by those who invoke the Invisible Hand, runs aground on the fact that Smith's conjecture, or rather formal demonstrations of its correctness, are flawed. The problem is not that the mathematics is wrong. It is that the model of a market economy for which the two theorems are provable fails to capture salient features of real-world market systems.

There are two kinds of difficulties. Those of one sort—I will call them the standard problems—have long been recognized. Their existence sustains a body of research that investigates the efficiency properties of departures from the general equilibrium model. The guiding idea has been to theorize economic structures that exemplify the key features of the mathematical model while, at the same time, avoiding some of its more unrealistic assumptions. The other sort of difficulty has only lately been acknowledged within the economics profession and its public policy extensions. It is not that these problems have just been discovered. But it is only recently that economists have succeeded in constructing formal models that take them into account and in proving results with a degree of acuity similar to work done within the general equilibrium paradigm. There is what the French call a *déformation profesionelle* to which economists are susceptible—a propensity to take seriously only what they are able to model. This fact, more than anything else, explains why difficulties of this second sort have only lately come into view in professional circles. It will be instructive to look briefly at these problems first. I will call them *information deficit* problems. Information deficit problems are, in the end, more devastating to neoclassical orthodoxy than the standard problems are. However, the standard problems have played a more prominent role in shaping contemporary thinking.

Information Deficits

Smith's conjecture and its modern mathematical reconstructions imply that there is social benefit in laissez-faire; that is, in treating market economies as self-regulating systems that are best left alone to follow their own internal dynamic. This conclusion is then taken to imply that state interferences with markets, however well intentioned, do harm because they impede the processes through which markets generate efficient outcomes. The newly discovered or newly modeled problems with the general equilibrium paradigm put this implication in question. They all have to do, in one way or another, with one of the standard model's deepest assumptions: that economic agents have perfect information. No one ever seriously believed this was the case. Until recently, it was considered a harmless idealization. It no longer is.

Consider market incompleteness. For the two fundamental theorems of welfare economics to obtain, there must be a complete set of markets; in other words, no demand—no preference backed by a willingness to spend (given budget constraints)—can go unmet. But this is not the case in real-world market systems, nor in all likelihood could it ever be. Imagine would-be borrowers without assets and with poor credit histories who want consumer loans. It should cost them more to borrow money than it would cost more credit worthy borrowers, because, assuming self-interest and means-ends rationality, lending institutions, in computing interest rates, have to take into account how likely they are to default on the loans. Lending institutions have no way to do this except to rely on statistical averages for borrowers in similar circumstances. A lending agency would therefore proceed on the assumption that it is taking a greater risk of not being repaid in their cases than it would were it to lend money to someone who is asset rich and who has an excellent credit history. But, according to the general equilibrium model, where there is a demand, as there is in this instance, there must be a supply. In most jurisdictions, there are laws that forbid charging usurious interest rates. In real-world cases, therefore, it may be impossible for persons whose credit profiles are poor to find lenders because the interest rates that lenders would want to charge for lending money to them would be unlawfully high. But even if, in the spirit of laissez-faire, legal restrictions on interest rates were removed, there could still be a demand for credit that would go unmet. As interest rates rise to compensate for the risk of loans going bad, the incentive not to repay would rise correspondingly, increasing the riskiness of the loans in question. Potential lenders might soon find there is no interest rate they could charge that would compensate for the risk of lending money to customers who fall into categories of borrowers likely to default.

To some degree, market incompletenesses are rectified, in practice, by extralegal, black market arrangements. By definition, loan-sharking is illegal and not just in consequence of laws proscribing usury. Because they operate outside the law, loan sharks are able to encourage borrowers to repay their debts in ways that legal lending institutions like banks cannot. No doubt, the prospect of being beaten, maimed, or killed increases borrowers' incentives to repay. It is very unlikely, however, that any state could tolerate these methods. Even one that is dedicated to leaving the economic sphere free to regulate itself, as laissez-faire requires, would still enforce criminal laws. But even in a hyperlibertarian state— one that, in its dedication to keeping the state out of economic life, tolerated even blatant criminality on the part of lenders—there might still be people who want loans but are unable to get them. Lacking perfect information, loan sharks too have to rely on imperfect indicators. On this basis, some individuals, including some who actually would repay their loans and who therefore *should* be able to borrow money at *some* interest rate, would find themselves unable to borrow money at any price.

This problem is a special case of a more general problem that afflicts the general equilibrium model. The model assumes that resources can be diverted costlessly from one use to another. If they cannot, economic activities incur transaction costs detrimental to efficiency; dead weight expenses that draw resources away from productive uses. Transaction costs are pervasive in real-world market economies. The cost of obtaining and processing information is an important component of them. This is the main reason why markets are difficult to establish. If, as the general equilibrium model requires, there were markets for everything, then so much of a society's resources would be absorbed in acquiring the information necessary for individuals and firms to act in a utility maximizing way that there would be little left over for anything else—including producing the goods and services that markets are supposed to provide in an efficient manner. Of course, if markets could be established at no cost, their proliferation would not drag the economy down. However, that would only be possible if information were free. This is assumed in formal demonstrations of the soundness of the Invisible Hand conjecture. But, in fact, information is seldom free. It can be and often is costly to obtain; in some cases, it may not be available at all.

Consider insurance markets. In view of our vulnerability to contingencies of all sorts, it is impossible, in practice, to insure against everything untoward that might happen. In most cases, there are sellers of insurance for likely misfortunes, because the demand for it is high enough to keep premiums low enough for suppliers to find buyers. Thus car rental agencies can easily insure themselves against thefts and accidents. But car rental agencies are affected not only by predictable events like these, but also by unpredictable ones—economic recessions, declines in rentals after terrorist attacks, or surges in fuel prices—and by idiosyncratic occurrences of all kinds. It is unlikely that firms wanting to buy insurance against these contingencies would be able to find insurers willing to sell it to them. Or consider that for financial markets to work their purportedly beneficial effects, there would have to be a complete set of futures markets. But, this is inconceivable. In addition to the expense of acquiring and processing the requisite information, there is another even more intractable problem in this case—the fact that there is literally an infinity of future dates. There is no way in principle to concoct futures markets for all of them.

To work with a picture of an economy that assumes that it is possible to do what is impossible and that treats what is often very costly as if it were costless is not, as was once believed, to introduce innocuous idealizations into a genuinely explanatory model. It is to introduce profound distortions into efforts to understand economic life. Thanks to progress in economic modeling, it is now possible to say, even to the satisfaction of those in the thrall of the economist's *déformation professionelle,* that these assumptions are not ingenious theoretical maneuvers, but significant mistakes.

Shades of Hayek

It is ironic that, until recently, the theorist best known for focusing on information deficits was Hayek.[4] Hayek's aim was to combat central planning, the ostensible alternative to market systems. To that end, he insisted, correctly, that there is information that bears on economic practices that is irreducibly local and therefore knowable only to those individuals or firms who are most immediately involved. For this reason, he maintained that it is often impossible for central planners to obtain the information they need to make decisions about how to allocate resources efficiently. To get the best or, rather, the most efficient outcomes, the information that economic agents themselves have, and that they alone can reliably obtain and process, is indispensable. Hayek therefore concluded that economic affairs are best left to these agents themselves, to individuals and firms, not to bureaucrats in planning ministries.

However sound Hayek's premise may be, his conclusion does not follow—unless, one assumes the pertinence of the two fundamental theorems of welfare economics and then maintains that if central planners are unable to access relevant information, there is no alternative other than to rely on the utility maximizing behavior of those economic agents who are directly involved. Because these assumptions are unwarranted, the faith that Hayek and his followers evince in laissez-faire is correspondingly groundless. More precisely, it is just that—a faith.

The fact that information asymmetries exist, so far from underwriting a case for laissez-faire, suggests the opposite—that judicious state interventions are indispensable for enhancing efficiency, especially in the long run. This is especially evident in the case of financial markets. It is by this means that market economies allocate investment resources and coordinate their activities. The fact that there is not, and cannot be, a complete set of futures markets is therefore very relevant to Hayek's brief for laissez-faire. If market prices provide information about efficient resource allocations—as neoclassical theory holds—where markets do not exist, the requisite information is lacking. Even so, individuals and firms must form expectations about future prices if they are to act rationally (by maximizing utility, subject to the constraints they confront). They must therefore rely on beliefs about what other individuals and firms are likely to do. But these beliefs can never be more than unreliable guesses. This is especially true because firms typically go to great lengths to conceal information about their future activities to prevent competitors from using it to their disadvantage. So far from coordinating rational investment decisions, real-world market economies establish obstacles in their way.

The threat to efficiency is mainly long term. In the short run, because most prices are posted, it is usually possible to plan from one time period to another. But what individuals and firms do now can have consequences extending into an indefinite future. Therefore, what may seem now like a good investment can turn out to have been a bad investment at a later date—thanks to unforeseeable changes in circumstances and thanks to what other economic agents do in the intervening period. Even if we ignore natural and political contingencies, and assume—as the neoclassical model does—that everyone makes means-ends rational choices, the long term future is still unpredictable. Small variations in investment strategies, following one fork in the road rather than another, can have significant ramifications down the line. This is why defenders of Smith's conjecture insist that, for investments to be coordinated efficiently in the long term, there must be financial futures markets for all periods. Again, this is impossible. It is possible, though, for the state to correct for this inevitable impediment to efficient investment at least to some extent—by implementing long term investment strategies and by providing information to firms and private investors. The laissez-faire policies that Hayek and his followers proposed do neither.

*   *   *

The neoclassical model postulates that large numbers of profit maximizing firms interacting with rational utility maximizing consumers in an economy in which there is a complete set of perfectly competitive markets will allocate resources in a Pareto optimal way, provided a host of background conditions obtain. In practice, some of these conditions may hold from time to time, but they almost never all obtain together. Even were we to ignore this fact or to discount its importance, the model would still fail. It would not take into account the devastating problems that arise in consequence of the absence of perfect information and the costs associated with information acquisition. These problems are especially acute in credit, insurance, and financial markets, for the reasons indicated above. Thus, they are especially disabling with respect to what matters most for the functioning of the system in the long run: social investment. This is why information deficit problems are more devastating to the neoclassical paradigm than criticisms of it that trade on the impossibility, in practice, of satisfying its other background assumptions. Problems of the latter sort can be glossed over to some extent by maintaining that real-world conditions approximate the ideal closely enough. The ineluctability of information deficits suggests a more radical conclusion: that the model is not only imperfectly realized in practice, but is flawed at its core.

Still, the standard problems with the fit between economic reality and economic theory are important in their own right. It will not be necessary to rehearse all of them. I will instead focus only on a few of the better known ones—those that arise out of so-called market failures and market incompetences and those that follow from the fact that many real-world markets are not even approximately competitive.

Externalities

Of market failures, perhaps the best known are so-called externalities or external effects. According to the neoclassical model, for optimal outcomes to emerge as unintended consequences of individuals' maximizing choices, individuals and firms must maximize utility based on information about real social costs. They must know what they have to give up in order to obtain what they want. This information is represented in the prices of goods and services. Therefore, to maximize utility properly, economic agents must confront prices that genuinely reflect social costs. But, this condition will not be satisfied when there are costs or benefits to individuals or firms that are not parties to the transactions in question. For example, if Jones buys coal from Smith to burn in his factory, the resulting pollution, which affects those residing near Jones's factory, is a cost that is not reflected in the price of the coal. On the other hand, the presence of Jones's factory in the neighborhood may attract other businesses, an unintended consequence from which some of his neighbors may benefit. These benefits are also not reflected in the price of the coal. Thus, the coal is incorrectly priced. This error leads to inefficiencies. In general, whenever there are costs or benefits that are not registered in market prices or whenever there are external effects of market transactions, the Pareto optimal structure that obtains in the absence of externalities is no longer secured.

The old orthodoxy maintained that, where externalities exist, there is a case for state intervention. On the whole, neoclassical theorists were of a mind to regret this necessity and eager to seek out alternatives. They were guided by the thought that market arrangements are preferable in principle—for efficiency's sake and often for other reasons as well. For some advocates of laissez-faire, including Hayek, one such nonefficiency reason had to do with freedom, understood as the absence of deliberate interferences with individuals' lives and behaviors. Market transactions are, by definition, voluntary and therefore, in this sense, free. As Hobbes made eminently clear (see Chapter 3), state interventions are not. They issue from authorities whose directives are backed by force. But when markets fail, as they do when externalities are present, market transactions can result in inefficient outcomes. In these circumstances, even those who are generally disposed to shelter the economic sphere from state interference will usually concede that the state ought to intervene. Defenders of laissez-faire have struggled valiantly over the years to contrive ways to diminish the need for state interventions in cases of market failure—to concoct market or market-like solutions for otherwise inefficient outcomes. They have never succeeded entirely, even by their own lights. Thus the principle remains: where markets fail, putting the efficiency of market-coordinated activities in jeopardy, state interventions, however regrettable, may sometimes be indispensable correctives.

Market Incompetences

As mechanisms for coordinating individuals' behaviors with a view to making them as well-off as can be, given their preferences, markets can do worse than fail—they can be outright incapable of producing certain socially desired goods. This was essentially the thought that motivated Hobbes's case for sovereignty. There, it was the inability of self-interested (or more precisely, "diffident, competitive, and vainglorious") rational agents to cooperate in a state of nature, to coordinate their behaviors by voluntarily deferring from doing what is individually best, that made a political (coercive) solution to the problems they confront necessary. As remarked, Hobbes's state of nature is the obverse of an Invisible Hand; it is a Prisoners' Dilemma game in which the unintended consequence of individuals' maximizing choices is, in the Paretian sense, suboptimal. Prisoners' Dilemmas exist in market economies too. Consider so-called public goods, goods that are generally desired and that are of such a nature that their benefits, if they exist at all, spill over to individuals irrespective of their contributions toward their production. According to the usual understanding of the term, public goods also require the contributions of many for their production. Defense against fire in congested areas is a textbook example. It is in the nature of fire fighting that to protect some individuals but not to protect their neighbors is either physically impossible or else is inordinately expensive (and therefore inefficient). It is also in the nature of this good that, in general, individuals cannot provide it for themselves; it must be, to some degree, jointly produced. In these circumstances, everyone who is self-interested and rational has an incentive not to purchase firefighting services. Everyone will want, instead, to "free-ride" on the contributions of others. But, then, the good will not be produced, even if, as in this case, everyone wants it—unless the state intervenes by coercing contributions from would-be free riders. This it does, typically, through the tax system; a political mechanism that unlike markets, but like other political instruments, ultimately relies on the use or threat of force.

Even those who are skeptical of the wisdom of state interventions intended to rectify market failures usually concede that public goods provision is a legitimate, perhaps the only legitimate, state function. Because goods with public goods structures almost always affect persons differently, unanimous support for their provision will generally not be forthcoming, as it is in the case of fire protection. It is therefore a matter for ordinary political processes to determine which, among goods with public goods structures, states should actually provide.

As remarked, Hobbes's account of the institution of sovereignty is, in effect, a special case of the more general argument that states legitimately supply public goods. According to Hobbes, individuals contract out of a state of nature for the sake of peace or security. Like fire protection in congested areas, security is a good the benefits of which, if they exist at all, spill over to everyone irrespective of their contributions toward it production. And, again like fire protection, it is a good that must be jointly produced. Thus it has a public goods structure. Unlike most other public goods, but like fire protection, security is unanimously preferred by individuals living in a state of nature. Indeed, if Hobbes's explanatory model was on track, it cannot fail to be desired by all of us, not just by some of us. It is, Hobbes insisted, "a general precept of reason," not an arbitrary preference, "to seek peace and follow it."[5]

For Hobbes and his successors—in this respect, everyone who endorses the state form of political organization is Hobbes's successor—public goods provision figures in political theory at two levels. First, it is the reason why states are necessary at all; why they cannot be replaced by laissez-faire arrangements that leave individuals free to do what they want with the resources they control in the circumstances they confront. And, then, after states exist, what they rightfully do, even in the view of those who would retract the state's role to its bare minimum, is what markets cannot: provide goods that have public goods structures.

Competition

The neoclassical model supposes perfect competition, which implies that firms and consumers are price takers—in other words, that they are not able directly to control the terms in which they obtain production factors or final consumption items. When they enter the marketplace, they are supposed to find posted prices. Then, taking these prices as given, they are supposed to maximize profits or utility subject to their budget constraints. This picture fails in two ways. First, real-world markets are almost never perfectly competitive. Therefore, it is seldom the case that economic agents genuinely are price takers in the requisite sense. Because, for so long, socialists and others—including, in the United States, Progressives and New Deal liberals—targeted monopolies, this fact has been known and appreciated for a long time. Where monopolies exist, economic agents are, so to speak, weighty enough to influence, to some degree, the terms under which they trade. This violates the neoclassical model's assumption that they be price takers. Even when monopolies compete, there are too few of them to meet the demands of the model. The fact that monopolization of one or another sort is the norm in capitalist economies has, from its inception, cast a shadow over the neoclassical case for laissez-faire. This is why even defenders of laissez-faire usually recognize the need for state interventions—to make markets competitive.[6]

Worries about the effects of monopolization on competition, though familiar, are not entirely independent of the concerns of those who take the reality of information deficits seriously. One reason why most markets are not as competitive as the theory demands is that, when information is imperfect and costly to obtain, those who hold it gain a certain degree of market power. This condition encourages the formation of monopolies. Even in markets that have numerous sellers, the effective monopolization of information introduces monopoly-like distortions into the marketplace. For example, if a firm raises its prices, not all the firm's customers will immediately be able to find a rival firm that charges a lower price for the same commodity: even if one exists, they will not know where to look. Similarly, if a firm lowers its prices, customers of higher priced firms are not always able to find this out. Because information is imperfect, search is costly. The neoclassical model assumes, to its detriment, that it is either unnecessary or free. To the degree that this unrealistic assumption fails to hold, so too do conclusions drawn from the competitive model.

In addition, transaction costs impede perfect competition. These too exist, in part, because of imperfect information. Not all fixed costs are overhead costs of running a firm or supplying a service; some are associated with acquiring information about how to do whatever the firm does. This is one reason why it is unlikely that there will be a large number of firms producing every quality of every good at every location at every date. With even small fixed costs of this sort, many markets will have relatively few suppliers. Thus, again, the requirements of the neoclassical model will fail to hold.

*   *   *

In real-world conditions, when one pays for a production factor or for a service, there are costs involved in monitoring the extent to which one gets what one pays for. There are, in other words, principal-agent problems that must be addressed. Often, these are best dealt with by deviating deliberately from the competitive model. For example, one strategy that is particularly effective for obtaining skilled labor inputs is to compensate workers for their services at levels higher than would be the case if managers simply relied on labor markets—by offering jobs to those (qualified) workers who are willing to work for less than others. The idea is that the workers they hire will then have an incentive to perform their functions well, even without vigilant monitoring. The more the workers—the agents—have to lose, the more reason they have to do what their principals—the employers—want. Thus when monitoring costs are taken into account, there are good efficiency reasons for not wanting markets—in this case, labor markets—to be perfectly competitive. Managers of businesses have known this forever. They have always been inclined to pay what is nowadays called an efficiency wage—a wage above the (competitive) market wage—especially to skilled and professional labor. And when they contract work out, it is often not to the lowest bidder, but to firms or individuals with whom they have established relationships and from whom they can therefore be confident of getting what they pay for. In short, they elevate labor costs to reduce monitoring costs. This is economically rational. But it is at odds with the ideal of perfect competition. It is only in recent years that standard economic theory has taken this fact of economic life into account.

Economies of Scale

There is one other long recognized problem with the neoclassical model that should be mentioned. The model assumes that prices reflect real social costs, taking individuals' preference and budget constraints as given, and ruling out exogenous interferences with the market system, like the introduction of new technologies. But in the real world, prices of many produced goods and of some services are affected by the size of the market. In general, the larger the market, the more so-called economies of scale affect prices—in part because overhead costs are often fixed, regardless of the scale of production, so that their importance in the pricing of commodities declines as the scale of production increases; and in part because larger markets provide incentives for investments in means of production and in new technologies that enhance worker productivity, thereby diminishing costs per unit. Economies of scale are inevitable in real-world economies. But their existence threatens the efficiency of market allocations. This is yet another reason why the neoclassical model is a defective idealization and why it justifies much less laissez-faire than appears.

Conclusions

What, then, can we conclude about Smith's Invisible Hand conjecture?

First, that it does hold for a highly stylized mathematical model of a market economy. This result, as it emerged in the first part of the twentieth century, was so stunning that it transformed economic theory and its policy extensions for decades. Whatever ideological effects this paradigm has had in real-world political affairs, there is no doubt that it facilitated an enormous body of productive research. Under its aegis, much was learned about how market systems with (or without) private property operate.

But it is also plain that the model is flawed—not just in the way that any idealization is, but in a more fundamental sense as well. All idealizations abstract away most of what is or can be observed, in order to focus on explanatorily relevant underlying processes. Everyone knew, from the beginning, that, in this respect, the general equilibrium model was no different. But now that economists and others have begun to take information deficit problems seriously, it has dawned that the general equilibrium model is not just abstract. It is wrong. It fails to represent real and explanatorily relevant processes correctly.

Finally, we can conclude, in light of these findings and contrary to what procapitalists who invoke Smith's conjecture claim, that the weight of economic theory as it stands today, so far from making a case for laissez-faire, actually justifies state interventions in market economies. So pervasive, however, are the ideological effects of Invisible Hand thinking, even among academic economists, that an extensive body of theory, dedicated to exploring how state interventions can best enhance efficiency, has yet to emerge. Thus, in the academy and throughout the larger political culture, Invisible Hand ideology continues to foster ways of thinking about economic affairs that stand in opposition to what the best economic theory today implies. This remarkable state of affairs puts its role in the American ideology in particularly sharp relief.[7]

5

Efficiency as Ideology

The Hobbesian notion of means-ends rationality and, along with it, the idea that rational agents are utility maximizers have become fixtures of our intellectual and political culture. These assumptions helped to nurture the development of economic theory. Then, in turn, economic theory reinforced the instrumentalist understanding of rationality at both the individual and societal (collective) level. We have seen how Smith's Invisible Hand conjecture played a role in this process. It helped to shape the view that a rational society is one that allocates goods and services in an efficient (Pareto optimal) way. This is not only a highly attenuated understanding of collective rationality; it is not even one that applies to real-world economies. Nevertheless, it is this account of Reason in society that has predominated for many decades. In recent years, it has become very nearly the only view there is.

How can we account for the dominance these ideas exercise over our intellectual and political culture? No doubt, part of the explanation has to do with the cogency of the reasoning that underwrites them. But more robust understandings of Reason in society are supported by cogent reasoning too. In any case, it does not seem that rationally persuasive arguments by themselves account for the influence the now dominant way of thinking enjoys. To explain this phenomenon, it is therefore necessary to focus too on how efficiency considerations operate in the real world; specifically, on how they function ideologically.

As remarked, ideology has acquired a range of not always compatible meanings. I use the term here to refer to a doctrine or collection of doctrines that enjoy the influence they do, not in consequence of their cognitive merit, but because they help to sustain or otherwise benefit social elites. With regard to truth and falsity, this usage is similar to Freud's use of illusion. In Freud's sense, illusions are not necessarily false beliefs and neither are false beliefs always illusions. An illusion is an expression of an (unconscious) wish. An illusion's existence is therefore explained by its role in the psychic economy of the individuals who endorse it, not by its connection to the world. It was in this sense that Freud depicted the principal convictions of theistic religions as illusions.[1]

The genealogy of efficiency thinking includes ideas that antedate the inception of the American republic and ideas that were developed beyond America's frontiers. Nevertheless, in the present conjuncture, efficiency thinking does service mainly to American elites. However, it has also figured in other ideological configurations—including one that, for many decades, opposed the interests the American ideology promotes. The better to grasp the nature of efficiency thinking, and its susceptibility to ideological appropriation, it is instructive to examine its role in this very different context.

Efficiency and the Soviet Model

An efficiency imperative is assumed by proponents of laissez-faire. It is also assumed, with more reason, by defenders of governmental interventions in capitalist economies. But efficiency thinking was also taken up by the majority of socialists in the early and middle decades of the twentieth century. This is why it is not nearly as paradoxical as may first appear that in twentieth century debates between socialists and capitalists, the socialist side not only came to adopt the dominant understanding of Reason in society, but even defended socialism on the grounds that it is better able than capitalism to approximate this ideal in real-world conditions. This stance would have been unthinkable for earlier generations of socialists. They wanted to install a form of society in which the very notion of an economic sphere, of an economy that stands apart from other aspects of collective life, would have no place. Not unrelated, they were committed to thicker understandings of rationality at the societal level—specifically, to notions of Reason in society derived from Hegelian philosophy and, more immediately, from Marx's critique of political economy. It was not until the twentieth century unfolded that ideas nineteenth-century socialists opposed found a home within the socialist fold.

For most of the twentieth century, as throughout the nineteenth, the majority of socialists harbored an almost visceral hostility toward market arrangements. But unlike their predecessors, they had an alternative in mind. With few exceptions, they endorsed central planning of the type developed after the Russian Revolution. Support for planning, like opposition to markets, was largely reflexive, but when socialist intellectuals defended the Soviet model, they did so mainly by appealing to its purported efficiency advantages. Therefore, their opposition was not exactly directed to markets as such. Their commitment to central planning followed from their conviction that, for efficiency's sake, states ought to play an active role in economic life. Thus their rationale, though extreme, was of a piece with mainstream thinking in the capitalist West. There it was standard to support state interventions to rectify market failures, to supply public goods, and to enhance competition. The socialists' idea was just that a state unencumbered by the need to sustain a private property regime would be able to do all this and more, more effectively.

The kind of state socialists favored was also supposed to act affirmatively to implement values other than efficiency. In this respect too, prosocialists and (most) procapitalists were of one mind. The second fundamental theorem of welfare economics implies that efficiency and equity concerns are distinct. For anyone who accepts its pertinence, it then follows that state policies can serve each of these independent ends. According to the mainstream view, this is precisely what states ought to do. In addition to correcting for inefficiencies in real-world market arrangements, they should implement policies that enhance equity or justice. Libertarians oppose this use of state power. But, in practice, their position has nearly always lost out—even nowadays, when the American ideology sustains policy prescriptions with a strong libertarian bent. All states in capitalist societies, including the United States, redistribute market-generated distributions for the sake of justice to some extent. They trade off equity and efficiency concerns. Nearly everywhere, but especially in the American case, the balance is struck to the detriment of the former. But, in principle, it could be struck anywhere. Thus, it appears that such differences as there were between twentieth-century defenders of socialism and their procapitalist counterparts had mainly to do with how best to achieve commonly recognized objectives. Socialists maintained that under socialism, state policies can implement efficiency and equity goals better than they can under capitalism.

It is therefore fair to say that, throughout most of the twentieth century, socialists' views about the proper role of the state differed from mainstream procapitalist positions in degree, not in kind. This difference was mainly evident in the economic arena. The predominant view among socialists was that the state should take over the job of allocating resources. Those who endorsed the Soviet model were usually little interested in democratizing governing institutions, economic or otherwise. This was a point of difference between them and democratic socialists. But, the democratizers focused mainly on the firm or on its subunits—its factories and shops. Hardly anyone challenged central planning itself. Even on the capitalist side, it was only a few farsighted thinkers, like Hayek, who questioned the ability of central planners to allocate resources efficiently.

There is no doubt that, in principle, central planning can solve the standard problems that market systems confront. Therefore the common wisdom, well into the 1960s, was that central planning would be the wave of the future, that capitalist economies would eventually adopt some of its key features, and that third world countries would develop by following the Soviet example. The available evidence seemed to bear out this speculation. It was not until the final two or three decades of the Soviet Union's existence that it did not outpace developed capitalist countries in economic growth, as measured by standard economic indicators. Well into the 1970s, some states that followed the Soviet model, like East Germany, seemed to do better economically than capitalist states, like Great Britain, that veered in the direction the American ideology suggests. Thus, even as socialism's commitment to the idea of a rational society devolved into the notion associated historically with proponents of laissez-faire, the socialist tradition's long-standing abhorrence of markets not only remained in force but actually came to exercise a growing influence over mainstream, procapitalist thinking.

By the end of the 1960s, however, it became clear that the vaunted dynamism of the Soviet economy was spent and that many of the purported efficiency advantages of central planning were illusory. As this thought registered in the ensuing decades, faith in planning waned, especially among dissident socialists. The problem was no longer just that existing planning regimes were undemocratic; it was that planning itself is inherently inefficient. Thus the table has turned. For good or ill, it has become part of the common sense of our time that central planning is inferior to market systems.

Problems of Planned Economies

Why the Soviet economy suffered the fate it did will require decades to sort out. But, it is interesting to observe that two kinds of explanations that have been offered so far touch on the now dominant understanding of what a rational society is. One resonates with current views about the inability of the neoclassical paradigm to deal with the inexorable reality of information deficits; the other is closer in spirit to the standard objections to the general equilibrium model.

Among explanations that take information deficit problems seriously are claims that the Soviet model is replete with perverse incentives or, what comes to the same thing, that it failed to address its principal-agent problems satisfactorily.[2] In the Soviet case—and, more generally, in economies that allocate resources without relying on markets—there is, first of all, a manager-worker, principal-agent problem. Then there is the principal-agent problem that links the central planning authority to plant or firm managers; and, finally, there is the state-central planning authority principal-agent problem. In each case, it is claimed, the Soviet model failed to provide agents with a proper structure of incentives. Agents therefore implemented their principals' directives poorly, with dire efficiency consequences.

It is then maintained that market incentives are more effective in getting agents to do what their principals want. To be sure, the principal-agent problems market economies pose are not quite the same as those that exist in planned economies, but there are similarities. Thus, there is a manager-worker problem similar to the one encountered in planned economies. And there is a shareholder-manager, principal-agent problem roughly analogous to the planner-manager problem of the Soviet model, but that is all. Neither in theory nor in practice is there anything analogous to the state-planner, principal-agent problem in planned economies. Corporations and other economic agents are not beholden to any higher authority, including the state. This fact is reflected in the policy prescriptions that economic theory continues to underwrite, even now that the orthodox view has been substantially revised. Although information deficit problems imply a need for state interventions in the economic sphere, no one concludes that states should direct economic activity. They may be called upon, *faute de mieux,* to rectify market failures and incompetences and perhaps to facilitate efficient investment choices. But the state intervenes to correct markets, not to impose a different developmental logic. The prevailing idea still is that if only the state would leave the incentive structures markets install basically intact, macrolevel outcomes will take care of themselves, as if by the workings of an Invisible Hand.

Explanations for the Soviet Union's fall that call on notions of a more traditional vintage maintain, in effect, that Hayek and others, who questioned the ability of central planners to allocate resources efficiently, were right. Hayek advanced this claim because of the importance he attached to local information, accessible to economic agents, but difficult, if not impossible, to transmit to central planners. However, there is a more fundamental problem long known to afflict central planning. The price of a commodity is supposed to represent its real social cost. But in complex industrial economies, prices have effects that resonate throughout the entire system. Suppose that the state conveys to its planning agency that it would like to produce, say, 300,000 automobiles per year. That decision will affect, among other things, how much steel must be produced, which will affect how much of all the production inputs to steel must be produced, and so on and on. In addition, how many automobiles are manufactured affects how much fuel will be needed; how much to invest in road building and maintenance, in hotels and restaurants, and, indeed, in everything affected by the existence of automobiles—which is to say, in almost everything. All of this information must be processed if planners are to ascertain the correct prices for all of the commodities affected by this one directive. But when everything depends on everything else, there is too much information to process—not just for planners operating in the primitive conditions the Soviet Union faced in its early years, but even with the most advanced computer technology. The problems are so complex that they will probably always remain unsolvable, especially when planning authorities seek to implement many directives simultaneously.[3]

On the other hand, when markets organize economic activity, this information processing problem is disaggregated. Economic agents, acting individually, process only that information that bears on their own microlevel maximizing choices. Then, according to the neoclassical view, a Pareto optimal outcome—or, allowing for all the ways in which the real world is not like the mathematical model assumed in neoclassical theory, something approximating it—will emerge at the macrolevel. This latter claim, we now know, is inapplicable to real-world market economies. However, the point about the intractability of the information processing problems planners confront is sound. Markets do decompose what would otherwise be overwhelmingly complex calculation problems into a myriad of solvable, individual level maximizing choices. Then, even if the Invisible Hand does not quite do the rest, the rest gets done well enough or as well as can be, because market prices do reflect social costs somewhat and because efforts to do better bureaucratically are bound to fail. The Soviet Union foundered, the argument goes, because its planners were unable in principle to do what markets do automatically.

Market Solutions

Socialists generally were hostile to markets but, almost from the moment the Soviet economic system came into existence, there were a few socialist economists who shared their opponents' faith in market mechanisms or, more precisely, in their belief that market prices represent real social costs and must therefore be employed if resources are to be allocated efficiently. Thus, as remarked (in Chapter 4), the prospect of market socialism was broached. As understood throughout the middle and later decades of the twentieth century, the term designates an economic system in which the state owns the means of production, as in the Soviet model, but uses market prices, not state directives to allocate resources. In a market socialist regime, managers would maximize profits, just as managers do under capitalism, and planners would set prices in ways that replicate the workings of markets in capitalist societies. The price system would therefore equilibrate supply and demand, just as it is supposed to do in capitalist economies. But instead of emerging spontaneously through the market interactions of self-interested owners of productive assets, market prices would be discovered by government planners. Precisely how they would determine what market prices are need not detain us. Suffice it to say that the techniques proposed were powerful and subtle. Market socialism's defenders demonstrated, even to the satisfaction of economists not friendly to socialism, that, in principle, planners can discover efficiency prices tolerably well. In theory, market socialism should be capable of doing at least as well as actually existing capitalism in approximating Pareto optimal outcomes. Thus, as a theory (for that is all that it has ever been), market socialism promises the best of both worlds—efficiency and equity—all within the purview of mainstream understandings of Reason in society.

Market socialists, like everyone else, identified social property with state property. They therefore maintained that the state should assume responsibility for allocating capital. Their thought was not just that its doing so is desirable for efficiency reasons, it was that state directed capital allocations are crucial for promoting equity or, what comes to the same thing for socialists, for enhancing equality. This is why market socialists generally treat capital markets differently from other markets. In that one domain, they do not seek to replicate the outcomes that would emerge under capitalism, if only the conditions assumed in the general equilibrium model obtained. But even the handful of market socialists who would accede to market discipline in this matter, defend market socialism on the grounds that, because it is socialist, it fulfills aspirations for equality better than any feasible alternative. Since capital is not in private hands, profits or returns on investment go to the state, not to shareholders. These monies can then be distributed by the state in accord with its equity goals. In a market socialist regime, the principal inequality generating mechanism affecting capitalist economies would be replaced by equality enhancing state polices.[4]

Market socialist doctrine, in its original versions, assumed that the neoclassical model was sound. It only sought to correct for some of the untoward dynamic efficiency and equity consequences that follow from utilizing markets as allocation mechanisms in private property regimes. Newer versions of market socialist theory that focus on getting incentive structures in principal-agent problems right are less wedded to this claim.[5] But, they share a fundamental conviction with their ancestor theories. They agree that rationality at the societal level involves nothing more than getting the economy to operate efficiently—that is, in a Pareto optimal way. For them—just as for mainstream economic theorists, whether they deploy the old, general equilibrium model or work instead in the new, information-centered paradigm—this is all the collective rationality there can be.

Efficiency Reified

In the *Economic and Philosophical Manuscripts of 1844*, the so-called *Paris Manuscripts*, Marx maintained that, under capitalism, the economic structure, in reality nothing more than a human creation, takes on a life of its own.[6] Human beings are therefore alienated from what human praxis has made. In consequence, the laws of capitalist development dominate the individuals whose behaviors they govern—to devastating effect. Some twentieth-century Marxists called the process that brings this unhappy state of affairs about *reification,* the making of a thing (*res*) out of that which, in reality, is not a thing, but, in this case, only a set of social practices.[7] Marx and his successors maintained that alienation is the most extreme, and most irrational, form of human unfreedom. Alienated men and women are thralls of economic exigencies. They are slaves of (reified) masters of their own making, obliged to set their respective courses according to the requirements of capitalist accumulation, not the dictates of their own free (autonomous) wills. Thus, under capitalism, the real order of things is inverted: means become ends, and persons, autonomous agents, become mere instrumentalities. Meanwhile, labor or productive activity, so far from liberating humankind from the yoke of necessity, becomes the principal source of human bondage.

In developing his account of alienated labor, Marx followed Hegel's lead. Like Hegel, he employed a richer conception of Reason in society than the one assumed nowadays by the intellectual descendants of Hobbes and Pareto. On this understanding, a world where alienation reigns is indictable on grounds of irrationality, regardless of how efficient it may be. But even proponents of mainstream understandings of collective rationality can see that the charge of reification rings true and that it helps to explain why the cardinal virtue of economic systems—efficiency—enjoys preeminence. Nevertheless, from all corners of the reigning intellectual and political culture, including its now nearly defunct socialist tributary, efficiency considerations do in fact rule.

To some extent, this phenomenon is explained by historical circumstances. Just as economists and policy makers who came of age during the Great Depression of the 1930s made unemployment their main focus, those whose ideas were formed in the period of the decline and fall of the Soviet Union have come to attach enormous importance to delivering the goods: in other words, to providing a level of economic well-being sufficient to keep people supportive of or at least not hostile to the regime in place. According to a widely accepted view, one reason why the Soviet Union and the "peoples' democracies" of Eastern Europe became undone is that their economies failed to deliver the goods as well as first world economies did. As this fact became evident to their populations—thanks to irrepressible advances in communication, transport, and tourism—the legitimacy of Soviet style communism was undermined. Thus a common theme in the writings of the handful of Left economists and political scientists who still defend socialism is that, to be feasible, socialism will have to deliver the goods at least as well as capitalist economies do.

But, it is not only, or mainly, socialists who have an interest in having the goods delivered well. Politicians in capitalist countries also need efficient, well functioning economies. For them, winning competitive elections depends, to a considerable extent, on the public's perception that the economy the government superintends is performing well in comparison to its own recent past and to the economies of peer countries. Nothing is as effective in encouraging this perception as the fact that the goods actually are delivered well. Thus, insofar as public opinion matters, as it does in all modern regimes, politicians' own self-interest also nourishes efficiency thinking.

Needless to say, delivering the goods and Pareto optimality are not identical notions. In practice, however, efficiency stands for both and more. Everywhere, the term is used vaguely and with reckless abandon. Even in quasi-technical writings, efficiency sometimes means nothing more than working effectively or well. Then, typically, this colloquial usage is confounded with Pareto optimality. What emerges is a rhetorically potent mix in which a legitimate concern that institutions do what they are supposed to do without wasting effort, time, or resources becomes invested with the prestige and assurance that attaches to mathematical pyrotechnics and formal demonstrations. At the same time, unworldly formal arguments purporting to establish the efficiency advantages of capitalist (or socialist) economic systems come to seem pertinent because they ostensibly connect with the reasonable popular aspiration that institutions and social practices live up to their self-representations.

The result is not just that efficiency considerations carry undue weight in policy deliberations involving trade-offs with equity. It is that efficiency becomes an end in itself; one that we reify and then allow to dominate us. Thus we turn ourselves into slaves of an efficiency imperative. A result of this sad turn of events is that economic affairs are increasingly immunized against the prospect of democratic control. Driven by the impersonal dictates of the efficiency standard, political economy has nearly lost its political dimension. The irony is extreme. In *The Anti-Dühring*, Friedrich Engels wrote that, under communism, after the state has "withered away," "the administration of things" would take the place of "the governance of men."[8] Under the aegis of the American ideology, we are witnessing a similar phenomenon—not in what Engels called "the realm of freedom," where the people (demos) rule, but as part of a sustained assault on democratic self-governance and popular empowerment. Where efficiency is reified, what is left for democratic deliberation and collective choice? In the economic sphere (and not only there), very little. Much like the weather, the economy becomes something to talk about, but not to do anything about and certainly not to change fundamentally for the better. The task instead is to accommodate to its exigencies: to make the best of them.

Thus efficiency, a defensible aspiration, having taken on a life of its own, militates against self-determination, not just at the individual level but at the level of the collectivity as well. It becomes an obstacle in democracy's way.

Who Benefits?

Who benefits? Whoever stands to lose as democracy advances. Thus the beneficiaries are, in the first instance, existing elites, especially economic elites—whether in capitalist countries, where property is privately owned, or, as in the former socialist states, where most productive assets were owned by the state but controlled by state and party functionaries. It serves their interests if it can be taken as given that their privileged role is a consequence of ineluctable economic forces, akin to laws of nature. When efficiency is reified, elites benefit; and everyone else or, more precisely, everyone who would do better if the power of these elites were diminished or broken, bears the cost.

The battle lines were once more clearly drawn. Democracy used to be perceived everywhere as a threat to property holders. Since, at the time, the defense of property rights was a prime concern of liberals, democracy and liberalism were generally in tension. In those days too, political theory, which seldom strays from representing the interests of elite social strata, reflected this opposition. This is why, until about the middle of the nineteenth century, it was commonplace for political theorists, liberal or not, to disparage democracy—in much the way that, nowadays, anarchy is disparaged. The idea, in both cases, was (or is) that these are extremal positions, useful to contemplate, but unreasonable to advocate or endorse. For democracy, this understanding became undone by events. Thanks to the revolutionary upheavals of the seventeenth and eighteenth centuries, culminating in the Revolution in France, the demos—the popular masses—entered the political arena irreversibly. Some measure of democracy—of government of, by, and for the people—thereafter became indispensable for ensuring the legitimacy of any regime that would rule effectively or even survive for all but the briefest period. Governing with the consent of the governed—or appearing to do so—has become a prerequisite for governing at all.

Thus, two old foes—liberals, with their concern for property rights, and democrats, intent on empowering the demos—had to join forces; or, more precisely, liberals had to readjust their sights to reconcile their concerns with the aspirations of demotic constituencies. Liberal democracy was the result. This fusion of liberal and democratic components was largely the work of liberals, not democrats. Thus it has always been more liberal than democratic. Liberal democracy is not, and never has been, what its name implies; it is not, except rhetorically, a fusion of liberal and democratic theory. Rather, it is liberalism with a democratic veneer. As the nineteenth century wore on, it became clear to liberals that a small measure of democracy was all they needed to take on board. Indeed, for the legitimacy of institutional arrangements in liberal democracies to be secure, it is enough, apparently, that citizens select their representatives in free, competitive elections. No matter that all the people do is ratify choices already made within the ruling structures of the regime. The idea, after all, was never really to empower the people. It was to employ a vague and highly attenuated notion of popular empowerment to legitimate elite control in developing capitalist economies. Since liberal protections are thought to be useful in these circumstances, they are generally secure, though always embattled, in liberal democracies. Real democracy, however, is barely in evidence.

In the distant past, liberals and others, even as they acquiesced in representative institutions and periodic elections, were especially intent on restricting the franchise to (male) property holders. The idea, presumably, was that property holders would not use their power to infringe property rights; while nearly everyone else, the vast majority, would. Before the emergence of liberal democratic institutions, with their anesthetizing effect on democratic aspirations, this was a reasonable fear. Locke's brief in defense of restricting the franchise illustrates this way of thinking with particular clarity.[9]

Locke favored restricting the franchise to adult male property holders. Although he defended paternal authority within the family, he offered no explicit arguments against extending the franchise to women. Perhaps it seemed obvious to him, as to nearly everyone else in his time, that women's place was in the private sphere of the family, not in public life. However, Locke did offer arguments for restricting the franchise to property holders. His idea was that only people who have the leisure to cultivate the capacities required to vote competently should be entitled to make collective choices for the whole community. Then, since the requisite degree and type of leisure is available only to those with income from property, especially landed property, only property holders should vote.

This position reflected both a remarkable class bias and a view of the condition of agricultural and urban workers that has long been out of date. But, Locke's was not an uncommon view among political thinkers in his time and it was not entirely groundless. Allowing that innate mental capacities are distributed more or less equally across social classes, a point Locke would probably not have conceded, the servile condition of the propertyless masses arguably did render them unfit either to vote competently or to govern. Because democratic impulses were still under-developed in those days, it did not occur to Locke or to those who thought like him that this observation might underwrite a call to improve the conditions of labor in order to enlighten and then empower the demos. It seems to have been their view that it is inevitable that the vast majority of human beings be assigned to lives of burdensome toil, that political competence will therefore always be the possession of the fortunate few, and that political institutions must accommodate to this inexorable fact.

For the past century and a half, if not longer, positions like Locke's have been unthinkable. Democratic convictions have become too deeply entrenched in the popular imagination. However, positions like Locke's have also became unnecessary. The institutions of representative government—above all, the party system, as it developed everywhere—channeled popular enthusiasms in directions that propertied interests had little reason to fear, even as the propertyless masses won the right to vote. As late as the 1840s, economic elites in Britain fought the Chartists' demand to extend the franchise. By the end of the century, with universal male suffrage nearly everywhere attained, parliamentary socialism, even in its most radical varieties, posed a far less menacing threat. In time, the idea that the existing order could be challenged fundamentally by electoral means came to seem entirely fanciful, both to those who would defend it and to its opponents. This is why the strategies adopted by revolutionary socialists for the past century and a half were, in the main, extraparliamentary. To be sure, all but some anarchists and a few sectarian socialist groups engaged, when they could, in electoral contestations. But, they saw electoral work as a form of organizing and consciousness raising; not as a means for assuming power and changing life. In these circumstances, legal restrictions on voting rights, of the kind that Locke and other early liberals favored, became pointless. To maintain the privileged positions of property holders, there was no longer any need to restrict the franchise or otherwise adopt explicitly antidemocratic measures. However the problem that genuine democracy poses for the beneficiaries of the system in place—still essentially the system Locke and his followers defended—remains.

The institutional arrangements characteristic of liberal democracies have done their job well. I would hazard, though, that they would not have been able to deflect democratic impulses as successfully as they did without the aid of efficiency thinking or—since this component of the American ideology did not fully come into its own until decades after liberal democracies first developed—its anticipations. But for the perception that the sphere of production and exchange had developed into a self-regulating system, governed by its own laws and accountable to itself alone, universal suffrage might indeed have challenged the dominance of economic elites, at least in liberal democracy's early days. In the aftermath of the revolutionary upheavals of the eighteenth century, the visible hand of political power did not lend itself to the task of keeping democratic impulses at bay. But the invisible hand of economic necessity did. Or so it came to be believed. With this conviction in tow, the aspiration of the demos to take their own affairs in hand could be stifled without excluding popular constituencies from the public arena; indeed, without anyone doing anything transparently undemocratic at all. In recent years, with efficiency thinking more fully developed, reification and its consequences have become, if anything, even more debilitating. In conjunction still with the institutional arrangements liberal democracies have developed over the years, it has become perhaps the most powerful force working to keep democratic impulses at bay.

Thus, it is widely believed nowadays that the so-called globalization of the world economy—its incorporation into an economic system organized and structured by international (mainly American) corporations and maintained by American military power—is inevitable. This perception is reinforced by the unrelenting insistence of intellectuals and others subservient to (mainly American) economic elites. Their watchword has become what Margaret Thatcher famously proclaimed, that "there is no alternative." This is why the conventional wisdom is that there is no point in challenging the emerging, U.S. dominated world order, except perhaps in marginal ways, to make it "kinder and gentler." At the same time, an increasingly disempowered demos—at home and abroad—suffers savagely on its account. This grim fact, even when acknowledged, changes nothing. Who would be so foolish as to try to combat an unyielding law of nature?

Even so, to a degree unknown in recent decades, the power of capitalist elites is again being contested, this time on a global scale. Could it be that the hold efficiency thinking has had over our collective consciousness for so long is weakening? Perhaps, but its day is far from over and it is far from certain that, without a deliberate and protracted struggle to end it, it ever will be.

A Vicious Circle

What can undo the pervasive reification of the efficiency imperative? In the final analysis, the answer is simple and obvious—more and deeper democracy. However, it is not obvious how to get from here to there. We are locked in a vicious circle. Everywhere, democracy is on the defensive. This is why, as the range and power of the American ideology grows in consequence of business domination of the American polity and of American economic and military domination of the world, the idea of an economic order under popular control and serving popular interests has become increasingly difficult to sustain.

The Left was hardly responsible for this state of affairs. But neither was it blameless. The idea that efficiency considerations are of overwhelming, even decisive, importance exerted a powerful influence on the historical Left. Its theoreticians promoted it. It even helped to shape the political and economic theory of socialism, especially in the years of socialism's decline. But socialists of all types, including market socialists, retained a connection, attenuated but real, to an alternative vision of public life, motivated by a more robust vision of Reason in society, that implies the extension of democratic rule into all regions of human life. Their commitment to social property, however poorly understood and inadequately theorized that notion was, ensured this linkage, even as the vicissitudes of Soviet communism obfuscated and then discredited it. Now that socialism has faded from the scene, a sense of what genuine democracy involves has become harder to recover and build upon. The consequences are especially salient in the liberal camp. Without a pole of attraction to its left, without any vision of a more rational social order than the Invisible Hand can provide, liberalism has rediscovered its vocation as an ideology in the service of private accumulation. Its already feeble connections with the democratic aspirations of the historical Left are therefore weakened further, with policy following in suit.

Meanwhile, the circle grinds on. Liberal democracy's denigration of its democratic component secures the subordination of economic affairs to an efficiency imperative. This process further enhances the reification of the economic order. Then the economy, increasingly a law unto itself and master of all there is, further diminishes democracy. Everywhere, the specter of inefficiency impedes the prospects for democratic renewal. But the fact remains: democracy is the cure, the only cure possible. The choice, then, is either to acquiesce in the spurious conviction that there is no alternative to the decline of democratic self-assertion or else to change course radically by mobilizing the demos to act in its own behalf. In this case, there truly is no other alternative.

Fortunately, the democratic impulse is not easily defeated. The burdens of life in regimes sustained by the American ideology generate discontents that even a full-fledged ideological assault cannot permanently quash. Blowback from imperialist ventures, awareness of the corruption inherent in unfettered capitalism, and a growing sense of the horrors that follow in the wake of corporate globalization and its military extensions are, by now, so stunningly obvious that they cannot be prevented from registering in the popular consciousness. Desperation is an inevitable response and there is no lack of it in our political culture. But there are contrary stirrings too. The pendulum is swinging back. If only unspeakable catastrophes can be avoided, the political climate is bound to become more propitious. The world is a more dangerous place than just a few years ago. The right wing of the American political class, in triumphalist fervor, has gone on the offensive. But, in doing so, they have inadvertently shattered old complacencies and reawakened the courage and generosity of spirit that once fed the historical Left. Thus, despite all obstacles, resistance is growing on a worldwide scale and, with it, the possibility that progressive, democratic forces will emerge strengthened and that democracy will again advance.

This outcome is not inevitable. What is sure is just that a reconstructed democratic theory can help to make it more likely; and that the reification of efficiency thinking is an obstacle in its way. It is not the only one, however. There is also the other component of the American ideology—the constellation of ideas that cluster around that other descendant of older, thicker conceptions of Reason in society—the reasonable.

6

The Reasonable

Rationality is a normative standard applicable, at the individual level, to beliefs and actions and, at the societal level, to institutional arrangements and social practices. Reasonableness is less demanding. Like the conception of social rationality admitted into the American ideology, it is susceptible to ideological appropriation. Like efficiency too, though more subtly, it can work to the detriment of democratic aspirations. The reasonable has long been a mainstay of Western jurisprudence. Partly in consequence of this history, it can be invoked to articulate a certain conception of democratic governance. It is by this route that it has come to play an ideological role.

Thanks to the work of Rawls and others, academic political philosophy has lately taken up the idea with a vengeance. In doing so, it has brought a degree of self-awareness to a form of governance that has become pervasive in the United States. It is the conception of the reasonable employed in this strain of philosophical philosophy that I will focus on here. It will be appropriate, following Rawls's lead, to call the body of theory I have in mind political liberalism. That term is sometimes used more narrowly to designate the account of political legitimacy elaborated by Rawls in his later work.[1] But since my aim is not to explicate that seminal thinker's views, but rather to investigate the ideological uses of an idea that he has perspicaciously developed, I will use the term more loosely to denote views about the nature and justification of political arrangements that reflect the underlying notions Rawls and his cothinkers deploy. As I will use the term, political liberalism is, above all, an account of what liberalism is. It is a theory about liberal theory, a second-order theory, that then has implications for reflections on liberal institutional arrangements; in other words, for first-order liberalism.

Liberalism

At least since the beginning of the eighteenth century, a political philosophy counted as liberal if it acknowledged principled limitations on the use of public coercive force; in other words, if it held that the state's authority over individuals' lives and behaviors ought to be subject to specifiable constraints. The kinds of interferences that liberalism proscribes are coercive. This is the point of Mill's well-known distinction, set forth in the first chapter of *On Liberty*, between "remonstrating," "reasoning," "persuading," and "entreating," on the one hand, and "compelling" an individual or "visiting him with (some) evil," on the other.[2] It is the latter type of interference that liberals are mainly concerned to restrict.

If we imagine that political authority is established by a social contract, as some but not all liberals have, then a regime is liberal if the social contract requires individuals to give up or alienate only some of the (unlimited) rights they enjoy over themselves in the state of nature—in other words, in the absence of political authority relations. What individuals do not alienate, political authorities cannot (rightfully) infringe. Locke is a liberal in this sense because the social contract he envisioned is partial, not total. Like Thomas Jefferson after him, Locke proclaimed some rights inalienable and therefore incapable of being contracted away. Principled limitations on the use of public coercive force can also be defended without recourse to inalienable rights or social contracts. Mill's own example is a case in point. Mill, a utilitarian, maintained that the principle of utility requires that a certain area of individuals' lives and behaviors be immune from public interference.

From the beginning, liberals have taken care to distinguish the state from civil society. In their view, the good life is attainable in and through civil society, not the state. In this respect, even in its most secular versions, liberalism falls within the Christian tradition in Western political thought. In contrast to the classical view, advanced by Aristotle and other Greek thinkers and by some political philosophers in modern times, the Christians denied that political activity is any part of the good for human beings. In the version of this idea epitomized in the writings of St. Augustine, Fallen Man is so corrupted by Original Sin that no good can come from earthly efforts. Some souls are nevertheless chosen to be saved through unmerited grace.[3] However, this good, salvation, awaits them in the world to come. It is not an earthly condition. But since a prerequisite for its attainment at the Final Judgment is the administration of the sacraments to the elect of all nations—a condition for which a measure of civil peace, enough to ensure the orderly growth of Church institutions, is indispensable—earthly means for ensuring order are required. This is what political authority does from the standpoint of Providential design. From a human standpoint, what political authority does is impede the free expression of (fallen) human nature. In this sense, it is an evil, an unnatural imposition upon the human race. These understandings converge in the idea that political institutions are punishments for Original Sin. Ironically, though, they are also palliatives for its consequences— quashing what would otherwise be a devastating war of all against all. Even from a human point of view, (coercive) political institutions are necessary. They are necessary evils.

With some conspicuous exceptions like Locke, most seventeenth- and eighteenth-century liberals were loathe to employ theological representations of philosophical positions. In any case, from the time that liberal theory revived in the aftermath of the French Revolution, it has been an unabashedly secular doctrine. Even so, it is important not to lose sight of its affinities with Christian political theory. A likeness is especially evident in the liberal account of the relation between the political realm and what makes life worth living. From its inception, liberalism assumed that the political sphere is a necessary evil because the state is and can only be opposed to the free expression of human nature. Thus, liberals denied Aristotle's contention that man is a political animal and agreed with Augustine's claim that nothing of fundamental value can be addressed in the political sphere. To be sure, they never relegated the good for human beings to a world to come. They thought it attainable here and now in civil society. This difference has far-reaching implications. But it is still the old Christian idea, shorn of its theological carapace. The role of political institutions, in the Augustinian scheme, was to make the Final Judgment and therefore the salvation of the elect possible. The role of the state in the liberal view is to superintend a civil society in which human beings can realize their interests as free beings. In both cases, politics plays no direct role in achieving the good. In both cases, however, political institutions are indispensable for obtaining what is of paramount importance outside the political realm.

In their view of the unnaturalness of political institutions, liberals follow the course set by the preeminent secular Christian political philosopher of the modern period, Hobbes (see Chapter 3). Hobbes was no liberal. He denied liberalism's defining doctrine, its support for limited sovereignty. But, Hobbes's rationale for the state is the one liberals assumed. The state is concocted by human beings to serve their interests—above all, their interest in blocking a "war of all against all." In this sense, its function is what Augustine said it was—to secure order. For Hobbes and the liberals, it was not Original Sin, but human nature that makes disorder our "natural condition"; and it was not Providential design, but universal human interests that make order the preeminent value. But, for Hobbes and the liberals, as much as for Augustine, order itself is neither a good, nor part of the good for humankind. It is only a way of mitigating an even greater bad. That greater bad is so bad that, as Hobbes would have it, it is a general precept of reason that we establish sovereignty and maintain it by all necessary means.

Hobbes argued that the sovereign's power must be absolute in principle. Nevertheless, there is a sense in which Hobbes's view of the role of political institutions in human life suggests a case for limited sovereignty. States restrict the free expression of human nature. But their existence does not entail that human nature can never be expressed freely anywhere. There would be no coercion in the City of God that Augustine envisioned for the end of time; with Fallen nature overcome, coercion would be neither necessary nor possible.[4] There is no coercion either in civil society. But for this sphere of human life to exist, it is necessary, first, to establish a framework in which self-interested human beings can interact in peace. For liberals, this is the mission of the state: it creates the conditions that make civil society possible for beings like ourselves. Thus the state exists to superintend a sphere outside itself, where human nature can be freely expressed. Because liberals also took over Hobbes' view of human nature, it was natural for them to suppose that civil society is basically commercial in nature; a view early liberals, like Locke, embraced. It was natural for them to infer too that, once a civil society is in place, the state that governs least or, rather, that governs as little as necessary for civil society to flourish, governs best. Liberalism therefore favors restricting the sovereign's power as much as possible. From this conviction, it is only a small step to the view that there are things that states ought never to do; that certain areas of individuals' lives and behaviors are, as a matter of right, immune from state interference.

It was probably inevitable that liberalism's commitment to limited sovereignty would eventually extend beyond the state into the larger public realm. Mill's insistence, in *On Liberty*, that "the moral coercion of public opinion" falls as much within the purview of liberal concerns as do state enforced legal sanctions was perhaps the first unequivocal expression of this view. Nowadays, it is pervasive. In a sense, this development turned liberalism into something more than a theory of limited sovereignty. But, it did not change liberalism's longstanding view of the political. To construe moral coercion as a form of public coercive force is to extend liberal protections into aspects of human life that the first liberals never contemplated. This is a momentous development. But, it leaves liberalism's affiliation with the Christian tradition in political thought intact. The political sphere is as much a necessary evil for liberals like Mill and his successors, as it was for those who came before them.

From Tolerance to Neutrality

Liberalism's commitment to limited sovereignty was, in part, a concession to the fact of religious pluralism. In the aftermath of the wars of religion that followed the Protestant Reformation, it appeared to liberalism's first exponents that tolerance of other faiths, however unpalatable, was preferable to never-ending strife. Thus, the first liberals maintained that political institutions should accommodate irreconcilable religious differences; that the sovereign's power should not extend into this domain. By this route, tolerance gained a foothold. But the tolerance the first liberals endorsed amounted to little more than a modus vivendi—a grudging acceptance of differences that were impossible to eradicate—except perhaps through endless repression and war.

In time, though, as liberalism evolved into more than just a theory of limited sovereignty, tolerance became increasingly central to its purpose. Liberalism became a theory of ideal political and social arrangements; one in which differences were not just accepted, but welcomed. What liberals came to want is a society in which individuals are as free as they can be to pursue their own ends—or, as Rawls would express it in his typically high-minded fashion, their individual conceptions of the good.

The freedom liberals had in mind was freedom from state interference and, usually too, from "the moral coercion of public opinion." The content of these freedoms has varied over time and, even today, there is no consensus. But, there are certain freedoms that modern liberals have always endorsed. Among them are civil liberties like freedom of thought and expression, the right of assembly, and freedom of religion. The first liberals and their libertarian successors also endorse so-called economic freedoms like the right to hold assets privately and to deploy them in production and trade. Libertarians regard these liberties as infrangible and (very nearly) absolute rights; other liberals are disposed to limit them in various ways. But, most liberals do endorse economic freedoms to some extent. In this way, liberalism is linked historically and conceptually with capitalism. However, it has long been a matter of controversy whether economic freedoms and civil liberties comprise a seamless web or whether it is possible consistently to support the one, but not the other. Nowadays, civil liberties are defended by all liberal writers, economic freedoms are not. It is therefore fair to say that freedom of speech, assembly, religion, and the like constitute the core of first-order liberal theory. Other, more contested freedoms, like those that join liberalism with capitalism, are peripheral.

From its beginnings, liberalism's aim has been to regulate fundamental political and perhaps also social practices. In this sense, it has always been a constitutionalist doctrine, not a theory of individual conduct, except derivatively. It was therefore as a matter of constitutional principle that liberals came to see value in diversity—in thought, in lifestyle, and in all aspects of human endeavor. Today, therefore, a liberal constitution is above all a tolerant one. Its watchword is laissez-vivre.

Laissez-vivre should not be confused with laissez-faire, even if there are liberals who believe that the one entails the other. Laissez-faire implies reliance on market arrangements and the exclusion of the state from economic affairs—except, of course, to the considerable degree that states are indispensable for maintaining market arrangements. Laissez-vivre implies openness to experimentation in those spheres of life that, according to liberal doctrine, ought to be immune from state and societal interference and also, as far as possible, in areas of human life that the state may rightfully regulate. Thus, tolerance in liberal theory often means something different from what it means in ordinary speech. Colloquially, the term suggests forbearance from repressing disapproved ideas and activities. Liberal tolerance, on the other hand, implies the active encouragement of diversity and dissent in pursuit of an ideal social order.

Within those areas of individuals' lives that liberalism immunizes from public regulation, individuals may be as ardent as they please in the pursuit of their own conceptions of the good. Their private commitments may, in turn, inform their interventions in the public arena, subject to constitutional constraints. It is only constitutional arrangements that must be free of partisanship. Robert Frost is reputed to have said that a liberal is someone who will not take his own side in an argument. He may have been right. But Frost's comment applies to liberals, not liberal theory. There is nothing in liberal doctrine that precludes individuals dedicating themselves wholeheartedly to contentious causes. All liberalism requires is that the state—which, according to Hobbes, organizes society directly through coercion—and civil society—insofar as its institutions are capable of moral coercion—not do so.

*   *   *

A way to articulate this position is to maintain that what liberalism demands is neutrality—of intent, not outcome—on the part of public, especially state, institutions. This characterization is Rawlsian in spirit.[5] The thought it conveys is integral to political liberalism, broadly construed.

In the essay that launched neutrality into recent political philosophy, Ronald Dworkin set out to explore the connections joining liberal theory, as it had developed under Rawls's influence, and liberal politics, as it is understood in the United States and similarly minded political cultures.[6] Writing at a time when it still had a public presence, Dworkin took the New Deal conception of liberal politics, with its commitment to an activist state, as a paradigm. By his reckoning, New Deal liberalism was one of a number of liberal "settlements" that coalesced in recent centuries. Like the others, it expressed what Dworkin called a "constitutive political morality"—one that supplies a particular interpretation to the widely held conviction that persons are free and equal moral agents, worthy of equal respect. Thus, on Dworkin's account, it is a commitment to the moral equality of persons, a commitment that Rawls emphasized repeatedly, that leads liberals to proscribe the use of public coercive force in behalf of particular conceptions of the good. To side for or against anything so fundamental to individuals' identities as moral personalities would be tantamount to siding for or against some individuals at the expense of others. This violates the norm of equal respect. Hence, neutrality is warranted. According to Dworkin, New Deal liberalism expressed this understanding by articulating what neutrality requires under the particular historical conditions that existed at the time of its emergence and tenure. In earlier times, liberalism's constitutive political morality underwrote different policy prescriptions, including some that were congenial to unregulated capitalism. One can infer that, in new conditions, Dworkin would predict that liberals would concoct yet unprecedented policies and institutional arrangements.

Dworkin's account of neutrality was importantly influenced by Rawls's contention, implicit in *A Theory of Justice* and developed expressly in papers written shortly thereafter (and incorporated into *Political Liberalism*) that principles of justice ought to treat rival conceptions of the good fairly. However, Rawls's aim was different from Dworkin's. It was not to identify underlying constitutive political moralities or to reveal the essential content of liberal settlements. His subject was political legitimacy. Rawls wanted to justify neutrality—the idea, not the term—in a way that is itself distinctively liberal. This is why he endeavored to wrest second-order liberal theory away from moral philosophy. The moral philosophical positions that defenders of first-order liberalism appealed to in the past derived, almost without exception, from the utilitarian and Kantian traditions. Rawls insisted that a genuinely liberal defense of liberalism cannot base its support for neutrality on the truth of these (or any other) "comprehensive doctrines." A liberal (neutral) defense of liberalism (neutrality) must be free standing.

The Neutral and the Reasonable

Since reasonableness, as Rawls uses the term, is mainly a property of comprehensive doctrines, we should take care to understand what Rawls meant by that idea. Here is his most complete account:

> A *"comprehensive doctrine"* includes conceptions of what is of value in human life, and ideals of personal character, as well as ideals of friendship and of familial and associational relationships, and much else that is to inform our conduct and in the limit to our life as a whole. A conception is fully comprehensive if it covers all recognized values and virtues within one rather precisely articulated system; whereas a conception is only partially comprehensive when it comprises a number of, but by no means all, nonpolitical values and virtues and is rather loosely articulated. Many religious and philosophical doctrines aspire to be . . . comprehensive.[7]

Rawls maintained that comprehensive doctrines, so conceived, are bound to be contentious. To appeal to them is therefore to defend first-order liberalism in a nonneutral way; in a way that fails to accord moral agents equal respect.

A properly neutral second-order defense of first-order neutrality would garner support for liberal institutions and practices on the basis of prin-

ciples that everyone—or, as we will see presently, a subset of everyone—
can accept, whether they are committed to liberal comprehensive
doctrines or not. These principles comprise a (notional) constitution.
Insofar as its tenets are consistent with the comprehensive doctrines that
"inform [the] conduct" of the relevant subset of persons, it is legitimate,
and individuals can be said to consent to its provisions.

It is clear, in retrospect, that it was this thought—or rather a less philosophical, ancestor version of it—that motivated the authors of the U.S.
Constitution. Their aim was to forge a union among constituencies
plagued by fundamental disagreements—not over comprehensive
doctrines, but over potentially divisive economic, political, and moral
issues like slavery. A full-fledged consensus was out of the question; the
divisions were too profound. Hence the goal became to forge a union
based on a limited consensus—organized around principles of sufficient
weight to join together all the interested parties, but not so weighty as to
preclude the adherence of any of them. Rawls's liberal second-order
defense of first-order liberalism generalizes this strategy and gives it theoretical expression.

The account of political legitimacy Rawls developed is ambiguous in
the sense that it conflates an account of de jure legitimacy, legitimacy in
right, with questions about political stability and other issues that bear on
the de facto legitimacy of political arrangements. Political arrangements
are de facto legitimate if they are believed to be de jure legitimate by most
of the people they affect. Thus political institutions can be de facto, but
not de jure, legitimate. In the main, it is Rawls's account of de jure legitimacy that unwittingly expresses a core component of the American
ideology. But, it can be useful to accede to the ambiguity of Rawls's own
formulations and not distinguish these issues meticulously. It is in this
spirit that one should take Rawls's contention that (most) people in societies like our own can be brought to endorse constitutional principles that
ensure neutrality on the part of public institutions.

Because it is supposed to follow from an (imputed) consensus that
could fail to exist, political liberalism is not, by its own lights, a universally applicable political philosophy. It is not timelessly true. Therefore,
unlike a utilitarian or Kantian liberal, a political liberal cannot claim that
political institutions ought to uphold neutrality in all times and places.
But a political liberal can say that liberal constitutional principles are
possible and desirable in the conditions that obtain in societies like our
own; that they are right for us and for other peoples similarly situated. In
this sense, political liberalism is a relativist doctrine; it holds that political

philosophies are true or false relative to those whose affairs they govern. But, it is not a relativist doctrine in the sense that it denies the pertinence of truth or falsity altogether, as some postmodernists do.

Because political stability was an objective of Rawls's, it was his intent that individuals enthusiastically favor neutral institutions. Passive acquiesce is not enough. Thus political liberalism suggests a political project—to secure the requisite support. Rawls would pursue this objective by building what he called an overlapping consensus—or, rather, by making a notional overlapping consensus actual. An overlapping consensus contrasts with a modus vivendi. Thus, like Mill and most other modern liberals, Rawls wanted more than an agreement somehow to get along in the face of contentious disputes over fundamental issues. A modus vivendi is not to be despised; especially when no stronger basis for social unity exists. However, in the end, it is too fragile a basis for the social unity liberals want because the stability it underwrites is prone to becoming undone as the balance of forces within a society changes. It is therefore better, for stability's sake, to base support for neutrality on convictions actively endorsed throughout the political community. The problem is that except for those citizens whose comprehensive doctrines are expressly liberal—utilitarians or Kantians— support for neutrality is, at best, only latent. The task, then, is to make it manifest. Rawls would do so by appealing to elements already present in the comprehensive doctrines individuals hold. This mission will be easier to execute the more that individuals are already won over to positions friendly to neutrality. But it is not necessary that they actually be philo-sophical liberals. What is necessary is only that the comprehensive doctrines they endorse not fall beyond the range of a potential overlapping consensus. If there is insufficient overlap, coercion, not consensus, would be the only way to ensure stability, insofar as a modus vivendi is not up to the task. This eventuality is unacceptable, but Rawls was convinced that it is avoidable. He was confident that the requisite consensus does exist in principle; that, in consequence of the cultural and political transforma-tions wrought by the Protestant Reformation, the Enlightenment, and the history of liberalism itself, an overlapping consensus is there to be forged.

*   *   *

Neutrality is and can only be a matter of intent, not of consequences. In practice, some conceptions of the good are bound to prevail over others. But even at the level of intent, it is plain that a state can never be quite so neutral as the word suggests. Liberal states can accommodate nonliberal comprehensive doctrines if they are compatible with a constitutional order that tolerates diverse conceptions of the good. But, expressly antiliberal positions raise problems for liberal regimes. They can hardly be neutral with respect to practices or activities that threaten to undo their own neutrality. Nor can liberal states be neutral with respect to ways of life that undermine the moral equality of persons, even if they are part of individuals' comprehensive doctrines. Thus liberals agree that states can rightfully prohibit slavery, even when it is allowed—or required—by particular religious or secular world views. Neutrality applies to whatever upholds, or at least does not undermine, the moral equality of persons. Within that range, liberals insist that state power not be used to favor some conceptions of the good over others.

But, of course there are always unintended consequences of legitimate state activities that advance some conceptions of the good at the expense of others—especially in regimes organized in accord with liberal settlements that imply an activist role for the state. Paradoxically too, some conceptions of the good are bound to prevail in consequence of the exercise of neutrality itself. Thus a neutral state could not employ state power to oppose, say, religious liberty or the right of a woman to an abortion—despite the fact that conceptions of the good supporting religious intolerance and the absence of reproductive freedom exist among the comprehensive doctrines that political liberals would organize into an overlapping consensus. Where neutrality reigns, tolerance is the default position. Proponents of conceptions of the good that actively endorse tolerance will therefore generally get their way; while proponents of conceptions that oppose laissez-vivre generally will not.

Social Unity

The political liberal account of de jure legitimacy puts the issue of political stability at center stage. But, unlike Hobbes, political liberals do not value stability for its own sake. Stability is vital, for them, when it helps to advance liberty and justice. Therefore, they want to enhance stability in liberal, but not necessarily in nonliberal, regimes. Thus they accord price of place to social unity in conditions that approximate the ideal. In those circumstances, the political liberal project devolves into an effort to advance social unity by making the (imputed) overlapping consensus supporting liberal constitutional principles explicit. Like all supporters of Hobbes's case for the state, political liberals accept the inevitability of coercive public institutions. They are not anarchists. But they want the constitutional provisions of liberal states to be sustained by freely conferred consent. They want individuals to accede to the rules of the game because they accept them, not because they fear the consequences of noncompliance. Social division is inimical to this objective. Social unity is instrumental for its advancement. It is, at once, a condition for the possibility of liberal regimes and a goal of political liberal politics.

For Rawls and the others, social unity operates very much like tolerance does in the case Mill made in its defense in *On Liberty*. In Mill's view, tolerance is justified for its beneficial effects; the more tolerant the practice, the better the utility consequences. But, as Mill made plain, a certain antecedent level of tolerance is necessary before the beneficial effects of tolerance kick in. Tolerance fosters the development of individuals' moral and intellectual capacities; in this way, it is an improver. But if these capacities are insufficiently developed, as they are in "children, idiots, and lunatics" and also in normal adult members of illiberal and therefore intolerant societies, tolerance can make outcomes worse. Beyond a relevant threshold, the more tolerance there is, the more beneficial it becomes. Below that threshold, it may not be beneficial at all. Similarly, a consensus in support of liberal constitutional arrangements presupposes a threshold level of social unity. When it exists, there can be liberal institutions that function well and, in turn, foster social unity, reinforcing the condition for their own possibility.

They do so by mitigating conflicts that threaten to exacerbate social divisions; conflicts that deliberative political institutions are unable to address without putting social unity in peril. Again, the model is the U.S. Constitution. Its authors aimed to transform potentially disruptive disagreements into disputes that could be settled juridically, according to principles that the interested parties could accept. There is a place for public deliberation and collective choice in this view. However, it is not as large a place as one might suppose in a democracy. This legacy has shaped the American political culture from its earliest years. The American state is unusual among liberal democracies for the extent to which it excludes wrenching public controversies from the sphere of public deliberation and collective choice. Political liberalism articulates the rationale behind this practice. It endorses the idea of settling conflicts administratively: by the proper application of constitutional precepts, adjudicated by a judicial or extrajudicial administrative system insulated from potentially divisive political pressures.[8]

Keeping this objective in mind, it is possible to reconstruct Rawls's position in a way that partially disentangles his accounts of de jure and de facto legitimacy. Rawls wanted the legitimacy of political institutions to be based upon the de facto legitimacy of the constitutional arrangements that sustain them; and he wanted de facto legitimacy to be based upon the fact that these institutions are legitimate de jure—in other words, upon the fact that people actually do endorse the regime, even when they do not like what it does. At the same time, he insisted that, in a free society, many different comprehensive doctrines will have adherents and that some of these comprehensive doctrines will be, by all appearances, non- or even antiliberal. In these circumstances, the requisite consensus on constitutional principles must be forged—not through coercion, but through rational persuasion. Is this possible? The conviction that motivates the political liberal project is that it is. If this conviction were mistaken, then the political liberal's account of de jure political legitimacy would fail. For it is not enough to show that legitimate authority is conceivable. One must also demonstrate that the concept is applicable in our time and place. Unless it does, the theory is not true for us.

The general strategy is plain: begin with extant and ostensibly opposed comprehensive doctrines, some of which may be illiberal; find higher-order commitments that proponents of all of these views can endorse; and then derive a consensus supporting liberal constitutional arrangements on the basis of these higher-order commitments. The foundational commitments that Rawls identified, and that all political liberals accept, are themselves uncontentious in the modern world: the idea that persons are morally equal in possessing capacities for a sense of justice and for conceptions of the good and that people have capacities for judgment, thought, and inference. However, the claim that recognition of these capacities can be fashioned into support for neutrality is more asserted than demonstrated. Neither Rawls nor anyone else has shown how an overlapping consensus can be forged out of actual comprehensive doctrines. What Rawls did instead was adduce (generally inconclusive) considerations in support of the claim that a subset of extant positions, the reasonable ones, can be dialectically shaped into a consensus of the requisite sort. Insofar as *reasonable* is defined independently, so that it is not true by definition that reasonable comprehensive doctrines (implicitly) support liberal constitutional principles, this conviction is an empirical speculation, not an incontrovertible fact. Evidently, political liberals believe that, in generally free societies, many (if not most) comprehensive doctrines will be reasonable. Otherwise, liberal institutions might survive—through fear or indifference on the part of the citizenry—but a well-ordered, flourishing liberal state, grounded in active support for its constitutional arrangements would remain an elusive ideal.

Reasonableness

In its commitment to constitutional provisions consistent with an over-lapping consensus of reasonable comprehensive doctrines, political liberalism effectively advances its own, distinctive conception of Reason in society. That conception is epitomized in its notion of the reasonable. But reasonable is a vague term, especially when applied to comprehensive doctrines.[9] It is also ambiguous. On the one hand, a position or comprehensive doctrine is reasonable if it can be modified or at least redescribed in a way that makes cooperation with others who hold different views possible on free and equal terms. In other words, a position is reasonable if it makes uncoerced tolerance possible. On the other hand, "reasonable" also means plausible, given the uncertainties that inevitably afflict human deliberations. Political liberals, following Rawls's lead, are extremely generous in their use of this description. For them, disagreements with respect to fundamental religious or moral issues are all reasonable, so long as their existence cannot be explained by willful blindness or blatant irrationality. The "burdens of judgment"—shortage of time, lack of decisive evidence, difficulties in prioritizing values and all the other un-certainties that afflict the use of rational powers in real-world condi-tions—make a range of conflicting and even incommensurable views plausible. Rawls insisted that reasonable disagreements, so understood, are permanent and ineradicable features of modern societies. The expec-tation that fundamental moral, philosophical, and religious differences will eventually disappear is therefore itself unreasonable (in the sense that contrasts with "plausible"). Thus most extant moral, philosophical, and religious doctrines meet this standard.

But can this conclusion be sustained? Can we say, for example, that someone is reasonable who believes in the existence of an omnipotent, omniscient, and perfectly good God when that person also believes, rightly or wrongly, that there are no considerations that weigh in favor of the existence of such a being and many that weigh against? Is it reason-able to believe in what one considers absurd or even, as some theists proclaim, to believe in God because the belief is absurd? Political liberals would say yes; a religious belief would have to be unimaginably bizarre before they would deem it unreasonable, irrespective of believers' reasons, if any, for holding the convictions they do. This is not surprising given liberalism's origins in the struggle for religious toleration. No second-order liberal theory could pass muster if it implied that this longstanding dedication is problematic. But it is surely irrational to find reasonable—or in light of the burdens of judgment, plausible—what we have good reason to think false or unworthy of serious consideration. Unless a political liberal is prepared to argue that the weaker standard—reasonableness—trumps the stronger one—rationality—this consideration should be decisive. Rawls never pressed this unlikely claim. What he did say was that when we take account of the fact that human beings are obliged to draw conclusions in the face of factors that render their judgments unsure, we can understand, despite our own convictions, that people can in good faith arrive at positions contrary to our own, and that they will not retreat voluntarily from their views. This understanding engenders a certain humility about our own convictions. The resulting sense of the world may not lead us to welcome the existence of views we think mistaken. However, it cannot fail to diminish our intolerance of them; in other words, to make us disposed to be reasonable (in the sense of flexible or cooperative). On this basis, Rawls concluded that, if we must go wrong, we ought to err on the side of generosity in deeming comprehensive doctrines and the positions they motivate reasonable.

Is this a defensible rejoinder? Surely it matters why we think a belief is false or not worth taking seriously. It is relevant that many of the beliefs upon which comprehensive doctrines rest can be reasonably (plausibly) dismissed for reasons that, if believed, plainly do trump other considerations. Thus, I would venture that theistic beliefs should be especially troubling for political liberals. Recall Freud's account, in *The Future of an Illusion*, according to which the belief in God—or, rather, the disposition to believe—arises from the same Oedipal conflicts that account for neuroses. This body of reasonable (plausible) theory underwrites the conclusion that belief in God is an illusion (see Chapter 2). It is an expression of an unconscious wish, in just the way that, according to an analogy Freud devised, a middle-class girl's belief that a prince will come to marry her would be. Freud expressly denied that theistic convictions are delusional. Unlike genuine delusions, they are not held in the face of overwhelming evidence to the contrary—as would be the case, for example, if the girl believed she was Cleopatra. Her belief about the prince would therefore satisfy the political liberal's criterion. But is the belief that a prince will come truly reasonable, given the burdens of judgment? It is relevant to take into account not only the improbability of what is believed, but also the nature of the causal mechanism that accounts for it. Then the answer is clear. The fact, if it is a fact, that the belief arises in a pathological way—or, more precisely, in the way that some clinically significant psychiatric pathologies arise—makes it unreasonable. But, Freud's point is that the same mechanism, and therefore the same implausibility, afflicts theistic belief. Whether or not he was right, this example makes the problematic role of reasonableness in the political liberal project clear. Freudians can hardly consider theists' views reasonable. They could, of course, still resolve to be reasonable themselves; that is to be flexible or cooperative. But, their resolution would not follow from the rationale Rawls advanced. Tolerance, in this instance, is not mandated by the inevitability of differences of opinion among human beings confronting the burdens of judgment. It would be based, instead, on a sense of the futility of trying to persuade others with whom one wants to get along. Thus political liberals who consider their opponents' views irrational or otherwise infirm, but who nevertheless support the reasonableness of the comprehensive doctrines they underwrite are, one suspects, guilty (perhaps inadvertently) of a conceptual slight of hand: identifying the reasonable with what they think ought to be protected from societal and state interference. In other words, they are confounding the policy they want to justify with the justification they provide.

Rawls effectively blurred the line between the various senses of reasonable by maintaining that, for the reason just indicated, a position is reasonable if its proponents recognize the hopelessness of trying to convert others to it noncoercively. His idea, it seems, is that people will moderate their claims for the sake of social cooperation whenever they acknowledge the futility of defeating conflicting or incommensurable comprehensive doctrines through the force of argument alone. The implicit contrast is with scientific communities in which a consensus around basic theoretical orientations is a fair expectation, at least in those hard sciences that are theoretically mature and relatively insulated from political and religious pressures. Rawls's thought, apparently, was that fundamental moral, philosophical, and religious differences can never be surmounted—unlike scientific disagreements which, when they occur, are temporary phenomena that the progress of science will eventually resolve.

To assume this contrast, it is not necessary to suppose that scientific theories develop continuously, propelled along by a universally acknowledged and incontrovertible scientific method. The hope for a rational consensus in the sciences is compatible with the influential view of

T. S. Kuhn according to which fundamental changes of theoretical orientation, paradigm shifts, seldom if ever result from the force of new evidence or theoretical argument.[10] According to Kuhn, science changes through scientific revolutions in which new and even incommensurable theories arise on the ashes of old paradigms, when new scientific communities or new strata within existing scientific communities supplant practitioners of prevailing orthodoxies. In consequence of the (largely extrarational) means through which old regimes are overthrown and replaced, a new consensus is forged in which fundamental differences eventually recede. Agreement is achieved, then, not because it is rationally necessitated, though it generally is retrospectively, but in consequence of institutional and social transformations within scientific communities. Even so, scientific revolutionaries seldom, if ever, rely on expressly illiberal means to achieve agreement. And, in any case, scientific revolutions are relatively brief discontinuities that punctuate the history of successive forms of "normal science" in which consensus is the norm. If Rawls was right, there is no similar prospect for the comprehensive doctrines that populate the intellectual and moral landscape of modern, liberal societies; no likelihood of a consensus emerging within the community at large. Liberals therefore cannot expect anything analogous to scientific progress to foster social unity. It was Rawls's belief, however, that in the absence of an overt consensus around constitutional principles for mediating disruptive conflicts, liberal institutions would be in peril. In those circumstances, so long as people care intensely about the (sometimes conflicting) comprehensive doctrines they support, order could only be imposed by force, in contravention of liberalism's basic rationale. Hence, the need to forge an overlapping consensus around constitutional principles that uphold neutrality as a principled conviction.

If the issue were just de facto legitimacy, Rawls's account would be exaggerated at best. To be sure, as secular, progressive alternatives to the system of world domination that the American ideology sustains have gone missing, religious fundamentalisms have taken hold in some of the most oppressed regions of the world and among subpopulations in the United States and other liberal democracies. Nevertheless, liberal democracies today are hardly riven by the threat of religious or civil war. Indifference about comprehensive doctrines, not fanatical adherence, has become the norm. This would seem to undo the need for an overlapping consensus. But, despite his own equivocations, Rawls's claims in behalf of forging one pertain mainly to de jure, not de facto legitimacy. The issue is not so much what is necessary for civil peace as what is required to legitimate the use of public coercive force.[11]

*   *   *

Political liberalism is not itself a comprehensive doctrine. It is only a theory about politics, one that underwrites a resolve to handle disagreements about fundamental commitments in a political way, reconciling differences—or, if necessary, evading them—by building on points of consensus. The idea is to underwrite liberal constitutional arrangements without appealing to contentious moral, philosophical, or religious beliefs. In their stead, political liberals would substitute a commitment on the part of the citizenry to these constitutional procedures themselves. Rawls made plain that for these procedures to serve this function, there must first be a threshold level of support for them. For that support to exist there must already be a threshold measure of social unity. Once this threshold is surpassed, how, in the political liberal view, does it register politically? How, in other words, is it expressed?

The answer, to which all political liberals advert, is that it can only be expressed democratically. Thus, political liberalism implies a democratic theory. Political liberals advocate deliberative democracy. To grasp the ideological role of the political liberal's purchase on the reasonable, it is therefore to the theory and practice of deliberative democracy that we must turn.

7

Deliberative Democracy

From the time the ancient Greeks coined the word, democracy meant "rule of the demos"—the popular masses. For millennia thereafter, the idea was understood to be a theoretical possibility, but not one that any sensible person would advocate. Over the past several centuries, the situation has changed—to the point that, today, democracy is universally endorsed. This is not to say that the rule of the demos is now an unchallenged ideal. Quite the contrary. The term—and therefore, to some extent, the idea it denotes—has become essentially contested. All political forces endeavor to enlist the word in their own behalf, even as disagreements rage over what democracy is.

This remarkable turn of events is a consequence of two general phenomena:

1. The irreversible entry of the demos into the political arena
2. The development of institutional means for rendering subversive demotic aspirations benign

The first of these great transformations was both a cause and effect of the revolutionary upheavals that shook the foundations of England, its North American colonies, and then France in the seventeenth and eighteenth centuries and that subsequently expanded to become a global phenomenon of unparalleled importance and depth. In consequence, today, everywhere, the demos, though hardly in power anywhere, is a political actor with which all regimes must contend and, in one way or another, accommodate. Meanwhile, the rise of liberal institutions, and their success in co-opting democratic aspirations, played a significant role in domesticating the demos, rendering its political presence harmless to entrenched elites. Outside the liberal ambit, similar phenomena occurred. Thus the regimes that followed the Soviet model described themselves as democracies too—peoples' democracies. This description was only a little more disingenuous than its liberal democratic counterpart was. After all, the peoples' democracies did overthrow the economic and political elites of the regimes they succeeded, even as they established alternative ruling structures that were ultimately as bad or worse for popular rule. To the profound misfortune of their subject populations, Soviet-style regimes were unconscionably illiberal. To tame democratic impulses while still using democratic aspirations to enhance their de facto legitimacy, they were therefore obliged to rely on institutional arrangements of a less savory, more authoritarian kind. The Soviet system of one party rule, wherein the party—or, rather, the leading strata of the party—substituted for the demos proved more than adequate for the task.

These broad historical processes were bound eventually to affect philosophical theories of democracy. Several distinct strains of democratic theory emerged—all of them only tenuously connected to the original idea of the people in power. The philosophical character of deliberative democracy, the democratic theory continuous with political liberalism, is best exposed in light of its affinities with, and differences from, these distinctively modern forms of democratic thought.

Collective Choice

All theories of democracy suppose the existence of some mechanism through which the will of the demos is ascertained. Almost without exception, that mechanism involves voting. Voting may be direct, as when the entire population decides measures; or indirect, when measures are enacted by legislators—a tiny, specially selected subset of the population. In liberal democracies, the constituents in competitive elections usually elect their legislators. Typically, however, the selection process accords citizens little control over outcomes—thanks, mainly, to the party system and, especially in recent years, the agenda-shaping operations of the mass media. But the election of legislators, though the norm, is not indispensable. Some democratic theorists, even today, look to so-called "Athenian democracy" for guidance.[1] In ancient Athens, representatives were selected by lot from among the (small) part of the population that enjoyed full citizenship rights. Even in the Athenian case, however, voting was part of the legislative process. After being selected, representatives voted to determine which of the alternatives in contention would prevail.

Voting systems are rules for making collective choices. The presumption is that a simple numerical majority of votes cast—or, more rarely, a numerical majority of all eligible voters—should suffice to select representatives and to enact measures or laws. However, in both theory and practice, this presumption is easily overridden. Thus, to make an enactment, it is often the case that more than a simple numerical majority is required. At the limit, unanimity may be necessary. Or, several votes, taken in different legislative bodies or in the same legislative body at different times, might be required. The former arrangement is the more usual one. Bicameral legislatures, as in the federal government of the United States and in all but one of its constituent states, are found throughout the world. These practices make change more difficult than it would be under simple majority rule voting. When larger majorities than 50% plus one are required to pass enactments, a minority of voters gain effective veto power over them. In the extreme case, when unanimity is the rule, a single individual can block a change. Similarly, the more legislative obstacles there are to overcome, the less likely it is that an enactment will pass. These familiar deviations from the method of majority rule introduce a bias in favor of the status quo. It is widely thought that this bias is desirable; that, for the sake of social stability, it is wise not to rely too much on decision procedures that are highly sensitive to potentially mercurial changes in popular attitudes. The guiding principle, then, is not exactly that the devil we know is better than the devil we do not. It is that stability is an important desideratum; therefore, whatever can disrupt order, as change often does, is best approached with caution.

Still, simple majority rule is the presumptive norm. In identifying different strains of democratic thought, there is therefore no harm in fixing on this voting rule. It will suffice to bear in mind that, for conservative or other extrademocratic reasons, it will often be best, in both theory and practice, to deviate from this procedure.

Rousseauean Theories

At one extreme, is the view of democratic collective choice advanced by Jean-Jacques Rousseau.[2] For Rousseau, it is a condition for the possibility of de jure political authority that the body politic be joined together by a strong consensus on ends, according to which each citizen-subject wills the same thing, the general will. In Rousseau's account, this consensus is notional, not actual, even in ideal conditions. Conditions are ideal when citizens, brought together in popular assemblies, deliberate and then vote disinterestedly. In other words, when they ask themselves "what is best for the political community of which I am an integral part?"; not "what is best for me individually?" When voters respond to the latter question, voting becomes a mechanism for aggregating private wills. In this respect, it resembles negotiating. For reasons that Rousseau labored to make plain, but that need not detain us here, it then fails to confer de jure legitimacy. It is only when votes represent opinions as to what the general will is that outcomes are legitimate de jure.

Even in ideal conditions, though, voters expressing their opinions about what the general will is may disagree. Public deliberation can diminish the extent of their disagreement, but it cannot be counted on to eliminate it altogether, especially because decisions must be made in a timely fashion. While everyone, by hypothesis, wants what is best for the whole community, some individuals may not know what that is. Rousseau insisted that majority rule voting could solve this problem; that it could discover the general will.

So far from resembling a negotiation, voting, in the Rousseauean scheme, is a truth discovery procedure analogous to the statistical pooling of expert, disinterested opinion. Jury voting was, apparently, Rousseau's model. When jurors vote, they express their opinion about a matter of fact—say, whether or not a defendant is guilty (or, in the American case, whether or not the defendant has been proven guilty "beyond a reasonable doubt"). This is not the same thing as expressing a preference for one or another outcome. A juror might wish that the defendant be innocent, but nevertheless believe that the burden of proof has been met. She is then obligated, as a member of the jury, to vote guilty. However, for the jury model to apply in the way Rousseau intended, there must really be a matter of fact for voters to discover. Rousseau's claim was that there is: that the general will is a matter of fact. Thus, for Rousseau, there is a right answer to the question "what ought we, the citizenry, to do?" that is logically independent of what anybody, including a majority of the voters, think it is. His contention was that the majority will discover the answer to this question, provided voters do indeed express their opinions as they deliberate and vote. This is why those who are in the minority on an issue decided by majority rule voting in a de jure legitimate state "obey only themselves," when they accede to the majority's decision—and therefore remain free (autonomous).[3] The majority discovers what everyone, including voters on the losing side, truly wants. Citizens in the minority are wrong about what they will as citizens; they have false beliefs about what their interests are.

What is especially problematic in Rousseau's position is the idea that there is a general interest. Despite what may at first appear, the other claim—that, if there is a general interest, the majority will discover it— is less doubtful. Rousseau did not expressly defend either claim. But, there is an argument for the second one. It was supplied by the Marquis de Condorcet.[4] Condorcet proved a theorem pertaining, not surprisingly, to the jury system. He demonstrated that if a juror has a better than 50% chance of being right, the probability that the vote of the entire jury will be right rises exponentially as the majority increases. More precisely, if each member of the group is right in proportion v *(verité)* of the cases and wrong in proportion e *(erreur)* so that v + e = 1, then if in a given instance h members of the group give one answer and k members another, where h > k, the probability that the h members are right is given by the expression:

$$\frac{v^{h-k}}{v^{h-k} + e^{h-k}}$$

For example, if v = 60% and e = 40%, and if h = 51 and k = 49, the probability that the majority h is right is:

$$\frac{60^2}{60^2 + 40^2}$$

or approximately 69%. A majority of only 2 therefore has a 9% greater chance of being right than a single individual in a group whose members have a 60% chance of being right. As the majority increases, the probability that it will be right rises exponentially—rapidly approaching (though never strictly reaching) unity. Condorcet's theorem does not establish the infallibility of majority rule voting, even when all voters attempt in a genuinely disinterested way to determine what the whole community ought to do; no probabilistic argument could do that. But, it does show that majority rule voting can be a highly reliable truth detector. We can therefore say, with some confidence, that if there is a general will, the majority will likely discover what it is.

But only if, in voting, they deliberate as integral members of the collective entity they comprise, not as discrete individuals with private wills.

Rousseau's case for this position follows, implicitly, from a fundamental concern with the moral equality of persons.[5] In this respect, he and the political liberals are of one mind. But political liberals think that when citizens place themselves "under the supreme direction of the general will," they fail to accord moral personality, in themselves and others, the respect it is due—because they subordinate their own interests to the interests of "the whole community." Rousseau's contention, on the other hand, was that subordinating one's private will to the general will—that is, to one's own will as a citizen—is indispensable for respecting moral personality in the political sphere. I will not try to defend his position here. But I would point out that it is not surprising that liberals, especially those who think that neutrality in the face of ineluctable disagreements is mandated by a notion of equal respect, would disagree with him. Their purchase on the notion of equal respect leads them to focus on what marks individuals off from the groups they constitute, not on what draws them together. This is why deliberative democrats do not fully accept Rousseau's account of democratic collective choice, even as they acknowledge its appeal.

Proceduralism

According to the main opposing view, voting does just what Rousseau claimed it must not: it aggregates private interests or, more exactly, expressions of preference for alternatives in contention. Those who understand voting this way also believe that individuals have a common, still private, interest in joining together to make collective choices. Thus, like everyone else (except anarchists), they endorse the Hobbesian case for sovereignty. And, like nearly everyone after Hobbes, they supplement it with the claim that the people themselves are sovereign. They then infer, not unreasonably, that, just as a Hobbesian sovereign does what he most wants, the popular sovereign ought to do what it most wants or what is most preferred by the individuals who comprise it.

Assuming, then, that individuals know best what their own preferences are and that they are means-ends rational, voting will register individuals' preferences. Thus it is assumed that, within the parameters established by a shared interest in maintaining their existence as a collectivity, individuals will seek to advance their own private interests. They will therefore endeavor, through voting, to have their preferences realized.[6] Thus, the ideal decision procedure will be the one that is most responsive to voters' choices. On this understanding, voting does resemble negotiating. So far from being a device that pools expert opinions, it combines interests that converge only on the idea that the system itself must be preserved. In all other respects, the interests votes express may, and often will, be at odds.

Voting, on this view, is a struggle for competitive advantage within a framework that everyone has an interest in maintaining. It is like a market transaction. Suppose an individual, Jones, wants to sell a car and another individual, Smith, wants to buy it. Suppose too that Jones is willing to sell the car for $5,000 or more and Smith is willing to buy it for $6,000 or less.[7] There is therefore a space between $5,000 and $6,000 within which both Jones and Smith are better off, given their interests, if a sale takes place than if it does not. Within that space, however, Jones is better off selling for more and Smith is better off buying for less. Therefore, a successful negotiation, one that does not break down, will settle on a selling price that is better or worse for one or the other of the transacting parties, but still advantageous for both. On the proceduralist view, this is just what happens in voting. By hypothesis, everyone, or nearly everyone, has a common (private) interest in maintaining the political community. Everyone therefore has an interest in maintaining the decision rule through which the community makes collective choices. However, within the space established by that common interest, individuals will seek the most advantageous outcomes for themselves.

On this understanding of what voting does, the method of majority rule is plainly superior to alternative collective choice rules. Imagine a constitutional convention in which individuals or groups of individuals seek to advance their private interests and in which no outcome can be reached unless everyone agrees. We can be sure that no decision procedure that fails to take everyone's interests into account will be selected, because anyone whose interests might be neglected would not agree to it. We can be equally sure that, if the convention is fair in the sense that the competing parties come together on free and equal terms, no agreement will be reached that advantages some individuals or groups over others. One person, one vote will therefore be the outcome. But, it will then remain to negotiate how these equally weighted votes should be counted. Insofar as the idea is to maximize overall preference satisfaction—in other words, to have individuals' preferences be as satisfied as can be, given that choices must be made collectively and that everyone's choice must count equally—the best decision procedure will be the one that best represents the actual distribution of preferences within the voting population. Because it alone is unbiased for or against the status quo, that can only be simple majority rule voting. Procedures that are consistent with the principle of one person, one vote, but that require larger majorities to pass enactments are biased against change; procedures requiring less than numerical majorities are biased against the status quo.[8] Therefore, simple majority rule voting will be the presumptive choice. This presumption may be countervailed for conservative or other reasons. But, insofar as the issue is how best to maximize preference satisfaction, the method of majority rule is what the constitution writers will choose.

In the procedural model, the role of public deliberation is problematic. Perhaps because popular and legislative assemblies have been thought of as public fora from time immemorial, procedural democrats do not exclude debate altogether. Thus it is permissible, in their view, and even desirable that legislators make speeches defending their positions before they vote and that they challenge their opponents' views. But, for proceduralists, what legitimates outcomes is the collective choice rule citizens employ, not the deliberations that precede its exercise. Proceduralists take preferences, represented in votes, as given. What matters to them is how votes are treated, not how preferences are formed. Before voting, voters can and do deliberate in their own minds and among themselves. In doing so, they may be impressed by arguments offered by others and change their minds accordingly. But, the role of public deliberation in the process of preference formation falls outside the purview of democratic theory, strictly speaking. In this respect, proceduralism is like mainstream microeconomic theory. Economists too acknowledge that tastes or preferences for alternatives in contention can be explained causally and that they are subject to change for a variety of reasons. However, their concern is with what happens to preferences after they are formed, not with the processes affecting their formation.[9] Even so, democracy, as proceduralists understand it, is not entirely continuous with the market. Because proceduralism is still a normative political theory, linked historically with ancestor theories that celebrate the forum and denigrate the market, it can hardly disparage public deliberation altogether. However, it is not clear what its role is. The contrast with the kind of democratic theory Rousseau's work epitomized could not be starker.

Nevertheless, proceduralism is widely believed to be more apt than its Rousseauean rival. The reason why, I think, is just that it accords better with lived experience. It is plain to everybody living in liberal democratic regimes that voting has more to do with aggregating competing interests than with discovering a (notional) consensus on ends. Thus, Rousseau's political philosophy strikes most readers as fanciful, if not utopian.

Because it shares Rousseau's aim of reaching a genuine consensus on ends, deliberative democracy is tarnished with the same brush. On the other hand, proceduralism seems more realistic, more in accord with the world as it is.

For proceduralists, there is no right answer to the question "what ought we to do?" Therefore, for them, voting cannot serve Truth, but it can serve Justice. The intuition is that all interests deserve fair representation. To the degree that collective choices represent voters' preferences, everyone counting equally, the outcomes of votes determined by majority rule voting will be fair—and, insofar as justice is fairness, just. Thus, proceduralism still offers an attractive ideal; one that underwrites the conclusion that we ought to do what the majority decides. On this, proceduralists and Rousseaueans agree. But, the reason why proceduralists think that the minority should accede to the majority's choice has nothing to do with the majority's ability to detect what everyone, including individuals in the minority, truly want. We ought to do what the majority decides because the method of majority rule is the fairest of all possible collective choice rules.

However, once it is conceded that verisimilitude is an appropriate standard for judging normative visions, we are on a slippery slope bound to undo proceduralism too. For the real world of liberal democratic politics, especially American politics, is hardly an arena in which free and equal citizens, with given preferences, vie for power within a framework that they all want to maintain. Our democracy is an oligarchy or, more precisely, a plutocracy in which moneyed elites, not undifferentiated citizens, endeavor to control the political process. Thanks to the irrevocable entry of the demos into the public sphere, these elites are obliged to contend with one another in ways that respect democratic forms. Thus, through various means, they attempt, usually with great success, to control the political agenda; and once the agenda is set, to manipulate a depoliticized and effectively disempowered citizenry to vote in ways that accord with their interests. Joseph Schumpeter argued long ago that it would be well to drop the pretense that democracy is or ought to be government of, by, and for the people. He thought that we should accede instead to this more realistic picture of what democracy is.[10] For obvious reasons, his position has seldom been advanced as a normative vision; even if its realism has been a perennial pole of attraction for some political theorists. After all, how can one defend the gross manipulation of a population equipped with democratic sensibilities to others with similar convictions?[11] It is plain that one cannot and still remain within the democratic fold. Schumpeter accepted this consequence. Thus, he proposed that we wrest the term away from normative political philosophy and use it instead to refer to regimes like our own, utilizing its prestige to help maintain the comparatively benign status quo these regimes superintend. Ordinary usage nowadays accords fairly well with this suggestion, even as the idea of democracy—of government of, by, and for the people—remains a force in our collective consciousness and therefore in our political life. Even the dull reality that afflicts our political culture cannot entirely extinguish normative visions and the aspirations that motivate them. Political philosophy refuses to die.

In any event, it was evidently the colloquial usage that Winston Churchill had in mind when, echoing Schumpeter's thought, he famously proclaimed that democracy is the worst form of government there is, except for all the others. Pessimists might take this *faute de mieux* argument to reflect a healthy skepticism about democratic objectives. Real democrats would insist instead that it reflects a failure of political imagination. But, even if Churchill and Schumpeter were right to reject real democracy, their thought is of little service to those who would justify elite rule at home and the unrestricted projection of American power abroad. To sell the American empire even to a compliant public disposed to acquiescence, a more appealing, more democratic, vision is needed. This is why, despite its unreality, deliberative democracy, not proceduralism and certainly not Schumpeterian democracy, has won a place in the American ideology.

Rousseau without the General Will

For Rousseau's account of political legitimacy to stand, it must be the case that what is best for the whole community is a matter of fact; that citizens want this outcome; and that they register this desire in their votes. Rousseau would have been the first to admit that the last two of these conditions are seldom, if ever, realized. In his view, "the exercise of the general will" has never been a fact and he was doubtful that it ever would be. It exists only in a notional sense and is therefore something permanently to aspire toward.

For a deliberative democrat, steeped in political liberalism, what is wrong with Rousseau's vision, conceived as an objective toward which to aspire, is just that it fails to take account of the ineradicability—in genuinely free conditions, where convictions are uncoerced—of fundamental disagreements about comprehensive doctrines and conceptions of the good. In other words, it errs in failing to acknowledge what Rawls called "the fact of reasonable pluralism." However, the rival proceduralist account—and, of course, its Schumpeterian extension—err even more grievously. The problem is not just that they implicitly denigrate public deliberation and debate. The more devastating reproach that deliberative democrats level against proceduralism and its extensions is that they fail to solve the problem that Rousseau correctly identified—the problem of justifying coercion. It is not enough, the deliberative democrat thinks, to consent to a procedure for making collective choices; it is necessary too, as Rousseau insisted, to consent to the outcomes these procedures generate. Proceduralism falls short on this account. On the other hand, Rousseau's solution to the problem he formulated is impeccable. Nevertheless, it is unworkable because it relies on an untenable assumption—that, for such beings as ourselves, a consensus on ends is indeed a notional possibility. That assumption runs aground on the fact of reasonable pluralism. What the deliberative democrat then sets out to do is to reconcile the Rousseauean criterion of legitimacy with this allegedly ineluctable fact.

It might seem that deliberative democracy is a mean between the twin extremes of Rousseauean and proceduralist democratic theories—that it strengthens the latter by according a preeminent role to deliberation and weakens the former by relaxing its purchase on the idea of a consensus on ends. But this description is misleading. Deliberative democrats are not interested in finding common ground between contending strains of democratic theory. Their aim instead is to defend a collective choice rule consistent with the principle that motivates political liberalism. In short, deliberative democracy is a response to the exigency that political liberalism puts at center stage: to accord peoples' diverse goals and values equal respect. To this end, it endeavors to marry Rousseau's account of the condition for de jure political legitimacy, that individuals obey only themselves, to Rawls's insistence on the fact of reasonable pluralism. This is an unlikely alliance and it is far from clear that it can be made to work. But the objective is plain: it is to do for collective choice what political liberalism does for liberal protections generally—to counteract the potentially divisive effects of reasonable pluralism by evading contentious and intractable moral, political, and social conflicts wherever possible, and mitigating the consequences of social division wherever evasion is not an option.

*　*　*

Rousseauean political philosophy has well-known illiberal implications. Among other things, it implies the suppression of partial associations that mediate between the individual and the state on the grounds that their existence is a threat to the exercise of the general will. The reason is that social groups have interests that can diverge from the general interest. Because legitimacy depends on individuals making the general interest their own, a wise state will enhance the likelihood of this eventuality by restricting rights of association. No doubt, this feature of Rousseau's political theory has helped to generate support for rival, proceduralist theories of democracy among liberal democrats. But, deliberative democracy is free of this taint. It helps to sustain first-order liberal theory as much as proceduralism and its Schumpeterian extension do. As Rawls made plain, any democratic practice capable of doing what deliberative democrats want would require equal protection of basic (political) rights at the greatest feasible level. There must therefore be freedom of speech and association, along with other political rights, including those that ensure freedom from fear of governmental authorities, plus suffrage rights that extend across the entire political community. Citizens must be free to engage in political life—to debate issues and, since representative government is presupposed, to question and criticize political figures. There must also be tolerance and the rule of law.

Following Rawls's lead, deliberative democrats are disinclined to view these and other freedoms as formal rights only. They are all sensitive to the hollowness of claims that freedoms exist when, for rectifiable social or economic reasons, individuals are unable to put them to use. Deliberative democrats therefore insist that, in a just society, basic rights and liberties be accorded what Rawls called their "fair value." For some, this requirement entails that background social and economic conditions be such that citizens enjoy equal opportunity for political influence. Others maintain that it suffices if a threshold level of political participation is feasible for everyone. On either understanding, democracy presupposes some considerable degree of equality in the distribution of those factors, including status and wealth, that affect individuals' abilities to exercise political rights.

Since deliberative democrats endorse Rousseau's commitment to the moral equality of persons, while believing, unlike Rousseau, that a rational consensus on fundamental valuational commitments is impossible, it follows that, for them, democratic processes ought to aim at compromises that respect moral equality. Since force is proscribed, the requisite meeting of minds can only be won through rational persuasion. It is at this point that the convergence between political liberalism and deliberative democracy becomes especially clear. Plato called the virtue of a thing that which allows it to perform its function well. Thus, reasonableness is the virtue of the liberal citizen. If we allow, as deliberative democrats do, that for a regime to be able legitimately to coerce its citizenry, its citizens must genuinely consent to being coerced, everyone—winners and losers—must actively endorse outcomes generated through democratic procedures. But given the ineradicable plurality of comprehensive doctrines and conceptions of the good, such endorsement is possible only if citizens are reasonable in at least one of the political liberal's senses of the term. They must be disposed to cooperate. To accord moral personality the respect it is due, citizens must want to arrive at outcomes cooperatively so much that they prefer compromise solutions reached through rational deliberation to the realization of the (pregiven) preferences they bring into the public forum.

If citizens are to be counted on to be reasonable in this sense, public deliberation and debate—public reason, as Rawls called it—must be respectful of the unavoidable differences that divide free people. Individuals' political commitments will be shaped by many factors, including their comprehensive doctrines and conceptions of the good. But, in pressing their case to others in the public arena, respect for others entails that arguments be fashioned in ways that address what citizens have in common, not what divides them. Thanks to the (putative) overlapping consensus of reasonable comprehensive doctrines, what they have in common is a commitment to the constitutional norms of the political community to which they belong. It is in these terms, then, that cases must be framed.

Thus, for the deliberative democrat, reasonableness is the virtue too of a democratic society. However, for reasonableness to flourish, citizens must evince a virtue of their own, an individual virtue—civility. Tolerance alone is not enough. All liberalisms, political or not, insist on the acceptance of diversity; some even welcome it enthusiastically. But, if public reason is to regulate public life, the form in which diversity is accepted matters. This is why deliberative democrats want citizens to treat their opponents as the moral personalities they are by addressing them in ways that acknowledge the reasonableness of the positions they hold. In this sense, democracy is a procedure, after all. But, it is not about aggregating pregiven preferences. Democracy is a procedure that aspires toward creating a rational consensus, even in the face of diversity. As such, it gives expression to the idea of political equality and the right of all citizens to equal consideration. It therefore works best when those who engage in it adhere to norms of conduct that express respect for one another. Civility helps keep conflicts in bounds and it facilitates managing them when they arise, as they inevitably will. In a word, it fosters reasonableness, the disposition to cooperate on free and equal terms.

Implementation

If civility is to be more than an estimable character trait, if it is to have political consequences, institutions must be contrived that encourage its development. Deliberative democrats therefore advocate social practices that foster it. This is why they urge individuals to adhere to the norms of public reason when they engage in public deliberations. But this insistence, by itself, is little more than an appeal for self-restraint. Citizens are enjoined to address each other in ways that abide by constitutional norms and that appeal to constitutional principles. They are told not, in any case, to make arguments that invoke considerations that others, with different comprehensive doctrines, cannot accept. Adherence to this advice can help to promote social order, but it can only go so far.

Common sense and conventional wisdom support this judgment. When individuals who disagree fundamentally are determined to get along—and especially when they are determined to get along well, by evincing respect for each other's views—it is often a bad idea for them to confront their differences directly, even if they do so civilly. Direct confrontations will seldom result in outcomes that each of the contending parties can actively endorse. More likely, they will strain relationships or lead to their dissolution. Thus, often without thinking about it, people agree to disagree; in other words, to evade contentious issues that threaten to divide them.

This is what the framers of the American Constitution tried to do. They knew that they confronted disagreements divisive enough to put the existence of the union itself in jeopardy. Slavery was the prime example. The framers dealt with it by enacting constitutional provisions that effectively removed the subject from the political arena. This strategy succeeded for more than half a century in keeping the union together. Then, as circumstances changed and opposition to slavery grew, the division between slave and free states could no longer be relegated to political oblivion. The question could only be resolved directly: not through democratic contestation, because legislative solutions were out of the question, but by war. Even allowing for the historical circumstances that shaped the founders' agreement to disagree about slavery, no deliberative democrat could endorse the settlement they reached. Slavery is incompatible with equal respect for persons; it is therefore always illegitimate. Although this particular settlement fails to pass muster and despite the fact that it served as a paradigm case, deliberative democrats support the idea that motivated it. Indeed, they raise it to the level of principle.

Here, again, it will be instructive to imagine a constitutional convention. If, for the participants, it is of preeminent importance that there be procedures that respect moral equality, and if they believe that there are fundamental but still reasonable divisions of opinion within the citizenry, then it would indeed be wise for them to remove deeply contentious issues from the legislative arena as much as they can. They should transfer the issues to an impartial judiciary with a mandate to find constitutional grounds for resolving the disputes that, despite their best efforts to suppress them, still inevitably arise.[12] They cannot relegate literally everything to a judicial branch, because the constitution writers would also realize that they must provide a space for democratic forms.

For the sake of de facto legitimacy, it must at least appear that collective choices are, to some degree, made by the people they affect. But, at the same time, the constitution writers would likely conclude that they ought not to go very far in extending the scope of collective decision making. To do so would put social unity in jeopardy. Their task, then, would be to design institutions that strike the right balance.

Where that balance is struck would depend on their assessment of the degree of social unity already in place. The framers might conclude that, apart from matters that pertain directly to individuals' rights, there is no reason, in real-world conditions, to restrict the scope of democratic collective choice in clear and infrangible ways, because there is little harm in allowing people or their representatives to legislate in most domains. On many issues, they might suppose that there actually will be a substantial measure of consensus. The question faced by voters, then, will be how best to implement their shared (or nearly shared) objectives—the very question that Rousseau thought voters would confront in the state he envisioned. And even when disagreements might threaten to pass into potentially divisive areas, the constitution writers might decide that the exercise of public reason would suffice to mitigate the dangers of untrammeled debate.

Consider the question of abortion. This is a topic on which adherents of different comprehensive doctrines, especially those associated with the major world religions, disagree. But if, as political liberals believe, these comprehensive doctrines, despite their differences, can all be brought together into an overlapping consensus substantive enough to support general constitutional principles, and if the debate about abortion can be cast in constitutional terms everyone reasonably accepts, then perhaps even this question could be admitted into the legislative arena without jeopardizing social unity based on mutual respect. It is worth recalling that in the American case, the legislative arena has not been, in the main, where questions pertaining to abortion have been decided. Legislatures have imposed their will on the margins of the abortion debate. But the basic decision to protect the right to an abortion was determined by the judicial system. If it is ever overturned, it will be the judicial system that reverses it.

The reason why the Supreme Court was right to come to the conclusion it did in the case of *Roe v. Wade*, the case that made abortion legal in the United States, is clear, even if the arguments advanced around this issue, with their emphasis on privacy rights, obfuscate the essential point. When some but not all ostensibly reasonable comprehensive doctrines enjoin restricting individuals' rights—in this case, the right of women to control their own bodies in matters pertaining to reproduction—the default position is always not to introduce the proscription. Neutrality requires this result; anything else would imply the imposition on (some) citizens of views derived from positions they reject. Thus a liberal constitution, dedicated to promoting neutrality, ought to relegate the question of abortion to individual conscience, not public policy. In deciding in favor of abortion rights, the Supreme Court justices represented themselves, not inaccurately, as interpreters of the Constitution, not as makers of new law. Of course, some abortion opponents, not liking their decision, disagree with the court. But it is telling that even they concede that the way the issue has so far been addressed is correct. It is for the courts to determine whether women have the right to have abortions. To settle this question, the courts must interpret the rules of the game to which Americans, by hypothesis, assent. It is as if everyone recognizes, wittingly or not, that the issue, being contentious, is best turned into a constitutional question because the risks to social unity of confronting it directly through democratic procedures are too great.

The U.S. Constitution does not strictly require that this issue be settled juridically. One could imagine a different history, consistent with the broad outlines of American constitutional government, according to which the courts remained silent, and the legislatures of the various states determined the outcome. This was, in fact, what was happening before *Roe v. Wade*. Recourse to the courts was a strategy pursued by all sides for their own reasons. Among them were the deliberative democrat's concerns: everyone, or nearly everyone, wanted to evade situations that might undermine social unity. However, things have not worked out that way. Constitutionalizing the issue has, if anything, exacerbated social divisions. The abortion issue, as it has evolved since *Roe v. Wade*, much like the case of slavery before the Civil War, illustrates a problem for the deliberative democratic program—that in real-world conditions, its means for advancing social unity can prove inadequate for the task.

Must We Retract Democracy to Save It?

Ultimately, social unity cannot be willed into existence. Deliberative democrats are painfully aware of this fact. And because they are—to a degree that is unusual for liberal democrats—genuinely committed to democratic values, they are—again to an unusual degree—disposed to want to shelter democratic institutions from the consequences of social divisions. This is why they would retract the scope of democratic collective choice by turning contentious issues over to the judiciary or to administrative agencies, where they can be evaded or ostensibly resolved by applying the rules of the game—or, rather, a highly interpreted version of those rules since they are almost always too indeterminate to apply literally.

This is how deliberative democrats would save democracy. Thus, despite their affinities with Rousseau and the tradition of radical democracy he inaugurated, deliberative democrats are not as friendly to democratic aspirations as may appear. But, to its credit, deliberative democracy does prescribe genuine deliberation. This fact alone, along with the background conditions necessary for making public deliberation practicable, would, if implemented, revitalize public life. The demos would be many steps further along the path to real empowerment if the deliberative democrat's ideal, or some close approximation, somehow replaced the actually existing democracy of the United States and other liberal democracies. In this sense, deliberative democracy is a progressive theory.

What makes it resonate with the ideological overtones it evinces in our time and place is therefore not so much its content as the background conditions in which it operates. In a sense, the deliberative democrat's ideal gives theoretical expression to the best face of American political institutions. It articulates a constitutional vision that, if realized, would go some considerable way toward advancing "liberty and justice for all." It celebrates the rule of law and the triumph of civility, conditions no one can fault. But in the real world of liberal democracy, especially in the United States, the conditions for realizing this vision hardly obtain. The culprit is not just reasonable pluralism. Of far greater importance is the economic structure itself, with its tendency to sort individuals out into social classes, producing social disunity systemically. In a word, capitalism makes deliberative democracy susceptible to being transformed into the ideological weapon it has become. With capitalist economic structures generating social divisions, the deliberative democrat's vision becomes every bit as utopian as Rousseau's. In these circumstances, it lends itself to employment as a snare and delusion, hiding the truth from everyone, at home and abroad, whose acquiescence to the predations of the American empire depend, in part, on believing its self-representations. Thus, so far from moving our political culture closer to its best face, making it all that it can be within its own institutional limits, the vision deliberative democrats advance, taken as an ideal that our institutions purport to approximate, sustains injustices that call for democratic redress.

Conclusion

Like political liberalism, deliberative democracy is a creature of the academy, with very little direct real-world impact. But the ideas Rawls and his followers have developed so perspicuously articulate a way of thinking about governance that is enormously influential, in part because, in existing conditions, it is useful to the interests of those who benefit most from the regime in place. It is not just that deliberative democracy puts a fine, if meretricious, face on a sordid reality. It is also that its policy implications directly serve the interests of those who benefit from the restriction of democracy's scope and depth. Because our world is one in which public opinion is a factor that our rulers must take into account, elites and their functionaries have much to gain from the pretense that our institutions approximate government of, by, and for the people. But, they have even more to gain by removing issues that matter fundamentally to them from the agenda of political contestation. In all likelihood, they can never succeed completely in this endeavor, because the de facto legitimacy of the regime from which they derive their power depends, in part, on the impression that the people rule, and it is difficult to sustain an impression that bears no connection at all to the facts on the ground. Nevertheless, in recent years, the rulers of the empire have been remarkably successful in ensuring that the only issues contested domestically are those that do not disturb their fundamental interests, however they are ultimately resolved. Deliberative democracy has come to function as the theory of this practice.

At root, the vision deliberative democratic theory promotes is the Rousseauean ideal of a community joined together by a consensus on ends, softened by a Rawlsian insistence on the (alleged) fact of reasonable pluralism. This is not an ideal that anyone with democratic sensibilities can reproach, except perhaps for its pessimism about the prospects for reaching a stronger consensus on ends. But, in a world that is far from united in the way Rousseau envisioned, a world in which social divisions are rampant and systemic, the real-world impact of the deliberative democrat's ideal has become nearly the opposite of what deliberative democrats intend. Long ago, Marx faulted Rousseau's notion of political equality by launching an attack on a descendant version of the just state Rousseau envisioned, the Hegelian *Rechtstaat*, a state grounded in universal principles of Right.[13] His contention was not that Hegel's account of universality was incoherent or undesirable. It was that the idea of Right, insofar as it came to be embodied in political institutions in a world riven by class divisions, works to the detriment of human emancipation by subordinating both the victims and the beneficiaries of the regime to a common set of laws that, thanks to background inequalities, reinforce the existing system of domination. Thus, it was not universality that Marx inveighed against, but spurious universality. His reason for opposing it had to do with its real-world effects. A similar point applies to the theory of deliberative democracy. The deliberative democrat's ideal of social unity is estimable. But with social divisions rife, deliberative democratic theory, like its Rousseauean ancestor, works to reinforce existing oppressions. In this sense, it too turns into the opposite of what it would be, if it could somehow be extracted from the world in which it operates.

To save democracy, what is needed is more democracy, not less. There is no other way to advance toward the vision the deliberative democrat embraces or, as far as feasible and desirable, to move beyond it. Ironically, this is just what deliberative democracy, or rather the way of thinking it articulates, militates against. Regardless of their intent, deliberative democrats who would retract democracy in order to save it or who advance ideas that imply that its retraction would be wise are obstacles's in democracy's way. The way to move democratic aspirations forward is to do just what the theory and practice of deliberative democracy recommends against doing. It is to expand democracy into the economic sphere, to the point that capitalism itself—the real villain—comes into question.

8

Which Way Forward?

Efficiency thinking promotes faith in inexorable economic laws and in the Invisible Hand of the market to the detriment of the visible hand of democratic deliberation and collective choice. Political liberalism and its cognate democratic theory make the restriction of public debate and collective choice a matter of principle, at the same time that they mask the substantial gulf that separates the self-representations of liberal democracies from their reality. These are reasons enough to conclude that the middle-range theories that cluster around the notions of the efficient and the reasonable are not up to the task of underwriting a practice capable of moving democracy forward—especially not into the economic sphere to the point that capitalism itself is seen as the problem for democracy that it is. To be sure, neither component of the American ideology is hostile to the kind or degree of democracy we already have. If anything, they encourage the best and most democratic aspects of our political life. But in the conditions that nowadays prevail, their most salient property is their usefulness to the beneficiaries of the system in place, elites whose power depends on keeping democracy in bounds.

Nevertheless, in view of the not inconsiderable merits of the theories that cluster around the notions of the efficient and the reasonable, one might think that there is nothing fundamentally wrong with these ideas; that the problem instead is the hypocrisy of those who invoke them for their own benefit. It would be difficult to overestimate hypocrisy's pervasiveness. Electoral institutions everywhere encourage it, nowhere more than in the United States, where the influence of moneyed interests is especially blatant and where deception and self-deception are rampant. No doubt, hypocrisy does partly explain how these offspring of the idea of Reason came to function as they do. But hypocrisy is not the whole story. I have suggested that efficiency and reasonableness are especially prone to ideological misappropriation—thanks to the distorting consequences of capitalism generally and, more particularly, to the exigencies of American capitalism today. To explain precisely how these underlying structural factors have turned good, but flawed, ideas into ideological weapons would require a close sociological and historical analysis of the real-world conditions in which these ways of thinking operate. But it is not necessary to have a fine grained understanding of how we arrived at our present situation to know what must be done to reach a more democratic conclusion. We must wrest the ideas that comprise the American ideology away from the interests they serve by retrieving what is sound in them and building a new life for them on that basis. In other words, we must rehabilitate them or—as I will say from now on—reconstruct them.

In the philosophy of the twentieth century, the term reconstruction was deployed in two distinct ways. By far the most familiar derives from the work of the logical positivists and their successors. For them, to reconstruct was to translate from a conceptual framework or discourse of one type to a discourse of another type in which everything that can be expressed in the former discourse can be restated in a more fundamental and perspicuous way. The paradigm is provided in Rudolph Carnap's *Logical Structure of the World*.[1] Using the tools of modern logic and set theory, Carnap translated talk of physical objects into a language that countenances immediate objects of sense experience only. Nowadays, the term is commonly used in a looser way, but still generally in Carnap's sense. To reconstruct a theory is to recast it in a form that renders it more susceptible than the original to rational adjudication and criticism.

The term was also used by some American pragmatists, most notably John Dewey.[2] Exactly what Dewey and the others had in mind is difficult to describe precisely. Unlike the logical positivists, they were not always disposed to define their terms carefully or to present their views in clear and unmistakable ways. But the general idea is plain enough. By way of conclusion, I will suggest that the best way forward for democrats is to reconstruct the component parts of the American ideology in this Deweyan sense.

Deweyan Reconstruction

For the Deweyan program to apply, it must be the case that received ideas meet two requirements that coexist in creative tension. The first is that the tradition in which they arose has importantly gone astray. I have tried to show that this is the case with the ideas that cluster around the notions of the efficient and the reasonable. At the same time, the tradition must contain resources sufficient for setting itself back on track. I would venture that this is also true of the American ideology. The doctrines examined in preceding chapters are therefore good candidates for reconstruction. The task, then, is to set them free from their ideological carapace and enlist them in a different project—one that serves democracy.

Key to this endeavor is the contention, articulated by Dewey and others, that in the final analysis democracy is not only a type of government, but also a form of civilization. This is also a position implicit in Rousseau's political philosophy and, therefore, in an attenuated way, in its Rawlsian descendant, deliberative democratic theory. For both Dewey and Rousseau, democracy does stand for government of, by, and for the people. But it also implies that the people constitute a community of equals joined together in a common endeavor. Thus, popular rule includes the function Hobbes identified—coordinating individuals' behaviors through the use or threat of force. But it also encompasses everything instrumental for making actual an order conducive to human flourishing in a democratic age. The objective for Dewey and Rousseau was therefore not, as it was for Hobbes, to create a minimal coercive framework sufficient for ending a war of all against all. Were citizens to stop where Hobbes recommended, individuals would be free to pursue their own disparate ends. But they would not be able to realize their destinies as free and equal beings. For that weightier goal to be achieved, Dewey, like Rousseau, thought it essential to make liberty, equality, and fraternity the cornerstones of communal life.

Dewey maintained that the emergence and development of democracy represented a breakthrough advance in what he deemed the most fundamental human activity—problem solving. Human communities face a variety of problems. To the degree that these communities differ, the problems they face differ correspondingly. To the degree that they overlap, their problems are shared. No doubt, there is more overlap than difference; especially nowadays, as capitalism, in its relentless destruction of everything that preceded it, has imposed (nearly) the same problems on everyone. Human communities are also integrated vertically, a condition that has become more significant with the progress of civilization. Today, even quite disparate peoples are joined together into ever larger communal configurations, culminating ultimately in the human community itself. To the degree that vertical integration is a fact of human life, the problems individuals and groups confront become increasingly common to all. Even so, distinct communities will have their own ways of dealing with their problems and their own particular solutions. But, for democratic communities, the way forward is, in all cases, the same: it is to put the intelligence of free and equal human beings to work together in an effort to change the world. Dewey insisted that there is no better way for human beings to solve the problems they share.

Rousseau pressed a similar point. For him, there is only one possible social contract, but the ways in which it can be implemented are as diverse as the populations that comprise the human race. Governmental forms and other institutional arrangements would, in his view, vary widely in just states—in consequence of the different traditions and circumstances of their respective citizenries. Still, in all cases, because there is ultimately only one social contract, the ways that collective solutions to problems, universal or not, would become manifest would be through a collective choice rule that respects the moral equality of persons. This procedure is necessary for de jure legitimacy, but it is also, at the same time, a condition for its possibility. Thus, just as democratic procedures, in the fullest sense of the term, guarantee that individuals, in placing themselves under the supreme direction of the general will remain free (autonomous), they turn individuals into the free and equal members of democratic communities that they must be for democracy to be more than a notional possibility.

What we must strive to do, then, is to enlist citizens in the project of implementing the values that we have come to recognize as truest to our natures and therefore to our common interests. These are the values embraced and propagated by the historical Left—liberty, equality, and fraternity. Insofar as there is a collective will to make them actual—to embody them in institutions and in ordinary human interactions—and insofar as the tradition has resources capable of doing so, there is, potentially, a democratic objective already in place around which human communities in all of their various configurations can coalesce. This is what Dewey and the others had in mind. The task, as they saw it, is to democratize the world we have inherited, not out of nothing, but out of the materials that progress has put at our disposal. Thus, Deweyan reconstruction is a bootstrapping operation. Unlike revolution, which aims to overthrow old regimes and then to build new worlds on their ashes, reconstruction supposes that what is already in place, flawed as it may be, provides the best basis for moving ahead.

So conceived, reconstruction is a liberal undertaking. It is liberal not just because it is committed to tolerance or to neutrality on the part of public, coercive institutions. It is liberal because it is part of an ongoing political tradition that, building on the doctrine of limited sovereignty, developed into a full-fledged political tendency in the aftermath of the French Revolution. *That* liberalism was, from the beginning, friendly to many of the causes the French revolutionaries advanced. But, it was hostile to the theory and practice of revolution itself. It was dedicated instead to permanent reform, to change—sometimes substantial, more usually incremental—imposed from above. Post-Revolutionary liberalism embraced the notion of progress implicit in contemporaneous understandings of the Revolution the liberals (ambivalently) disavowed. But, unlike the more radical revolutionaries in France and their successors in the socialist movements that emerged in the nineteenth century, post-Revolutionary liberals were dedicated to changing the world from the top down, within the framework of existing legal and institutional structures. For them, the agent of change ought always to be enlightened leaders, not insurrectionary masses. These leaders would engineer improvements in accord with a design that was more or less worked out, but in a piecemeal way; not, like revolutionaries, by taking on the old regime in its totality.

Despite this dedication to change imposed from the top down, post-Revolutionary liberalism was more continuous with socialism than is generally assumed. Both political tendencies agreed on ultimate objectives—they wanted to enhance liberty, equality, and fraternity to the greatest extent possible. From the moment it first appeared, liberalism has stood for liberty. Since the Revolution, it has stood for equality and fraternity too. Its purchase on these notions has not always been recognizably continuous with Revolutionary and later socialist understandings. But, it was still robust enough to make post-Revolutionary liberalism a part of the historical Left, albeit of the Left's right wing.

This was the tradition Dewey joined and substantially transformed. It was his view that, more than a century after the French Revolution, American society was already somewhat democratic.[3] In these circumstances, Dewey concluded that the alternative to permanent revolution was no longer just permanent reform imposed by enlightened leaders. There was another way. That way involved building on the foundations of what had already been achieved, by joining people together to enhance the democracy they already enjoyed. Dewey's liberalism falls within the liberal tradition in the sense that it is a non- and even antirevolutionary doctrine. However, he adapted the thinking of his predecessors to the unprecedented circumstances of the world in which he lived. His liberalism was the liberalism of permanent reform—reconstructed.

Rousseau's aim was not very different from Dewey's. They both wanted to overcome conflicts of private interests with a view to joining citizens together in a common, democratic project. Neither is Dewey's insistence on the efficacy of creative intelligence all that different from the understanding of public deliberation and collective choice advanced by Rousseau. His idea was that collectively citizens should endeavor to solve the problems they confront—though deliberative means, but also in ways less immediately connected to questions of governance. For this strategy to work there must already be a general disposition on the part of the citizenry to address their problems in ways that do not privilege particular interests, but that look instead to the good of the whole community. Dewey believed that this was already the case, at least to some degree, in the America of his time. Rousseau was of a very different mind about his own and other European societies. This is why he relegated general will deliberation to a (notional) just state. He seems to have believed that Europe was so corrupted by civilization that the prospects for instituting the sovereignty of the general will there were almost nil. The only exceptions were territories whose inhabitants had managed to remain close to their primitive condition—Corsica being the example upon which he lavished the most attention.[4] Dewey turned Rousseau on his head. For Rousseau, the encroachments of civilization undermined the prospects for the full fruition of democratic ideals. For Dewey, the progress of civilization had the opposite effect. It laid the foundations for a democratic order, encompassing the entire demos, capable of pulling itself up collectively by its own bootstraps to a place where the values he and Rousseau shared could finally govern human affairs.[5]

My aim, in preceding chapters, was to scrutinize the ideas that comprise the American ideology by analyzing some of their principal features and tracing their roots. There is still a great deal of philosophical and genealogical work of this kind to do. There are also sociological and historical investigations to undertake to account for how these ideas have so to speak, gone bad. Their reconstruction is yet another, more urgent matter. To that end, it is necessary, first, to determine what is retrievable in the American ideology. I will conclude by offering a few general thoughts on this question.

Democratizing the Economic Sphere

The tradition of thought that underlies efficiency thinking has never outgrown its origins in utilitarian philosophy; not even as it transformed itself into the very different, analytical framework within which Smith's Invisible Hand conjecture was finally established. Even now, with the neoclassical model partially superseded by economic theories that take account of market incompletenesses and information asymmetries, the connection with utilitarianism remains. The utilitarian's core idea—that institutional arrangements, economic and otherwise, are justified to the extent that they advance the well-being of the individuals they affect—is still intact. Thus, even as the actively promoted claim that there is no alternative to the current domestic and international agenda of the American Right is heard everywhere, the theory that underlies this unhappy, and unnecessary, assessment still implies that economic and social institutions only exist to further well-being. This is true even for adherents of philosophical views expressly opposed to utilitarianism. Perhaps the most antiutilitarian social philosophers today are those libertarians who, following Locke's lead, believe that there are premoral property rights that institutions must accommodate at all costs.[6] It is noteworthy that even they acknowledge that, so long as property rights are respected, institutions should maximize welfare overall by making individuals as well off as they can be.

It would be fair to say that the conviction that institutions should be welfare-enhancing has become second nature. It is certainly the default position in ongoing policy deliberations: the rule that dictates outcomes when no contravening considerations trump it. But it is not obviously true and it has not always governed thinking about economic and social life. For the intuition underlying utilitarianism to have become hegemonic, it first required that those who think about policy matters philosophically adopt the distinctively modern understanding that what matters, ultimately, in justifying social and political arrangements are the interests of the individuals they affect, and then that the right way to attend to individuals' interests is to maximize interest satisfaction overall. These positions have become part of our intellectual legacy to a degree that, for good or ill, they operate almost spontaneously. At some future time, if more robust understandings of Reason in society again assert themselves, it might be necessary to rethink them and perhaps even to try to dislodge their hold. But, for now and the foreseeable future, they are good enough to work with. A reconstructed democratic theory ought to build upon them.

It ought also to welcome the policy implications of the new, information centered paradigm. We have seen that state interventions into the workings of market economies are necessary to counter the effects of market incompletenesses and information asymmetries. Democratic citizens, deploying their collective intelligence creatively, will probably want to accord a significant role to markets nevertheless. However, it is unlikely, in light of what is now understood, that they will allow markets to operate without extensive and direct public oversight, as if a beneficent Invisible Hand could better serve human interests than human beings themselves when they employ their intelligence collectively and with regard for the public good. It has long been a mainstay of mainstream policy thinking that markets, by themselves, cannot address equity concerns satisfactorily. We now know that the Invisible Hand cannot be counted on, in real-world conditions, even to enhance efficiency. Public authorities must intervene, not just to trade off equity and efficiency, but to promote efficiency itself.

This conclusion raises the prospect of a more radical democratization of the economic sphere than most twentieth-century theorists, including market socialists and defenders of central planning, were prepared to defend. On the understanding that the best social science forces upon us, it no longer makes sense to imagine that a blind mechanism—the self-regulating market—will enhance efficiency if only interferences with its workings are minimized or eliminated or, as socialists intended, mimicked. What equity requires has always been considered a matter for the public to decide. It now seems that what the state ought to do to enhance efficiency is too. Once everything is thrown into the same cauldron, policy deliberations can bear on the entire range of topics affected by production, distribution, and exchange; everything economic becomes susceptible to the problem solving intelligence of an engaged citizenry, pursuing democratic ends. In these circumstances, planning would almost certainly come back in—not the kind of planning, replete with perverse incentives, that has become discredited, but planning that addresses pertinent principal-agent problems creatively. For as long as the Soviet Union served as a model, plans were deemed alternatives to markets. The way is now clear to overcome this "untenable dualism," as Dewey might have called it, by joining markets and plans together in unprecedented and largely uncharted ways.

The point is not just to democratize planning, however important that may be. It is to transcend the parameters of the old debate. The old discussion focused on the efficiency advantages and shortcomings of these ways of coordinating economic affairs. In that context, the question of the relevance of markets and plans to solving the problems real people confront became obscured, as the contending sides focused on formal aspects of their respective cases. This way of looking at the economy did lead to important breakthroughs and to the development of useful methods of economic analysis. It also turned attention away from facts on the ground that highly abstract and stylized models do little to explain. A more pragmatic approach would not ignore questions of intellectual coherence or denigrate demonstrations of formal cogency. But it would not focus on these aspects of economic theorizing to the exclusion of everything else. What matters, in the end, is what advances the values efficiency thinking presupposes. This focus is easily deflected. It must be kept ever in mind.

I would hazard, finally, that reconstructing this component of the American ideology is bound to put existing property relations in question. Reconstruction would therefore renew, in a different context and perhaps in a different guise, the old contest between socialism and capitalism. How that debate, if and when it is engaged again, will unfold cannot be predicted with certainty. But it is plain that there is little reason for supporting untrammeled private control and revenue rights over productive resources. Some form of social property is almost certain, therefore, to come back onto the agenda and with it, a revival of the venerable struggle of the Left to transform capitalism into a radically different economic order.

Reconstructing Rawls

The virtues of reasonableness and civility plainly have a role to play in a fully realized democratic order; a fact that ought to weigh on the deliberations of a pragmatically minded, democratic citizenry. In societies like our own, where these virtues are honored, in word if not always in deed, they can be important too, not just for their own sake but also for moving from where we now are to where we want to go. Incivility can become an issue in its own right, a distraction that impedes constructive change. But incivility can also have the opposite effect. Especially in the United States, where the political class is bent on pursuing a project of world domination by any means necessary, moral outrage is frequently the only appropriate response. Sometimes it is the most efficacious response too. In real-world conditions, it is sometimes necessary to breach the rules of the game in indecorous ways even to be heard and certainly to have any hope of forcing the regime to change course. To imply, as political liberalism and deliberative democratic theory do, that individuals ought to act here and now in the ways that they should in less outrageous circumstances is, often, to reinforce the conditions that adherents of these doctrines oppose.

There is more to the Rawlsian legacy than the virtues it promotes. Rawls and his successors want to join the Rousseauean tradition in political philosophy with the dominant strain of liberal theory and practice, the strain that privileges tolerance and neutrality on the part of coercive public institutions. Some of the positions Rawls developed in the course of executing this project are problematic. But it is an eminently worthwhile objective; one that reconstructers of democratic theory would almost certainly want to adopt. To this end, Rawls's work provides an indispensable starting point. Not just because of its perspicuity, but because Rousseauean thought, untempered by Rawls's concerns, can have powerfully illiberal consequences.

Rousseau's illiberalism can and has helped to nurture tyrannies even more detrimental to the values he promoted than the regime the American ideology sustains today. The reason why is clear.[7] To the extent that political legitimacy depends on a consensus on ends, whatever imperils consensus formation is a threat to legitimacy. Rousseau therefore wanted differences minimized, not welcomed in the way that liberals recommend. To this end, he thought it important to suppress the formation of social groups. Individual particularities are bad enough. Group identifications are worse, because communities within communities deflect citizens away from the communal identification indispensable for de jure legitimacy. They function as alternatives to what Rousseau called "the whole community" (of undifferentiated citizens). Rousseau was worried most about groupings based on status and wealth. This concern extended back into the feudal past and forward into the capitalist future. For Rousseau knew well that economies based on private property and market exchange generate systemic differences unrelentingly—class differences. Since he defended private property and markets—or, more precisely, since he saw no workable alternative to them—he concluded that a just state would have to take positive steps to nullify their effects. In practice, these measures are bound to be illiberal, touching on some of the most fundamental political freedoms. Rousseau also advocated uses of state power that are patently nonneutral. Conceding that only so much can be done to counter the tendency of civil society (in private property regimes) to draw people apart, he insisted that the effects of the economic and social order on opinion be countered by a state organized offensive. Thus, the state Rousseau envisioned would take charge of everything affecting opinion, from education to religion to the organization of public spectacles intended to promote patriotism and virtue. Since even these interventions would be insufficient, it would also have at its disposal a coercive apparatus for repressing ideas at odds with the general will.

Before the French Revolution, these measures and others in a similar vein might have seemed plausible to democrats. In the twenty-first century, they no longer can. To have any chance of success, Rousseau's political program requires leaders with (nearly) unrestricted power and with the steadfastness of will and purity of spirit not to succumb to its temptations—leaders who are incorruptible. During the most radical phase of the French Revolution, Robespierre and his fellow Jacobins, inspired by Rousseau, aspired to fulfill these obligations. They failed and were overthrown. Their successors' failures, in the Soviet Union and elsewhere, were even more palpable and damaging to Left ideals. It is now clear that any political program, no matter how radical, that is not also liberal has no chance of gaining adherents and even less of leading to outcomes that genuinely do respect the moral equality of persons. A principled accommodation to the fact of reasonable pluralism and, along with it, support for tolerance and neutrality has become mandatory for any future Left.

The task today is to build on the theoretical resources Rawlsians have provided, without succumbing to their illusions about the pacificity and overall beneficence of American capitalism and of American political institutions. Since political liberal and deliberative democratic ideas articulate, in an unusually perspicacious way, the theory and practice of American constitutional government, this is tantamount to saying that the task is to take over what is genuinely democratic and also liberal in our political culture, in order to concoct a more thoroughly democratic civilization on that basis. This is what Dewey envisioned for the more inchoate strands of liberal and democratic thought of his own time. Any serious attempt at democratic reconstruction, attuned to contemporary social, political, and economic realities would assume a similar posture.

There is an important caveat, however. Like Rousseau and like many of Dewey's contemporaries, Dewey was cognizant of class inequalities. He was also sensitive to the problems faced by immigrant populations. But, like almost everyone else in his time and place, he was inclined to ignore the legacies of slavery and manifest destiny and the problems women faced in patriarchal societies. It would be an exaggeration to say that he saw only the bright side of his America. But some of his country's most profound and damaging faults did elude his attention. Today, with imperialist ambitions waxing large, American democrats must do better. The traditions Americans inherit are estimable in many ways, as much now as a century ago. But these traditions have also sustained ways of thinking and acting that must be confronted, denounced, and excised. This is what reconstruction calls for. To execute the project Dewey launched, we must become more Deweyan than Dewey himself. We must not only build on what we have inherited; we must ruthlessly and unapologetically discard everything in it that works to the detriment of our ideals.

What Is to Be Done?

To the extent that the American ideology has creditable aspects, as it plainly does, it is susceptible to being reconstructed. But for this project to succeed, a *Gestalt* change must occur. To carry the project of reconstruction forward, we must be prepared to act on the belief the American ideology militates against: that democracy can and should breed more democracy. This conviction implies that we work to ensure that the democratic processes we already have be as unfettered as possible by our governing institutions, and that we then deploy our problem solving intelligence, individually and collectively, to deepen and extend democracy's scope into the sphere of production, distribution, and exchange. In a word, we should endeavor to turn neoliberal economic doctrine on its head. Its proponents argue for self-regulating markets, free from state interferences (except those that further their own interests). Disingenuously but zealously, they advocate laissez-faire in modern dress. This prescription, we know, is based on a needlessly attenuated conception of Reason in society and on an illusory faith in the workings of real-world market arrangements. Democrats evince a more reasonable faith in self-regulating democratic polities. To advance fundamental human interests, they would rely on an enlightened demos—on people adept at finding their own collective way and should they go astray, at correcting their own course.

To see that faith vindicated in the future, it is imperative, here and now, to struggle against all those policies the American ideology sustains that impede or distort the spontaneously democratizing tendencies present already in the existing order. Some of these impedances are institutional—winner-take-all electoral systems, for example, and constitutional and statutory provisions that violate the principle of one person, one vote. Of particular salience, in the American case, is the virtual abdication by Congress of its constitutional authority, not only in matters of war and peace, but in other areas too, including almost everything that bears on so-called national security and homeland defense. In recent years, in the absence of concerted opposition, the presidency has assumed many of the powers constitutionally allotted to the legislative branch. This phenomenon must be resisted. More generally, the revitalization of institutions that give the people voice ought to be high on the agenda of any social movement intent on moving democracy forward. In reconstructing the American ideology, this exigency should be borne ever in mind.

The main problems facing our polity, the road blocks that must be removed first, are the factors that allow economic inequalities, objectionable in their own right, to spill over into the political sphere, impeding even distant approximations of that equality of political influence that deliberative democratic theory celebrates. Moneyed interests have always been with us; they have always threatened what little democracy we have. But, their power has grown in recent years. There are many reasons why this has happened. High on the list, in the American case, is the fact that the judiciary, the model for so much that Rawlsians admire, has blocked far-reaching efforts to control the financing of electoral campaigns—not so much for principled reasons, but in ways that belie the faith political liberals and deliberative democrats express for the vaunted independence of those assigned the task of ascertaining the rules of the game. Today, the United States, more than at any time in the past, has a political class beholden, almost entirely, not to the people who elect them, but to those "malefactors of great wealth," as they were known in Dewey's time, who finance their campaigns. Meanwhile, the unprecedented concentration of media ownership, in conjunction with the exponential growth of media influence over daily life, has narrowed the political agenda to a remarkable degree. The American ruling class has always been adept at suppressing dissent without relying, as their counterparts in police states do, on overt repression. But never has the range of mainstream discourse been more constricted than it now is. In Rawlsian theory, the reasonable encompasses nearly everything that is not plainly delusional. In the real world of American politics, almost everything that fails to accord with the interests of the few who run the show is relegated to the margins of political life—as if it, not mainstream political discourse, were wildly at odds with overwhelming evidence and common sense. It would be no exaggeration to say that our political life is locked into a delusional state. Or, to turn from a Freudian to an Hegelian idiom, we might say that we are in a situation where the actual is the (metaphorical) inverse of the real. It is urgent that we break out of this miasma and that we reintroduce transparency and intellectual honesty into our political life.

*   *   *

The American ideology helps to sustain this unhappy state of affairs. It is therefore part of the problem. Reconstructing it can be part of the solution. But it must be a radical reconstruction, joined integrally to the larger reconstruction of the entire social order. To that end, it is well past time to rest content with the conceptions of Reason in society that nourish efficiency thinking and Rawlsian liberalism. Efficiency and reasonableness are too insubstantial, as normative standards and as ideals, to propel a robustly democratic vision forward. For democracy's sake, the idea of Reason must be paid its due, in both theory and practice.

Only then can the collective intelligence of democratic citizens be freed from the integuments of the American ideology and the remnants of that ideological configuration, the part that is sound, be put to work addressing the increasingly serious problems Americans confront and the potentially devastating problems American economic and military power poses for the world.

Incurable romantics will find this a less inspiring prospect than the centuries old revolutionary call to build a new, more rational order on the ashes of the old. But it will almost certainly involve as profound a transformation of the old regime. Revolutions destroy in order to rebuild. There is much that ought to be destroyed, but wisdom dictates caution, lest events run out of control, as they do in revolutionary situations. Revolution can be a way to move history forward; but it is a fitful way, prone to long and sometimes permanent setbacks. In any case, the revolutionary movement that began in the seventeenth century and continued into the twentieth is now almost certainly off the historical agenda. With the fall of the Soviet Union and the social system it spawned, changes that were once thought irreversible have been reversed, casting discredit on the most ostensibly successful of the revolutionary ventures of the past century. Moreover, it has been plain for many decades that there is no longer any hope of consolidating a class with "radical chains," as Marx put it, capable of changing society radically and for the better. Oppression is everywhere on the rise. But there is no agent of revolutionary change, strategically located within the old regime, able and willing to install new, freer social relations to replace those under which so many suffer. In Marx's time, the nascent proletariat could plausibly be thought to occupy such a position and therefore to have the historical mission Marx imputed to it. Today, the workers of the world, especially those in the imperial center, have a good deal more to lose than their chains. In consequence, few of them have any inclination to assume the risks attendant upon assaulting entrenched power. Indeed, the overwhelming majority no longer have any desire to change the world fundamentally at all. Decades ago, it was believed by some that there were forces in the Third World that could take their place. No one believes that now. In retrospect, Third Worldism appears to have been yet another illusion. Revolution is off the agenda, not just because past revolutionary ventures have ended in profound disappointment, but because the prospect of revolutionary change now seems plainly unfeasible.

On the other hand, reconstruction is eminently feasible, notwithstanding the often repeated shibboleth that there is no alternative to the world the American ideology is invoked to defend. The reconstruction of middle-range theories clustering around the notions of the efficient and the reasonable can help this larger, world transforming project to take shape. It can begin right away. The theories in question are vulnerable to criticism on their own terms, as well as from perspectives outside their conceptual horizons. But they also contain a great deal that democrats can retrieve and build upon. In the spirit of Dewey and his cothinkers, the task is to refashion what is salvageable in them into something radically different and better—something more attuned to human needs and therefore more in line with what Reason, our longest standing and most bedrock normative standard, requires.

Notes

Introduction

1. It would not be unfair to surmise that it is because political liberalism developed and matured in the decades when the U.S. judiciary was, for the most part, on the side of the angels that political liberals take an especially sanguine view of this branch of government.

Chapter 1. Reason

1. The nature of the difference, if any, between morality and rationality is a philosophical question. Morality is best understood as a deliberative attitude: one that enjoins us, in those circumstances where it is appropriate, to do what the Golden Rule commands—"to do unto others as we would have others do unto ourselves." It requires that, in our deliberations, we abstract away whatever distinguishes ourselves from others and take into account only what we have in common. The moral point of view is one of generality or impartiality. It is agent neutral in the sense that it adopts no particular deliberative vantage point, not even the vantage point of the deliberator. To deliberate morally, then, is to deliberate from the point of view of agency as such. Immanuel Kant, perhaps the greatest moral philosopher in the history of Western philosophy, in consequence of protracted investigations of moral deliberation and of reason in its application to action, concluded that morality just is rationality. However, not all philosophers agree. It should also be noted that there are normative standards besides rationality and morality—aesthetic standards, for example.

2. Because rational arguments, like moral arguments, are objective in this sense, Kant ultimately identified these ostensibly different normative standards. (See Note 1).

3. Ironically, in view of its dedication to Reason, Socrates' position resembles that of the early Christian martyrs. For different reasons than his—because they were taught "to render unto Caesar the things that are Caesar's, and unto God, the things that are God's"—Christians were obliged not to resist those authorities who commanded them to transgress their faith, but also not to accede to their commands. Thus the early Christians, like Socrates, thought themselves obliged

to obey the authorities in all cases but this one and, in no case, to challenge existing authorities (Christian or pagan) in any way. They therefore believed, like Socrates, that when ordered to do what their faith would not allow, they had no choice but to disobey and then resign themselves to the punishment— almost always death—that the authorities chose to visit upon them.

4. Like efficiency and reasonableness, diversity is another good idea gone bad—not entirely, but enough to warrant skepticism wherever it is invoked. However, unlike those other ideas, diversity has little directly to do with maintaining American capitalism or projecting its influence globally. It functions more at a psychological level—among the remnants of the Left (or, more precisely, the New Left)—enabling erstwhile radicals who endorse it to reconcile themselves to their roles in running the leading institutions of the state and civil society. In the United States, the call for diversity is especially evident in university milieus, in the media, and in Democratic Party circles. Supporting diversity enables former militants for radical causes to think of themselves, despite everything, as still true to their original calling. Less disingenuously, the term is also advocated by far-sighted adherents of the (respectable) Right for its usefulness in promoting competitiveness and social stability. It should surprise no one that similar considerations are advanced by erstwhile Leftists too. Support for diversity is one thing; its actual implementation is something else. Hypocrisy engulfs the celebrations of diversity that proliferate throughout the political landscape, as its purported beneficiaries cannot fail to notice.

5. The connections are particularly evident in Marxist theory and practice. Marx combined a vision of ideal (rational) institutional arrangements with an account of history's internal dynamic, according to which the agents of Reason were "the wretched of the earth" or, more precisely, the proletariat—the direct producers of wealth in capitalist societies who, in the words of the old labor song "Solidarity Forever," stand "outcast and starving, midst the wonders [they] have made," and who therefore, as Marx and Engels proclaimed in *The Communist Manifesto,* "have nothing to lose but their chains."

6. There is a strain of recent scholarship, motivated in part by anti-Eurocentric thinking, which purports to deconstruct received understandings of the West by focusing on African and Asian sources of Hellenic culture. The best known example is Martin Bernal's *Black Athena: The Afroasiatic Roots of Classical Civilization,* Vol. 1: The Fabrication of Ancient Greece 1785–1985 (New Brunswick, NJ: Rutgers University Press, 1987). The scholarship underlying Bernal's work has been extensively criticized. See, for example, the papers collected in Mary R. Lefkowitz and Guy MacLean Rogers, *Black Athena Revisited* (Chapel Hill, NC: The University of North Carolina Press, 1996). But his central point—that the idea of the West is, to some considerable extent, an ideologically motivated and intellectually untenable social construction—remains intact. However, this claim hardly impugns the idea of Reason. If ancient Greece was more a part of Asia and Africa than those who concocted the idea of the West maintained, then, the idea of Reason is less a distinctively Western idea than anti-Eurocentrists suppose. Then to the degree that it matters where it came from or where it took root early on, the validity of the idea would be enhanced. However, this inference is as otiose as it is contrary. Where and when the idea of Reason arose, and by whose hands, does not matter one way or the other.

7. This is the position taken by Richard Rorty. See, for example, *Philosophy and the Mirror of Nature* (Princeton, NJ: Princeton University Press, 1979) and *Contingency, Irony and Solidarity* (Cambridge and New York: Cambridge University Press, 1989).

Chapter 2. Ideology

1. Max Weber, Talcott Parsons, trans., *The Protestant Ethic and the Spirit of Capitalism* (New York: Charles Scribner's Sons, 1958). This work was originally published in 1904–1905 as a two-part article in the *Archiv für Sozialwissenschaft und Sozialpolitik*.

2. Readers interested in Marx's position should consult G.A. Cohen, "Restricted and Inclusive Historical Materialism," reprinted in *History, Labour and Freedom: Themes from Marx* (Oxford: Oxford University Press, 1988) and Erik Olin Wright, Andrew Levine, and Elliott Sober, *Reconstructing Marxism* (London & NY: Verso, 1992), Chapter 5.

3. See, for example, Noam Chomsky and Edward Herman, *Manufacturing Consent: The Political Economy of the Mass Media* (New York: Pantheon, 1988) and John C. Stauber, *Toxic Sludge is Good for You: Lies, Damn Lies and the Public Relations Industry* (Monroe, ME: Common Courage Press, 1995).

4. Their asceticism is not, however, the only reason that capitalists consume proportionately less of the economic surplus than, say, feudal lords. It is also relevant that there is much more surplus to consume, thanks to the expansion of productive capacities under capitalism. Thus, even if capitalists generally consume more than, say, feudal lords in an absolute sense, as they surely do (by most plausible measures), they consume less proportionately.

5. It is important to bear in mind that the capitalism Weber described was classical capitalism—not the capitalism of the late twentieth or early twenty-first centuries. Weber's capitalists would be appalled by the behavior of their counterparts in contemporary consumerist societies. But contemporary capitalism is overripe, because, contrary to most contemporaneous expectations (including Weber's), capitalism was able to survive even after it had outlived its usefulness for fostering economic growth. To nearly everyone's surprise, it succeeded in fighting back revolutionary challenges. Thus, under capitalism's aegis, productive capacities have developed beyond the point at which the spirit of capitalism is instrumental for addressing the previously compelling human interest in further development. Thanks to capitalism's own success, enough wealth already exists to make forms of economic life that are more compatible with human nature—with what we might think of as a natural human desire for spontaneous enjoyment and freedom from burdensome toil—possible. Thus, with capitalism having survived beyond the point where it is necessary for growth, the spirit of capitalism became increasingly irrational in a somewhat different sense from the one Weber intended. Because postclassical capitalist societies have too much productive capacity— not in the sense that human beings have everything they want or need, but in the sense that capitalist property relations cannot accommodate further growth without augmenting demand beyond the limits imposed by need or spontaneous desire—worldly asceticism has become counterproductive. This is why, nowadays, instilling demands for products no one living in a society more consonant with human nature would want, has become indispensable for capitalism's survival. Along with nonproductive and wasteful spending, consumerism has become a pillar of our postclassical or late capitalist order.

6. It is therefore not surprising that monasticism has been, at most, only a marginal phenomenon in the Protestant tradition.

Chapter 3. Means-End Rationality

1. Hobbes inveighed against Aristotelean understandings of causality most famously in *De Corpore*: 15:3.

2. Thomas Hobbes, *The Leviathan* (1651).

3. Max Weber, "Politics as a Vocation" in Hans H. Gerth and C. Wright Mills, Eds., *From Max Weber: Essays in Sociology* (Oxford: Oxford University Press, 1958).

4. External relations contrast with internal relations. Being a brother is an internal relation because an individual cannot be a brother except in relation to another individual, the one whose brother he is. Hobbes would not deny that internal relations exist in a state of nature. Even there, some individuals are brothers. However, Hobbes would say that in the state of nature—and in real-world political communities too, because the state of nature is just the actual world with political authority relations and all their effects subtracted away—such internal relations as there may be have nothing to do with what makes individuals the individuals they are.

5. Socrates denied the possibility of going wrong in this last way, insisting that failing to act on one's own true ends is always a consequence of failing to know what one's true ends are. Aristotle disagreed. After Aristotle, the reality of the phenomenon he called *akrasia,* "weakness of will," has been widely accepted in philosophical circles. Without entering into a discussion of this condition—one that Aristotle and Socrates both acknowledged, but then described and accounted for differently—it is fair to observe that the judgment that Aristotle was right and Socrates wrong accords with widespread intuitions about what is the case. Perhaps these intuitions are as they are because Aristotle's distinction between theoretical and practical reason, a distinction unknown to Socrates or Plato, has won the day. Or perhaps it is because, regardless of philosophical assumptions, the idea that the will can be weak, not just ill informed, seems to capture a phenomenon we have all encountered in ourselves and in others.

6. Thomas Hobbes, *The Leviathan,* Chapter 14.

7. G.E. Moore, *Principia Ethica* (Cambridge and New York: Cambridge University Press, 1903) and *Ethics* (Oxford: Oxford University Press, 1912).

8. Had Pareto realized that utilitarians need not identify the good with a conscious state, the measurement problems he thought fatal to utilitarianism would not immediately go away. What would it mean, for example, to measure desire-satisfaction interpersonally? What metric would be appropriate for comparing degrees of directly apprehended goodness? Perhaps one could motivate interpersonal comparisons of objective conditions in a way that would avoid Pareto's Cartesian concerns, especially if these conditions are conceived in a way that makes no essential reference to individuals' states of mind. But even though this prospect is available to utilitarians, the utilitarian welfare economists who were Pareto's principal adversaries knew nothing of it. As Pareto supposed, they were basically of the same view as Bentham.

9. Similarly, temperature measures heat by assigning cardinal numbers to different heat levels. Were the numbers assigned arbitrarily, the resulting measurements would be of no interest. It was therefore an achievement of some moment when, for example, Fahrenheit succeeded in assigning cardinal numbers to differences in heat levels in a theoretically well motivated way. It is worth noting that temperature measurement is less demanding than utility measurement. Unlike utilities, temperatures are not additive. When you combine, say, a substance at 10 degrees Fahrenheit with another at 20 degrees Fahrenheit, you do not get 30 degrees of temperature on the Fahrenheit scale. On the other hand, the difference between, say, 80 degrees Fahrenheit and 70 degrees Fahrenheit is in a theoretically meaningful sense the same as the difference between 30 degrees and 20 degrees. In this respect, temperature measurement is more like intrapersonal utility measurement than like utility measurement *tout court.*

10. Public goods provision is an example. See Chapter 4.
11. The classic account is R. Duncan Luce and Howard Raiffa, *Games and Decisions: Introduction and Critical Survey* (New York: John Wiley and Sons, 1957).
12. Adam Smith, *The Wealth of Nations* (New York: The Modern Library, 1937). Originally published in 1776.

Chapter 4. The Invisible Hand

1. The emphasis economists and others nowadays give to getting incentives right is compatible with Weber's account of the genesis of the spirit of capitalism (see Chapter 2). It is only beings imbibed with that spirit—or individuals who are already equipped with the motivational structures economic theory presupposes—who will be disposed to respond to the incentives economists discuss.
2. Because real-world economies are dynamic and not divided into discrete trading cycles—in other words, because there is no actual time at which trading begins or ends—the idea of an initial distribution, much like the idea of a general equilibrium, is a theoretical abstraction.
3. Precisely what counts as a harm can be controversial. The basic idea is that individuals are harmed whenever nontrivial interests of theirs are infringed in ways that are deleterious to their well-being. Because it is unclear what interests ought to count in identifying instances of harm, the concept invites endless debate. Even so, the general idea is clear enough. With respect to control rights, for example, if I own an automobile, I can do what I want with it. I can even destroy it, if I choose. But I cannot rightfully run anyone over with it or burn it in a way that sets off toxic fumes that others are likely to breathe.
4. See, especially, W.W. Bartley III, Ed., *Fatal Conceit: The Errors of Socialism* (Chicago: University of Chicago Press, 1989); Peter G. Klein, Ed., *Fortunes of Liberalism: Essays on Austrian Economics, and the Ideal of Freedom* (Chicago: University of Chicago Press, 1997); and *New Studies in Philosophy, Politics, Economics and the History of Ideas* (Chicago: University of Chicago Press, 1978). Hayek's best known works include *The Constitution of Liberty* (Chicago: University of Chicago Press, 1960) and *The Road to Serfdom* (Chicago: University of Chicago Press, 1944).
5. Thomas Hobbes, *The Leviathan*, Chapter 14.
6. For a similar reason, the efficiency of outcomes is put in jeopardy by the existence of monopsonies, situations in which there are very few (or, at the limit, only one) purchasers for particular goods or services.
7. Insofar as market socialists maintained that, with socialist property relations, closer approximations of the general equilibrium model could be obtained, their arguments too are put in jeopardy by the shortcomings of the general equilibrium model. See Joseph E. Stiglitz, *Whither Socialism?* (Cambridge, MA: MIT Press, 1995). However, market socialism was never more than a marginal strain of socialist theory. This is why the general equilibrium model never functioned ideologically for elites in self-described socialist regimes in quite the way that it does for elites in capitalist countries.

Chapter 5. Efficiency as Ideology

1. See Sigmund Freud, *The Future of an Illusion* in James Strachey, Ed., *The Standard Edition of the Complete Psychological Works of Sigmund Freud*, Vol. 21 (London: Hogarth Press and the Institute of Psycho-Analysis, 1961).
2. See chapter 4. Whenever individuals or groups—principals—rely on other indi-

viduals or groups—agents—they must somehow get their agents to do their will. They then face a principal-agent problem. In contrast to feudal or slave societies, principal-agent problems under capitalism—and socialism—are usually addressed without overt coercion, through the establishment of appropriate incentive structures.

3. The Soviet model derived more from the experience of Germany's economy during the First World War than from Marxist or other economic theories. For a long time, it was a commonly accepted, mainstream belief that planning bests markets when, as in war time conditions, there is an urgent need to increase production of relatively few products—tanks and guns, for example, or steel and basic foodstuffs. The problem comes when there are many production targets. Then the inability to get pricing decisions right becomes disabling.

4. Wage inequalities would still remain; though it could also be state policy to flatten wage differences. Or a state might attempt to advance equality in other ways—for example, by providing an unconditional basic income to each of its citizens. This option is available both under capitalism and under socialism. In either case, monies used for basic income grants might be collected through taxation. In socialist regimes, they might also be deducted from the dividends from investments in state-owned property.

5. See, for example, John Roemer, *A Future for Socialism* (London: Verso, 1994).

6. Karl Marx, Friedrich Engels, *Collected Works*, Vol. 3 (New York: International Publishers, 1975).

7. See, for example, "Reification and the Consciousness of the Proletariat" in Georg Lukács, *History and Class Consciousness* (London: Merlin, 1971).

8. See Marx, Engels, *Collected Works*, Vol. 25 (New York: International Publishers, 1976), p. 268.

9. See C.B. Macpherson, *The Political Theory of Possessive Individualism: Hobbes to Locke* (Oxford: Oxford University Press, 1962). Macpherson's reconstruction of Locke's case for restricting the franchise draws mainly on the *Second Treatise of Government* (1690) and "Some Considerations of the Consequences of the Lowering of Interest and Raising the Value of Money" in *Works*, 6th ed., Vol. 2 (1759).

Chapter 6. The Reasonable

1. See John Rawls, *Political Liberalism* (New York: Columbia University Press, 1993).

2. See John Stuart Mill, *On Liberty* (New York: Hackett, 1982). Originally published, 1859.

3. Shorn of its political implications, this is the theological doctrine that gave rise to the Protestant ethic and therefore to the spirit of capitalism. See Chapter 2 of this book. Augustine's views are set forth in *The City of God* (New York: Random House, 1950). The text was written between 413–427 CE.

4. It is because Fallen Man loves the things of this earth that he can be coerced by the threat of their removal. Similarly, for Hobbes, it is because human beings are, by nature, diffident, competitive, and vainglorious that they are susceptible to being controlled.

5. However, "neutrality" was not Rawls's term. In fact, he expressly distanced himself from it—see, for example, *Political Liberalism*, pp. 190–195.

6. Ronald Dworkin, "Liberalism," in Stuart Hampshire, Ed., *Public and Private Morality* (Cambridge and New York: Cambridge University Press, 1978).

7. Rawls, *Political Liberalism*, p. 13.

8. See Introduction, Note 1.

9. Even Rawls concedes that it is "deliberately loose." He concedes this point after providing the following gloss on the idea:

   ... Reasonable comprehensive doctrines ... have three main features. One is that a reasonable doctrine is an exercise of theoretical reason: it covers the major religious, philosophical, and moral aspects of human life in a more or less consistent and coherent manner. It organizes and characterizes recognized values so that they are compatible with one another and express an intelligible view of the world. Each doctrine will do this in ways that distinguish it from other doctrines, for example, by giving certain values a particular primacy and weight. In singling out which values to count as especially significant and how to balance them when they conflict, a reasonable comprehensive doctrine is also an exercise of practical reason. ... Finally, a third feature is that while a reasonable comprehensive doctrine is not necessarily fixed and unchanging, it normally belongs to, or draws upon, a tradition of thought and doctrine. Although stable over time, and not subject to sudden and unexplained changes, it tends to evolve slowly in the light of what, from its point of view, it sees as good and sufficient conditions. *Political Liberalism*, p. 59.

10. Thomas S. Kuhn, *The Structure of Scientific Revolutions* (Chicago: University of Chicago Press, 1962).

11. With regard to de facto legitimacy, even political liberals should acknowledge that an overlapping consensus is not necessary for disposing citizens to support regimes that uphold neutrality. No doubt, recognition of the fact that human beings make fundamental commitments in the face of conditions that render definitive conclusions elusive can encourage tolerance. But so can a belief in the intractable irrationality of one's compatriots. Those who, for example, think that Freud's account of the psychological function of theism is sound may be as confident as any political liberal of the impossibility of changing the minds of most adherents of rationally indefensible, theistically based comprehensive doctrines. Freudians would, in fact, be even more disinclined than political liberals to expect a rational consensus to emerge in this instance, because, in their view, theism is appealing in consequence of unsatisfactory resolutions of unavoidable Oedipal conflicts, not contingent information deficits or time constraints. They believe that a propensity to accept theistic beliefs is hardwired into most of us. What chance is there, then, of persuading large numbers of people to convert to sounder doctrines? Thus this line of thought leads to the same conclusion that political liberalism does: a rational consensus is unachievable. Therefore, the wisest posture for first-order liberals is to recognize the futility of trying to forge one and to be satisfied instead with constitutional arrangements that encourage citizens to try to get along as best they can. In short, de facto legitimacy does not depend on the viability of the political liberal project.

Chapter 7. Deliberative Democracy

1. See, for example, John Burnheim, *Is Democracy Possible?* (Berkeley and Los Angeles: University of California Press, 1985). Much as the "council communists" did decades before, Burnheim proposed substituting legislatures composed of elected representatives from geographically based districts with legislatures made up of representatives selected randomly from functionally identified constituencies.

2. See, especially, *The Social Contract* (first published, 1754). For elaboration of what follows, see my *The General Will: Rousseau, Marx, Communism* (Cambridge and New York: Cambridge University Press, 1993) and *Engaging*

Political Philosophy: Hobbes to Rawls (Boston, Blackwell Publishers, 2001), Chapter 2.

3. The argument is given in *The Social Contract*, Book IV, Chapter 2.
4. Condorcet's work was published after *The Social Contract*, but it is believed that the general idea illustrated here was in circulation long before its publication. In any case, the earliest published version of this theorem occurs in his *Essai sur l'Application de l'Analyse à la Probabilité des Décisions Rendue à la Pluralité des Voix* (Paris: 1785), pp. 10–11.
5. It was this side of Rousseau's thought that appealed particularly to Immanuel Kant, the philosopher who brought the moral equality of persons into the forefront of philosophical thought. I investigate Rousseau's rationale in *The Politics of Autonomy: A Kantian Reading of Rousseau's "Social Contract"* (Amherst, MA: University of Massachusetts Press, 1976).
6. This is an oversimplification. In real-world voting situations, voters will often vote strategically and may therefore not vote for the candidate they most prefer to help prevent the election of someone they like even less.
7. In the usual case, neither party knows the other's threat point—the point beyond which the negotiation will break down.
8. Because they smack of dictatorship, decision rules of this sort, methods of minority rule, are seldom, if ever, attractive to democrats. Moreover, because change is typically unsettling, minority rule voting is more detrimental to stability than majority rule voting is. This is another reason why it is seldom contemplated.
9. This concern may be ill-chosen, because it is plain that preferences are affected by the nature and range of the choices agents confront. Among the first to recognize the importance of this phenomenon was Jon Elster. See *Sour Grapes: Studies in the Subversion of Rationality* (Cambridge and New York: Cambridge University Press, 1983).
10. See Joseph Schumpeter, *Capitalism, Socialism, Democracy* (New York: Harper and Brothers, 1942).
11. Schumpeter did try, as we will see presently. For a candid, recent effort to defend Schumpeterian democracy as a normative theory, see Richard A. Posner, *Law, Pragmatism, and Democracy* (Cambridge, MA: Harvard University Press, 2003).
12. I have already suggested (see Introduction, Note 1) that the Rawlsians' faith in the judicial branch may be, in large part, a consequence of the fact that Rawlsian political philosophy developed in a period when the U.S. judiciary generally was progressive. However, from a longer historical perspective or from today's vantage point, the belief that the courts can be relied upon to advance liberty, equality, and fraternity and not to impede democratization seems to be more of a hope than a reasonable expectation. In Freud's sense (see Chapter 7), it is an illusion.
13. See, especially, *The Critique of "Hegel's Philosophy of Right"* (1843).

Chapter 8. Which Way Forward?

1. See Rudolph Carnap, *The Logical Structure of the World: Pseudoproblems in Philosophy*, translated by Rolf A. George (Berkeley and Los Angeles: University of California Press, 1967). Originally published in 1928.
2. See, for example, John Dewey, *Reconstruction in Philosophy* (New York: Henry Holt and Company, 1920).
3. It was also a patriarchal society with a subjugated population only recently freed from slavery and an aboriginal population still facing genocidal annihilation.

Dewey, like most of his contemporaries, was generally insensitive to these and other dilemmas of American democracy.

4. Thus, in 1764, Rousseau worked on an (unfinished) constitution for Corsica. It was published, eventually, in 1861, under the title *Project for a Constitution for Corsica*.

5. Deliberative democrats, despite their connections to Rousseau, are not so much pessimistic about the feasibility of their vision as oblivious to the entire issue. Being accountable mainly to disciplinary and academic constituencies, they proceed as if the radical disconnect between their theory and the world in which it operates is of no philosophical consequence. Thus their picture of democratic deliberation, governed by public reason and respectful of the moral equality of persons, proceeds as if particular, especially elite, interests did not render their vision otiose in practice.

6. The best known recent example is Robert Nozick. See *Anarchy, State, Utopia* (New York: Basic Books, 1974).

7. I elaborate on the claims advanced in this paragraph and the next in *The Politics of Autonomy*, Chapter 4 and Chapter 5 and in *The General Will Rousseau, Marx, Communism* (Cambridge and New York: Cambridge University Press, 1993), Chapter 7.

Index